DARING DEEDS OF DERRING-DO
AS TOLD BY AWARD-WINNING, BESTSELLING
MASTERS OF FANTASY, INCLUDING:

"Gwydion and the Dragon" by C.J. Cherryh: *Once upon a time there was a dragon, and once upon that time a prince who undertook to win the hand of the elder and fairer of two princesses. Not that this prince wanted either of Madog's daughters . . .*

"Chivalry" by Neil Gaiman: *Mrs. Whitaker found the Holy Grail; it was under a fur coat . . .*

"The Bully and the Beast" by Orson Scott Card: *There is a flame at the heart of every dragon. It doesn't come from the dragon's mouth or the dragon's nostrils. If he burns you, it won't be with his breath . . .*

"The Land Beyond the World" by Michael Moorcock: *Elric dreamed. He dreamed that he had dreamed of the Dark Ship and Tanelorn and Agak and Gagak while he lay exhausted upon a beach somewhere beyond the borders of Pikarayd . . .*

. . . and many more.

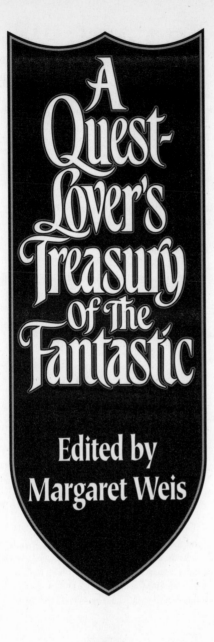

A Quest-Lover's Treasury Of The Fantastic

Edited by Margaret Weis

ASPECT®

WARNER BOOKS

An AOL Time Warner Company

"Introduction" by Margaret Weis. Copyright © 2002 by Margaret Weis.

"Gwydion and the Dragon" by C.J. Cherryh. Copyright © 1991 by C.J. Cherryh. First published in *Once Upon a Time*. Reprinted by permission of the author.

Copyright information continued on page 310.

Aspect® name and logo are registered trademarks of Warner Books, Inc.

Warner Books, Inc., 1271 Avenue of the Americas, New York, NY 10020

Visit our Web site at www.twbookmark.com.

An AOL Time Warner Company

Printed in the United States of America

First Printing: May 2002

10 9 8 7 6 5 4 3 2 1

Library of Congress Cataloging-in-Publication Data

A quest lover's treasury of the fantastic / edited by and with an introduction by Margaret Weis.
    p. cm.
    "Aspect."
    Contents: Gwydion and the dragon / C.J. Cherryh—Misericorde / Karl Edward Wagner—The barbarian / Poul Anderson—The silk and the song / Charles L. Fontenay—Mirror, mirror on the lam / Tanya Huff—Chivalry / Neil Gaiman—Firebearer / Lois Tilton—The bully and the beast / Orson Scott Card—A time for heroes / Richard Parks—The cup and the cauldron / Mercedes Lackey—The lands beyond the world / Michael Moorcock.
    ISBN 0-446-67927-5
    1. Fantasy fiction, American. 2. Quests (Expeditions)—Fiction. I. Weis, Margaret.

PS509.F3 Q47 2002
813'0876608—dc21
                                        2001056871

Contents

Introduction

❖

Margaret Weis

 once heard author Gary Paulsen tell a group of children that the very first authors were those who flung the wolfskins over their heads and crouched in the firelight to tell their tales to the tribe. I am certain that among the tales these early storytellers told their people were those of men and women who set off on quests.

The quest story has been handed down through time because it is story to which each one of us can relate. The quest story mirrors the journey of our lives. From the moment of our birth, we begin the great quest that ends in this world with our death and, perhaps, at that point starts anew.

One might say that almost every story ever written or told is a quest story in one form or another. Sherlock Holmes quested for truth and justice. Elizabeth Bennet set out upon a famous quest for love. D'Artagnan took the road to Paris in search of adventure and honor. Mr. Pickwick left London to discover humanity (and good food!).

Quests are not relegated to days past. We read tales of ancient heroes who set about searching for the golden fleece and tales of modern heroes who take up the quest for golden medals at once-ancient games.

Most important, the quest story involves a search for self.

Charles Dickens wrote in *David Copperfield*: "Whether I shall turn out to be the hero of my own life, or whether that station will be held by anybody else, these pages must show."

We turn to quest stories to learn how to be the heroes of our own lives. Quest stories show us how other people live their lives, face their challenges, and deal with their problems. We may emulate them or shun them, pity them or admire them, hate them or weep for them, but we always learn something from them.

In each story we read, whether it is the quest for the Holy Grail or the search for the Hound of the Baskervilles, we are studying mankind. We are studying ourselves and examining our own quests. In this book, you will find some of your favorite fantasy authors writing stories of men and women questing, striving, seeking, finding.

Each day begins a new quest for each of us. Take along this book of some of my favorite quest stories on yours.

A Quest-Lover's Treasury of the Fantastic

Gwydion and the Dragon

❖

C.J. Cherryh

nce upon a time there was a dragon, and once upon that time a prince who undertook to win the hand of the elder and fairer of two princesses.

Not that this prince wanted either of Madog's daughters, although rumors said that Eri was as wise and as gentle, as sweet and as fair as her sister, Glasog, was cruel and ill-favored. The truth was that this prince would marry either princess if it would save his father and his people; and neither if he had had any choice in the matter. He was Gwydion ap Ogan, and of princes in Dyfed he was the last.

Being a prince of Dyfed did not, understand, mean banners and trumpets and gilt armor and crowds of courtiers. King Ogan's palace was a rambling stone house of dusty rafters hung with cooking pots and old harnesses; King Ogan's wealth was mostly in pigs and pastures—the same as all Ogan's subjects; Gwydion's war-horse was a black gelding with a crooked blaze and shaggy feet, who had fought against the bandits from the high hills. Gwydion's armor, serviceable in that perpetual warfare, was scarred leather and plain mail, with new links bright among the old; and lance or pennon he

1

had none—the folk of Ogan's kingdom were not lowland knights, heavily armored, but hunters in the hills and woods, and for weapons this prince carried only a one-handed sword and a bow and a quiver of gray-feathered arrows.

His companion, riding beside him on a bay pony, happened through no choice of Gwydion's to be Owain ap Llodri, the hound-master's son, his good friend, by no means his squire: Owain had lain in wait along the way, on a borrowed bay mare—Owain had simply assumed he was going, and that Gwydion had only hesi-tated, for friendship's sake, to ask him. So he saved Gwydion the necessity.

And the lop-eared old dog trotting by the horses' feet was Mili: Mili was fierce with bandits, and had respected neither Gwydion's entreaties nor Owain's commands thus far: stones might drive her off for a few minutes, but Mili came back again, that was the sort Mili was. That was the sort Owain was too, and Gwydion could refuse neither of them. So Mili panted along at the pace they kept, with big-footed Blaze and the bow-nosed bay, whose name might have been Swallow or maybe not—the poets forget—and as they rode Owain and Gwydion talked mostly about dogs and hunting.

That, as the same poets say, was the going of Prince Gwydion into King Madog's realm.

Now no one in Dyfed knew where Madog had come from. Some said he had been a king across the water. Some said he was born of a Roman and a Pict and had gotten sorcery through his mother's blood. Some said he had bargained with a dragon for his sorcery—certainly there was a dragon: devastation followed Madog's conquests, from one end of Dyfed to the other.

Reasonably reliable sources said Madog had applied first to King Bran, across the mountains, to settle at his court, and Bran having once laid eyes on Madog's elder daughter, had lusted after her beyond all good sense and begged Madog for her.

Give me your daughter, Bran had said to Madog, and I'll give you your heart's desire. But Madog had confessed that Eri was be-trothed already, to a terrible dragon, who sometimes had the form of a man, and who had bespelled Madog and all his house: if Bran could overcome this dragon he might have Eri with his blessings, and his gratitude and the faithful help of his sorcery all his life; but if he died childless, Madog, by Bran's own oath, must be his heir.

That was the beginning of Madog's kingdom. So smitten was Bran that he swore to those terms, and died that very day, after which Madog ruled in his place.

After that Madog had made the same proposal to three of his neighbor kings, one after the other, proposing that each should ally with him and unite their kingdoms if the youngest son could win Eri from the dragon's spell and provide him an heir. But no prince ever came back from his quest. And the next youngest then went, until all the sons of the kings were gone, so that the kingdoms fell under Madog's rule.

After them, Madog sent to King Ban, and his sons died, last of all Prince Rhys, Gwydion's friend. Ban's heart broke, and Ban took to his bed and died.

Some whispered now that the dragon actually served Madog, that it had indeed brought Madog to power, under terms no one wanted to guess, and that this dragon did indeed have another form, which was the shape of a knight in strange armor, who would become Eri's husband if no other could win her. Some said (but none could prove the truth of it) that the dragon-knight had come from far over the sea, and that he devoured the sons and daughters of conquered kings, that being the tribute Madog gave him. But whatever the truth of that rumor, the dragon hunted far and wide in the lands Madog ruled and did not disdain to take the sons and daughters of farmers and shepherds too. Devastation went under his shadow, trees withered under his breath, and no one saw him outside his dragon shape and returned to tell of it, except only Madog and (rumor said) his younger daughter, Glasog, who was a sorceress as cruel as her father.

Some said that Glasog could take the shape of a raven and fly over the land choosing whom the dragon might take. The people called her Madog's Crow, and feared the look of her eye. Some said she was the true daughter of Madog and that Madog had stolen Eri from Faerie, and given her mother to the dragon; but others said they were twins, and that Eri had gotten all that an ordinary person had of goodness, while her sister, Glasog—

"Prince Gwydion," Glasog said to her father, "would have come on the quest last year with his friend Rhys, except his father's refusing him, and Prince Gwydion will not let his land go to war if he can find another course. He'll persuade his father."

"Good," Madog said. "That's very good." Madog smiled, but Glasog did not. Glasog was thinking of the dragon. Glasog harbored no illusions: the dragon had promised Madog that he would be king of all Wales if he could achieve this in seven years; and rule for seventy and seven more with the dragon's help.

But if he failed—failed by the seventh year to gain any one of the kingdoms of Dyfed, if one stubborn king withstood him and for one day beyond the seven allotted years, kept him from obtaining the least, last stronghold of the west, then all the bargain was void and Madog would have failed in everything.

And the dragon would claim a forfeit of his choosing.

That was what Glasog thought of, in her worst nightmares: that the dragon had always meant to have all the kingdoms of the west with very little effort—let her father win all but one and fail, on the smallest letter of the agreement. What was more, all the generals in all the armies they had taken agreed that the kingdom of Ogan could never be taken by force: there were mountains in which resistance could hide and not even dragonfire could burn all of them; but most of all there was the fabled Luck of Ogan, which said that no force of arms could defeat the sons of Ogan.

Watch, Madog had said. And certainly her father was astute, and cunning, and knew how to snare a man by his pride. There's always a way, her father had said, to break a spell. This one has a weakness. The strongest spells most surely have their soft spots.

And Ogan had one son, and that was Prince Gwydion.

Now we will fetch him, Madog said to his daughter. Now we will see what his luck is worth.

The generals said, "If you would have a chance in war, first be rid of Gwydion."

But Madog said, and Glasog agreed, there are other uses for Gwydion.

"It doesn't *look* different," Owain said as they passed the border stone.

It was true. Nothing looked changed at all. There was no particular odor of evil, or of threat. It might have been last summer, when the two of them had hunted with Rhys. They had used to hunt together every summer, and last autumn they had tracked the bandit Llewellyn to his lair, and caught him with stolen sheep. But in the spring Ban's sons had gone to seek the hand of Madog's daughter, and one by one had died, last of them, in early summer, Rhys himself.

Gwydion would have gone, long since, and long before Rhys. A score of times Gwydion had approached his father, King Ogan, and his mother, Queen Belys, and begged to try his luck against Madog, from the first time Madog's messenger had appeared and challenged the kings of Dyfed to war or wedlock. But each time Ogan had refused him, arguing in the first place that other princes, accustomed to warfare on their borders, were better suited, and better armed, and that there were many princes in Dyfed, but he had only one son.

But when Rhys had gone and failed, the last kingdom save that of King Ogan passed into Madog's hands. And Gwydion, grief-stricken with the loss of his friend, said to his parents, "If we had stood together we might have defeated this Madog; if we had taken the field then, together, we might have had a chance; if you had let me go with Rhys one of us might have won and saved the other. But now Rhys is dead and we have Madog for a neighbor. Let me go when he sends to us. Let me try my luck at courting his daughter. A war with him now we may not lose, but we cannot hope to win."

Even so Ogan had resisted him, saying that they still had their mountains for a shield, difficult going for any army; and arguing that their luck had saved them this far and that it was rash to take matters into their own hands.

Now the nature of that luck was this: that of the kingdoms in Dyfed, Ogan's must always be poorest and plainest. But that luck meant that they could not fail in war nor fail in harvest: it had come down to them from Ogan's own great-grandfather Ogan ap Ogan of Llanfynnyd, who had sheltered one of the Faerie unaware; and only faithlessness could break it—so great-grandfather Ogan had said. So: "Our luck will be our defense," Ogan argued with his son. "Wait and let Madog come to us. We'll fight him in the mountains."

"Will we fight a dragon? Even if we defeat Madog himself, what of our herds, what of our farmers and our freeholders? Can we let the land go to waste and let our people feed this dragon, while we hide in the hills and wait for luck to save us? Is that faithfulness?" That was what Gwydion had asked his father, while Madog's herald was in the hall—a raven black as unrepented sin . . . or the intentions of a wizard.

"Madog bids you know," this raven had said, perched on a rafter of Ogan's hall, beside a moldering basket and a string of garlic, "that he has taken every kingdom of Dyfed but this. He offers you what he offered others: if King Ogan has a son worthy to win Madog's daughter and get an heir, then King Ogan may rule in peace over his kingdom so long as he lives, and that prince will have titles and the third of Madog's realm besides. . . .

"But if the prince will not or cannot win the princess, then Ogan must swear Madog is his lawful true heir. And if Ogan refuses this, then Ogan must face Madog's army, which now is the army of four kingdoms each greater than his own. Surely," the raven had added, fixing all present with a wicked, midnight eye, "it is no great endeavor Madog asks—simply to court his daughter. And will so many die, and so much burn? Or will Prince Gwydion win a realm wider than your own? A third of Madog's lands is no small dowry and inheritance of Madog's kingdom is no small prize."

So the raven had said. And Gwydion had said to his mother, "Give me your blessing," and to his father, Ogan: "Swear the oath Madog asks. If our luck can save us it will save me and win me this bride; but if it fails me in this it would have failed us in any case."

Maybe, Gwydion thought as they passed the border, Owain was a necessary part of that luck. Maybe even Mili was. It seemed to him now that he dared reject nothing that loved him and favored him, even if it was foolish and even if it broke his heart: his luck seemed so perilous and stretched so thin already he dared not bargain with his fate.

"No sign of a dragon, either," Owain said, looking about them at the rolling hills.

Gwydion looked about him too, and at the sky, which showed only the lazy flight of a single bird.

Might it be a raven? It was too far to tell.

"I'd think," said Owain, "it would seem grimmer than it does."

Gwydion shivered as if a cold wind had blown. But Blaze plodded his heavy-footed way with no semblance of concern, and Mili trotted ahead, tongue lolling, occasionally sniffing along some trail that crossed theirs.

"Mili would smell a dragon," Owain said.

"Are you sure?" Gwydion asked. He was not. If Madog's younger daughter could be a raven at her whim he was not sure what a dragon might be at its pleasure.

That night they had a supper of brown bread and sausages that Gwydion's mother had sent, and ale that Owain had with him.

"My mother's brewing," Owain said. "My father's store." And Owain sighed and said: "By now they must surely guess I'm not off hunting."

"You didn't tell them?" Gwydion asked. "You got no blessing in this?"

Owain shrugged, and fed a bit of sausage to Mili, who gulped it down and sat looking at them worshipfully.

Owain's omission of duty worried Gwydion. He imagined how Owain's parents would first wonder where he had gone, then guess, and fear for Owain's life, for which he held himself entirely accountable. In the morning he said, "Owain, go back. This is far enough."

But Owain shrugged and said, "Not I. Not without you." Owain rubbed Mili's ears. "No more than Mili, without me."

Gwydion had no least idea now what was faithfulness and what was a young man's foolish pride. Everything seemed tangled. But Owain seemed not in the least distressed.

Owain said, "We'll be there by noon tomorrow."

Gwydion wondered, Where is this dragon? and distrusted the rocks around them and the sky over their heads. He felt a presence in the earth—or thought he felt it. But Blaze and Swallow grazed at their leisure. Only Mili looked worried—Mili pricked up her ears, such as those long ears could prick, wondering, perhaps, if they were going to get to bandits soon, and whether they were, after all, going to eat that last bit of breakfast sausage.

"He's on his way," Glasog said. "He's passed the border."

"Good," said Madog. And to his generals: "Didn't I tell you?"

The generals still looked worried.

But Glasog went and stood on the walk of the castle that had been Ban's, looking out over the countryside and wondering what the dragon was thinking tonight, whether the dragon had foreseen this as he had foreseen the rest, or whether he was even yet keeping some secret from them, scheming all along for their downfall.

She launched herself quite suddenly from the crest of the wall, swooped out over the yard and beyond, over the seared fields.

The dragon, one could imagine, knew about Ogan's luck. The dragon was too canny to face it—and doubtless was chuckling in his den in the hills.

Glasog flew that way, but saw nothing from that cave but a little curl of smoke—there was almost always smoke. And Glasog leaned toward the west, following the ribbon of a road, curious, and wagering that the dragon this time would not bestir himself.

Her father wagered the same. And she knew very well what he wagered, indeed she did: duplicity for duplicity—if not the old serpent's aid, then human guile; if treachery from the dragon, then put at risk the dragon's prize.

Gwydion and Owain came to a burned farmstead along the road. Mili sniffed about the blackened timbers and bristled at the shoulders, and came running back to Owain's whistle, not without mistrustful looks behind her.

There was nothing but a black ruin beside a charred, brittle orchard.

"I wonder," Owain said, "what became of the old man and his wife."

"I don't," said Gwydion, worrying for his own parents, and seeing in this example how they would fare in any retreat into the hills.

The burned farm was the first sign they had seen of the dragon, but it was not the last. There were many other ruins, and sad and terrible sights. One was a skull sitting on a fence row. And on it sat a raven.

"This was a brave man," it said, and pecked the skull, which rang hollowly, and inclined its head toward the field beyond. "That was his wife. And farther still his young daughter."

"Don't speak to it," Gwydion said to Owain. They rode past, at Blaze's plodding pace, and did not look back.

But the raven flitted ahead of them and waited for them on the stone fence. "If you die," the raven said, "then your father will no longer believe in his luck. Then it will leave him. It happened to all the others."

"There's always a first," said Gwydion.

Owain said, reaching for his bow: "Shall I shoot it?"

But Gwydion said: "Kill the messenger for the message? No. It's a foolish creature. Let it be."

It left them then. Gwydion saw it sometimes in the sky ahead of them. He said nothing to Owain, who had lost his cheerfulness, and Mili stayed close by them, sore of foot and suspicious of every breeze.

There were more skulls. They saw gibbets and stakes in the middle of a burned orchard. There was scorched grass, recent and powdery under the horses' hooves. Blaze, who loved to snatch a bite now and again as he went, moved uneasily, snorting with dislike of the smell, and Swallow started at shadows.

Then the turning of the road showed them a familiar brook,

and around another hill and beyond, the walled holding that had been King Ban's, in what had once been a green valley. Now it was burned, black bare hillsides and the ruin of hedges and orchards.

So the trial they had come to find must be here, Gwydion thought, and uneasily took up his bow and picked several of his best arrows, which he held against his knee as he rode. Owain did the same.

But they reached the gate of the low-walled keep unchallenged, until they came on the raven sitting, whetting its beak on the stone. It looked at them solemnly, saying, "Welcome, Prince Gwydion. You've won your bride. Now how will you fare, I wonder."

Men were coming from the keep, running toward them, others, under arms, in slower advance.

"What now?" Owain asked, with his bow across his knee; and Gwydion lifted his bow and bent it, aiming at the foremost.

The crowd stopped, but a black-haired man in gray robes and a king's gold chain came alone, holding up his arms in a gesture of welcome and of peace. Madog himself? Gwydion wondered, while Gwydion's arm shook and the string trembled in his grip. "Is it Gwydion ap Ogan?" that man asked—surely no one else but Madog would wear that much gold. "My son-in-law to be! Welcome!"

Gwydion, with great misgivings, slacked the string and let down the bow, while fat Blaze, better trained than seemed, finally shifted feet. Owain lowered his bow too, as King Madog's men opened up the gate. Some of the crowd cheered as they rode in, and more took it up, as if they had only then gained the courage or understood it was expected. Blaze and Swallow snorted and threw their heads at the racket, as Gwydion and Owain put away their arrows, unstrung their bows and hung them on their saddles.

But Mili stayed close by Owain's legs as they dismounted, growling low in her throat, and barked one sharp warning when Madog came close. "Hush," Owain bade her, and knelt down more than for respect, keeping one hand on Mili's muzzle and the other in her collar, whispering to her, "Hush, hush, there's a good dog."

Gwydion made the bow a prince owed to a king and prospective father-in-law, all the while thinking that there had to be a trap in this place. He was entirely sorry to see grooms lead Blaze and Swallow away, and kept Owain and Mili constantly in the tail of his eye as Madog took him by the arms and hugged him. Then Madog said, catching all his attention, eye to eye with him for a moment, "What a well-favored young man you are. The last is always best. —So you've killed the dragon."

Gwydion thought, Somehow we've ridden right past the trial we should have met. If I say no, he will find cause to disallow me; and he'll kill me and Owain and all our kin.

But lies were not the kind of dealing his father had taught him; faithfulness was the rule of the house of Ogan; so Gwydion looked the king squarely in the eyes and said, "I met no dragon."

Madog's eyes showed surprise, and Madog said: "Met no dragon?"

"Not a shadow of a dragon."

Madog grinned and clapped him on the shoulder and showed him to the crowd, saying, "This is your true prince!"

Then the crowd cheered in earnest, and even Owain and Mili looked heartened. Owain rose with Mili's collar firmly in hand.

Madog said then to Gwydion, under his breath, "If you had lied you would have met the dragon here and now. Do you know you're the first one who's gotten this far?"

"I saw nothing," Gwydion said again, as if Madog had not understood him. "Only burned farms. Only skulls and bones."

Madog turned a wide smile toward him, showing teeth. "Then it was your destiny to win. Was it not?" And Madog faced him about toward the doors of the keep. "Daughter, daughter, come out!"

Gwydion hesitated a step, expecting he knew not what—the dragon itself, perhaps: his wits went scattering toward the gate, the horses being led away, Mili barking in alarm—and a slender figure standing in the doorway, all white and gold. "My elder daughter," Madog said. "Eri."

Gwydion went as he was led, telling himself it must be true, after so much dread of this journey and so many friends' lives lost—obstacles must have fallen down for him, Ogan's luck must still be working. . . .

The young bride waiting for him was so beautiful, so young and so—kind—was the first word that came to him—Eri smiled and immediately it seemed to him she was innocent of all the grief around her, innocent and good as her sister was reputed cruel and foul.

He took her hand, and the folk of the keep all cheered, calling him their prince; and if any were Ban's people, those wishes might well come from the heart, with fervent hopes of rescue. Pipers began to play, gentle hands urged them both inside, and in this desolate land some woman found flowers to give Eri.

"Owain?" Gwydion cried, looking back, suddenly seeing no sign of him or of Mili: "Owain!"

He refused to go farther until Owain could part the crowd and reach his side, Mili firmly in hand. Owain looked breathless and frightened. Gwydion felt the same. But the crowd pushed and pulled at them, the pipers piped and dancers danced, and they brought them into a hall smelling of food and ale.

It can't be this simple, Gwydion still thought, and made up his mind that no one should part him from Owain, Mili, or their swords. He looked about him, bedazzled, at a wedding feast that must have taken days to prepare.

But how could they know I'd get here? he wondered. Did they do this for all the suitors who failed—and celebrate their funerals, then . . . with their wedding feast?

At which thought he felt cold through and through, and found Eri's hand on his arm disquieting; but Madog himself waited to receive them in the hall, and joined their hands and plighted them their vows, to make them man and wife, come what might—

"So long as you both shall live," Madog said, pressing their hands together. "And when there is an heir Prince Gwydion shall have the third of my lands, and his father shall rule in peace so long as he shall live."

Gwydion misliked the last—Gwydion thought in alarm: As long as he lives.

But Madog went on, saying, "—be you wed, be you wed, be you wed," three times, as if it were a spell—then: "Kiss your bride, son-in-law."

The well-wishes from the guests roared like the sea. The sea was in Eri's eyes, deep and blue and drowning. He heard Mili growl as he kissed Eri's lips once, twice, three times.

The pipers played, the people cheered, no few of whom indeed might have been King Ban's, or Lugh's, or Lughdan's. Perhaps, Gwydion dared think, perhaps it was hope he brought to them, perhaps he truly had won, after all, and the dreadful threat Madog posed was lifted, so that Madog would be their neighbor, no worse than the worst they had had, and perhaps, if well-disposed, better than one or two.

Perhaps, he thought, sitting at Madog's right hand with his bride at his right and with Owain just beyond, perhaps there truly was cause to hope, and he could ride away from here alive—though he feared he could find no cause to do so tonight, with so much prepared, with an anxious young bride and King Madog determined to indulge his beautiful daughter. Women hurried about with flowers and with torches, with linens and with brooms and platters and plates, tumblers ran riot, dancers leaped and cavorted—one of whom came to grief against an ale-server. Both went down, in Madog's very face, and the hall grew still and dangerous.

But Eri laughed and clapped her hands, a laughter so small and faint until her father laughed, and all the hall laughed; and Gwydion remembered then to breathe, while Eri hugged his arm and laughed up at him with those sea-blue eyes.

"More ale!" Madog called. "Less spillage, there!"

The dreadful wizard could joke, then. Gwydion drew two easier breaths, and someone filled their cups. He drank, but prudently: he caught Owain's eye, and Owain his—while Mili having found a bone to her liking, with a great deal of meat to it, worried it happily in the straw beneath the table.

There were healths drunk, there were blessings said, at each of which one had to drink—and Madog laughed and called Gwydion a fine son-in-law, asked him about his campaign against the bandits and swore he was glad to have his friends and his kin and anyone he cared to bring here: Madog got up and clapped Owain on the shoulder too, and asked was Owain wed, and, informed Owain was not, called out to the hall that here was another fine catch, and where were the young maids to keep Owain from chill on his master's wedding night?

Owain protested in some embarrassment, starting to his feet—

But drink overcame him, and he sat down again with a hand to his brow, Gwydion saw it with concern, while Madog touched Gwydion's arm on the other side and said, "The women are ready," slyly bidding him finish his ale beforehand.

Gwydion rose and handed his bride to her waiting women. "Owain!" Gwydion said then sharply, and Owain gained his feet, saying something Gwydion could not hear for with all the people cheering and the piper starting up, but he saw Owain was distressed. Gwydion resisted the women pulling at him, stood fast until Owain reached him, flushed with ale and embarrassment. The men surrounded him with bawdy cheers and more offered cups.

It was his turn then on the stairs, more cups thrust on him, Madog clapping him on the shoulder and hugging him and calling him the son he had always wanted, and saying there should be peace in Dyfed for a hundred years . . . unfailing friendship with his father and his kin—greater things, should he have ambitions. . . .

The room spun around. Voices buzzed. They pushed him up the stairs, Owain and Mili notwithstanding, Mili barking all the while. They brought him down the upstairs hall, they opened the door to the bridal chamber.

On pitch dark.

Perhaps it was cowardly to balk. Gwydion thought so, in the instant the laughing men gave him a push between the shoulders. Shame kept him from calling Owain to his rescue. The door shut at his back.

He heard rustling in the dark and imagined coils and scales. Eri's soft voice said, "My lord?"

A faint starlight edged the shutters. His eyes made out the furnishings, now that the flare of torches had left his sight. It was the rustling of bedclothes he heard. He saw a woman's shoulder and arm faintly in the shadowed bed, in the scant starshine that the shutter let through.

He backed against the door, found the latch behind him, cracked it the least little bit outward and saw Owain leaning there against his arm, facing the lamplit wall outside, flushed of face and ashamed to meet his eyes at such close range.

"I'm here, m'lord," Owain breathed, on ale-fumes. Owain never called him lord, but Owain was greatly embarrassed tonight. "The lot's gone down the stairs now. I'll be here the night. I'll not leave this door, nor sleep, I swear to you."

Gwydion gave him a worried look, wishing the two of them dared escape this hall and Madog's well-wishes, running pell-mell back to his own house, his parents' advice, and childhood. But, "Good," he said, and carefully pulled the door to, making himself blind in the dark again. He let the latch fall and catch.

"My lord?" Eri said faintly.

He felt quite foolish, himself and Owain conspiring together like two boys at an orchard wall, when it was a young bride waiting for him, innocent and probably as anxious as he. He nerved himself, walked up by the bed and opened the shutters wide on a night sky brighter than the dark behind him.

But with the cool night wind blowing into the room he thought of dragons, wondered whether opening the window to the sky was wise at all, and wondered what was slipping out of bed with the whispering of the bedclothes. His bride forwardly clasped his arm, wound fingers into his and swayed against him, saying how beautiful the stars were.

Perhaps that invited courtly words. He murmured some such. He found the courage to take Madog's daughter in his arms and kiss her, and thereafter—

He waked abed with the faint dawn coming through the window, his sword tangled with his leg and his arm ensnared in a woman's unbound hair—

Hair raven black.

He leaped up trailing sheets, while a strange young woman sat up to snatch the bedclothes to her, with her black hair flowing about her shoulders, her eyes dark and cold and fathomless.

"Where's my wife?" he cried.

She smiled, thin-lipped, rose from the bed, drawing the sheets about her like royal robes. "Why, you see her, husband."

He rushed to the door and lifted the latch. The door did not budge, hardly rattled when he shoved it with all his strength. "Owain?" he cried, and pounded it with his fist. "Owain!"

No answer came. Gwydion turned slowly to face the woman, dreading what other shape she might take. But she sat down wrapped in the sheets with one knee on the rumpled bed, looking at him. Her hair spread about her like a web of shadows in the dawn. As much as Eri had been an innocent girl, this was a woman far past Eri's innocence or his own.

He asked, "Where's Owain? What's become of him?"

"Guesting elsewhere."

"Who are you?"

"Glasog," she said, and shrugged, the dawn wind carrying long strands of her hair about her shoulders. "Or Eri, if you like. My father's elder daughter and younger, all in one, since he has none but me."

"Why?" he asked. "Why this pretense if you were the bargain?"

"People trust Eri. She's so fair, so kind."

"What do you want? What does your father want?"

"A claim on your father's land. The last kingdom of Dyfed. And you've come to give it to us."

Gwydion remembered nothing of what might have happened last night. He remembered nothing of anything he should have heard or done last night, abed with Glasog the witch, Madog's raven-haired daughter. He felt cold and hollow and desperate, asking, "On your oath, *is* Owain safe?"

"And would you believe my oath?" Glasog asked.

"I'll see your father," Gwydion said shortly. "Trickery or not, he swore me the third of his kingdom for your dowry. Younger or elder, or both, you're my wife. Will he break his word?"

Glasog said, "An heir. Then he'll release you and your friend, and your father will reign in peace . . . so long as he lives."

Gwydion walked to the open window, gazing at a paling, still sunless sky. He feared he knew what that release would be—the release of himself and Owain from life, while the child he sired would become heir to his father's kingdom with Madog to enforce that right.

So long as his father lived . . . so long as that unfortunate *child* might live, for that matter, once the inheritance of Ogan's line and Ogan's luck passed securely into Madog's line—his father's kingdom taken and for no battle, no war, only a paltry handful of lies and lives.

He looked across the scorched hills, toward a home he could not reach, a father who could not advise him. He dared not hope that Owain might have escaped to bring word to his father: I'll not leave this door, Owain had said—and they would have had to carry Owain away by force or sorcery. Mili with him.

It was sorcery that must have made him sleep and forget last night. It was sorcery he must have seen when he turned from the window and saw Eri sitting there, rosy-pale and golden, patting the place beside her and bidding him come back to bed.

He shuddered and turned and hit the window ledge, hurting his hand. He thought of flight, even of drawing the sword and killing Madog's daughter, before this princess could conceive and doom him and his parents. . . .

Glasog's voice said, slowly, from Eri's lips, "If you try anything so rash, my father won't need your friend any longer, will he? I certainly wouldn't be in his place then. I'd hardly be in it now."

"What have you done with Owain?"

Eri shrugged. Glasog's voice said, "Dear husband—"

"The marriage wasn't consummated," he said, "for all I remember."

It was Glasog who lifted a shoulder. Black hair parted. "To sorcery—does it matter?"

He looked desperately toward the window. He said, without looking at her: "I've something to say about that, don't you think?"

"No. You don't. If you wouldn't, or couldn't, the words are said, the vows are made, the oaths are taken. If not your child—anyone's will do, for all men know or care."

He looked at her to see if he had understood what he thought he had, and Glasog gathered a thick skein of her hair—and drew it over her shoulder.

"The oaths are made," Glasog said. "Any lie will do. Any child will do."

"There's my word against it," Gwydion said.

Glasog shook her head gravely. "A lie's nothing to my father. A life is nothing." She stood up, shook out her hair, and hugged the sheets about her. Dawn lent a sudden and unkind light to Glasog's face, showing hollow cheeks, a grim mouth, a dark and sullen eye that promised nothing of compromise.

Why? he asked himself. Why this much of truth? Why not Eri's face?

She said, "What will you, husband?"

"Ask tonight," he said, hoping only for time and better counsel.

She inclined her head, walked between him and the window, lifting her arms wide. For an instant the morning sun showed a woman's body against the sheets. Then—it might have been a trick of the eyes—black hair spread into the black wings, something flew to the window and the sheet drifted to the floor.

What about the dragon? he would have asked, but there was no one to ask.

He went to the door and tried it again, in case sorcery had ceased. But it gave not at all, not to cleverness, not to force. He only bruised his shoulder, and leaned dejectedly against the door, sure now that he had made a terrible mistake.

The window offered nothing but a sheer drop to the stones below, and when he tried that way, he could not force his shoulders through. There was no fire in the room, not so much as water to drink. He might fall on his sword, but he took Glasog at her word: it was the form of the marriage Madog had wanted, and they would only hide his death until it was convenient to reveal it. All the house had seen them wed and bedded, even Owain—who, being honest, could swear only what he had seen and what he had guessed—but never, never to the truth of what had happened and not happened last night.

Ogan's fabled luck should have served him better, he thought, casting himself onto the bedside, head in hands. It should have served all of them better, this luck his great-grandfather had said only faithlessness could break—

But was Glasog herself not faithlessness incarnate? Was not Madog?

If that was the barb in great-grandfather's blessing—it had done nothing but bring him and his family into Madog's hands. But it seemed to him that the fay were reputed for twists and turns in their gifts, and if they had made one such twist they might make another: all he knew was to hew to the course Ogan's sons had always followed.

So he had come here in good faith, been caught through abuse of that faith, and though he might perhaps seize the chance to come at Madog himself, that was treachery for treachery and if he had any last whisper of belief in his luck, that was what he most should not do.

"Is there a child?" Madog asked, and Glasog said, "Not yet. Not yet. Be patient."

"There's not," Madog said testily, "forever. Remember that."

"I remember," Glasog said.

"You wouldn't grow fond of him—or foolish?"

"I?" quoth Glasog, with an arch of her brow. "I, fond? Not fond of the dragon, let us say. Not fond of poverty—or early dying."

"We'll not fail. If not him—"

"Truly, do you imagine the dragon will give you *anything* if the claim's not legitimate? I think not. I do think not. It must be

Gwydion's child—and *that*, by nature, by Gwydion's own will. That *is* the difficulty, isn't it?"

"You vaunt your sorcery. Use it!"

Glasog said, coldly, "When needs be. If needs be. But it's myself he'll have, *not* Eri, and for myself, not Eri. That's my demand in this."

"Don't be a fool."

Glasog smiled with equal coldness. "This man has magical protections. His luck is no illusion and it's not to cross. I don't forget that. Don't you. *Trust* me, Father."

"I wonder how I got you."

Glasog still smiled. "Luck," she said. "You want to be rid of the dragon, don't you? Has my advice ever failed you? And isn't it the old god's bond that he'll barter for questions?"

Her father scowled. "It's *my* life you're bartering for, curse your cold heart. It's my life you're risking with your schemes—a life from each kingdom of Dyfed, *that's* the barter we've made. We've caught Gwydion. We can't stave the dragon off forever for your whims and your vapors, Daughter. Get me a grandson—by whatever sorcery—and forget this foolishness. Kill the dragon . . . do you think I've not tried that? All the princes in Dyfed have tried that."

Glasog said, with her grimmest look: "We've also Gwydion's friend, don't we? And isn't he of Ogan's kingdom?"

Gwydion endured the hours until sunset, hungry and thirsty and having nothing whatever to do but to stare out the slit of a window, over a black and desolate land.

He wondered if Owain was even alive, or what had become of Mili.

Once he saw a raven in flight, toward the south; and once, late, the sky growing dimly copper, he saw it return, it seemed more slowly, circling always to the right.

Glasog? he wondered—or merely a raven looking for its supper?

The sky went from copper to dusk. He felt the air grow chill.

He thought of closing the shutters, but that was Glasog's access. So he paced the floor, or looked out the window or simply listened to the distant comings and goings below which alone told him that there was life in the place.

Perhaps, he thought, they only meant him to die of thirst and hunger, and perhaps he would never see or speak to a living soul again. He hoped Glasog would come by sunset, but she failed that; and by moonrise, but she did not come.

At last, when he had fallen asleep in his waiting, a shadow swept in the window with a snap and flutter of dark wings, and Glasog stood wrapped only in dark hair and limned in starlight.

He gathered himself up quickly, feeling still that he might be dreaming. "I expected you earlier," he said.

"I had inquiries to make," she said, and walked to the table where—he did not know how, a cup and a silver pitcher gleamed in reflected starlight. She lifted the pitcher and poured, and oh, he was thirsty. She offered it, and it might be poisoned for all he knew. At the very least it was enchanted, and perhaps only moon-dust and dreams. But she stood offering it; he drank, and it took both thirst and hunger away.

She said, "You may have one wish of me, Gwydion. One wish. And then I may have two from you. Do you agree?"

He wondered what to say. He put down the cup and walked away to the window, looking out on the night sky. There were a hundred things to ask: his parents' lives; Owain's; the safety of his land—and in each one there seemed some flaw.

Finally he chose the simplest. "Love me," he said.

For a long time Glasog said nothing. Then he heard her cross the room.

He turned. Her eyes flashed at him, sudden as a serpent's. She said, "Dare you? First drink from my cup."

"Is this your first wish?"

"It is."

He hesitated, looking at her, then walked away to the table and reached for the shadowy cup, but another appeared beside it, gleaming, crusted with jewels.

"Which will you have?" she asked.

He hoped then that he understood her question. And he picked up the cup of plain pewter and drank it all.

She said, from behind him, "You have your wish, Gwydion."

And wings brushed his face, the wind stirred his hair, the raven shape swooped out the window.

"Owain," a voice said—the raven's voice, and Owain leaped up from his prison bed, such as he could, though his head was spinning and he had to brace himself against the wall. It was not the raven's first visit. He asked it, "Where's my master? What's happened to him?"

And the raven, suddenly no raven, but a dark-haired woman: "Wedlock," she said. "Death, if the dragon gets his due—as soon he may."

"Glasog," Owain said, chilled to the marrow. Since Madog's men had hauled him away from Gwydion's door he had had this dizziness, and it came on him now. He felt his knees going and he caught himself.

"You might save him," Glasog said.

"And should I trust you?" he asked.

The chains fell away from him with a ringing of iron, and the bolts fell from the door.

"Because I'm his wife," she said. Eri stood there. He rubbed his eyes and it was Glasog again. "And you're his friend. Isn't that what it means, friendship? Or marriage?"

A second time he rubbed his eyes. The door swung open.

"My father says," Glasog said, "the dragon's death will free Prince Gwydion. You may have your horse, your dog, your armor and your weapons—or whatever you will, Owain ap Llodri. But for that gift—you must give me one wish when I claim it."

In time—Gwydion was gazing out the window, he had no idea why, he heard the slow echo of hoofbeats off the wall.

He saw Owain ride out the gate; he saw the raven flying over him.

"Owain," he cried. "Owain!"

But Owain paid no heed. Only Mili stopped, and looked up at the tower where he stood.

He thought—Go with him, Mili, if it's home he's bound for. Warn my father. There's no hope here.

Owain never looked back. Gwydion saw him turn south at the gate, entirely away from home, and guessed where Owain was going.

"Come back," he cried. "Owain! No!"

It was the dragon they were going to. It was surely the dragon Owain was going to, and if Gwydion had despaired in his life, it was seeing Owain and Mili go off in company with his wife.

He tried again to force himself through the window slit. He tried the door, working with his sword to lift the bar he was sure was in place outside.

He found it and lifted it. But it stopped with the rattle of chain.

They found the brook again, beyond the hill, and the raven fluttered down clumsily to drink, spreading a wing to steady herself.

Owain reined Swallow in. He had no reason to trust the raven in any shape, less reason to believe it than anything else that he had seen in this place. But Mili came cautiously up to it, and suddenly it was Glasog kneeling there, wrapped only in her hair, with her back to him, and Mili whining at her in some distress.

Owain got down. He saw two fingers missing from Glasog's right hand, the wounds scarcely healed. She drank from her other hand, and bathed the wounded one in water. She looked at Owain and said, "You wished to save Gwydion. You said nothing of yourself."

Owain shrugged and settled with his arm around Mili's neck.

"Now you owe me my wish," Glasog said.

"That I do," he said, and feared what it might be.

She said, "There's a god near this place. The dragon overcame him. But he will still answer the right question. Most gods will, with proper sacrifice."

Owain said, "What shall I ask him?"

She said, "I've already asked."

Owain asked then, "And the answers, lady?"

"First that the dragon's life and soul lies in his right eye. And second that no man can kill him."

Owain understood the answer then. He scratched Mili's neck beneath the collar. He said, "Mili's a loyal dog. And if flying tires you, lady, I've got a shoulder you can ride on."

Glasog said, "Better you go straightaway back to your king. Only lend me your bow, your dog, and your horse. *That* is my wish, ap Llodri."

Owain shook his head, and got up, patting Mili on the head. "All that you'll have by your wish," Owain said, "but I go with them."

"Be warned," she said.

"I am that," said Owain, and held out his hand. "My lady?"

The raven fluttered up and settled on his arm, bating as he rose into the saddle. Owain set Swallow on her way, among the charred, cinder-black hills, to a cave the raven showed him.

Swallow had no liking for this place. Owain patted her neck, coaxed her forward. Mili bristled up and growled as they climbed. Owain took up his bow and drew out an arrow, yelled, "Mili! Look out!" as fire billowed out and Swallow shied.

A second gust followed. Mili yelped and ran from the roiling smoke, racing ahead of a great serpent shape that surged out of the cave; but Mili began to cross the hill then, leading it.

The raven launched itself from Owain's shoulder, straighter than Owain's arrow sped.

A clamor rose in the keep, somewhere deep in the halls. It was dawn above the hills, and a glow still lit the south, as Gwydion watched from the window.

He was watching when a strange rider came down the road, shining gold in the sun, in scaled armor.

"The dragon!" he heard shouted from the wall. Gwydion's heart sank. It sank further when the scale-armored rider reached the gate and Madog's men opened to it. It was Swallow the dragon-knight rode, Swallow with her mane all singed; and it was Mili who limped after, with her coat all soot-blackened and with great sores showing on her hide. Mili's head hung and her tail drooped and the dragon led her by a rope, while a raven sat perched on his shoulder.

Of Owain there was no sign.

There came a clattering in the hall. Chain rattled, the bar lifted and thumped and armed men were in the doorway.

"King Madog wants you," one said. And Gwydion—

"Madog will have to send twice," Gwydion said, with his sword in hand.

The dragon rode to the steps and the raven fluttered to the ground as waiting women rushed to it, to bring Princess Glasog her cloak—black as her hair and stitched with spells. The waiting women and the servants had seen this sight before—the same as the men at arms at the gate, who had had their orders should it have been Owain returning.

"Daughter," Madog said, descending those same steps as Glasog rose up, wrapped in black and silver. Mili growled and bristled, suddenly strained at her leash—

The dragon loosed it and Mili sprang for Madog's throat. Madog fell under the hound and Madog's blood was on the steps—but his neck was already broken.

Servants ran screaming. Men at arms stood confused, as if they had quite forgotten what they were doing or where they were or what had brought them there, the men of the fallen kingdoms all looking at one another and wondering what terrible thing had held them here.

And on all of this Glasog turned her back, walking up the steps.

"My lady!" Owain cried—for it was Owain wore the armor; but it was not Owain's voice she longed to hear.

Glasog let fall the cloak and leaped from the wall. The raven glided away, with one harsh cry against the wind.

In time after—often in that bitter winter, when snows lay deep and wind skirled drifts about the door—Owain told how Glasog had pierced the dragon's eye; and how they had found the armor, and how Glasog had told him the last secret, that with the dragon dead, Madog's sorcery would leave him.

That winter, too, Gwydion found a raven in the courtyard, a crippled bird, missing feathers on one wing. It seemed greatly confused, so far gone with hunger and with cold that no one thought it would live. But Gwydion tended it until spring and set it free again.

It turned up thereafter on the wall of Gwydion's keep—King Gwydion, he was now—lord of all Dyfed. "You've one wish left," he said to it. "One wish left of me."

"I give it to you," the raven said. "Whatever you wish, King Gwydion."

"Be what you wish to be," Gwydion said.

And thereafter men told of the wisdom of King Gwydion as often as of the beauty of his wife.

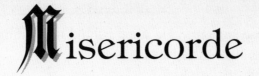

Misericorde

❖

Karl Edward Wagner

he close chamber smelled of stale flowers and staler love.

Tamaslei shook the agate phial petulantly, found it drained of her favorite scent. Crossing her bedchamber with long-limbed strides, she ripped aside a silken curtain and tossed the phial through the window. She drew a deep breath. Chill mountain air puckered her bare nipples. Distantly the phial smashed against stone.

"I will not love a coward," she said to the night.

Upon her bed, Josin stirred uneasily. The agate phial of scented oil had been another of his gifts. He had given it to her the night before he had killed her previous lover.

"I would do whatever you wish. You know that."

"Do I?" Tamaslei laughed derisively and considered her reflection in the dressing-table mirror. Her glossy black hair hung in tangled masses. She flung its coils back across her white shoulders and gathered them at her nape with a gold-chased cord. Tamaslei studied her eyes, as her strong fingers crushed belladonna berries against an onyx mortar.

Josin arose anxiously. He stood behind her, hiding his sudden detumescence from the mirror.

"What you ask is death."

"What I ask is danger. A risk. Surely no *man* would hide his face and creep away on his belly at a simple request from his lady?"

"You ask—you demand," Josin lowered his voice as he glanced at the opened window, "that I steal the ducal crown of Harnsterm from the Vareishei clan."

"*They* stole it easily enough when milord Lonal was fool enough to lead an expedition against them."

"Stripping a coronet from a dead man's bloody pate is a bloody different game from stealing it from an outlaw stronghold."

"You always *said* you were the cleverest thief of all Chrosanthe." Tamaslei discovered an errant eyelash, pitilessly plucked it.

"And so I am," Josin reassured her.

"It's only a dingy old fortress," Tamaslei pressured him, "an uncouth band of robbers."

"Who have held these mountains under their command since the assassination of King Janisavion ten years ago," Josin reminded her.

"Who wears the coronet might well claim rulership of Harnsterm," Tamaslei mused. "Our lamented duke was slain without a direct heir. It will be years before Chrosanthe has exhausted all plots and deposed all pretenders. What the people want now is power—rather, the assurance of power, the symbols of power. I need not remind you that my own family is one of our city's oldest, for all our fall from grace during these recent civil troubles.

"With the ducal crown—*and* an alliance with the man bold enough to wrest it from these mountain bandits . . ." Tamaslei applied scent to the vale of her breasts.

"The Vareishei guard their stolen treasures well."

"And you say that you are a thief."

"I say that I am your lover."

"And I say that I will not love a coward."

Josin shrugged his capable shoulders. His mustache made a sad smile into the mirror. He had climbed this far. Dare he climb farther still? He *was* the best. Of thieves. Of lovers. Of ambitious adventurers. Of all this he was certain. Against the Vareishei? No man had ever won out.

"You shall have this coronet," Josin promised.

"And you shall have my love."

It was a fortnight later.

Two ravens had been cawing at her window.

Tamaslei at last awoke. She climbed from her cold bed. Upon her window ledge rested a shriveled lump of muscle.

She knew it for her lover's heart even before she learned that his head stood atop a pole just beyond the walls of Harnsterm.

It was then that she sought out Kane.

I. Four Names in Blood

"I AM TOLD," TAMASLEI SAID TO THE HALF-BLIND LAMPLIGHTER, "that for a certain amount of gold one may procure the fulfillment of her most fanciful wishes, here in the back streets of Harnsterm."

The lamplighter trimmed the wick and applied his flame. Closing the lozenge-shaped pane, he stepped down from his footstool and hefted his can of oil. He stank of oil and soot, and it seemed that a chance spark might set the old man and his tattered garments ablaze.

"There are many wishes."

"My wish is to speak with a certain man. His name is Kane."

"Dead. Dead, so I have heard. Dead, these many years."

Tamaslei counted gold coins from one palm to another. Josin had once told her that the old lamplighter knew more of the affairs of Harnsterm's underworld than did its denizens.

"But then," said the lamplighter, flipping back his eyepatch to gloat upon the roll of gold pieces, "I *might* know someone who *might* know where Kane *might* be found . . ."

Tamaslei permitted a gold piece to drip from her fingers. It rolled into a pile of horse dung beside the old man's filthy boots.

"When I have spoken with Kane in my chambers in the

Tameiral Mansion," she said, nodding toward the decaying district where Harnsterm's wealth once dwelt, "you shall have five golden companions to clink against this one."

The lamplighter grubbed for the coin as she turned away. "If you live past that tête-à-tête," he mumbled to his beard.

Tamaslei tossed her cloak to a maid and entered her private chambers. She considered the muck that smeared her boots and decided that a bath might remove the stench of the streets from her nostrils. First, though, a drink to calm her unease.

Crossing to the decanter of brandy upon the sideboard, Tamaslei started to pour for herself—some indication of the urgency of her need—when she noticed that one of the matched set of crystal goblets was missing. In vexation, she glanced about the chamber, already preparing a tonguelashing for the servant who had not cleansed and replaced the goblet—and a worse sort of lashing if it had been broken.

The goblet, intact and only just now emptied, was held in a hand that almost engulfed it. Tamaslei splashed brandy onto the sideboard, staring openmouthed at the man who watched her from the shadows of her chamber.

He was huge—it seemed incredible that she hadn't noticed him instantly upon entering the room until she thought of how beasts of prey seem to merge with their surroundings. He was dressed entirely in black, from his high boots and leather trousers to his close-fitting leather jacket. As he leaned against the wall, a sword hilt protruded above his right shoulder, showing a complex filigree against the dark panels. A closely trimmed red beard softened the planes of a brutal face, but the cold blue eyes that studied her from the shadow made Tamaslei choke back the outcry that shuddered in her throat.

"Shall I pour?" suggested Kane.

Regaining her composure, Tamaslei promised herself to take pains with the servant who had failed to inform her of Kane's presence. "You came here quickly."

"Bad news travels quickly." Kane measured brandy into their

goblets. Close to her, his size was even more forbidding, which made the polished grace of his movements all the more sinister.

"You are Kane." Tamaslei's inflection was not questioning. "Josin spoke of you to me. He called you his friend."

"A man of great promise—and, one would have thought, of keener judgment than to attempt to steal from the Vareishei clan. I drink to a comrade departed."

"And I, to a lover." Tamaslei briefly touched her lips to her goblet. "I imagine you will have guessed why I have summoned you here."

Above the rim of his goblet, Kane's eyes were watchful.

"Josin told me that you were the best, the very best. He said that just as he was the greatest of thieves because he stole for the thrill of it, so were you the greatest of assassins because you killed men for the sport."

"And for a price," Kane reminded her.

"They say that for ten marks of gold one may purchase a life from you—the life of anyone."

Kane set aside his goblet. Tamaslei looked into his eyes, and no other answer was needed.

"I wish to purchase a life," she said, "Four lives."

She unclasped a key from the belt of her gown and unlocked the iron-bound door of a massive oaken aumbry. From within she withdrew a pair of leather almoners. Carrying one in either hand, she deposited them upon the sideboard. Returning to the aumbry, she placed two more heavy purses beside the first pair. The decanter and crystal goblets vibrated in elfin cries to the sullen clink of gold coins.

"Each purse contains ten marks in golden coins. For each purse, I demand a life. When four lives are taken, these four purses shall be yours." Her smile challenged him. "Or would you think to take them from me now?"

"I did not come here to steal," Kane told her.

"Because even assassins have their code—and their pride—just as thieves like Josin do."

"Certain rules of the game are essential," Kane replied. "Otherwise it isn't a game. For the true adept, wealth is not the object. If I am offered a fee to perform a certain assignment, I will not accept that fee until I have accomplished it. Taking a fee by force—or accepting an assignment without the certainty that it will be carried out—would be pointless, a bore."

"Then you *will* accept this assignment?"

"I am bored with the ordinary, and already this problem has surpassed the ordinary. It remains for you to tell me the names of the four lives you desire, and the problem shall be solved."

"Josin once told me that a certain etiquette is involved," Tamaslei said. "I, too, believe in doing things correctly."

She thrust her hand into her boot-top and unsheathed a thin-bladed dagger. Setting its point to her thumb, Tamaslei drew a bright rivulet of blood. Using the dagger as a pen, she wrote a name in blood upon each leather almoner.

Wenvor. Ostervor. Sitilvon. Puriali.

"The Vareishei clan." Kane's face showed interest.

"The Vareishei clan." Tamaslei's eyes were as pitiless as Kane's. "They killed my lover. I want their lives."

"I'm fascinated." Kane's smile suggested some secret jest.

"Further," Tamaslei chose her words carefully, "there is the matter of a certain crown that dear Josin sought to steal for me. Should you chance upon the ducal crown of Harnsterm after the Vareishei no longer have need of it, I shall pay you a most generous price."

"So be it," Kane agreed. "You have purchased four lives—and a crown. I had meant to conclude other business this night, but instead I shall give immediate attention to this problem."

"You will find me most appreciative," promised Tamaslei.

II. Fortress of Fear

NORTHWEST OF THE SOUTHERN KINGDOMS, CHROSANTHE WAS A heavily forested, mountainous region of many small villages, usually situated within the protection of an overlord's fortress. Over the years, some of these clustered villages had grown together into fortified cities under the general control of the lord of the castle, who now vied for power with the city mayors. Such a city was Harnsterm, well isolated within the deep valleys and rocky summits of the Altanstand Mountains, but a city of wealth and power because it had developed along the main trade routes through the mountain passes and across the frontier.

It was a land where central power was difficult to maintain, and only the strongest of kings had ever successfully controlled the wealthy cities and the mountain-guarded fortresses of the powerful lords. Since the assassination of King Janisavion a decade before, Chrosanthe had known only anarchy and civil war that threatened to endure forever. Beyond the security of city walls, Chrosanthe was a lawless wilderness, ravaged by the private armies of the powerful lords and plundered by marauding bands of outlaws. Often the distinction was of little consequence, if it could be drawn at all: the Vareishei were a case in point.

It was generally agreed that Altharn Keep had guarded the major pass through the Altanstand Mountains between Harnsterm and the frontier for centuries before Harnsterm had grown into a city. Other legends, according to one's credulity, suggested that the stone fortress had always scowled down from the precipice there, that its ancient walls were raised upon older walls and yet older foundations—a monastery abandoned for uncertain reasons, a temple to a forgotten deity, a castle raised and toppled in an age lost to history, perhaps a prehuman edifice from the ruins of Elder Earth. Whatever its history, Altharn Keep was not a congenial locale, and the lords of Harnsterm had not been long in shifting the seat of their authority to a new castle built along the trade routes somewhat farther within the lands of Chrosanthe, which with the passage of generations became the city of Harnsterm. Altharn Keep, of undeniable strategic importance, had remained under the control of Harnsterm—the command of the fortress and its garrison usually bestowed upon lesser scions of the ruling house.

It was not a holding younger sons plotted murder to possess. In the settled years of King Janisavion, no one thought it unusual that Lonal, duke of Harnsterm, had given command of Altharn Keep to a bastard brother, Vareishei. Presumably Vareishei's excesses would have soon demanded intervention, even had not civil war and its ensuing anarchy given Vareishei a free hand to indulge his despotic whims. To pass beyond the Altanstand Mountains meant to pass below Altharn Keep; where previous wardens had collected taxes and duties, Vareishei took whatever he desired. As lawlessness spread and caravans grew fewer, Vareishei turned his attentions to the surrounding countryside and villages, extending his depredations to the shadow of Harnsterm's walls. Lonal at last had led an expedition against his mutinous half-brother. Some of his army returned with tales of red massacre beneath the somber heights; Lonal never returned at all.

Vareishei might well have claimed lordship of Harnsterm, had he long survived his half-brother. Popular ballads had it that Lonal had given Vareishei his death wound, that their skeletons lay locked together in eternal combat upon the field of battle. Those who claimed to have fought in the battle swore that Vareishei had ridden away unscathed. Regardless, Vareishei had not been seen again following that battle, and some said he had died of his wounds, and some said he had vanished from his chambers on a stormy moonless night. Some few hinted that his children might know the truth of Vareishei's fate, but this was never said above a whisper, and often not a second time.

For some years now Altharn Keep had been held by the Vareishei clan. There were four. Wenvor was the oldest son, powerfully built and a man to be feared in battle. Sitilvon, the sole daughter, was of a subtle mind, and her poisons were subtler still. Ostervor, her younger brother, had some of Wenvor's talents and some of Sitilvon's, and it was not wise to turn a back to him. The fourth, Puriali, was a half-brother, born to a girl Vareishei had abducted from a lonely mountain cottage. Puriali was the only one of his bastards that Vareishei knowingly spared, and some said it was out of love for his mother and others said it was out of fear of her. It may have been out of fear of Puriali, for his mother had guided his footsteps upon darker paths.

As central power and the rule of law fast became a distant memory, much as a cancer victim dimly recalls a life without pain, the Vareishei clan assumed absolute rule of the mountains beyond Harnsterm. Altharn Keep was unassailable; Harnsterm dared not spare more of its soldiers to defend its holdings. The Vareishei demanded heavy tribute from those they spared, and those they chose not to spare might only beg for a quick death. Where their father had been ruthless, the Vareishei clan were malevolent. The people of Harnsterm looked to their walls and prayed against the evil day when tribute would not suffice.

Kane smelled death long before he came upon the caravan. The fresh mountain breeze brought the musty scent of stale blood, the sweetness of torn flesh, and an acrid stench of burning. Moving silently beneath the stars, Kane's black stallion stepped from the edge of the forest and onto the weed-grown trail. Once this had been a well-traveled road, but that had been in days when corpses did not dangle from tree limbs to mark the way.

As Kane passed between the rows of the dead, he heard the sound of hoarse breathing and paused. One, a boy barely into his teens, was still alive—although from the blood that yet trickled from his mutilated loins down his legs and into the earth, he would not see the sunrise. Kane cut him down from the limb over which they had bound him. His eyes opened as Kane stretched him out upon the trampled ground.

"The Vareishei?" Kane asked, more to prompt than to question.

The boy answered mechanically, like someone speaking from a trance. "We thought to slip past them under cover of darkness. They caught us at daybreak. They said they would leave us here as warning to those who would cross their domain without paying tribute."

"And afterward?"

"They carried away all to Altharn Keep. They took my sister."

"Doubtless to be held for ransom. Now, let this powder dissolve upon your tongue; it will ease the pain."

The first was a lie, and the last was not, for Kane was seldom needlessly cruel. The artery beneath his fingertips pulsed weakly until he had counted to twenty-seven, then the heart shuddered and stopped.

Remounting, Kane resumed his journey to Altharn Keep. The clods of turf torn by his stallion's hooves fell soundlessly, for the dead cannot hear.

Puriali absently chewed a tidbit of raw liver as he searched the girl's entrails. His surgery was quite precise, for all that his captive had continued to struggle until a moment gone. Her virgin blood made scarlet rivulets across the polished slab of pale pink marble.

"There is danger for us."

His half-sister licked her lips. "Do you actually give credence to augury such as this?"

"Not really, Sitilvon," murmured Puriali. "But I know that it pleases me. And you."

Puriali wiped his hands against his trouser legs, mingling red with less certain stains as he stared upward into the night skies enclosing the tower's summit. "Merely a supportive exercise. The stars cannot lie. They warn of death."

Wenvor snorted and tightened his fist about his sword hilt. Ostervor shifted his feet and considered his wine cup. The brothers were both tall and black-bearded, though Wenvor's meaty shoulders would have made two of Ostervor; their sister might have been a clean-shaven twin of the younger brother. Puriali, who somewhat favored his mother, was shorter, slighter, with a spiky shock of reddish hair and a face too pockmarked to grow a full beard. The two brothers wore leather trousers and stained hacquetons, having shed their mail. Sitilvon had thrown a fur cloak about her ankle-length gown, but Puriali stood bare-chested despite the chill mountain wind.

"The stars cannot lie," Puriali repeated.

"Another thief?" Wenvor laughed and nudged his sister. "I hope better sport than the last."

Ostervor did not share their mirth. "I have heard certain reports that Josin's bereaved mistress has made inquiries about Kane."

There was no more laughter.

"Kane may well be dead," Wenvor scoffed finally. "Nothing has been heard of Kane in years now. Some say he's fled the land; some say he's grown old and left his trade."

"And some say he's withdrawn solely to perfect his art," Ostervor said.

"Whatever arts they may be," added Puriali.

"Does it matter?" sneered Sitilvon. "Kane or any other foe—if they come against us, they die. If the stars give us warning, then let us heed them. Let him enter Altharn Keep, if he dare. Others who have tried have scarcely outstayed their welcome."

Puriali pointed upward. "Look."

As if swept over by a black wave of mist, the stars had vanished. Only a pallid sickle of moon interrupted the absolute darkness that enclosed Altharn Keep.

III. The Summoning

WENVOR HUNCHED HIS BROAD SHOULDERS AND BLEW UPON HIS hands. Beneath the flaring cressets, frost sparkled upon the massive stones of the merlons. The eldest Vareishei scorned cloak or gauntlets as he continued to pace the darkened battlements of Altharn Keep. Save the measured challenge of an unseen sentry, the thin scuff of his boots marked the only sound of his progress.

Altharn Keep controlled the gorge through the Altanstand Mountains from atop a high cliff, beneath which a narrow roadway crowded passage between sheer walls of stone and thunderous white-water rapids. More than two-thirds of the fortress walls rose above a breathless precipice falling several hundred feet onto the eroded boulders where the river pounded through its bend. Approach to Altharn Keep's heavily fortified entrance curled along the steep ridge that completed its perimeter. Armies had attempted assault along this slope throughout the ages, and their bleached bones could be found entangled in the thickets of heather and rhododendron.

No one in memory had forced the gates of Altharn Keep.

Guards had always maintained harsh vigilance over those who were permitted to pass through its gates, and with the deepening civil chaos their attentions only grew less restrained. Josin had managed to scale the walls with a climbing rope, but this initial success had not repaid him. It was always possible—just possible—that an intruder might attempt to enter Altharn Keep by ascending the sheer face of the escarpment and scaling the less well-guarded battlements that crested the precipice. Over the ages a few rash fools had attempted this, and where the river had rolled their shattered bones no one knew.

Wenvor, while he might not be his siblings' equal in guile, was never one to misjudge an enemy, and he did not discount the tales he had heard of Kane. Thus, Wenvor permitted himself a thin smile of vindication when he heard the soft clink of metal against stone.

With surprising stealth for a man of his bulk, Wenvor closed upon the source of the sound: a darkened stretch of the parapet, a hundred feet or more between sentry posts, guarding the most treacherous face of the precipice. Only an eye alert to discover that which the mind knew must be there would have seen it: a steel grapnel lodged against one crenel.

"I would have expected no less of you," Wenvor said softly, even as his broadsword swung downward through the darkness and parted the taut cord of knotted silk. The cord sang like a snapped bowstring, the slack grapnel fell to the parapet with a tiny clatter, and the rush of the river swallowed the sounds of whatever might have fallen far below.

Wenvor sighed and straightened.

He heard again the soft scrape of metal against stone.

Wenvor turned. The sickle moon and distant cressets together gave light enough to see the hulking figure in black, idly touching the tip of his broadsword to the battlement. Eyes of the coldest blue caught the wan light as chillingly as did the frost.

"Your sentry," said Kane.

"Damn you!" said Wenvor, and lunged.

Wenvor's only emotion as Kane's blade checked his own downward stroke was one of rage. While Kane's physical presence was formidable, Wenvor was himself a man of overawing stature, and he had never seen his equal in swordplay. Their broadswords warred together as if the storm gods gave battle above the clouds—flickering sudden explosions of bright sparks, shattering the night's stillness with tearing clangor of steel against steel. Driving against each other, their powerful two-handed blows jarred through muscle and bone with stunning force, all but smashing sword hilts from nerveless fists.

Wenvor's breath shook in hoarse gasps, and, as he began to listen for the clamor of onrushing guardsmen, he knew that he felt fear. And with that knowledge, Wenvor's desperate parry failed by a fraction of a second, and Kane's blade drove into his shoulder with crushing force.

Even the best mail cannot withstand stress beyond its limits; enough links held to save dismemberment, but Kane's sword bit deep into Wenvor's flesh with bone-shattering force. Wenvor's blade rang against the parapet, even as he was driven to his knees. Numbing, sickening pain racked him, and he knew instinctively that in another instant would be surcease.

Kane, however, disdained the killing blow. Weaponless, his hands reached out for Wenvor.

"Wenvor, come with me."

Ostervor held his breath, gradually increasing the pressure of his shoulder against the black oak panel. He felt his bones begin to creak in protest, then the section of wall pivoted inward, corroded hinges rasping under their first movement in more than a century. Cobwebs hung with the dust of another's ancestors curtained the aperture, but the darkness within welled outward with the cold breath of frosted night beyond.

Ostervor smeared sweat from his forehead with a dusty forearm, considering the three depressed inlays in the parquetry of the chamber's floor. Reputedly haunted, the north wing of Altharn Keep had remained untenanted throughout living memory. Ostervor, who had long ago mastered the hidden passageways that crept through the other sections of the fortress, congratulated himself upon his having solved this final mystery. The doggerel inscription upon the chamber's mantel—*One for the Bold, Two for the Gold, Three for to Hold*—had seemed nonsensical to generations of inhabitants. Recent perusal of a centuries-old journal in Altharn Keep's moldering library had provided Ostervor the essential clue, with its archaic pun on *bold* and *hold* in reference to the coat-of-arms stylized in the parquetry. Other allusions to the treacherous pitfalls within the north wing's secret ways had determined Ostervor to pursue its exploration after appropriate deliberation. However . . .

Ostervor did not discount his half-brother's premonition of doom anymore than he dismissed his own spies' reports that Josin's mistress had sought out Kane. Granting Kane a cunning almost equal to his own—if the lurid tales bore any credence—Ostervor hardly expected their nemesis to present his shield at the fortress gate. Given Kane's reputation—even allowing for the inevitable exaggerations and embellishments—Ostervor assumed that the assassin would seek to enter Altharn Keep by stealth of the most devious sort. The ancient citadel was honeycombed with hidden passageways, all of which (now that the north wing had given up its secrets) were intimately known to Ostervor. It would be a fatal underestimation of their enemy to assume that Kane would not be privy to these secret ways as well.

Nonetheless, it quite unnerved Ostervor to discern recent footprints etched upon the passageway whose dust should not have been disturbed in more than a century.

Ostervor hesitated, scowling at the damp boot prints that strode boldly through the smear of light his candle shed. He had already seen to the citadel's other hidden passages, most of which were known only to himself; a score of deadly traps—six of his own devising and installation—meant certain death for any intruder. Yet, here in this passageway whose secrets Ostervor himself had only lately mastered, another had already gained entry.

Ostervor touched a finger to one boot print, recovering a fragment of lichen, flakes of frost still melting upon it. The intruder had passed this way only a moment before. Ostervor pulled off his boots and unbuckled his sword. The narrow passage was no field for swordplay, and the heavy dirk that he now drew had served him well in close quarters many times before. He placed his candle upon the floor outside the pivoted doorway. Silently, unseen, Ostervor would follow Kane through the north wing passages, trusting to his own fragmentary knowledge of its pitfalls. Kane obviously could not attempt their traverse in darkness; he must show a light, and then Ostervor would creep upon him from behind.

Ostervor, however, had not expected the panel to swing shut as he passed through it.

He counted slowly to fifty, his eyes pressed shut, before he moved. Other than the spectral groan of hinges as the doorway closed, there was no other sound. At least, he told himself, he wasn't backlighted by the feeble glow of the candle in the chamber behind the wall. Kane—and Ostervor had earlier peered into the passage for a gleam of the assassin's light—had likely passed beyond hearing in search of a hidden entrance to the Vareishei's private quarters. Ostervor withdrew a fresh candle from a pouch at his belt—there was yet another, and a tinderbox to strike fire—and tied a neckscarf about it for bulk. This he wedged against the now-closed doorway, marking its location. Silently counting his paces, Ostervor felt his way along the pitch-dark passageway, following the direction Kane's footprints had taken.

He had counted only seven paces when Ostervor's outthrust fingers encountered a stone wall.

Ostervor halted before the unexpected barrier, puzzled by its presence. He knew to expect the trapdoor paving at thirty paces, to be wary of the pivoting steps midway down the first staircase, to avoid the spring-loaded spears just beyond the second turning— these and other deathtraps were described in the fragmentary journals he had discovered. There was no reference to a blank wall, such as he now confronted.

A later modification, Ostervor decided. At some point the citadel's master had walled off this series of passageways. And yet,

Kane's footprints had led this way. It was impossible that Kane could have passed him upon returning; therefore the assassin must have known of another exit from the passage. Or had his returning footprints, no longer damp from the night beyond, left marks unnoticed at Ostervor's first glance?

Stealthily Ostervor retraced his way along the passage, seeking Kane in the other direction. Ten paces beyond the point of his entrance, Ostervor's outthrust fingers encountered a stone wall.

Ostervor swore silently, beginning to know fear. Feeling his way carefully across the blank wall and back down the passageway, his toes nudged the candle knotted within its scarf.

The flicker of his tinderbox was blinding, and his hand shook as he applied its flame to candlewick. Its light was more than sufficient to disclose that the passageway had been walled up at either end.

The doorway by which Ostervor had entered the passage refused to open for all his cunning attempts to activate its hidden mechanism, nor did the thick oaken panels yield to his frantic pounding.

Ostervor wasted most of his one remaining candle seeking some other means of egress. Kane's bootprints, maddeningly obscured by his own footprints, somehow seemed to lead in either direction and into nowhere. Giving it up, Ostervor began to hew upon the oaken panels through which he had entered. His last candle gave light long enough to disclose the steel plating sandwiched within the paneling, but it was little joy to Ostervor that he had solved the mystery of the hidden doorway's solidity.

In the long darkness that followed, Ostervor's kicking and pounding brought no more response than did his screams. The north wing, of course, was reputedly haunted, and seldom was it visited. In time his shouts became a hoarse croaking, his hands raw and bleeding, his body an agonizing mass of bruises from useless rushes against the unyielding walls.

The choking dust only made his throat come upon him the sooner, so that the torture of his thirst for some time obscured the realization that the air in the passage was growing bad. Whatever circulation might exist, it was inadequate for his needs, and Ostervor was slowly suffocating inside this crypt. He lay motionless, conserving strength, only his brain furiously at work on the problem of escape. Time became a meaningless interval between useless efforts to open the door; it may be that he slept, for the choking darkness gave no indication of the hours that passed. The poisoned air now hurt his lungs worse than the agony of his parched throat.

Rising from a hopeless stupor, Ostervor knew his strength was failing. He forced stale air into his chest for one last jagged howl of despair and flung his pain-racked body against the unyielding doorway.

The doorway instantly pivoted before his weight, and Ostervor fell headlong into the chamber beyond. Upon the floor beside his face, the candle he had placed there was still burning.

"Time, after all," said Kane, reaching down for him, "is only relative."

Ostervor's hoarse breath melted the flecks of frost upon Kane's boots.

"Ostervor, come with me."

Sitilvon liked to refer to the cellar chamber as her studio. Seated at her writing table, she stared thoughtfully at the half-covered page of parchment before her. Her pen had dried again, and she absently wet its tip with her tongue to keep it from blotting—a habit that left her with a blotchy sort of mustache when she kept late hours in her studio. She considered the now-still body of the youth strapped head down upon an X-shaped frame in the center of the chamber. Beneath his dangling head a large silver bowl was nearly filled with blood-tinged vomit. Sitilvon reread her notes of earlier that evening, then dipped her clean pen into her inkwell and concluded her notes.

"Subject 3 is young male of sound physique and good health. Force-fed vomitus concentration from Subject 2, placed upon frame. Severe convulsions observed by second hour, increasing intensity with total vomiting of stomach contents by third hour, decreasing soon thereafter. No observable signs of life after fourth hour."

Sitilvon frowned and continued to write.

"There seems little point in continuing this line of study. Despite common belief, it is demonstrable that a combination of arsenic and mercuric salt does not increase in toxicity as the poison is recovered from the vomitus of one victim to the next."

"Obviously you were only diluting its virulence," commented Kane, reading over her shoulder. "One might as well maintain that a blade grows sharper each time it hews flesh and bone."

Sitilvon's pen shook a spatter of ink upon the page, but she gave no other outward sign of disquiet.

"The poison might have absorbed certain essences of death from each victim," she said calmly.

"What? Heavy metal salts?" Kane was derisive. "Rank superstition."

She rose slowly from her chair and faced Kane, gaining considerable assurance from the fact the assassin had not simply cut her throat once he had crept upon her unseen.

"I had thought I had given orders not to be disturbed. Shall I call in my guardsmen?"

"They are rather less capable of obeying you now," Kane said.

"What do you want?"

"I should think you must know that answer."

Sitilvon knew, but she also knew that while they talked, she remained alive. She smoothed the folds of her gown across her hips and faced him coolly. While she scorned to take pains with her appearance, she knew her features were good, her figure exciting to her occasional lovers—and Kane, after all, was only a man.

"You are no common assassin," she told him, "or you would have slain me from behind."

"I was interested in your conclusions to this experiment," Kane said. "I had earlier amused myself by reading through your journal. Truly remarkable."

"One would assume an assassin would be interested in the

practical, if not the theoretical aspects of toxicology," Sitilvon smiled, edging toward a credenza. "May I drink a glass of wine?"

"It would be rude to refuse you," Kane acceded. "The notes where you established the toxic characteristics of each portion of the monkshood plant were particularly methodical. Forty children—fascinating!"

"Will you drink a glass with me?" Sitilvon invited. "This vintage has lain in our cellars since it was pillaged before my father's day. None of us has been able to identify it."

She poured two ice-clear goblets with heavy, tawny wine, and then handed one to Kane.

Kane had been watching her every movement. "The other goblet, if you please," he said, ignoring the one she proferred.

Sitilvon shrugged and made the exchange. "As you please."

She took a luxuriant sip from her goblet, then noticed that Kane was still watching her, his own wine untasted.

"I'm sure you'll understand if I exchange goblets with you once again," Kane smiled, giving Sitilvon his wine and taking hers.

"Under the circumstances, I can understand your caution." Sitilvon returned his smile above her goblet. She drank deeply, and Kane followed suit.

Sitilvon drowned her laughter in the wine. Both of their glasses were poisoned, for the decanter from which she poured was steeped with enough distillate of the amber poppy to kill a hundred men. Sitilvon, whose addiction to the same rare drug had established an enormous tolerance, considered this tainted liqueur no more than a pleasant nightcap. For Kane, the sleep would never be broken.

Kane drained his goblet. "This is one of the sweet white wines that could be had from regional vineyards where the Southern Kingdoms border Chrosanthe," Kane decided, "until the killing blight of a century past destroyed the grapes there. Its precise vineyard and perhaps its exact year I might have told you, had the wine not been so heavily laced with a tincture of amber poppies."

Sitilvon's eyes grew wide with fear.

"The stimulant I swallowed as you poured for us is quite sufficient an antidote," Kane said gently. "After all, I've had time enough to peruse your journal—and to partake of your sideboard. The opium of the amber poppy is no stranger to me."

Sitilvon realized that her heartbeat was too rapid, too erratic, even for fear. Pain lanced through her chest.

"When you switched goblets with me . . ."

"Actually, it was in your inkwell," Kane explained.

Her pulse was shaking her entire body. Sitilvon clutched at her writing table, her legs nerveless. Kane's hands reached out for her.

"Sitilvon, come with me."

Puriali dipped his brush of maidens' eyelashes into the jade cup of infant's blood and completed the final astrological symbol within the pentacle's inner circle an instant before the last weakened cry of the newborn. Difficult in the extreme each step had been, but then the stakes were the highest, and Puriali knew he was too accomplished an adept to fail. He gathered his magician's robes close to his bony knees—it would be catastrophic should one of the lines be obliterated at this hour—and stepped carefully outside of the pentacle. Its outermost circle of power touched the threshold of the tower chamber's door and encompassed half the room. Puriali seated himself at his desk in view of the only door. A block of tarry substance with which he had formed the outer circle lay in his fingers, and his hand hung down only inches from a short gap that broke the outer circle. His lips barely seemed to move as he crooned a low chant in an archaic tongue.

The wait was longer than Puriali had anticipated, but in time Kane slipped past the open doorway and stepped into the circle of the pentacle. Puriali lashed out with his dubious chalk and closed the circle. Kane halted at the sudden movement, watching the sorcerer.

Puriali nodded a complacent greeting. "By now," he said urbanely, "it would no doubt be facetious to inquire after the wellbeing of my paternal siblings."

"Do you really want to know?" Kane asked.

"Surely you couldn't have thought I bore them any brotherly

affection. They would have rid themselves of me long ago had we not needed one another. The solution to the problem is that *I* was first to realize the others were superfluous."

Puriali's smirk bespoke private jests. He watched Kane pace about the pentacle, seemingly studying its artistry with the detachment of the connoisseur.

"I imagine you may be curious as to why I have summoned you to me," Puriali suggested.

Kane ceased his pacing and regarded the sorcerer attentively. "I was awaiting a polite opportunity to ask."

"I know everything about you, of course," Puriali assured him with benign humor. "Everything."

"Everything?"

"Which is both why *and* how I summoned you here." Puriali held up a hand to forestall protest. "No doubt you are thinking that you were sent here to carry out the vendetta of some bereaved whore with grandiose dreams. You should have understood by now that apparent free will is only a delusion.

"You were summoned here through my own arts, Kane. I knew my half-siblings hated me, plotted as one to be rid of me whenever it seemed that my arts were more of a danger to them than an asset. Why not? Together we killed our father when his usefulness was outlived. But this time theirs was the error of judgment. I was already too powerful to require their continued existence."

Puriali withdrew a glittering coronet from beneath his robes and jammed it down upon his shock of red hair. "The ducal crown of Harnsterm," he crowed, regarding Kane through over-bright blue eyes. "Fits rather well, don't you agree?"

"Gold can be bent to any shape," Kane remarked.

"Very pithy, to be sure. No doubt your unsuspected wit will provide me with much needed amusement while you serve my will."

"You were about to explain . . . ?"

"Why, I should imagine it is all obvious to you by now, Kane." Puriali adjusted the crown. "Who else could have murdered Wenvor and Ostervor and lovely Sitilvon? They were far too vigilant to give me the chance."

"And now?"

"And now you should serve me. With the others dead I shall require a loyal henchman—one who can lead men into battle as expertly as he can weave political intrigue. For this reason I have spared you. With you to carry out my commands, Harnsterm is only the first step toward conquest of this strife-torn land."

"An ambitious scheme," Kane commented, "if not particularly original. However, I regret that my own immediate assignments will make such an alliance impossible."

"Alliance?" Puriali laughed. "Not so. It is servitude I demand of you, Kane—although you will find that I am a kind master to those who serve me well."

He rose to his feet and gestured sweepingly. "By now you will have examined the pentacle into which you so obligingly blundered. Still believe in freedom of will, Kane? I summoned you tonight, willing you to slay the others, then to come to me in my tower. You are imprisoned now within the pentacle, held there by the symbols of power that represent the innermost secrets of your existence. You cannot escape the pentacle until I set you free, Kane—and this I will do only after I have bound you to me through certain irrevocable oaths and pacts that not even you dare break."

Puriali savored his triumph. "You see, Kane, I know that you are no common assassin and adventurer, no matter how uncommon your abilities. I *know* who you are."

The sorcerer gestured impressively. "Kane, son of Adam and born of Eve, you are within my power and my power alone. For centuries beyond counting you have followed your accursed fate, but after this night you shall follow only the dictates of my will. I have seen your destiny in the stars, and the astrological symbols of your nativity bind you powerless within the pentacle."

"Most impressive," Kane admitted. "Your work would do credit to a far older sorcerer whose wisdom would transcend this provincial backwater. You have committed only a few mistakes, but regrettably this is not an art in which one learns through experience.

"In time even the stars change," Kane explained, casually stepping out of the pentacle, "and yours are not the constellations of my birth."

Puriali shrank back against the tower wall, seeking in vain for an avenue of escape.

"And it's ironic that you hadn't known Eve was only my stepmother," Kane continued, reaching out for Puriali, "inasmuch as I rather suspect there's some trace of my blood in your veins.

"Puriali, come with me."

IV. Payment in Full

TAMASLEI AWOKE FROM DREAMS OF JOSIN TO DISCOVER KANE SEATED beside her bed. It was not a pleasant prospect, and she clutched the fur robes protectively about her silk-clad shoulders. Remembering the thin-bladed dagger sheathed just behind the headboard, she regained composure.

"What do you want, Kane?" Her voice was surprisingly level.

"Payment. I have completed my part of our bargain."

Tamaslei turned up the wick of her bedside lamp, increasing its companionable glow to brightness that split the chamber into shadows. Her figure was supple beneath the translucent silk.

"No doubt there is proof?" Tamaslei's eyes were upon the large bag that Kane carried. Its leather folds seemed too flaccid to contain the evidences she expected.

Kane's tone was formal, but held neither rancor nor scorn. "Tamaslei, I give these to you in accordance with our agreement."

He took her hand and dropped several bright objects onto her palm.

Tamaslei's first thought was that they were jewels, then she saw they were something more. They were four oblong sigils carved of some crystal resembling jet, approximately the size of the first joint of her thumb, unusually heavy for their size and curiously warm to the touch. Each bore a carving upon its flattened side, and each carved figure was different: a dragon, a spider, a serpent, and a scorpion.

"I'm not certain I understand the jest, Kane. I hired you to kill the Vareishei clan, and unless you have brought me their heads as proof that you have fulfilled our bargain, I insist upon awaiting news of their deaths before I give you payment."

She had expected protest, but Kane's voice was patient. "You did not ask me to kill the Vareishei clan; you said you wished to purchase their lives. You were most explicit."

"Come to the point of your jest, Kane."

"There is no jest. You made a contract to purchase four lives. I took four lives. You hold them in your hand: Wenvor, Ostervor, Sitilvon, Puriali."

"Do you think me a fool!" Tamaslei slid closer to the hidden dagger.

Kane took the serpent-carven sigil from her hand and pressed it to her forehead. Tamaslei stiffened for a moment, then flung herself away with a violent shudder.

"The secret is all but lost," Kane said, "but I assumed you understood when you agreed to our contract, and I took from them their lives as I promised to do."

"And what of their physical bodies?" Tamaslei no longer doubted.

Kane shrugged. "Lifeless carrion. Perhaps their followers were of a mind to burn their bodies upon a pyre of their stolen riches, perhaps they left them for the ravens. Their life-force remains imprisoned within these sigils."

"And what shall I do with them?"

"Whatever you wish."

"If I smash the sigils?"

"Their life-force would be released to reanimate their former flesh, such as may remain of it. However transient that experience might be, it cannot be a pleasant one."

Tamaslei rose from her bed and seated herself at her dressing table. One by one she dropped each sigil into her onyx mortar, smashing brutally downward with its pestle. The crystals shattered under her determined blows, suddenly disintegrating into thousands of dull granules. The sound of their shattering was like a cry of anguish.

When she had finished, Tamaslei seemed to remember Kane's presence, like one recalling a long-ago dream. "And the coronet?" she asked, coming to herself.

Kane produced the crown of Harnsterm from the depths of his bag. "The Vareishei no longer had need of it."

Tamaslei snatched it from his hand and gazed into her mirror. Her eyes glowed as she adjusted the crown upon her head.

"There remains the matter of payment," Kane reminded her.

"Of course! And you shall find me more than generous."

"I only demand payment as agreed upon. A game is pointless if one disregards its rules."

Tamaslei unlocked the iron-bound door of her aumbry, as Kane held open his bag. One by one she drew them out: four bulging leather almoners, a name written in blood upon each heavy purse. One by one they disappeared into the black depths of Kane's bag.

"I have kept these forty marks of gold in readiness for you, as promised," Tamaslei explained. "I insist on paying you full value for this crown as well. However, I don't have enough gold on hand to make fair payment. Tomorrow evening, when you call upon me, I shall have obtained the full payment you have earned."

Tamaslei judged that by that time she could obtain half a dozen sufficiently competent and considerably less expensive assassins to lie in wait for Kane.

"The crown is yours to keep," Kane said unexpectedly. "I rather think Josin would have wanted you to have it."

He pointed toward the depths of the aumbry. "If you will just pull out the false nailheads immediately above and below the middle shelf at the left, that will release the lock on the false bottom. Hand me as payment what you find within, and this most interesting assignment will be completed."

Tamaslei bit her lip in anger, wondering how Kane could know of the aumbry's secret compartment. But he was not as clever as he thought, for the false bottom concealed nothing of real value—it was luck that Kane had not learned of the hidden space beneath the hearth.

To her surprise, her fingers closed upon a thick leather purse. In wonder she dragged it out. It was a fat almoner, heavy with gold, just the same as the other four. Tamaslei gaped at it, turning it about in her hands.

There was a name written in blood: *Tamaslei*.

She remembered the thin-bladed dagger beside her bed, then saw that it was now held in Kane's hand.

"Josin knew you were sending him to almost certain death," Kane told her, stepping near. "Josin came to me before he set out, and we made a contract."

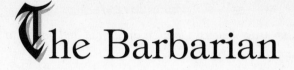

The Barbarian

❖

Poul Anderson

ince the Howard-de Camp system for deciphering preglacial inscriptions first appeared, much progress has been made in tracing the history, ethnology, and even daily life of the great cultures which flourished till the Pleistocene ice age wiped them out and forced man to start over. We know, for instance, that magic was practiced; that there were some highly civilized countries in what is now Central Asia, the Near East, North Africa, southern Europe, and various oceans; and that elsewhere the world was occupied by barbarians, of whom the North Europeans were the biggest, strongest, and most warlike. At least, so the scholars inform us, and being of North European ancestry they ought to know.

The following is a translation of a letter recently discovered in the ruins of Cyrenne. This was a provincial town of the Sarmian Empire, a great though decadent realm in the eastern Mediterranean area, whose capital, Sarmia, was at once the most beautiful and the most lustful, depraved city of its time. The Sarmians' northern neighbors were primitive horse nomads and/or Centaurs; but to the east lay the Kingdom of Chathakh, and to the south was the Herpetarchy of Serpens, ruled by a priestly cast of snake worshippers—or possibly snakes.

The letter was obviously written in Sarmia and posted to Cyrenne. Its date is approximately 175,000 B.C.

Maxilion Quaestos, sub-sub-sub-prefect of the Imperial Waterworks of Sarmia, to his nephew Thyaston, Chancellor of the Bureau of Thaumaturgy, Province of Cyrenne:

Greetings!

I trust this finds you in good health, and that the gods will continue to favor you. As for me, I am well, though somewhat plagued by the gout, for which I have tried [*here follows the description of a home remedy, both tedious and unprintable*]. This has not availed, however, save to exhaust my purse and myself.

You must indeed have been out of touch during your Atlantean journey, if you must write to inquire about the Barbarian affair. Now that events have settled down again, I can, I hope, give you an adequate and dispassionate account of the whole ill-starred business. By the favor of the Triplet Goddesses, holy Sarmia has survived the episode; and though we are still rather shaken, things are improving. If at all times I seem to depart from the philosophic calm I have always tried to cultivate, blame it on the Barbarian. I am not the man I used to be. None of us are.

To begin, then, about three years ago the war with Chathakh had settled down to border skirmishes. Now and then a raid by one side or the other would penetrate deeply into the countries themselves, but with no decisive effect. Indeed, since these operations yielded a more or less equal amount of booty for both lands, and the slave trade grew brisk, it was good for business.

Our chief concern was the ambiguous attitude of Serpens. As you well know, the Herpetarchs have no love for us, and a major object of our diplomacy was to keep them from entering the war on the side of Chathakh. We had, of course, no hope of making them our allies. But as long as we maintained a posture of strength, it was likely that they would at least stay neutral.

Thus it stood when the Barbarian came to Sarmia.

We had heard rumors of him for a long time. An accurate description was available. He was a wandering soldier of fortune from some kingdom of swordsmen and seafarers up in the northern forests. He had drifted south, alone, in search of adventure or perhaps only a better climate. Seven feet tall, and broad in proportion, he was one mass of muscle, with a mane of tawny hair and sullen blue eyes. He was adept with any weapon, but preferred a four-foot double-edged sword with which he could cleave helmet, skull, neck, and so on down at one blow. He was also said to be a drinker and lover of awesome capacity.

Having overcome the Centaurs singlehanded, he tramped down through our northern provinces and one day stood at the gates of Sarmia herself. It was a curious vision—the turreted walls rearing up over the stone-paved road, the guards with helmet and shield and corselet, and the towering near-naked giant who rattled his blade before them. As their pikes slanted down to bar his way, he cried in a voice of thunder:

"I yam Cronkheit duh Barbarian, an' I wanna audience widjer queen!"

His accent was so ludicrously uneducated that the watch burst into laughter. This angered him; flushing darkly, he drew his sword and advanced stiff-legged. The guardsmen reeled back before him, and the Barbarian swaggered through.

As the captain of the watch explained it to me afterward: "There he came, and there we stood. A spear length away, we caught the smell. Ye gods, *when* did he last bathe?"

So with people running from the streets and bazaars as he neared, Cronkheit made his way down the Avenue of Sphinxes, past the baths and the Temple of Loccar, till he reached the Imperial Palace. Its gates stood open as usual, and he looked in at the gardens and the alabaster walls beyond, and grunted. When the Golden Guardsmen approached him upwind and asked his business, he grunted again. They lifted their bows and would have made short work of him, but a slave came running to bid them desist.

You see, by the will of some malignant god, the Empress was standing on a balcony and saw him.

As is well known, our beloved Empress, Her Seductive Majesty the Illustrious Lady Larra the Voluptuous, is built like a mountain highway and is commonly believed to be an incarnation of her tutelary deity, Aphrosex, the Mink Goddess. She stood on the balcony with the wind blowing her thin transparent garments and thick black hair, and a sudden eagerness lit her proud lovely face. This was understandable, for Cronkheit wore only a bearskin kilt.

So the slave was dispatched, to bow low before the stranger and say: "Most noble lord, the divine Empress would have private speech with you."

Cronkheit smacked his lips and strutted into the palace. The chamberlain wrung his hands when he saw those large muddy feet treading priceless rugs, but there was no help for it, and the Barbarian was led upstairs to the Imperial bedchamber.

What befell there is known to all, for of course in such interviews the Lady Larra posts mute slaves at convenient peepholes, to summon the guards if danger seems to threaten; and the courtiers have quietly taught these mutes to write. Our Empress had a cold, and had furthermore been eating a garlic salad, so her aristocratically curved nose was not offended. After a few formalities, she began to pant. Slowly, then she held out her arms and let the purple robe slide down from her creamy shoulders and across the silken thighs.

"Come," she whispered. "Come, magnificent male."

Cronkheit snorted, pawed the ground, rushed forth, and clasped her to him.

"Yowww!" cried the Empress as a rib cracked. "Leggo! Help!"

The mutes ran for the Golden Guardsmen, who entered at once. They got ropes around the Barbarian and dragged him from their poor lady. Though in considerable pain, and much shaken, she did not order his execution; she is known to be very patient with some types.

Indeed, after gulping a cup of wine to steady her, she invited Cronkheit to be her guest. After he had been conducted off to his rooms, she summoned the Duchess of Thyle, a supple, agile little minx.

"I have a task for you, my dear," she murmured. "You will fulfill it as a loyal lady in waiting."

"Yes, Your Seductive Majesty," said the Duchess, who could well guess what the task was and thought she had been waiting long enough. For a whole week, in fact. Her assignment was to take the edge off the Barbarian's impetuosity.

She greased herself so she could slip free if in peril of being crushed, and hurried to Cronkheit's suite. Her musky perfume drowned out his odor, and she slipped off her dress and crooned with half-shut eyes: "Take me, my lord!"

"Yahoo!" howled the warrior. "I yam Cronkheit duh Strong, Cronkheit duh Bold, Cronkheit what slew a mammot' single-handed an' made hisself chief o' duh Centaurs, an' dis's muh night! C'mere!"

The Duchess did, and he folded her in his mighty arms. A moment later there was another shriek. The palace attendants were treated to the sight of a naked and furious greased Duchess speeding down the jade corridor.

"Fleas he's got!" she cried, scratching as she ran.

So all in all, Cronkheit the Barbarian was no great success as a lover. Even the women in the Street of Joy used to hide when they saw him coming. They said they'd been exposed to clumsy technique before, but this was just too much.

However, his fame was so great that the Lady Larra put him in command of a brigade, infantry and cavalry, and sent him to join General Grythion on the Chathakh border. He made the march in record time and came shouting into the city of tents which had grown up at our main base.

Now admittedly our good General Grythion is somewhat of a dandy, who curls his beard and is henpecked by his wives. But he has always been a competent soldier, winning honors at the Academy and leading troops in battle many times before rising to the strategic-planning post. One could understand Cronkheit's incivility at their meeting. But when the general courteously declined to go forth in the van of the army and pointed out how much more valuable he was as a coordinator behind the lines—that was no excuse for Cronkheit to knock his superior officer to the ground and call him a coward, damned of the gods. Grythion was thoroughly justified in having him put in irons, despite the casualties involved. Even as it was, the spectacle had so demoralized our troops that they lost three important engagements in the following month.

Alas! Word of this reached the Empress, and she did not order Cronkheit's head struck off. Indeed, she sent back a command that he be released and reinstated. Perhaps she still cherished him enough to be an acceptable bed partner.

Grythion swallowed his pride and apologized to the Barbarian, who accepted with an ill grace. His restored rank made it necessary to invite him to a dinner and conference in the headquarters tent.

It was a flat failure. Cronkheit stamped in and at once made sneering remarks about the elegant togas of his brother officers. He belched when he ate and couldn't distinguish the product of one vineyard from another. His conversation consisted of hour-long monologues about his own prowess. General Grythion saw morale zooming downward, and hastily called for maps and planning.

"Now, most noble sirs," he began, "we have to lay out the summer campaign. As you know, we have the Eastern Desert between us and the nearest important enemy positions. This raises difficult questions of logistics and catapult emplacement." He turned politely to the Barbarian. "Have you any suggestion, my lord?"

"Duh," said Cronkheit.

"I think," ventured Colonel Pharaon, "that if we advanced to the Chunling Oasis and dug in there, building a supply road—"

"Dat reminds me," said Cronkheit. "One time up in duh Norriki marshes, I run acrost some swamp men an' dey uses poisoned arrers—"

"I fail to see what that has to do with this problem," said General Grythion.

"Nuttin'," admitted Cronkheit cheerfully. "But don't innerup' me. Like I was sayin'—" And he was off for another dreary hour.

At the end of a conference which had gotten nowhere, the general stroked his beard and said shrewdly: "Lord Chronkheit, it appears your abilities are more in the tactical than the strategic field."

The Barbarian snatched for his sword.

"I mean," said Grythion quickly, "I have a task which only the boldest and strongest leader can accomplish."

Cronkheit beamed and listened closely for a change. He was to be sent out with his men to capture Chantsay. This was a fort in the mountain passes across the Eastern Desert, and a major obstacle to our advance. However, in spite of Grythion's judicious flattery, a full brigade should have been able to take it with little difficulty, for it was known to be undermanned.

Cronkheit rode off at the head of his men, tossing his sword in the air and bellowing some uncouth battle chant. Then he was not heard of for six weeks.

At the close of that time, the ragged, starving, fever-stricken remnant of his troops staggered back to the base and reported utter failure. Cronkheit, who was in excellent health himself, made some sullen excuses. But he had never imagined that men who march twenty hours a day aren't fit for battle at the end of the trip—the more so if they outrun their own supply train.

Because of the Empress's wish, General Grythion could not do the sensible thing and cashier the Barbarian. He could not even reduce him to the ranks. Instead, he used his well-known guile and invited the giant to a private dinner.

"Obviously, most valiant lord," he purred, "the fault is mine. I should have realized that a man of your type is too much for us decadent southerners. You are a lone wolf who fights best by himself."

"Duh," agreed Cronkheit, ripping a fowl apart with his fingers and wiping them on the damask tablecloth.

Grythion winced, but easily talked him into going out on a one-man guerrilla operation. When he left the next morning, the officers' corps congratulated themselves on having gotten rid of the lout forever.

In the face of subsequent criticism and demands for an investigation, I still maintain that Grythion did the only rational thing under the circumstances. Who could have known that Cronkheit the Barbarian was so primitive that rationality simply slid off his hairy skin?

The full story will never be known. But apparently, in the course of the following year, while the border war continued as usual, Cronkheit struck off into the northern uplands. There he raised a band of horse nomads as ignorant and brutal as himself. He also rounded up a herd of mammoths and drove them into Chathakh, stampeding them at the foe. By such means, he reached their very capital, and the King offered terms of surrender.

But Cronkheit would have none of this. Not he! His idea of warfare was to kill or enslave every last man, woman, and child of the enemy nation. Also, his irregulars were supposed to be paid in loot. Also, being too unsanitary even for the nomad girls, he felt a certain urgency.

So he stormed the capital of Chathakh and burned it to the ground. This cost him most of his own men. It also destroyed several priceless books and works of art, and any possibility of tribute to Sarmia.

Then he had the nerve to organize a triumphal procession and ride back to our own city!

This was too much even for the Empress. When he stood before her—for he was too crude for the simple courtesy of a knee bend—she exceeded herself in describing the many kinds of fool, idiot, and all-around blockhead he was.

"Duh," said Cronkheit. "But I won duh war. Look, I won duh war, I did. I won duh war."

"Yes," hissed the Lady Larra. "You smashed an ancient and noble culture to irretrievable ruin. And did you know that one half our peacetime trade was with Chathakh? There'll be a business depression now such as history has never seen before."

General Grythion, who had returned, added his own reproaches. "Why do you think wars are fought?" he asked bitterly. "War is an extension of diplomacy. It's the final means of making somebody else do what you want. The object is *not* to kill them all off—how can corpses obey you?"

Cronkheit growled in his throat.

"We would have negotiated a peace in which Chathakh became our ally against Serpens," went on the general. "Then we'd have been safe against all comers. But *you*— You've left a howling wilderness which we must garrison with our own troops lest the nomads take it over. Your atrocities have alienated every civilized state. You've left us alone and friendless. You've won this war by losing the next one!"

"And on top of the depression which is coming," said the Empress, "we'll have the cost of maintaining those garrisons. Taxes down and expenditures up— It may break the treasury, and then where are we?"

Cronkheit spat on the floor. "Yuh're all decadent, dat's what yuh are," he snarled. "Be good for yuh if yer empire breaks up. Yuh oughtta get dat city rabble o' years out in duh woods an' make hunters of 'em, like me. Let 'em eat steak."

The Lady Larra stamped an exquisite gold-shod foot. "Do you think we've nothing better to do with our time than spend the whole day hunting, and sit around in some mud hovel at night licking the grease off our fingers?" she cried. "What the hell do you think civilization is for, anyway?"

Cronkheit drew his great sword so it flashed before their eyes. "I hadda nuff!" he bellowed. "I'm t'rough widjuh! It's time yuh was all wiped off duh face o' duh eart', an I'm jus' duh guy t' do it!"

And now General Grythion showed the qualities which had raised him to his high post. Artfully, he quailed. "Oh no!" he whimpered. "You're not going to—to—to fight on the side of Serpens?"

"I yam," said Cronkheit. "So long." The last we saw of him was a broad, indignant, flea-bitten back, headed south, and the reflection of the sun on a sword.

Since then, of course, our affairs have prospered and Serpens is now frantically suing for peace. But we intend to prosecute the war till they meet our terms. We are most assuredly not going to be ensnared by their treacherous plea and take the Barbarian back!

The Silk and the Song

❖

Charles L. Fontenay

I

lan first saw the Star Tower when he was twelve years old. His young master, Blik, rode him into the city of Falklyn that day.

Blik had to argue hard before he got permission to ride Alan, his favorite boy. Blik's father, Wiln, wanted Blik to ride a man, because Wiln thought the long trip to the city might be too much for a boy as young as Alan.

Blik had his way, though. Blik was rather spoiled, and when he began to whistle his father gave in.

"All right, the human is rather big for its age," surrendered Wiln. "You may ride it if you promise not to run it. I don't want you breaking the wind of any of my prize stock."

So Blik strapped the bridle-helmet with the handgrips on Alan's head and threw the saddle-chair on Alan's shoulders. Wiln saddled up Robb, a husky man he often rode on long trips, and they were off to the city at an easy trot.

The Star Tower was visible before they reached Falklyn. Alan could see its spire above the tops of the ttornot trees as soon as they emerged from the Blue Forest. Blik saw it at the same time. Holding onto the bridle-helmet with one four-fingered hand, Blik poked Alan and pointed.

"Look, Alan, the Star Tower!" cried Blik. "They say humans once lived in the Star Tower."

"Blik, when will you grow up and stop talking to the humans?" chided his father. "I'm going to punish you severely one of these days."

Alan did not answer Blik, for it was forbidden for humans to talk in the Hussir language except in reply to direct questions. But he kept his eager eyes on the Star Tower and watched it loom taller and taller ahead of them, striking into the sky far above the buildings of the city. He quickened his pace, so that he began to pull ahead of Robb, and Robb had to caution him.

Between the Blue Forest and Falklyn, they were still in wild country where the land was eroded and there were no farms and fields. Little clumps of ttornot trees huddled here and there among the gullies and low hills, thickening back toward the Blue Forest behind them, thinning toward the northwest plain, beyond which lay the distant mountains.

They rounded a curve in the dusty road, and Blik whistled in excitement from Alan's shoulders. A figure stood on a little promontory overhanging the road ahead of them.

At first Alan thought it was a tall, slender Hussir, for a short jacket partly concealed its nakedness. Then he saw it was a young human girl. No Hussir ever boasted that mop of tawny hair, that tailless posterior curve.

"A Wild Human!" growled Wiln in astonishment. Alan shivered. It was rumored the Wild Humans killed Hussirs and ate other humans.

The girl was looking away toward Falklyn. Wiln unslung his short bow and loosed an arrow at her.

The bolt exploded the dust near her feet. With a toss of bright hair, she turned her head and saw them. Then she was gone like a deer.

When they came up to where she had stood, there was a

brightness in the bushes beside the road. It was a pair of the colorful trousers such as Hussirs wore, only trimmer, tangled inextrica-
bly in a thorny bush. Evidently the girl had been caught as she
climbed up from the road, and had had to crawl out of them.

"They're getting too bold," said Wiln angrily. "This close to
civilization, in broad daylight!"

Alan was astonished when they entered Falklyn. The streets
and buildings were of stone. There was little stone on the other
side of the Blue Forest, and Wiln Castle was built of polished
wooden blocks. The smooth stone of Falklyn's streets was hot
under the double sun. It burned Alan's feet, so that he hobbled a
little and shook Blik up. Blik clouted him on the side of the head
for it.

There were so many strange new things to see in the city that
they made Alan dizzy. Some of the buildings were as much as three
stories high, and the windows of a few of the biggest were covered,
not with wooden shutters, but with a bright, transparent stuff that
Wiln told Blik was called "glaz." Robb told Alan in the human
language, which the Hussirs did not understand, that it was rumored humans themselves had invented this glaz and given it to
their masters. Alan wondered how a human could invent anything, penned in open fields.

But it appeared that humans in the city lived closer to their
masters. Several times Alan saw them coming out of houses, and a
few that he saw were not entirely naked, but wore bright bits of
cloth at various places on their bodies. Wiln expressed strong disapproval of this practice to Blik.

"Start putting clothing on these humans and they might get
the idea they're Hussirs," he said. "If you ask me, that's why city
people have more trouble controlling their humans than we do.
Spoil the human and you make him savage, I say."

They had several places to go in Falklyn, and for a while Alan
feared they would not see the Star Tower at close range. But Blik
had never seen it before, and he begged and whistled until Wiln
agreed to ride a few streets out of the way to look at it.

Alan forgot all the other wonders of Falklyn as the great monument towered bigger and bigger, dwarfing the buildings around it, dwarfing the whole city of Falklyn. There was a legend that humans had not only lived in the Star Tower once, but that they had built it and Falklyn had grown up around it when the humans abandoned it. Alan had heard this whispered, but he had been warned not to repeat it, for some Hussirs understood human language and repeating such tales was a good way to get whipped.

The Star Tower was in the center of a big circular park, and the houses around the park looked like dollhouses beneath it. It stretched up into the sky like a pointing finger, its strange dark walls reflecting the dual sunlight dully. Even the flying buttresses at its base curved up above the big trees in the park around it.

There was a railing around the park, and quite a few humans were chained or standing loose about it while their riders were looking at the Star Tower, for humans were not allowed inside the park. Blik was all for dismounting and looking at the inside of the tower, but Wiln would not hear of it.

"There'll be plenty of time for that when you're older and can understand some of the things you see," said Wiln.

They moved slowly around the street, outside the rail. In the park, the Hussirs moved in groups, some of them going up or coming down the long ramp that led into the Star Tower. The Hussirs were only about half the size of humans, with big heads and large pointed ears sticking straight out on each side, with thin legs and thick tails that helped to balance them. They wore loose jackets and baggy, colored trousers.

As they passed one group of humans standing outside the rail, Alan heard a familiar bit of verse, sung in an undertone:

> Twinkle, twinkle, golden star,
> I can reach you, though you're far.
> Shut my mouth and find my head,
> Find a worm—

Wiln swung Robb around quickly and laid his keen whip viciously across the singer's shoulders. Slash, slash, and red welts sprang out on the man's back. With a muffled shriek, the man ducked his head and threw up his arms to protect his face.

"Where is your master, human?" demanded Wiln savagely, the whip trembling in his four-fingered hand.

"My master lives in Northwesttown, your greatness," whimpered the human. "I belong to the merchant Senk."

"Where is Northwesttown?"

"It is a section of Falklyn, sir."

"And you are here at the Star Tower without your master?"

"Yes, sir. I am on free time."

Wiln gave him another lash with the whip.

"You should know humans are not allowed to run loose near the Star Tower," Wiln snapped. "Now go back to your master and tell him to whip you."

The human ran off. Wiln and Blik turned their mounts homeward. When they were beyond the streets and houses of the town and the dust of the roads provided welcome relief to the burning feet of the humans, Blik asked: "What did you think of the Star Tower, Alan?"

"Why has it no windows?" Alan asked, voicing the thought uppermost in his mind.

It was not, strictly speaking, an answer to Blik's question, and Alan risked punishment by speaking thus in Hussir. But Wiln had recovered his good humor with the prospect of getting home in time for supper.

"The windows are in the very top, little human," said Wiln indulgently. "You couldn't see them, because they're inside."

Alan puzzled over this all the way to Wiln Castle. How could windows be inside and none outside? If windows were windows, didn't they always go through both sides of a wall?

When the two suns had set and Alan was bedded down with the other children in a corner of the meadow, the exciting events of the day repeated themselves in his mind like a series of colored pictures. He would have liked to question Robb, but the grown men and older boys were kept in a field well separated from the women and children.

A little distance away the women were singing their babies to sleep with the traditional songs of the humans. Their voices drifted to him on the faint breeze, with the perfume of the fragrant grasses.

> Rock-a-bye, baby, in mother's arm,
> Nothing's nearby to do baby harm.
> Sleep and sweet dreams, till both suns arise,
> Then will be time to open your eyes.

That was a real baby song, the first he ever remembered. They sang others, and one was the song Wiln had interrupted at the Star Tower.

> Twinkle, twinkle, golden star,
> I can reach you, though you're far.
> Shut my mouth and find my head,
> Find a worm that's striped with red,
> Feed it to the turtle shell,
> Then go to sleep, for all is well.

Half asleep, Alan listened. That song was one of the children's favorites. They called it "The Star Tower Song," though he had never been able to find out why.

It must be a riddle, he thought drowsily. "Shut my mouth and find my head . . ." Shouldn't it be the other way around—"Find my head (first) and shut my mouth . . ."? Why wasn't it? And those other lines. Alan knew worms, for he had seen many of the creepy, crawly creatures, long things in many bright colors. But what was a turtle?

The refrain of another song reached his ears, and it seemed to the sleepy boy that they were singing it to him.

Alan saw a little zird,
Its wings were all aglow.
He followed it away one night.
It filled his heart with woe.

Only that wasn't the last line the children themselves sang. Optimistically, they always ended that song ". . . to where he liked to go."

Maybe he was asleep and dreamed it, or maybe he suddenly woke up with the distant music in his ears. Whichever it was, he was lying there, and a zird flew over the high fence and lit in the grass near him. Its luminous scales pulsed in the darkness, faintly lighting the faces of the children huddled asleep around him. It opened its beak and spoke to him in a raucous voice.

"Come with me to freedom, human," said the zird. "Come with me to freedom, human."

That was all it could say, and it repeated the invitation at least half a dozen times, until it grated on Alan's ears. But Alan knew that, despite the way the children sang the song, it brought only sorrow to a human to heed the call of a zird.

"Go away, zird," he said crossly, and the zird flew over the fence and faded into the darkness.

Sighing, Alan went back to sleep to dream of the Star Tower.

II

BLIK DIED THREE YEARS LATER. THE YOUNG HUSSIR'S DEATH BROUGHT sorrow to Alan's heart, for Blik had been kind to him and their relationship was the close one of well-loved pet and master. The deprivation always would be associated to him with another emotional change in his life, for Blik's death came the day after Wiln caught Alan with the blonde girl down by the stream and transferred him to the field with the older boys and men.

"Switch it, I hope the boy hasn't gotten her with child," grumbled Wiln to his oldest son, Snuk, as they drove Alan to the new meadow. "I hadn't planned to add that girl to the milking herd for another year yet."

"That comes of letting Blik make a pet out of the human," said Snuk, who was nearly grown now and was being trained in the art of managing Wiln Castle to succeed his father. "It should have been worked while Blik has been sick, instead of allowed to roam idly around among the women and children."

Through the welter of new emotions that confused him, Alan recognized the justice of that remark. It had been pure boredom with the play of the younger children that had turned his interest to more mature experimentation. At that, he realized that only the aloofness he had developed as a result of being Blik's pet had prevented his being taken to the other field at least two years earlier.

He looked back over his shoulder. The tearful girl stood forlornly, watching him go. She waved and called after him.

"Maybe we'll see each other again at mating time."

He waved back at her, drawing a sharp cut across the shoulders from Snuk's whip. They would not turn him in with the women at mating time for at least another three years, but the girl was almost of mating age. By the time she saw him again, she probably would have forgotten him.

His transfer into adulthood was an immediate ordeal. Wiln and Snuk remained just outside the fence and whistled delightedly at the hazing Alan was given by the men and older boys. The ritual would have been more difficult for him had it not been so long delayed, but he found a place in the scheme of things somewhat high for a newcomer because he was older than most of them and big for his age. Scratched and battered, he gained the necessary initial respect from his new associates by trouncing several boys his own size.

That night, lonely and unhappy, Alan heard the keening of the Hussirs rise from Wiln Castle. The night songs of the men, deeper and lustier than those of the women and children, faded and stopped as the sound of mourning drifted to them on the wind. Alan knew it meant that Blik's long illness was over, that his young master was dead.

He found a secluded corner of the field and cried himself to sleep under the stars. He had loved Blik.

After Blik's death, Alan thought he might be put with the laboring men, to pull the plows and work the crops. He knew he did not have the training for work in and around the castle itself, and he did not think he would be retained with the riding stock.

But Snuk had different ideas.

"I saw your good qualities as a riding human before Blik ever picked you out for a pet," Snuk told him, laying his pointed ears back viciously. Snuk used the human language, for it was Snuk's theory that one could control humans better when one could listen in on their conversations among themselves. "Blik spoiled all the temper out of you, but I'll change that. I may be able to salvage you yet."

It was only a week since Blik's death, and Alan was still sad. Dispiritedly, he cooperated when Snuk put the bridle-helmet and saddle-chair on him, and knelt for Snuk to climb on his back.

When Alan stood up, Snuk jammed spurs savagely into his sides.

Alan leaped three feet into the air with an agonized yell.

"Silence, human!" shouted Snuk, beating him over the head with the whip. "I shall teach you to obey. Spurs mean go, like so!"

And he dug the spurs into Alan's ribs again.

Alan twisted and turned momentarily, but his common sense saved him. Had he fallen to the ground and rolled, or tried to rub Snuk off against a ttornot tree, it would have meant death for him. There was no appeal from his new master's cruelty.

A third time Snuk applied the spurs and Alan spurted down the tree-lined lane away from the castle at a dead run. Snuk gave him his head and raked his sides brutally. It was only when he slowed to a walk, panting and perspiring, that Snuk pulled on the reins and turned him back toward the castle. Then the Hussir forced him to trot back.

Wiln was waiting at the corral when they returned.

"Aren't you treating it a little rough, Snuk?" asked the older

Hussir, looking the exhausted Alan up and down critically. Blood streamed from Alan's gashed sides.

"Just teaching it right at the outset who is master," replied Snuk casually. With an unnecessarily sharp rap on the head, he sent Alan to his knees and dismounted. "I think this one will make a valuable addition to my stable of riders, but I don't intend to pamper it like Blik."

Wiln flicked his ears.

"Well, you've proved you know how to handle humans by now, and you'll be master of them all in a few years," he said mildly. "Just take your father's advice, and don't break this one's wind."

The next few months were misery to Alan. He had the physical qualities Snuk liked in a mount, and Snuk rode him more frequently than any of his other saddle men.

Snuk liked to ride fast, and he ran Alan unmercifully. They would return at the end of a hot afternoon, Alan bathed in sweat and so tired his limbs trembled uncontrollably.

Besides, Snuk was an uncompromising master with more than a touch of cruelty in his makeup. He would whip Alan savagely for minor inattention, for failure to respond promptly to the reins, for speaking at all in his presence. Alan's back was soon covered with spur scars, and one eye often was half-closed from a whiplash across the face.

In desperation, Alan sought the counsel of his old friend, Robb, whom he saw often now that he was in the men's field.

"There's nothing you can do," Robb said. "I just thank the Golden Star that Wiln rides me and I'll be too old for Snuk to ride when Wiln dies. But then Snuk will be master of us all, and I dread that day."

"Couldn't one of us kill Snuk against a tree?" asked Alan. He had thought of doing it himself.

"Never think such a thought," warned Robb quickly. "If that happened, all the riding men would be butchered for meat. The Wiln family has enough money to buy new riding stables in Falklyn if they wish, and no Hussir will put up with a rebellious human."

* * *

That night Alan nursed his freshest wounds beside the fence closest to the women's and children's field and gave himself up to nostalgia. He longed for the happy days of his childhood and Blik's kind mastery.

Across the intervening fields, faintly, he heard the soft voices of the women. He could not make out the words, but he remembered them from the tune:

> Star light, star bright,
> Star that sheds a golden light,
> I wish I may, I wish I might,
> Reach you, star that shines at night.

From behind him came the voices of the men, nearer and louder:

> Human, see the little zird,
> Its wings are all aglow.
> Don't follow it away at night,
> For fear of grief and woe.

The children had sung it differently. And there had been a dream . . .

"Come with me to freedom, human," said the zird.

Alan had seen many zirds at night—they appeared only at night—and had heard their call. It was the only thing they said, always in the human language: "Come with me to freedom, human."

As he had before, he wondered. A zird was only a scaly-winged little night creature. How could it speak human words? Where did zirds come from, and where did they go in the daytime? For the first time in his life, he asked the zird a question.

"What and where is freedom, zird?" Alan asked.

"Come with me to freedom, human," repeated the zird. It flapped its wings, rising a few inches above the fence, and settled back on its perch.

"Is that all you can say, zird?" asked Alan irritably. "How can I go with you when I can't fly?"

"Come with me to freedom, human," said the zird.

A great boldness surged in Alan's heart, spurred by the dreary prospect of having to endure Snuk's sadism again on the morrow. He looked at the fence.

Alan had never paid much attention to a fence before. Humans did not try to get out of the fenced enclosures, because the story parents told to children who tried it was that strayed humans were always recaptured and butchered for meat.

It was the strangest coincidence. It reminded him of that night long ago, the night after he had gone into Falklyn with Blik and had first seen the Star Tower. Even as the words of the song died away in the night air, he saw the glow of the zird approaching. It lit on top of the fence and squawked down at him.

The links of the fence were close together, but he could get his fingers and toes through them. Tentatively, he tried it. A mounting excitement taking possession of him, he climbed.

It was ridiculously easy. He was in the next field. There were other fences, of course, but they could be climbed. He could go into the field with the women—his heart beat faster at the thought of the blonde girl—or he could even climb his way to the open road to Falklyn.

It was the road he chose, after all. The zird flew ahead of him across each field, lighting to wait for him to climb each fence. He crept along the fence past the crooning women with a muffled sigh, through the field of ripening akko grain, through the waist-high sento plants. At last he climbed the last fence of all.

He was off the Wiln estate. The dust of the road to Falklyn was beneath his feet.

What now? If he went into Falklyn, he would be captured and returned to Wiln Castle. If he went the other way the same thing would happen. Stray humans were spotted easily. Should he turn back now? It would be easy to climb his way back to the men's field—and there would be innumerable nights ahead of him when the women's field would be easily accessible to him.

But there was Snuk to consider.

For the first time since he had climbed out of the men's field, the zird spoke.

"Come with me to freedom, human," it said.

It flew down the road, away from Falklyn, and lit in the dust, as though waiting. After a moment's hesitation, Alan followed.

The lights of Wiln Castle loomed up to his left, up the lane of ttornot trees. They fell behind and disappeared over a hill. The zird flew, matching its pace to his slow trot.

Alan's resolution began to weaken.

Then a figure loomed up beside him in the gloom, a human hand was laid on his arm and a female voice said: "I thought we'd never get another from Wiln Castle. Step it up a little, fellow. We've a long way to travel before dawn."

III

THEY TRAVELED AT A FAST TROT ALL THAT NIGHT, THE ZIRD LEADING the way like a giant firefly. By the time dawn grayed the eastern sky they were in the mountains west of Falklyn, and climbing.

When Alan was first able to make out details of his nocturnal guide, he thought for a minute she was a huge Hussir. She wore the Hussir loose jacket, open at the front, and the baggy trousers. But there was no tail, and there were no pointed ears. She was a girl his own age.

She was the first human Alan had ever seen fully clothed. Alan thought she looked rather ridiculous and, at the same time, he was slightly shocked, as by sacrilege.

They entered a high valley through a narrow pass and slowed to a walk. For the first time since they left the vicinity of Wiln Castle, they were able to talk in other than short, disconnected phrases.

"Who are you, and where are you taking me?" asked Alan. In the cold light of dawn he was beginning to doubt his impetuousness in fleeing the castle.

"My name is Mara," said the girl. "You've heard of the Wild Humans? I'm one of them, and we live in these mountains."

The hair prickled on the back of Alan's neck. He stopped in his tracks, and half turned to flee. Mara caught his arm.

"Why do all you slaves believe those fairy tales about cannibalism?" she asked scornfully. The word *cannibalism* was unfamiliar to Alan. "We aren't going to eat you, boy, we're going to make you free. What's your name?"

"Alan," he answered into a shaky voice, allowing himself to be led onward. "What is this freedom the zird was talking about?"

"You'll find out," she promised. "But the zird doesn't know. Zirds are just flying animals. We train them to say that one sentence and lead slaves to us."

"Why don't you just come into the fields yourselves?" he asked curiously, his fear dissipating. "You could climb the fences easily."

"That's been tried. The silly slaves just raise a clamor when they recognize a stranger. The Hussirs have caught several of us that way."

The two suns rose, first the blue one, the white one only a few minutes later. The mountains around them awoke with light.

In the dawn, he had thought Mara was dark, but her hair was tawny gold in the pearly morning. Her eyes were deep brown, like the fruit of the ttornot tree.

They stopped by a spring that gushed from between huge rocks, and Mara took the opportunity to appraise his slender, well-knit frame.

"You'll do," she said. "I wish all of them we get were as healthy."

In three weeks, Alan could not have been distinguished from the other Wild Humans—outwardly. He was getting used to wearing clothing and, somewhat awkwardly, carried the bow and arrows with which he was armed. He and Mara were ranging several miles from the caves in which the Wild Humans lived.

They were hunting animals for food, and Alan licked his lips in anticipation. He liked cooked meat. The Hussirs fed their human herds bean meal and scraps from the kitchens. The only meat he had ever eaten was raw meat from small animals he had been swift enough to catch in the fields.

They came up on a ridge and Mara, ahead of him, stopped. He came up beside her.

Not far below them, a Hussir moved, afoot, carrying a short, heavy bow and a quiver of arrows. The Hussir looked from side to side, as if hunting, but did not catch sight of them.

A quiver of fear ran through Alan. In that instant, he was a disobedient member of the herd, and death awaited him for his escape from the fields.

There was a sharp twang beside him, and the Hussir stumbled and fell, transfixed through the chest with an arrow. Mara calmly lowered her bow and smiled at the fright in his eyes.

"There's one that won't find Haafin," she said. "Haafin" was what the Wild Humans called their community.

"The—there are Hussirs in the mountains?" he quavered.

"A few. Hunters. If we get them before they run across the valley, we're all right. Some have seen us and gotten away, though. Haafin has been moved a dozen times in the last century, and we've always lost a lot of people fighting our way out. Those little devils attack in force."

"But what's the good of all this, then?" he asked hopelessly. "There aren't more than four or five hundred humans in Haafin. What good is hiding, and running somewhere else when the Hussirs find you, when sooner or later there'll come a time when they'll wipe you out?"

Mara sat down on a rock.

"You learn fast," she remarked. "You'll probably be surprised to learn that this community has managed to hang on in these mountains for more than a thousand years, but you've still put your finger right on the problem that has faced us for generations."

She hesitated and traced a pattern thoughtfully in the dust with a moccasined foot.

"It's a little early for you to be told, but you might as well start keeping your ears open," she said. "When you've been here a year, you'll be accepted as a member of the community. The way that's done is for you to have an interview with the Refugee, the leader of our people, and he always asks newcomers for their ideas on the solution of that very problem."

"But what will I listen for?" asked Alan anxiously.

"There are two major ideas on how to solve the problem, and I'll let you hear them from the people who believe in them," she said. "Just remember what the problem is: to save ourselves from death and the hundreds of thousands of other humans in the world from slavery, we have to find a way to force the Hussirs to accept humans as equals, not as animals."

Many things about Alan's new life in Haafin were not too different from the existence he had known. He had to do his share of work in the little fields that clung to the edges of the small river in the middle of the valley. He had to help hunt animals for meat, he had to help make tools such as the Hussirs used. He had to fight with his fists, on occasion, to protect his rights.

But this thing the Wild Humans called "freedom" was a strange element that touched everything they were and did. The word, Alan found, meant basically that the Wild Humans did not belong to the Hussirs, but were their own masters. When orders were given, they usually had to be obeyed, but they came from humans, not Hussirs.

There were other differences. There were no formal family relationships, for there were no social traditions behind people who for generations had been nothing more than domestic animals. But the pressure and deprivations of rigidly enforced mating seasons were missing, and some of the older couples were mated permanently.

"Freedom," Alan decided, meant a dignity which made a human the equal of a Hussir.

The anniversary of that night when Alan followed the zird came, and Mara led him early in the morning to the extreme end of the valley. She left him at the mouth of a small cave, from which presently emerged the man of whom Alan had heard much but whom he saw now for the first time.

The Refugee's hair and beard were gray and his face was lined with years.

"You are Alan, who came to us from Wiln Castle," said the old man.

"That is true, your greatness," replied Alan respectfully.

"Don't call me 'your greatness.' That's slave talk. I am Roand, the Refugee."

"Yes, sir."

"When you leave me today, you will be a member of the community of Haafin, the only free human community in the world," said Roand. "You will have a member's rights. No man may take a woman from you without her consent. No one may take from you the food you hunt or grow without your consent. If you are first in an empty cave, no one may move into it with you unless you give permission. That is freedom.

"But, as you were no doubt told long ago, you must offer your best idea on how to make all humans free."

"Sir—" began Alan.

"Before you express yourself," interrupted Roand, "I'm going to give you some help. Come into the cave."

Alan followed him inside. By the light of a torch, Roand showed him a series of diagrams drawn on one wall with soft stone, as one would draw things in the dust with a stick.

"These are maps, Alan," said Roand, and he explained to the boy what a map was. At last Alan nodded in comprehension.

"You know by now that there are two ways of thinking about what to do to set all humans free, but you do not entirely understand either of them," said Roand. "These maps show you the first one, which was conceived a hundred and fifty years ago but which our people have not been able to agree to try.

"This map shows how, by a surprise attack, we could take Falklyn, the central city of all this Hussir region, although the Hussirs in Falklyn number almost ten thousand. Holding Falklyn, we could free the nearly forty thousand humans in the city and we would have enough strength then to take the surrounding area and strike at the cities around it, gradually, as these other maps show."

Alan nodded.

"But I like the other way better," Alan said. "There must be a reason why they won't let humans enter the Star Tower."

Roand's toothless smile did not mar the innate dignity of his face.

"You are a mystic, as I am, young Alan," he said. "But the tradition says that for a human to enter the Star Tower is not enough. Let me tell you of the tradition.

"The tradition says that the Star Tower was once the home of all humans. There were only a dozen or so humans then, but they had powers that were great and strange. But when they came out of the Star Tower, the Hussirs were able to enslave them through mere force of numbers.

"Three of those first humans escaped to these mountains and became the first Wild Humans. From them has come the tradition that has passed to their descendants and to the humans who have been rescued from Hussir slavery.

"The tradition says that a human who enters the Star Tower can free all the humans in the world—if he takes with him the Silk and the Song."

Roand reached into a crevice.

"This is the Silk," he said, drawing forth a peach-colored scarf on which something had been painted. Alan recognized it as writing, such as the Hussirs used and were rumored to have been taught by humans. Roand read it to him, reverently.

"'REG. B-XII. CULTURE V. SOS.'"

"What does it mean?" asked Alan.

"No one knows," said Roand. "It is a great mystery. It may be a magical incantation."

He put the Silk back into the crevice.

"This is the only other writing we have handed down by our forebears," said Roand, and pulled out a fragment of very thin, brittle, yellowish material. To Alan it looked something like thin cloth that had hardened with age, yet it had a different texture. Roand handled it very carefully.

"This was torn and the rest of it lost centuries ago," said Roand, and he read. "'October 3, 2 . . . ours to be the last . . . three lost expeditions . . . too far to keep trying . . . how we can get . . .'"

Alan could make no more sense of this than he could of the words of the Silk.

"What is the Song?" asked Alan.

"Every human knows it from childhood," said Roand. "It is the best known of all human songs."

"'Twinkle, twinkle, golden star,'" quoted Alan at once, "'I can reach you, though you're far . . .'"

"That's right, but there is a second verse that only the Wild Humans know. You must learn it. It goes like this:

"Twinkle, twinkle, little bug,
Long and round, of shiny hue.
In a room marked by a cross,
Sting my arm when I've found you.
Lay me down, in bed so deep,
And then there's naught to do but sleep."

"It doesn't make sense," said Alan. "No more than the first verse—though Mara showed me what a turtle looks like."

"They aren't supposed to make sense until you sing them in the Star Tower," said Roand, "and then only if you have the Silk with you."

Alan cogitated a while. Roand was silent, waiting.

"Some of the people want one human to try to reach the Star Tower and think that will make all humans miraculously free," said Alan at last. "The others think that is but a child's tale and we must conquer the Hussirs with bows and spears. It seems to me, sir, that one or the other must be tried. I'm sorry that I don't know enough to suggest another course."

Roand's face fell.

"So you will join one side or the other and argue about it for the rest of your life," he said sadly. "And nothing will ever be done, because the people can't agree."

"I don't see why that has to be, sir."

Roand looked at him with sudden hope.

"What do you mean?"

"Can't you or someone else order them to take one course or another?"

Roand shook his head.

"Here there are rules, but no man tells another what to do," he said. "We are free here."

"Sir, when I was a small child, we played a game called Two Herds," said Alan slowly. "The sides would be divided evenly, each with a tree for a haven. When two of opposite sides met in the field, the one last from his haven captured the other and took him back to join his side."

"I've played that game, many years ago," said Roand. "I don't see your point, boy."

"Well, sir, to win, one side had to capture all the people on the other side. But, with so many captures back and forth, sometimes night fell and the game was not ended. So we always played that, then, the side with the most children when the game ended was the winning side."

"Why couldn't it be done that way?"

Comprehension dawned slowly in Roand's face. There was something there, too, of the awe-inspiring revelation that he was present at the birth of a major advance in the science of human government.

"Let them count those for each proposal, eh, and agree to abide by the proposal having the greatest support?"

"Yes, sir."

Roand grinned his toothless grin.

"You have indeed brought us a new idea, my boy, but you and I will have to surrender our own viewpoint by it, I'm afraid. I keep close count. There are a few more people in Haafin who think we should attack the Hussirs with weapons than believe in the old tradition."

IV

WHEN THE ARMED MOB OF WILD HUMANS APPROACHED FALKLYN IN the dusk, Alan wore the Silk around his neck. Roand, one of the oldsters who stayed behind at Haafin, had given it to him.

"When Falklyn is taken, my boy, take the Silk with you into the Star Tower and sing the Song," were Roand's parting words. "There may be something to the old traditions after all."

After much argument among those Wild Humans who had given it thought for years, a military plan had emerged blessed with all the simplicity of a nonmilitary race. They would just march into the city, killing all Hussirs they saw, and stay there, still killing all Hussirs they saw. Their own strength would increase gradually as they freed the city's enslaved humans. No one could put a definite finger on anything wrong with the idea.

Falklyn was built like a wheel. Around the park in which stood the Star Tower the streets ran in concentric circles. Like spokes of the wheel, other streets struck from the park out to the edge of the city.

Without any sort of formation, the humans entered one of these spoke streets and moved inward, a few adventurous souls breaking away from the main body at each cross street. It was suppertime in Falklyn, and few Hussirs were abroad. The humans were jubilant as those who escaped their arrows fled, whistling in fright.

They were about a third of the way to the center of Falklyn when the bells began ringing, first near at hand and then all over the city. Hussirs popped out of doors and on to balconies, and arrows began to sail in among the humans to match their own. The motley army began to break up as its soldiers sought cover. Its progress was slowed, and there was some hand-to-hand fighting.

Alan found himself with Mara, crouching in a doorway. Ahead of them and behind them, Wild Humans scurried from house to house, still moving forward. An occasional Hussir hopped hastily across the street, sometimes making it, sometimes falling from a human arrow.

"This doesn't look so good," said Alan. "Nobody seemed to

think of the Hussirs being prepared for an attack, but those bells must have been an alarm system."

"We're still moving ahead," replied Mara confidently.

Alan shook his head.

"That may just mean we'll have more trouble getting out of the city," he said. "The Hussirs outnumber us twenty to one, and they're killing more of us than we're killing of them."

The door beside them opened and a Hussir leaped all the way out before seeing them. Alan dispatched him with a blow from his spear. Mara at his heels, he ran forward to the next doorway. Shouts of humans and whistles and cries of Hussirs echoed back and forth down the street.

The fighting humans were perhaps halfway to the Star Tower when from ahead of them came the sound of shouting and chanting. From the dimness it seemed that a solid river of white was pouring toward them, filling the street from wall to wall.

A Wild Human across the street from Alan and Mara shouted in triumph.

"They're humans! The slaves are coming to help us!"

A ragged shout went up from the embattled Wild Humans. But as it died down, they were able to distinguish the words of the chanting and the shouting from that naked mass of humanity.

"Kill the Wild Humans! Kill the Wild Humans! Kill the Wild Humans!"

Remembering his own childhood fear of Wild Humans, Alan suddenly understood. With a confidence fully justified, the Hussirs had turned the humans' own people against themselves.

The invaders looked at each other in alarm and drew closer together beneath the protection of overhanging balconies. Hussir arrows whistled near them unheeded.

They could not kill their enslaved brothers, and there was no chance of breaking through that oncoming avalanche of humanity. First by ones and twos, and then in groups, they turned to retreat from the city.

But the way was blocked. Up the street from the direction in which they had come moved orderly ranks of armed Hussirs. Some of the Wild Humans, among them Alan and Mara, ran for the nearest cross streets. Along them, too, approached companies of Hussirs.

The Wild Humans were trapped in the middle of Falklyn.

Terrified, the men and women of Haafin converged and swirled in a helpless knot in the center of the street. Hussir arrows from nearby windows picked them off one by one. The advancing Hussirs in the street were almost within bowshot, and the yelling, unarmed slave humans were even closer.

"Your clothes!" shouted Alan, on an inspiration. "Throw away your clothes and weapons! Try to get back to the mountains!"

In almost a single swift shrug, he divested himself of the open jacket and baggy trousers and threw his bow, arrows and spear from him. Only the Silk still fluttered from his neck.

As Mara stood openmouthed beside him, he jerked at her jacket impatiently. Suddenly getting his idea, she stripped quickly. The other Wild Humans began to follow suit.

The arrows of the Hussir squads were beginning to fall among them. Grabbing Mara's hand, Alan plunged headlong toward the avalanche of slave humans.

Slowed as he was by Mara, a dozen other Wild Humans raced ahead of him to break into the wall of humanity. Angry hands clutched at them as they tried to lose themselves among the slaves, and Alan and Mara, clinging to each other, were engulfed in a sudden swirl of shouting confusion.

There were naked, sweating bodies moving on all sides of them. They were buffeted back and forth like chips in the surf. Desperately they gripped hands and stayed close together.

They were crowded to one side of the street, against the wall. The human tide scraped them along the rough stone and battered them roughly into a doorway. The door yielded to the tremendous pressure and flew inward. Somehow, only the two of them lost their balance and sprawled on the carpeted floor inside.

A Hussir appeared from an inside door, a barbed spear upraised.

"Mercy, your greatness!" cried Alan in the Hussir tongue, groveling.

The Hussir lowered the spear.

"Who is your master, human?" he demanded.

A distant memory thrust itself into Alan's mind, haltingly.

"My master lives in Northwesttown, your greatness."

The spear moved in the Hussir's hand.

"This is Northwesttown, human," he said ominously.

"Yes, your greatness," whimpered Alan, and prayed for no more coincidences. "I belong to the merchant Senk."

The spear point dropped to the floor again.

"I felt sure you were a town human," said the Hussir, his eyes on the scarf around Alan's neck. "I know Senk well. And you, woman, who is your master?"

Alan did not wait to find out whether Mara spoke Hussir.

"She also belongs to my lord Senk, your greatness." Another recollection came to his aid, and he added, "It's mating season, your greatness."

The Hussir gave the peculiar whistle that served for a laugh among his race. He beckoned to them to rise.

"Go out the back door and return to your pen," he said kindly. "You're lucky you weren't separated from each other in that herd."

Gratefully, Alan and Mara slipped out the back door and made their way up a dark alley to a street. He led her to the left.

"We'll have to find a cross street to get out of Falklyn," he said. "This is one of the circular streets."

"I hope most of the others escape," she said fervently. "There's no one left in Haafin but the old people and the small children."

"We'll have to be careful," he said. "They may have guards at the edge of the city. We outtalked that Hussir, but you'd better go ahead of me till we get to the outskirts. It'll look less suspicious if we're not together."

At the cross street they turned right. Mara moved ahead about thirty feet, and he followed. He watched her slim white figure swaying under the flickering gaslights of Falklyn and suddenly he laughed quietly. The memory of the blonde girl at Wiln Castle had returned to him, and it occurred to him, too, that he had never missed her.

The streets were nearly empty. Once or twice a human crossed ahead of them at a trot, and several times Hussirs passed them. For a while Alan heard shouting and whistling not far away, then these sounds faded.

They had not been walking long when Mara stopped. Alan came up beside her.

"We must have reached the outskirts," she said, waving her hand at the open space ahead of them.

They walked quickly.

But there was something wrong. The cross street just ahead curved too much, and there was the glimmer of lights some distance beyond it.

"We took the wrong turn when we left the alley," said Alan miserably. "Look—straight ahead!"

Dimly against the stars loomed the dark bulk of the Star Tower.

V

THE GREAT METAL BUILDING STRETCHED UP INTO THE NIGHT SKY, losing itself in the blackness. The park around it was unlighted, but they could see the glow of the lamps at the Star Tower's entrance, where the Hussir guards remained on duty.

"We'll have to turn back," said Alan dully.

She stood close to him and looked up at him with large eyes.

"All the way back through the city?" There was a tremor in her voice.

"I'm afraid so." He put his arm around her shoulders and they turned away from the Star Tower. He fumbled at his scarf as they walked slowly back down the street.

His scarf! He stopped, halting her with a jerk. The Silk!

He grasped her shoulders with both hands and looked down into her face.

"Mara," he said soberly, "we aren't going back to the mountains. We aren't going back out of the city. We're going into the Star Tower!"

They retraced their steps to the end of the spoke street. They raced across the last and smallest of the circular streets, vaulted the rail, slipped like wraiths into the shadows of the park.

They moved from bush to bush and from tree to tree with the quiet facility of creatures born to nights in the open air. Little knots of guards were scattered all over the park. Probably the guard had been strengthened because of the Wild Humans' invasion of Falklyn. But the guards all had small, shaded lights, and Hussirs could not see well in the dark. The two humans were able to avoid them easily.

They came up behind the Star Tower and circled it cautiously. At its base, the entrance ramp was twice Alan's height. There were two guards, talking in low tones under the lamps that hung on each side of the dark, open door to the tower.

"If we could only have brought a bow!" exclaimed Alan in a whisper. "I could handle one of them without a weapon, but not two."

"Couldn't both of us?" she whispered back.

"No! They're little, but they're strong. Much stronger than a woman."

Against the glow of the light something projected a few inches over the edge of the ramp above them.

"Maybe it's a spear," whispered Alan. "I'll lift you up."

In a moment she was down again, the object in her hands.

"Just an arrow," she muttered in disgust. "What good is it without a bow?"

"It may be enough," he said. "You stay here, and when I get to the foot of the ramp, make a noise to distract them. Then run for it—"

He crept on his stomach to the point where the ramp angled to the ground. He looked back. Mara was a lightness against the blackness of the corner.

Mara began banging against the side of the ramp with her fists and chanting in a low tone. Grabbing their bows, both Hussir guards moved quickly to the edge. Alan stood up and ran as fast as he could up the ramp, the arrow in his hand.

Their bows were drawn to shoot down where Mara was, when they felt the vibration of the ramp. They turned quickly.

Their arrows, hurriedly loosed, missed him. He plunged his own arrow through the throat of one and grappled with the other. In a savage burst of strength, he hurled the Hussir over the side to the ground below.

Mara cried out. A patrol of three Hussirs had been too close. She had nearly reached the foot of the ramp when one of them plunged from the darkness and locked his arms around her hips from behind. The other two were hopping up the ramp toward Alan, spears in hand.

Alan snatched up the bow and quiver of the Hussir he had slain. His first arrow took one of the approaching Hussirs, halfway down the ramp. The Hussir that had seized Mara hurled her away from him to the ground and raised his spear for the kill.

Alan's arrow only grazed the creature, but it dropped the spear, and Mara fled up the ramp.

The third Hussir lurched at Alan behind its spear. Alan dodged. The blade missed him but the haft burned his side, almost knocking him from the ramp. The Hussir recovered like lightning, poised the spear again. It was too close for Alan to use the bow, and he had no time to pick up a spear.

Mara leaped on the Hussir's back, locking her legs around its body and grappling its spear arm with both her hands. Before it could shake her off, Alan wrestled the spear from the Hussir's hand and dispatched it.

The other guards were coming up from all directions. Arrows rang against the sides of the Star Tower as the two humans ducked inside.

There was a light inside the Star Tower, a softer light than the gas lamps but more effective. They were inside a small chamber, from which another door led to the interior of the tower.

The door, swung back against the wall on its hinges, was two feet thick and its diameter was greater than the height of a man. Both of them together were unable to move it.

Arrows were coming through the door. Alan had left the guards' weapons outside. In a moment the Hussirs would gain courage to rush the ramp.

Alan looked around in desperation for a weapon. The metal walls were bare except for some handrails and a panel from which projected three metal sticks. Alan wrenched at one, trying to pull it loose for a club. It pulled down and there was a hissing sound in the room, but it would not come loose. He tried a second, and again it swung down but stayed fast to the wall.

Mara shrieked behind him, and he whirled.

The big door was closing, by itself, slowly, and outside the ramp was raising itself from the ground and sliding into the wall of the Star Tower below them. The few Hussirs who had ventured onto the end of the ramp were falling from it to the ground, like ants.

The door closed with a clang of finality. The hissing in the room went on for a moment, then stopped. It was as still as death in the Star Tower.

They went through the inner door, timidly, holding hands. They were in a curved corridor. The other side of the corridor was a blank wall. They followed the corridor all the way around the Star Tower, back to the door, without finding an entrance through that inner wall.

But there was a ladder that went upward. They climbed it, Alan first, then Mara. They were in another corridor, and another ladder went upward.

Up and up they climbed, past level after level, and the blank inner wall gave way to spacious rooms in which was strange furniture. Some were compartmented, and on the compartment doors for three levels, red crosses were painted.

Both of them were bathed with perspiration when they reached the room with the windows. And here there were no more ladders.

"Mara, we're at the top of the Star Tower!" exclaimed Alan.

The room was domed, and from head level all the dome was windows. But, though the windows faced upward, those around the lower periphery showed the lighted city of Falklyn spread below them. There was even one of them that showed a section of the park, and the park was right under them, but they knew it was the park because they could see the Hussirs scurrying about in the light of the two gas lamps that still burned beside the closed door of the Star Tower.

All the windows in the upper part of the dome opened onto the stars.

The lower part of the walls was covered with strange wheels and metal sticks and diagrams and little shining circles of colored lights.

"We're in the top of the Star Tower!" shouted Alan in a triumphant frenzy. "I have the Silk and I shall sing the Song!"

VI

ALAN RAISED HIS VOICE AND THE WORDS REVERBERATED AT THEM from the walls of the domed chamber.

> Twinkle, twinkle, golden star,
> I can reach you, though you're far.
> Shut my mouth and find my head,
> Find a worm that's striped with red,
> Feed it to the turtle shell,
> Then go to sleep, for all is well.

Nothing happened.

Alan sang the second verse, and still nothing happened.

"Do you suppose that if we went back out now the Hussirs would let all humans go free?" asked Mara doubtfully.

"That's silly," he said, staring at the window where an increasing number of Hussirs was crowding into the park. "It's a riddle. We have to do what it says."

"But how can we? What does it mean?"

"It has something to do with the Star Tower," he said thought-fully. "Maybe the 'golden star' means the Star Tower, though I always thought it meant the Golden Star in the southern sky. Anyway, we've reached the Star Tower, and it's silly to think about reaching a real star.

"Let's take the next line. 'Shut my mouth and find my head.' How can you shut anyone's mouth before you find their head?"

"We had to shut the door to the Star Tower before we could climb to the top," she ventured.

"That's it!" he exclaimed. "Now, let's 'find a worm that's striped with red'!"

They looked all over the big room, in and under the strange crooked beds that would tilt forward to make chairs, behind the big, queer-looking objects that stood all over the floor. The bottom part of the walls had drawers and they pulled these out, one by one.

At last Mara dropped a little disc of metal and it popped in half on the floor. A flat spool fell out, and white tape unrolled from it in a tangle.

"Worm!" shouted Alan. "Find one striped with red!"

They popped open disc after metal disc—and there it was: a tape crossed diagonally with red stripes. There was lettering on the metal discs and Mara spelled out the letters on this one.

"EMERGENCY. TERRA. AUTOMATIC BLASTDOWN."

Neither of them could figure out what that meant. So they looked for the "turtle shell," and of course that would be the transparent dome-shaped object that sat on a pedestal between two of the chair-beds.

It was an awkward job trying to feed the striped worm to the turtle shell, for the only opening in the turtle shell was under it and to one side. But with Alan lying in one cushioned chair-bed and Mara lying in the other, and the two of them working together, they got the end of the worm into the turtle shell's mouth.

Immediately the turtle shell began eating the striped worm with a clicking chatter that lasted only a moment before it was drowned in a great rumbling roar from far down in the bowels of the Star Tower.

Then the windows that looked down on the park blossomed into flame that was almost too bright for human eyes to bear, and the lights of Falklyn began to fall away in the other windows around the rim of the dome. There was a great pressure that pushed them mightily down into the cushions on which they lay, and forced their senses from them.

Many months later, they would remember the second verse of the song. They would go into one of the chambers marked with a cross, they would sting themselves with the bugs that were hypodermic needles and sink down in the sleep of suspended animation.

But now they lay, naked and unconscious, in the control room of the accelerating starship. In the breeze from the air conditioners the silken message to Earth fluttered pink against Alan's throat.

Mirror, Mirror on the Lam

❖

Tanya Huff

he turquoise house on the headland had stood empty for some weeks. The wind off the sea whistled forlornly through the second floor cupola, tried each of the shuttered windows in turn, and finally, in a fit of pique, tossed a piece of forgotten garden furniture into what appeared to be a halfhearted attempt at shrubbery.

The green-and-gold lizard crouched under a wilting bayberry scrambled to safety just in time. Racing counterclockwise up the nearest palm, it stopped suddenly, lifted its head, and tested the air.

Someone was coming.

Ciro had left his donkey and cart carefully hidden at the foot of the hill. Although he doubted that any of the inhabitants of the nearby fishing village would venture so far from the cove, he never took risks he could avoid. As his dear old white-haired mother had told him, right before her public and very well-attended execution, chance favors the pessimist.

He'd have preferred a faster form of transportation, but since his current employer had been somewhat vague on the size of the object he was to acquire, he'd erred on the side of caution. If he couldn't deliver, he wouldn't get paid.

For safety's sake, he avoided paths and moved, where he could, from one patch of rock to the next. As he approached the house, the vegetation grew more lush, easier to hide behind if harder to move through. At the edge of the garden, he paused and studied the structure, a little taken aback by the extraordinary color. It was smaller than he'd expected, but perhaps the most powerful wizard in the world had no need for ostentatious display.

To his surprise, the kitchen door was not only unlocked but, if the crystal his employer had given him was to be trusted, also unwarded. As he crossed the kitchen floor, Ciro sincerely hoped that the shadows dancing in the corners owed more to the way the louvered shutters filtered light than to anything the wizard may have left behind.

Stepping out into a large square hall, he found himself facing three identical doors. As he moved forward, eyes half closed against the brilliant sunshine blazing through the circular skylight, the kitchen door closed behind him.

Four identical doors.

The door on his right led to a bedroom. The bed—a huge, northern-style four-poster that overwhelmed the southern decor—had been left unmade. Ciro pulled a sandal from the closest pile of clothing and used it to block the door open before he stepped cautiously forward.

The door closed.

No need to panic, he told himself. *You can always go out the window.*

A cloak, in a particularly vibrant shade of orange, had been draped over the large oval mirror. Standing safely to one side, he tugged at the cloth and took a quick look into the glass as it fell. A man of average height, his light brown hair and beard a little darker than his skin and a little lighter than his eyes, looked back at him. He frowned and his reflection echoed the movement. Either he'd lost weight or the mirror made him look thinner.

It was the only mirror in the room.

The door proved to be unlocked. It opened when he lifted the latch and, as he stepped back into the hall, it closed behind him.

Continuing to his right, Ciro opened the next door and found himself staring into the kitchen.

This time, he closed the door on his own.

The door to his left should now lead to the bedroom but he was no longer willing to take that for granted. He checked the crystal. The wizardry moving the house about was not directed at him—a mixed blessing at best. For lack of a better plan, he continued moving to the right.

A spare room. An unmade bed and empty wardrobe. One mirror, not very large and not what he was searching for.

The kitchen again. With luck, the shadows had changed only because the light had.

A spiral staircase leading up to the cupola, a small square room containing only a pile of multicolored cushions. Peering through one of the louvered shutters that made up the bulk of the walls, Ciro found himself staring out at a view from some fifty feet above the house. Without actually lifting his feet from the floor, the thief backed up and made his way carefully down the short—the far too short—flight of stairs.

The wizard's bedroom.

A bathing room. A dolphin mosaic decorated the tiles surrounding the sunken tub. The drying cloths were large, thick, and soft. From the variety of soaps and lotions, it was obvious that the wizard was no ascetic. There was no mirror.

He hadn't found a workshop yet but figured that he would in time. He'd never known a wizard who wasn't happiest puttering about with foul smelling potions and exploding incantations.

The kitchen.

The staircase.

The bedroom.

A sitting room. Big brightly colored cushions were piled high on round bamboo chairs. A carafe, two glasses, and a pile of withered orange peels had been left on a low table. On one wall, floor-to-ceiling shelves had been messily stuffed with scrolls and books and the occasional wax tablet. There were more shelves on the opposite wall, but they were less regular. Most held a variety of ornaments ranging, in Ciro's professional opinion, from the incredibly tacky to the uniquely priceless. Out of habit, he tucked a few of the latter in his pockets.

In the exact center of the wall was an open section. In it, covered in a black cloth, was an oval object about two feet across at its widest and three feet long. Holding his breath, Ciro flipped the cloth to one side.

Even knowing what to expect, he almost jumped back.

The demon trapped in the mirror snarled in fixed impotence as it had for decades.

Ciro smiled, rewrapped the mirror in the cloth, tucked the bundle under his arm, unlatched one of the large windows, and stepped out into the garden, politely closing and relatching the window behind him.

He never noticed the watching lizard.

"Well, Emili, did you miss me?"

The tiny gray cat cradled in Magdelene's arms hunkered down and growled.

"Because you're too old to leave by yourself, that's why. You're lucky Veelma was willing to take care of you."

The path from the beach to the top of the headland was both steep and rocky although generations of use had worn off the more treacherous edges. As the wizard climbed in breathless silence, the cat kept up a constant litany of complaint, squirming free with a final wail the moment the summit was reached and disappearing under a tangle of vegetation the moment after.

"I know exactly how you feel," Magdelene muttered, sagging against the end of the seawall and pushing a heavy fall of damp chestnut hair back off her face. "There's no place like home."

Magdelene seldom traveled. It needed far more exertion than she was usually willing to expend and experience had taught her that the easier she made it for herself, the more exertion it invariably required. This particular trip had been precipitated by an extremely attractive young man who'd come a very long way to request her assistance—and had cleverly exploited one of her weaknesses by making the request on his knees. He'd almost made it worth her while.

Reluctantly rousing herself, she crossed to the kitchen door, latched it open, and went inside. The wind followed her, only to be chased back outside where it belonged.

Sometime later, cleaned, changed, and holding a tall glass of iced fruit juice, Magdelene entered the sitting room and rolled her eyes dramatically when the opened shutters exposed a fine patina of dust.

"I've got to get another housekeeper," she muttered, dragging a finger along the edge of a shelf and frowning at the resulting cap of gray fuzz. The problem was, every time she got used to a housekeeper, they died. Antuca had been with her the longest and the fifty years they'd shared would make it even harder to replace her.

"On the other hand," Magdelene told herself philosophically, "someone has to do the cooking." Taking a long swallow of the juice, she crossed to the other side of the room. "Well, H'sak, did you . . . ?"

The section of wall was empty. Even the black cloth she'd thrown over the mirror before she'd left had been taken.

"Oh, lizard piss," said the most powerful wizard in the world.

The Five Cities were five essentially independent municipal areas set around a huge shallow lake. Reasoning they had more in common with each other than with the countries at their backs, they'd formed a loose alliance that had held for centuries. The Great Lake was the area's largest resource and the agreement allowed them to exploit it equally. Overly ambitious city governors were traditionally replaced with more pragmatic individuals practically before the body had cooled.

Two weeks to the day after the thief had stolen the mirror and twenty minutes after she'd dropped the cat back at Veelma's, Magdelene appeared in Talzabadhar, the Third City, clutching a black velvet pillow in both hands. Gratefully discovering that the contents of her stomach had traveled with her, she released the breath she'd been holding and took a quick look around.

The picture embroidered on the pillow over the barely legible words "A Souvenir of Scenic Talzabadhar" had been more or less accurate. The small stone shrine, five pillars holding apart a floor and a roof, had been rendered admirably true to life. Unable to anchor the transit spell in a place she'd never seen, Magdelene had taken a huge chance using the pillow for a reference. Fortunately, it appeared to have paid off.

Unfortunately, the shrine was not standing in isolation on a gentle green hill as portrayed but in the center of a crowded market square and the clap of displaced air that had heralded Magdelene's appearance had attracted the attention of almost everyone present. Fidgeting under the weight of an expectant silence, Magdelene looked out at half a hundred curious eyes.

Then a voice declaimed, "She has returned!" and everyone fell to their knees, hands over their faces, foreheads pressed against the ground.

Obviously, it was a case of mistaken identity. Magdelene, who had no time to be worshiped—although she had nothing actually against it—ran for an alley on the north side of the square.

Someone peeked.

"She goes!"

Experience having taught her how quickly a crowd can become a mob, Magdelene ran faster. Ducking into the mouth of the alley, she tossed the pillow back over her shoulder.

"A relic!"

"I saw it first!"

The sounds of a fight replaced the sounds of pursuit and Magdelene used the time gained to cover the length of the alley, round a corner, and run smack into a religious procession. By the time the first of her pursuers had come into sight, she'd borrowed a tambourine and an orange veil and was dancing away down the road, indistinguishable from any other acolyte.

At the first cross street, she returned her disguise, regretfully declined an invitation to lunch, and went looking for a member of the city guard.

"Excuse me, Sergeant?" When he glanced down, dark eyes stern and uncompromising under the edge of his helm, Magdelene gave him an encouraging smile. "I was wondering, who would you consider the best thief in the Five Cities?"

"Ciro Rasvona." His dark gaze grew a little confused, as though he wasn't entirely certain why he'd answered so readily.

"And where would I find him?"

The sergeant snorted. "If I knew that, I'd find him there myself."

"Maybe later," the wizard promised. "I meant, which of the Five Cities does he use as his base?"

"This one."

"This one? My, my." Magdelene was a big believer in luck—luck, coincidence and just generally having life arrange itself in her favor. It made everything much less work and she was a *really* big believer in that.

"If there's nothing else I can do for you . . ."

"Maybe later," she promised again and reluctantly let him walk on.

Ciro Rasvona had an average set of rooms in an average neighborhood under another, average name. His neighbors, when they thought of him at all, assumed he worked for the city government, a belief he fostered by living as outwardly boring a life as possible. He met his clients in public places and he brought neither friends nor lovers home.

His own mother hadn't known where he lived. This was fortunate since, during the trial, she'd cheerfully implicated everyone she knew in the hopes of clemency.

All things considered then, Ciro was astonished when he opened his door and saw an attractive woman in foreign clothes sitting in his favorite chair absently fondling his rosewood flute. Leaving the door open in the unlikely event she turned out to be a constable and he had to make a run for it, he took a step forward, smiled pleasantly and said, "Excuse me. Do I know you?"

Behind him, the door closed.

Heart pounding, he whirled around, yanked it open, and ran back into his rooms, ending up considerably closer to the woman in the chair before he could stop.

"I've come for the mirror," Magdelene told him.

His jaw dropped. "You . . . ? You're . . . ?"

"The most powerful wizard in the world," Magdelene finished when it seemed as though he wouldn't be able to get it out.

"But you're . . . I mean . . ." He swallowed and waved one hand between them for no good reason. "You, uh, you don't look like a wizard."

"Yeah, yeah, I know. No pointy hat, no robe, no staff." Magdelene sighed. "If I had a grain of sand for every time I've heard that, I'd have a beach. But we're not here to talk about me." She leaned forward. "Let's talk about the mirror."

"I don't have it."

"You've sold it *already*?"

"Not exactly." When her gray eyes narrowed, he felt compelled to add, "I was hired to steal it."

"For who?"

"My clients don't tell me their names."

"Oh, please."

Ciro supposed he might be reading a little too much into the way the wizard's hand closed around the shaft of his flute, but it sure looked uncomfortably like a warning to him. "All right, I know who he is. But I can't give you his name," he added hurriedly. "I took an oath."

"You also took my mirror."

"It was a blood oath."

"A blood oath?" Magdelene repeated. When he nodded, she sighed and massaged the bridge of her nose. The thief had turned out to be attractive, in an unprincipled sort of a way, with good teeth, broad shoulders, and lovely strong looking hands. *And* he played the flute. In a just world, she would have found him, retrieved her mirror, and suggested a way he could begin making amends. But he didn't have the mirror and a blood oath, unbreakable by death, or even Death, put a distinct crimp in her plans.

Then, suddenly, she had an idea. "Could I hire you to steal the mirror back?"

Ciro shook his head, a little surprised that he wanted the answer to be different. "I'd never be able to get it."

"You got it from me."

"Your pardon, Lady Wizard, but your door wasn't even locked. You relied too much on your reputation to protect you, forgetting that a reputation can also attract unwanted attention."

"Like yours?" Magdelene muttered.

He bowed. "Like mine."

In the silence that followed, Magdelene considered her options and found herself a little short. Magical artifacts were essentially null and void as far as wizardry was concerned, and she couldn't force the thief to tell her where it was. Tossing the flute onto the table, she stood. "Looks like I'll have to do this the hard way."

Suddenly drenched in sweat, Ciro took a step back. "Lady Wizard, I beg you . . ."

"Relax. I haven't time to deal with you right now." She paused, one hand on the door and half turned to face him. "But I know you, Ciro Rasvona." Her voice lingered over his name, sending not entirely unpleasant chills up and down his spine. "When this is over, I can always find you again."

A thief had no need for a conscience, but a remarkably well developed sense of self-preservation made a handy substitute. "I could *show* you where the mirror is. Actually taking you there wasn't covered by the oath," he explained when both her brows rose. As they slowly began to lower again, he smiled nervously. "I, uh, guess I should've mentioned that before."

Wondering what had happened to his policy of never taking risks he could avoid—*She'd been about to leave, you yutz!*—Ciro led the way down the stairs and out onto the street, exchanging a silent bow with a neighbor in front of the building. When that neighbor raised a scandalized middle-class brow at the sight of his companion, he took her elbow and began hurrying her toward one of the hub streets, aware of eyes watching from curtained windows.

"Did you really want to spend the rest of your life as a cockroach?" Magdelene asked conversationally.

"Sorry." Praying he was imagining the tingle in his fingers, he released her arm. "It's just that I've worked very hard at remaining unnoticeable and you're attracting attention."

A little surprised, Magdelene tossed her hair back off her face and turned to stare at him. "I'm not doing anything."

Ciro sighed. "You don't have to."

"They're not used to seeing wizards around here?"

She was wearing an orange, calf-length skirt, red leather sandals, and a purple, sleeveless vest held closed with bright yellow frogging. "Yeah. That's it."

"I guess you should've considered the consequences before you stole my mirror."

"I took every precaution. You shouldn't have been able to track me."

"I didn't. You're dangling a Five Cities talisman from your left ear, so I came directly here."

Unable to stop himself, Ciro clutched at the earring. So much for that protective crystal he'd been carrying. "You had a spell on the house to capture my image."

"No. I had a lizard."

Both sides of the hub street were lined with shops, merchandise spilling out onto the cobblestones. Magdelene shook her head as she followed the thief through the glittering displays. "This is really unfair," she muttered. "First time I make it to one of the Five Cities, and I'm here on business."

Ciro deftly snagged an exotic bloom from a hanging basket, tossing the vender a copper coin in almost the same motion. "Perhaps when you've brought your business to a close," he said, presenting the flower with a flourish, "I can show you around."

"Are you sucking up?"

"Is it working?"

"Not yet."

"Should I keep trying?"

"Couldn't hurt." He really did have a very charming smile, Magdelene decided, tucking the blossom into her hair, and she'd never been very good at holding a grudge. "Is the mirror in the city?"

"I can't tell you that, Lady Wizard."

"Call me Magdelene." Titles implied a dignity she certainly wouldn't bother living up to. Stepping over a pile of mollusk shells, their pearly interiors gleaming in the sunlight, she rearranged the question. "Are we staying in the city?"

"Yes."

"Good. I might just find H'sak in ti . . ."

"It is Her!"

"Oh, nuts." Grabbing Ciro's arm, she ducked into the nearest shop.

"What's going on?"

"I'll explain later."

"How may I help you, Gracious Lady?"

Magdelene flashed the shopkeeper a somewhat preoccupied smile. "Does this place have a back door?"

"But of course," he nodded toward a beaded curtain nearly hidden behind bolts of brightly colored fabric. "And on your way through, perhaps I can interest you in this lovely damask? Sale priced at only two dramils a measure. I offer a fine exchange rate on coin not of the Five Cities, and I deliver."

The most powerful wizard in the world hesitated, then sighed and shook her head. "Unfortunately, we're in a bit of a hurry."

"Because of the demon?" Ciro asked in an undertone as she pushed him through the curtain.

From outside the shop came an excited babble of voices, growing louder.

"Yeah. Him, too."

*   *   *

"You appeared in the Hersota's shrine?" Ciro tapped his forehead twice with the first three fingers of his right hand—just in case. "No wonder you caused so much excitement. Her return has been prophesied by three separate sects."

"I didn't know it was her shrine, did I? It was just the only reference point I had in any of the Five Cities." She peered around the corner, then led the way back onto the hub street some blocks from where they'd left it. "So what was the Hersota like?"

"According to her believers, she was a stern and unforgiving demiurge who preached that hard work and chastity were the only ways to enlightenment."

Magdelene stared at him in astonishment. "And they want her to come back?"

"I never said that I was waiting for her."

He sounded so affronted that Magdelene chuckled and tucked her hand into the crook of his elbow. There was muscle under the modest sleeve of his cream-colored shirt she noted with approval, and when he shot her a questioning glance, she answered it with her second best smile.

Her fingers were warm even through the cloth, and for a moment her smile drove the thought of unimportant bodily functions, like breathing, right out of Ciro's mind. He'd felt safer while she'd been threatening him. "I, uh, stole your mirror," he said. It seemed important that she remember that.

Magdelene waved off the reminder. "Now you're helping me find it."

"I broke into your home."

"I should've locked the door."

Wondering if he might not be better off finding a member of the city guard and turning himself in, Ciro escorted the wizard out into the Hub and around the civic fountain. "We're here."

"This is the government building."

"That's right."

"The mirror's in there?"

"I can't tell you that."

"I guess it is, then."

The government had outgrown its building a number of times, adding larger and equally unattractive structures as needed. The result looked pretty much exactly like what it was, architecture by committee—or, more precisely, a series of committees.

Shaking her head, Magdelene released Ciro's arm. "This is the ugliest pile of rock I've ever seen," she told him, walking toward it. "And I saw Yamdazador before the desert sands engulfed it."

Around the Great Lake, time had downgraded that ancient city's sudden and inexplicable disappearance from legend to parental warning: "*I swear by all the gods, if you don't stop stuffing beans up your brother's nose, I'm sending you to Yamdazador.*"

Running to catch up, Ciro gasped, "*You* were at Yamdazador?"

"I don't care what you heard, it wasn't my fault."

After a moment, he decided he didn't really want to know.

"So, now you're here, what's your plan?" he asked as they reached the stairs.

"My plan?" Pausing by the entrance a more practical administration had cut into the huge, brass double doors, Magdelene turned to face the thief. "I plan on getting my mirror back before H'sak is either purposefully or inadvertently released, and then I plan on making your client very, very sorry he ever hired you."

Ciro winced. "Good plan."

"I thought so. Let's get going."

It took a moment for the words to sink in, and when they did, he actually felt the blood drain from his face. It was an unpleasant feeling. "You want me to go with you."

"I might need your help."

"But I already told you, I won't be able to get near the mirror; it'll be too well guarded."

"You can't get near it on your own, but you don't know *what* you're capable of when you're with me." She winked and led the way inside.

While his mind was still busy trying to plan an escape route, his body happily followed. *Oh, sure,* he told it, as they crossed the atrium. *One lousy double entendre and you're willing to walk into the lion's den.* "Magdelene, this is a big place and I can't lead you any closer. If you can't scan for it, you'll never find the mirror."

"Of course I will. This is a government building, isn't it?" Slipping deftly between the constant stream of robed officials crossing and recrossing the atrium, Magdelene made her way to the desk at the center of all the activity. "Excuse me, could you please tell me if any of the senior officials has recently put him or herself incommunicado? Still in the building but not to be disturbed under any circumstances?"

The clerk glanced up from the continual flow of parchment, papyrus, and wax tablets crossing his desk, pale features twisted into an impatient scowl. "Who are you?"

"If you must know, I'm the most powerful wizard in the world."

He leaned far enough out to get a good look at her. "I find that highly unlikely," he sniffed.

"Why would he just give you that information?" Ciro demanded as they hurried through the halls.

"Successful government employees survive by recognizing power and responding to it."

"You mean kissing up to it."

"If you like."

According to the clerk, Governor Andropof had spent the day conducting research in the old library and was so insistent on not being disturbed that he'd put guards on all the entrances. *"He was in there this morning when I got to work, and he hasn't been out since. Please stop melting my wax. His assistant took him lunch, cold fish cakes and steamed dulce, but I don't know if he ate it."*

Which was a little more information than Magdelene had required but, happily, it had segued into directions. *"Go through that door, second right, past roads and public works, up the stairs, go right again, it's at the end of the long hall, and I'd be very grateful, Lady Wizard, if you could return my export documents to a recognizable language."*

"Wait a minute! You can't go in there!"

About to follow Ciro into one of the older parts of the building, Magdelene turned to see a clerk, identical but for gender to the clerk in the atrium, hurrying toward them.

"Tourists," she forced the word through stiff lips, "are only permitted in the designated areas."

"I'm on my way to see the governor."

"Have you got an appointment?"

"Have you got a desire to have a demon eat your liver?" Her tone made it clear that this was not a rhetorical question.

"Another successful government employee?" Ciro asked as they trotted up the forbidden flight of stairs.

Magdelene nodded. "I'm quite impressed by the state of your civil service, no wonder Talzabad-har runs so smoothly. I *am* a little disappointed in the governor, though."

"You're disappointed in the governor? Why?"

"Why? He hired a thief, and he's planning to use a demon for political gain."

Ciro turned to stare at her in amazement, tripped over the top step, and would've fallen had she not caught him. "Magdelene, he's a politician!"

"And?"

"You don't get out much, do you? This is normal behavior for a politician. In fact," he added as she set him back on his feet, "by Five Cities standards, he's a bit of an underachiever."

"I've never understood this obsessive power-seeking thing," Magdelene mused as they turned the last corner and started down a long, narrow hall, barely lit by tiny windows up under the ceiling.

"That's because you've got as much of it as you could ever want." Ciro waved toward the pair of city guards standing shoulder to shoulder in front of a square, iron bound door. "This looks like the place. What are we going to do about them?"

"Not a problem."

"I was hoping you'd say that." Thankful that the light was so bad, the thief kept his head down as they approached. The last thing he needed was some bright boy in the guards remembering his face. He needn't have worried, they were both watching Magdelene.

"Hi. Is this where the governor is?"

"Yes, ma'am," said the taller of the two.

"But we can't let you go in," added his companion.

She smiled sympathetically up at them. "It sure must be boring guarding this old door. You look like you could use a nap."

There's just something about men in uniform. Attempting to put her finger on just what that something was, she watched the two topple over in a tangle of tanned, muscular legs and short uniform kilts. *Oh, yeah, now I remember.* . . .

The door wasn't warded, but it was locked. Blowing it off its hinges in a blast of eldritch fire, announcing her presence, as it were, with authority, had its merits, but she didn't want to startle the governor into doing something he'd regret. He'd only regret it for about fifteen or twenty seconds depending on which end H'sak started with, but since she'd then be the one who had to deal with the demon there'd probably be less trauma all around if she merely . . .

"Magdelene?" Ciro straightened, slipped his lock pick back into the seam of his trousers, and pulled the door open a finger's width. "We can go in now."

The door opened onto a second floor balcony about eight feet long by six feet wide in one end of a large rectangular room. To both the left and the right, curved stairs led down to the floor. The library shelves had been emptied of books, and any lingering odors of paper and dust had surrendered to the swirling clouds of smoke that rose from a dozen incense burners. Motioning for Ciro to be quiet, Magdelene crept forward, peered over the balcony railing, and stiffened.

In the center of the floor was a multicolored pentagram. In the center of the pentagram, suspended horizontally some four feet above ground was an unconscious, seven-foot-tall, green-scaled demon. Standing beside the demon was a short, slight, balding man wearing what were traditionally thought of as wizard's robes.

As Magdelene's jaw dropped, he raised his arms into the air

with a flourish worthy of a stage magician. In his right hand he held a dagger and in his left, an ebony bowl. Something green and moist coated the edge of the dagger blade.

"Oh, shit!"

Governor Andropof's head jerked up and around toward the balcony. "Whoever you are, you're too late!" Laughing maniacally, he bent to hold the bowl under the demon's throat, then vanished.

The chime of the dagger hitting the floor hadn't quite faded when Magdelene reached the edge of the pentagram, Ciro, fighting every instinct, close behind her.

"Where's the governor?" he panted.

"The middle of the Great Lake."

"What's he doing there?"

"Probably treading water." Circling the pentagram, Magdelene frowned down at the design.

"Why would he send himself . . . ?"

"He didn't. I did. In another minute he'd have completed the sacrifice, and we don't want that."

"We don't?"

"Trust me." Inspecting the last of the five points, she nodded in satisfaction and stepped over to H'sak's side.

Magdelene!" Ciro spun around searching, unsuccessfully, for something to hide behind.

"Relax. This is an exact copy of one of the great pentagrams from *The Booke of Demonkind*." She had to admit that the governor had done impressive research for, as far as Magdelene knew, there were only two copies of that book still in existence, and she had one of them—it had been rather drastically overdue when the library'd burned down, so she'd kept it. "Unfortunately, the author had a tendency to choose art over craft, and all of her illustrations are completely inaccurate—but then what else can you expect from someone who spells book with an 'e'?"

"Well if the pentagram isn't holding the demon, what is?" He couldn't prevent his voice from rising rather dramatically on the last word although, when he noticed he was doing it, he did manage to stop wringing his hands.

"This."

This, was a glowing length of delicate silver chain.

"That's the Blazing Chain of Halla Hunta," the wizard explained as Ciro cautiously approached, drawn by the glint of a precious metal.

"Halla who?"

"Ancient warrior; nice buns, no manners. He had the chain forged, link by link, in volcanic fire, specifically to hold demons. It's why I didn't realize H'sak was out of the mirror; the chain's working the same way."

"Is it holding him up as well?" Ciro wondered, leaning closer.

"No. There's a Lombardi Floating Disk under his head and another under his feet, and I'd love to know how Governor Andropof got a pair away from Vince. You didn't . . . ?"

"No."

"Then it looks like you weren't the only thief he employed." Her eyes narrowed as she bent and scooped the dagger off the floor. "This is the Fell Dagger of Connackron, also called Demonsbane. And this . . ." With her free hand, she removed a cross section of bone from a hollow between the short horns extending out of the demon's forehead. ". . . is a piece of the thighbone of Mighty Manderkew. You haven't seen the sacrificial bowl from the destroyed Temple of the Darkest Night, have you?"

"It's under . . ." Ciro waved a hand more or less up and down the length of H'sak's body. ". . . him."

"Could you get it?"

Common sense suggested he point-blank refuse to crawl under an unconscious demon confined by no more than two ounces of silver chain and held off the floor in the center of an inoperative pentagram by artifacts he couldn't see. Unfortunately, common sense got overruled by a desire not to look like a wuss in front of an attractive woman. It didn't help that green slime had dripped all over the floor from a wound in the demon's throat.

When he emerged, bowl clasped between sweaty hands, Magdelene took a quick look inside it, sighed with relief, and shook her head. "I don't know whether to be impressed or appalled. Governor Andropof must've been gathering this crap for years."

"Not quite." Recognition steadying his nerves, Ciro managed a matter-of-fact tone. "I stole this last summer from an inn in the Fourth City. They were using it as a serving bowl."

"They have much business?"

"Actually, no."

"Can't say as I'm surprised."

"Was the governor a wizard then?"

"No. Just a cheap opportunist. The power's intrinsic to the artifacts. Demon blood shed with this knife into that bowl will open the way for one of the Demon Princes to leave the Netherhells. Once he gets here, the piece of thighbone's a promissory note."

Mouth suddenly dry, Ciro stared into the bowl.

"Relax, I stopped him in time and H'sak's almost healed." Magdelene rapped the demon almost fondly on the chest with the knuckles of the hand holding the bone. "Of course, after the note's redeemed, there'd be a Demon Prince loose in the world."

"He wouldn't just go home?"

"Not likely; demons gain rank through slaughter."

"I didn't know that," he said, wishing he'd never had the opportunity to find out. "Now what?"

"Now, I think you'd better hold these for me." She held out the dagger and the bone. "H'sak seems to be waking up."

"I thought the chain was holding him?"

"It is. But he was unconscious because he'd had his throat slit." A waggle of the dagger she was still holding out toward him, directed Ciro's attention to the demon blood staining the blade. "It takes a lot to kill the demonkind and unsuccessful attempts make them cranky. Now, if you don't mind, I may need both hands free."

On cue, H'sak's lips drew back off his teeth. A shudder ran the length of his body like a small wave.

"Both hands free," Ciro repeated. "Good idea." Sacrificial bowl from the destroyed Temple of the Darkest Night in his left hand, the Fell Dagger of Connackron and the thighbone of Mighty Manderkew in his right, he backed out of the pentagram and continued moving back until his shoulder blades hit the wall.

Magdelene glanced up at the impact. "What are you doing all the way over there?"

"I'm a thief," Ciro reminded her. "I'm not good at confrontation."

"Whatever. Just hang onto that stuff until I get time to destroy it."

"Couldn't you just, you know, poof? Like the governor?"

"The governor wasn't a magical artifact. Wizardry doesn't affect them, it's why I had to come after the mirror myself."

"Then how?"

"I was thinking of using a hammer. Now, if you don't mind . . ." She turned her attention back to the demon.

Ciro watched the eight-inch claws flexing at the end of arms that no longer looked quite so limp and decided that being able to raise even one hand in his own defense was better than nothing at all. He dropped the bone and the dagger into the bowl.

A barely viscous drop of demon blood rolled off the blade.

H'sak jerked. His eyes blazed red. "The way is open!"

In the silence that followed, Ciro was pretty sure he heard his heart stop beating.

"You know," Magdelene told him, "I *had* pretty much decided that bringing me here and opening the door made up for stealing my mirror."

The demon turned toward her. "You!"

"Who else?"

"There was a man . . . Oh, wait," he snorted, "if there was a man, I should've expected you to show up."

"You're in no position to make smart-ass comments. A Prince approaches, compelled to answer a summons from the mortal world, and your blood was the instrument of his summoning. He's going to be royally pissed."

H'sak struggled impotently within the chain. "Your death will follow mine, Wizard," he growled. "And I will die happy knowing you are about to be torn limb from limb!"

"Suppose neither of us has to die?"

Ciro, who'd been watching a speck of darkness grow to the size of a dinner plate, cleared his throat as a cold wind began to blow from the center of it. "Uh, Magdelene, you'd better hurry."

"H'sak?"

"You're the most powerful wizard in the world," he sniffed, "you close the way."

"I can't close the way against the Prince's power."

"So?"

"So this is no time to sulk about being stuck in that mirror!"

The demon's lips drew back, exposing a double row of fangs. "I've been forced to endure your singing for almost two hundred years. *I* think this is a fine time to sulk."

"Suit yourself. Ciro, find the mirror, it has to be in the library." She smiled down at the demon as the thief began to search. "I'm thinking of studying opera."

H'sak cringed. "You win. What's the plan?"

"I release you from the chain so I can use it on his Highness, and you don't attack me from behind until I've finished with him."

"And what if he finishes you?"

"Then at least you're facing him on your feet."

"Deal."

Grasping one end of the chain, Magdelene began to unwind it.

With one eye on the circle of darkness, now the size of a wagon wheel, Ciro sidled toward the pentagram. "I found the mirror," he muttered, lips close to Magdelene's ear. "It's in pieces."

She leaned closer. "Don't tell H'sak."

"Hadn't planned on it." He took a deep breath and lightly gripped her shoulders. "Magdelene, in case I don't get a chance to say this later, I'm sorry I took your mirror. I'm sorry about putting the bloody dagger in the bowl."

He looked so miserable she couldn't stay angry. Her expression softened. "I'd better send you away."

"Like the governor?"

"Only drier."

"No." The rising wind from the dark gate whipped her hair

into her face. He caught a strand and tucked it gently behind her ear. "I'm responsible for this, it's only fair I stay."

Eyes half lidded, Magdelene sighed. "I only regret that . . ."

"Wizard! You haven't got time!" H'sak kicked his feet, jerking the chain still in Magdelene's hand. "And don't raise those eyebrows at me! You *know* what you haven't got time for! After two hundred years," he muttered as she took a quick look at the nearly open gate and began to frantically unwind the chain, "you'd think that the novelty would've worn off."

Free, the demon rolled off the Lombardi Disks as the darkness fully dilated. Hooking his claws in the back of Ciro's shirt, he yanked the thief to the far side of the room and dropped him. "The man is out of the way," he hissed as a pale figure began to take shape in the gateway. "You'll only get one chance. Don't screw it up."

In answer, Magdelene leaned into the wind, and snapped the chain out to its full length. Wrapped around H'sak, the links had only gleamed but now, they blazed. She waited, eyes locked on the materializing Prince, noting the full thick fall of golden hair, the broad shoulders, the rippled stomach, the slender waist, the . . .

"What are you doing?" H'sak shrieked. "Waiting to see the whites of his eyes?"

"Not quite," Magdelene murmured and flicked the chain forward.

The Prince howled with laughter as the delicate links traced a spiral around him from neck to knees. "Foolish little wizard, you cannot hold . . ." His eyes widened, showing only onyx from lid to lid. "This is impossible! This toy is intended to contain the lesser demons!" He writhed in place. "I am a Prince!"

Trying very hard not to be distracted by the writhing, Magdelene held out her arms at shoulder height and brought her palms together. The gate began to close.

He stopped struggling. The perfect lines of his face smoothed out as he began to concentrate. The light of the chain began to dim. "You think you have power enough to keep me from this world?" he sneered as link after link went dark. "You think you can defeat m . . ."

The gate closed.

"Apparently," Magdelene said, twitching her skirt back into place.

Remembering how to use his legs, Ciro leaped to his feet and started forward. "Magdelene, you were magnificen . . ."

Magdelene turned, knowing exactly what she'd see.

"Now, we make a new bargain," H'sak announced, claws forming a cage around Ciro's head, their tips just barely into the skin of his throat.

Magdelene sighed. "You may find this hard to believe, H'sak, but I'm going to miss you."

The demon frowned. "I have the man."

Folding her arms over the purple vest, she tapped one red leather sandal against the floor.

H'sak withdrew his claws one at a time. Slowly. So that it didn't look as if he were making any sudden moves.

"Thank you."

Ciro's heels thumped back onto the floor, and he swayed in the rush of air that filled the space where the demon had been. "Where did you send him?"

"The Netherhells." She pursed her lips sympathetically at the collar of shallow punctures. "I'd have done it years ago but I didn't know the way."

"And now you do?" He glanced over to where the gate had been.

"Now I do."

Ciro managed a shaky smile. "That ought to terrify them."

"I don't see why it should," Magdelene protested. "If they don't bother me, I won't bother them. Shall we gather up the bits and pieces and get out of here?"

The guards were still asleep outside the library door. Magdelene woke them, helped them up onto their feet, and made a suggestion Ciro was rather glad he hadn't heard given the reaction of two strong men.

No one tried to stop them from leaving the building. No one paid them any attention at all until they were past the civic fountain.

"My eyes see Her!"

"Hard work and chastity," sighed the most powerful wizard in the world. "I don't think so." She squeezed Ciro's hand, and disappeared.

A heartbroken wail went up from the crowd. A weeping woman grabbed the thief's arm. "You were with Her! Tell us, tell us, will She return?"

Gently, but firmly, he disentangled himself. And then he smiled. "You can bet on it."

It took her a week to notice.

Ciro winced at the crack of displaced air and hoped the neighbors weren't home. This was exactly the sort of thing to get a normally quiet man an undeserved reputation. "Good afternoon, Magdelene."

"Don't good afternoon me, Ciro Rasvona, you little shit! You stole the gold hieroglyph of my name!"

He got slowly to his feet and held out his hand, the small gold plaque lying across his palm. "What," he asked, "can I possibly do to make amends?"

Cut off in mid rant, Magdelene looked down at the plaque, up at the thief, and the corners of her mouth turned up into her best smile. "I'll think of something," she promised, stepping forward. "That had better be a lock pick in your trousers, 'cause you don't seem very happy to see me . . . oh, wait a minute . . . my mistake."

"I also took that big blue pearl," he murmured when he could catch his breath.

"And the crystal gryphon?"

"No, but I'm willing to go back for it. . . ."

Chivalry

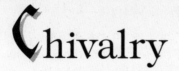

Neil Gaiman

rs. Whitaker found the Holy Grail; it was under a fur coat.

Every Thursday afternoon Mrs. Whitaker walked down to the post office to collect her pension, even though her legs were no longer what they were, and on the way back home she would stop in at the Oxfam Shop and buy herself a little something.

The Oxfam Shop sold old clothes, knickknacks, oddments, bits and bobs, and large quantities of old paperbacks, all of them donations: second-hand flotsam, often the house clearances of the dead. All the profits went to charity.

The shop was staffed by volunteers. The volunteer on duty this afternoon was Marie, seventeen, slightly overweight, and dressed in a baggy mauve jumper which looked like she had bought it from the shop.

Marie sat by the till with a copy of *Modern Woman* magazine, filling out a Reveal Your Hidden Personality questionnaire. Every now and then she'd flip to the back of the magazine, and check the relative points assigned to an A), B) or C) answer, before making up her mind how she'd respond to the question.

Mrs. Whitaker pottered around the shop.

They still hadn't sold the stuffed cobra, she noted. It had been there for six months now, gathering dust, glass eyes gazing balefully at the clothes racks and the cabinet filled with chipped porcelain and chewed toys.

Mrs. Whitaker patted its head as she went past.

She picked out a couple of Mills & Boon novels from a bookshelf—*Her Thundering Soul* and *Her Turbulent Heart,* a shilling each—and gave careful consideration to the empty bottle of Mateus Rose with a decorative lampshade on it, before deciding she really didn't have anywhere to put it.

She moved a rather threadbare fur coat, which smelled badly of mothballs. Underneath it was a walking stick, and a water-stained copy of *Romance and Legend of Chivalry* by A.R. Hope Moncrieff, priced at five pence. Next to the book, on its side, was the Holy Grail. It had a little round paper sticker on the base, and written on it, in felt pen, was the price: 30p.

Mrs. Whitaker picked up the dusty silver goblet, and appraised it through her thick spectacles.

"This is nice," she called to Marie.

Marie shrugged.

"It'd look nice on the mantelpiece."

Marie shrugged again.

Mrs. Whitaker gave fifty pence to Marie, who gave her ten pence change and a brown paper bag to put the books and the Holy Grail in. Then she went next door to the butcher's and bought herself a nice piece of liver. Then she went home.

The inside of the goblet was thickly coated with a brownish-red dust. Mrs. Whitaker washed it out with great care, then left it to soak for an hour in warm water with a dash of vinegar added.

Then she polished it with metal-polish until it gleamed, and she put it on the mantelpiece in her parlour, where it sat between a small, soulful, china basset hound and a photograph of her late husband, Henry, on the beach at Frinton in 1953.

She had been right: it did look nice.

For dinner that evening she had the liver fried in breadcrumbs, with onions. It was very nice.

The next morning was Friday; on alternate Fridays Mrs. Whitaker and Mrs. Greenberg would visit each other. Today it was Mrs. Greenberg's turn to visit Mrs. Whitaker. They sat in the parlour and ate macaroons and drank tea. Mrs. Whitaker took one sugar in her tea, but Mrs. Greenberg took sweetener, which she always carried in her handbag in a small plastic container.

"That's nice," said Mrs. Greenberg, pointing to the Grail. "What is it?"

"It's the Holy Grail," said Mrs. Whitaker. "It's the cup that Jesus drunk out of at the Last Supper. Later, at the crucifixion, it caught his precious blood, when the centurion's spear pierced his side."

Mrs. Greenberg sniffed. She was small and Jewish and didn't hold with unsanitary things. "I wouldn't know about that," she said, "but it's very nice. Our Myron got one just like that when he won the swimming tournament, only it's got his name on the side."

"Is he still with that nice girl? The hairdresser?"

"Bernice? Oh yes. They're thinking of getting engaged," said Mrs. Greenberg.

"That's nice," said Mrs. Whitaker. She took another macaroon.

Mrs. Greenberg baked her own macaroons and brought them over every alternate Friday: small sweet light-brown biscuits with almonds on top.

They talked about Myron and Bernice, and Mrs. Whitaker's nephew Ronald (she had had no children), and about their friend Mrs. Perkins who was in hospital with her hip, poor dear.

At midday Mrs. Greenberg went home, and Mrs. Whitaker made herself cheese on toast for lunch, and after lunch Mrs. Whitaker took her pills: the white and the red and two little orange ones.

The doorbell rang.

Mrs. Whitaker answered the door. It was a young man with

shoulder-length hair so fair it was almost white, wearing gleaming silver armour, with a white surcoat.

"Hello," he said.

"Hello," said Mrs. Whitaker.

"I'm on a quest," he said.

"That's nice," said Mrs. Whitaker, noncommittally.

"May I come in?" he asked.

Mrs. Whitaker shook her head. "I'm sorry, I don't think so," she said.

"I'm on a quest for the Holy Grail," the young man said. "Is it here?"

"Have you got any identification?" Mrs. Whitaker asked. She knew that it was unwise to let unidentified strangers into your home, when you were elderly and living on your own. Handbags get emptied, and worse than that.

The young man went back down the garden path. His horse, a huge grey charger, big as a shire-horse, its head high and its eyes intelligent, was tethered to Mrs. Whitaker's garden gate. The knight fumbled in the saddlebag, and returned with a scroll.

It was signed by Arthur, King of All Britons, and charged all persons of whatever rank or station to know that here was Galaad, Knight of the Table Round, and that he was on a Right High and Noble Quest. There was a drawing of the young man below that. It wasn't a bad likeness.

Mrs. Whitaker nodded. She had been expecting a little card with a photograph on it, but this was far more impressive.

"I suppose you had better come in," she said.

They went into her kitchen. She made Galaad a cup of tea, then she took him into the parlour.

Galaad saw the Grail on her mantelpiece, and dropped to one knee. He put down the teacup carefully on the russet carpet. A shaft of light came through the net curtains and painted his awed face with golden sunlight and turned his hair into a silver halo.

"It is truly the Sangrail," he said, very quietly. He blinked his pale blue eyes three times, very fast, as if he were blinking back tears.

He lowered his head as if in silent prayer.

Galaad stood up again, and turned to Mrs. Whitaker. "Gracious lady, keeper of the Holy of Holies, let me now depart this place with the Blessed Chalice, that my journeyings may be ended and my geas fulfilled."

"Sorry?" said Mrs. Whitaker.

Galaad walked over to her and took her old hands in his. "My quest is over," he told her. "The Sangrail is finally within my reach."

Mrs. Whitaker pursed her lips. "Can you pick your teacup and saucer up, please?" she said.

Galaad picked up his teacup, apologetically.

"No. I don't think so," said Mrs. Whitaker. "I rather like it there. It's just right, between the dog and the photograph of my Henry."

"Is it gold you need? Is that it? Lady, I can bring you gold . . ."

"No," said Mrs. Whitaker. "I don't want any gold, thank *you*. I'm simply not interested."

She ushered Galaad to the front door. "Nice to meet you," she said.

His horse was leaning its head over her garden fence, nibbling her gladioli. Several of the neighbourhood children were standing on the pavement watching it.

Galaad took some sugar lumps from the saddlebag, and showed the braver of the children how to feed the horse, their hands held flat. The children giggled. One of the older girls stroked the horse's nose.

Galaad swung himself up onto the horse in one fluid movement. Then the horse and the knight trotted off down Hawthorne Crescent.

Mrs. Whitaker watched them until they were out of sight, then sighed and went back inside.

The weekend was quiet.

On Saturday Mrs. Whitaker took the bus into Maresfield to visit her nephew Ronald, his wife, Euphonia, and their daughters,

Clarissa and Dillain. She took them a currant cake she had baked herself.

On Sunday morning Mrs. Whitaker went to church. Her local church was St. James the Less, which was a little more "don't think of this as a church, think of it as a place where like-minded friends hang out and are joyful" than Mrs. Whitaker felt entirely comfortable with, but she liked the Vicar, the Reverend Bartholemew, when he wasn't actually playing the guitar.

After the service, she thought about mentioning to him that she had the Holy Grail in her front parlour, but decided against it.

On Monday morning Mrs. Whitaker was working in the back garden. She had a small herb garden she was extremely proud of: dill, vervain, mint, rosemary, thyme and a wild expanse of parsley. She was down on her knees, wearing thick green gardening gloves, weeding, and picking out slugs and putting them in a plastic bag.

Mrs. Whitaker was very tender-hearted when it came to slugs. She would take them down to the back of her garden, which bordered on the railway line, and throw them over the fence.

She cut some parsley for the salad. There was a cough behind her. Galaad stood there, tall and beautiful, his armour glinting in the morning sun. In his arms he held a long package, wrapped in oiled leather.

"I'm back," he said.

"Hello," said Mrs. Whitaker. She stood up, rather slowly, and took off her gardening gloves. "Well," she said, "now you're here, you might as well make yourself useful."

She gave him the plastic bag full of slugs, and told him to tip the slugs out over the back of the fence.

He did.

Then they went into the kitchen.

"Tea? Or lemonade?" she asked.

"Whatever you're having," Galaad said.

Mrs. Whitaker took a jug of her homemade lemonade from the fridge and sent Galaad outside to pick a sprig of mint. She selected two tall glasses. She washed the mint carefully and put a few leaves in each glass, then poured the lemonade.

"Is your horse outside?" she asked.

"Oh yes. His name is Grizzel."

"And you've come a long way, I suppose."

"A very long way."

"I see," said Mrs. Whitaker. She took a blue plastic basin from under the sink and half-filled it with water. Galaad took it out to Grizzel. He waited while the horse drank, and brought the empty basin back to Mrs. Whitaker.

"Now," she said. "I suppose you're still after the Grail."

"Aye, still do I seek the Sangrail," he said. He picked up the leather package from the floor, put it down on her tablecloth and unwrapped it. "For it, I offer you this."

It was a sword, its blade almost four feet long. There were words and symbols traced elegantly along the length of the blade. The hilt was worked in silver and gold, and a large jewel was set in the pommel.

"It's very nice," said Mrs. Whitaker, doubtfully.

"This," said Galaad, "is the sword Balmung, forged by Wayland Smith in the dawn times. Its twin is Flamberge. Who wears it is unconquerable in war, and invincible in battle. Who wears it is incapable of a cowardly act or an ignoble one. Set in its pommel is the sardonyx Bircone, which protects its possessor from poison slipped into wine or ale, and from the treachery of friends."

Mrs. Whitaker peered at the sword. "It must be very sharp," she said, after a while.

"It can slice a falling hair in twain. Nay, it could slice a sunbeam," said Galaad, proudly.

"Well, then, maybe you ought to put it away," said Mrs. Whitaker.

"Don't you want it?" Galaad seemed disappointed.

"No, thank you," said Mrs. Whitaker. It occurred to her that her late husband, Henry, would have quite liked it. He would have hung it on the wall in his study next to the stuffed carp he had caught in Scotland, and pointed it out to visitors.

Galaad rewrapped the oiled leather around the sword Balmung, and tied it up with white cord.

He sat there, disconsolate.

Mrs. Whitaker made him some cream cheese and cucumber sandwiches, for the journey back, and wrapped them in greaseproof paper. She gave him an apple for Grizzel. He seemed very pleased with both gifts.

She waved them both goodbye.

That afternoon she took the bus down to the hospital to see Mrs. Perkins, who was still in with her hip, poor love. Mrs. Whitaker took her some homemade fruit cake, although she had left out the walnuts from the recipe, because Mrs. Perkins's teeth weren't what they used to be.

She watched a little television that evening, and had an early night.

On Tuesday, the postman called. Mrs. Whitaker was up in the box-room at the top of the house, doing a spot of tidying, and, taking each step slowly and carefully, she didn't make it downstairs in time. The postman had left her a message which said that he'd tried to deliver a packet, but no one was home.

Mrs. Whitaker sighed.

She put the message into her handbag, and went down to the post office.

The package was from her niece Shirelle in Sydney, Australia. It contained photographs of her husband, Wallace, and her two daughters, Dixie and Violet; and a conch shell packed in cotton wool.

Mrs. Whitaker had a number of ornamental shells in her bedroom. Her favourite had a view of the Bahamas done on it in enamel. It had been a gift from her sister, Ethel, who had died in 1983.

She put the shell and the photographs in her shopping bag. Then, seeing that she was in the area, she stopped in at the Oxfam shop on her way home.

"Hullo, Mrs. W," said Marie.

Mrs. Whitaker stared at her. Marie was wearing lipstick (possibly not the best shade for her, nor particularly expertly applied, but thought Mrs. Whitaker, that would come with time), and a rather smart skirt. It was a great improvement.

"Oh. Hello, dear," said Mrs. Whitaker.

"There was a man in here last week, asking about that thing you bought. The little metal cup thing. I told him where to find you. You don't mind, do you?"

"No, dear," said Mrs. Whitaker. "He found me."

"He was really dreamy. Really, really dreamy," sighed Marie, wistfully. "I could of gone for him. And he had a big white horse and all," Marie concluded. She was standing up straighter as well, Mrs. Whitaker noted approvingly.

On the bookshelf Mrs. Whitaker found a new Mills & Boon novel—*Her Majestic Passion*—although she hadn't yet finished the two she had bought on her last visit.

She picked up the copy of *Romance and Legend of Chivalry*, and opened it. It smelled musty. *Ex Libris Fisher*, was neatly handwritten at the top of the first page, in red ink.

She put it down where she had found it.

When she got home, Galaad was waiting for her. He was giving the neighbourhood children rides on Grizzel's back, up and down the street.

"I'm glad you're here," she said. "I've got some cases that need moving."

She showed him up to the box-room in the top of the house. He moved all the old suitcases for her, so she could get to the cupboard at the back.

It was very dusty up there.

She kept him up there most of the afternoon, moving things around while she dusted.

Galaad had a cut on his cheek, and he held one arm a little stiffly.

They talked a little, while she dusted and tidied. Mrs. Whitaker told him about her late husband, Henry; and how the life insurance had paid the house off; and how she had all these things but no one really to leave them to, no one but Ronald really and his wife only liked modern things. She told him how she had met Henry, during the war, when he was in the A.R.P. and she hadn't closed the kitchen blackout curtains all the way; and about the sixpenny dances they went to in the town; and how they'd gone to London when the war had ended, and she'd had her first drink of wine.

Galaad told Mrs. Whitaker about his mother, Elaine, who was flighty and no better than she should have been and something of a witch to boot; and his grandfather, King Pelles, who was well-meaning although at best a little vague; and of his youth in the Castle of Bliant on the Joyous Isle; and his father, whom he knew as "Le Chevalier Mal Fet," who was more or less completely mad, and was in reality Lancelot du Lac, greatest of knights, in disguise and bereft of his wits; and of Galaad's days as a young squire in Camelot.

At five o'clock Mrs. Whitaker surveyed the box-room and decided that it met with her approval; then she opened the window so the room could air, and they went downstairs to the kitchen, where she put on the kettle.

Galaad sat down at the kitchen table.

He opened the leather purse at his waist and took out a round white stone. It was about the size of a cricket ball.

"My lady," he said, "this is for you, and you give me the Sangrail."

Mrs. Whitaker picked up the stone, which was heavier than it looked, and held it up to the light. It was milkily translucent, and deep inside it flecks of silver glittered and glinted in the late afternoon sunlight. It was warm to the touch.

Then, as she held it, a strange feeling crept over her: deep inside she felt stillness and a sort of peace. *Serenity:* that was the word for it; she felt serene.

Reluctantly she put the stone back on the table.

"It's very nice," she said.

"That is the Philosopher's Stone, which our forefather Noah hung in the ark to give light when there was no light; it can transform base metals into gold; and it has certain other properties,"

Galaad told her, proudly. "And that isn't all. There's more. Here." From the leather bag he took an egg, and handed it to her.

It was the size of a goose egg, and was a shiny black colour, mottled with scarlet and white. When Mrs. Whitaker touched it the hairs on the back of her neck prickled. Her immediate impression was one of incredible heat and freedom. She heard the crackling of distant fires, and for a fraction of a second she seemed to feel herself far above the world, swooping and diving on wings of flame.

She put the egg down on the table, next to the Philosopher's Stone.

"That is the Egg of the Phoenix," said Galaad. "From far Araby it comes. One day it will hatch out into the Phoenix Bird itself; and when its time comes, the bird will build a nest of flame, lay its egg, and die, to be reborn in flame in a later age of the world."

"I thought that was what it was," said Mrs. Whitaker.

"And, last of all, lady," said Galaad, "I have brought you this."

He drew it from his pouch, and gave it to her. It was an apple, apparently carved from a single ruby, on an amber stem.

A little nervously, she picked it up. It was soft to the touch— deceptively so: her fingers bruised it, and ruby-coloured juice from the apple ran down Mrs. Whitaker's hand.

The kitchen filled, almost imperceptibly, magically, with the smell of summer fruit, of raspberries and peaches and strawberries and red currants. As if from a great way away she heard distant voices raised in song, and far music on the air.

"It is one of the apples of the Hesperides," said Galaad, quietly. "One bite from it will heal any illness or wound, no matter how deep; a second bite restores youth and beauty; and a third bite is said to grant eternal life."

Mrs. Whitaker licked the sticky juice from her hand. It tasted like fine wine.

There was a moment, then, when it all came back to her— how it was to be young: to have a firm, slim body that would do whatever she wanted it to do; to run down a country lane for the simple unladylike joy of running; to have men smile at her just because she was herself and happy about it.

Mrs. Whitaker looked at Sir Galaad, most comely of all knights, sitting fair and noble in her small kitchen.

She caught her breath.

"And that's all I have brought for you," said Galaad. "They weren't easy to get, either."

Mrs. Whitaker put the ruby fruit down on her kitchen table. She looked at the Philosopher's Stone, and the Egg of the Phoenix, and the Apple of Life.

Then she walked into her parlour and looked at the mantelpiece: at the little china basset hound, and the Holy Grail, and the photograph of her late husband, Henry, shirtless, smiling, and eating an ice cream, in black and white, almost forty years away.

She went back into the kitchen. The kettle had begun to whistle. She poured a little steaming water into the teapot, swirled it around, and poured it out. Then she added two spoonfuls of tea and one for the pot, and poured in the rest of the water. All this she did in silence.

She turned to Galaad then, and she looked at him.

"Put that apple away," she told Galaad, firmly. "You shouldn't offer things like that to old ladies. It isn't proper."

She paused, then. "But I'll take the other two," she continued, after a moment's thought. "They'll look nice on the mantelpiece. And two for one's fair, or I don't know what is."

Galaad beamed. He put the ruby apple into his leather pouch. Then he went down on one knee, and kissed Mrs. Whitaker's hand.

"Stop that," said Mrs. Whitaker. She poured them both cups of tea, after getting out the very best china, which was only for special occasions.

They sat in silence, drinking their tea.

When they had finished their tea they went into the parlour.

Galaad crossed himself, and picked up the Grail.

Mrs. Whitaker arranged the Egg and the Stone where the

Grail had been. The Egg kept tipping on one side, and she propped it up against the little china dog.

"They do look very nice," said Mrs. Whitaker.

"Yes," agreed Galaad. "They look very nice."

"Can I give you anything to eat before you go back?" she asked. He shook his head.

"Some fruit cake," she said. "You may not think you want any now, but you'll be glad of it in a few hours' time. And you should probably use the facilities. Now, give me that, and I'll wrap it up for you."

She directed him to the small toilet at the end of the hall, and went into the kitchen, holding the Grail. She had some old Christmas wrapping paper in the pantry, and she wrapped the Grail in it, and tied the package with twine. Then she cut a large slice of fruit cake, and put it in a brown paper bag, along with a banana and a slice of processed cheese in silver foil.

Galaad came back from the toilet. She gave him the paper bag, and the Holy Grail. Then she went up on tiptoes and kissed him on the cheek.

"You're a nice boy," she said. "You take care of yourself."

He hugged her, and she shooed him out of the kitchen, and out of the back door, and she shut the door behind him. She poured herself another cup of tea, and cried quietly into a kleenex, while the sound of hoofbeats echoed down Hawthorne Crescent.

On Wednesday Mrs. Whitaker stayed in all day.

On Thursday she went down to the post office to collect her pension. Then she stopped in at the Oxfam Shop.

The woman on the till was new to her. "Where's Marie?" asked Mrs. Whitaker.

The woman on the till, who had blue-rinsed grey hair, and blue spectacles that went up into diamante points, shook her head and shrugged her shoulders. "She went off with a young man," she said. "On a horse. Tch. I ask you. I'm meant to be down in the Healthfield shop this afternoon. I had to get my Johnny to run me up here, while we find someone else."

"Oh," said Mrs. Whitaker. "Well, it's nice that she's found herself a young man."

"Nice for her, maybe," said the lady on the till, "but some of us were meant to be in Healthfield this afternoon."

On a shelf near the back of the shop Mrs. Whitaker found a tarnished old silver container with a long spout. It had been priced at 60 pence, according to the little paper label stuck to the side. It looked a little like a flattened, elongated teapot.

She picked out a Mills & Boon novel she hadn't read before. It was called *Her Singular Love*. She took the book and the silver container up to the woman on the till.

"Sixty-five pee, dear," said the woman, picking up the silver object, staring at it. "Funny old thing, isn't it? Came in this morning." It had writing carved along the side in blocky old Chinese characters, and an elegant arching handle. "Some kind of oil can, I suppose."

"No, it's not an oil can," said Mrs. Whitaker, who knew exactly what it was. "It's a lamp."

There was a small metal finger-ring, unornamented, tied to the handle of the lamp with brown twine.

"Actually," said Mrs. Whitaker, "on second thought, I think I'll just have the book."

She paid her five pence for the novel, and put the lamp back where she had found it, in the back of the shop. After all, Mrs. Whitaker reflected, as she walked home, it wasn't as if she had anywhere to put it.

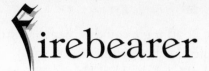irebearer

❖

Lois Tilton

n those distant ages when gods made war on gods, the skies were shattered by thunderbolts, the seas were breached, the earth itself was laid open and brought forth flame. Mountains were broken and raised up as the immortals strove against one another, the old against the new, Titans and their rebellious brood. In the end Keraunos prevailed: the Thunderer, the Cloud-gatherer, hurling the Titans from heaven with his thunderbolts and binding them in chains beneath the weight of the mountains, where they lay groaning and lamenting their loss.

Into a world newly remade humanity crept forth at last, trembling in fear and awe at the upheaval of the earth. But even as they crouched at their hearthfires, from the towering heights of a bare and desolate crag came the echo of ringing hammer-blows.

There were mornings when a silence lay on the Scythian coast before the sun rose above the mountaintops to burn away the mist, a stillness that seemed to chill the human heart. On such mornings the harsh scream of an eagle could be heard as it circled lower, descending upon one cloud-piercing crag.

The cry made Melas shudder. He stood in the doorway of his father's forge, which had been his father's before him. "Carrion bird!" he cursed the distant wheeling speck, but he spoke under his breath, for a man is rash who openly defies the gods.

The eagle's cry echoed from the mountain, followed by a low moan, a sound of hopeless torment.

The tale was old. Melas had heard it from his father by this very forge, when he had first asked as a boy, "Why does the mountain cry out in pain?"

Then his father's hand had tightened around his hammer. "It isn't the mountain that cries out so, but the Firebearer, chained at the peak."

At the god's name, the smith's hammer struck the bronze he was working a ringing blow. He likewise was called Melas, and was well named, for his hair and beard were dark and the smoke of the forge had blackened his face. To his son, he seemed the image of Hephaistos himself. But there was yet another, older god of the forge, who had taught Hephaistos his craft. "Up there? The Firebearer?" the younger Melas asked.

Again, hammer rang against bronze. "Aye, Pyrophoros, who brought the gift of fire to men and taught the crafts of metalwork, defying Keraunos," his father said grimly. "He was fettered naked to the mountain for it. But this wasn't punishment enough to satisfy the Thunderer."

By this time the hammer-strokes were a rhythmic counterpoint to the ancient tale. "Every day he sends his eagle to feed on the Titan's flesh, so men and gods alike will hear his cries and learn the price of defiance."

Young Melas had raised his eyes in horror to the mountaintop where the Firebearer suffered for the crime of bringing fire and knowledge to mankind. He cried, "Is there no one who could set him free?"

The hammer-blows paused briefly, then resumed their rhythm.

"The gods themselves were afraid to speak out against his punishment, for fear they might end up sharing it."

And as young Melas had watched, the eagle rose from the crag, its crop heavy with flesh, wheeled in the air, and flew into the distance, back to its master.

Melas had since grown to manhood, the muscles of his back and arm to a smith's strength. Soon the forge would be his, to be passed on to a son of his own. But on this morning he stood, the forge forgotten, and listened to the echoes of anguish from the mountain. Each time he saw the eagle descend upon the peak his heart would contract in pain and sympathy. His better sense argued that this was an affair of gods, not men, but always his soul cried out that such suffering was a shame to mankind, for whose sake it was endured.

On this morning he knew he could not bear it any longer. Grimly determined, he strode into the forge and began to throw his tools into a leather bag.

The old smith followed him inside and asked in a worried voice, "Where are you going?"

Melas's eyes turned to the mountain. "There."

"Fool!" his father groaned. "What do you think you can do against the will of the gods? Are you a hero? No! You're a simple bronzesmith, as your fathers were before you. Who is going to work this forge when you die on that mountain without leaving a son behind you?"

"I know what I am," Melas flung back. "But if it were you chained up there, by the will of the gods or no, how could I live day after day hearing your groans, doing nothing? How can I do less for the father of our craft?"

The old smith said nothing while Melas packed the tools with which he hoped to free the Titan from his chains. Then he lifted his hammer, passed on to him from his own father, and his father before him. "Here," he told his son, "take this. The tale has it that this hammer was forged in the very fire Pyrophoros brought from heaven. It may help."

Melas took the hammer reverently, stroked the face, felt the well-worn shaft in his hand. Tears stood in his father's eyes, and his hard calloused palms clasped his son's shoulders. "Perhaps a smith can breed a hero, after all," he said at last.

And tears rose in Melas, too, as he embraced his father, seeing him standing empty-handed by the cooling forge. Only the sight of the morning-lit peak behind him restored his resolve.

News of his intentions had spread by the time he departed, and the villagers stood in silence watching him approach the foot of the haunted crag, bearing little more than his bag of tools and a bow across his back. To some, the ancient tales of the god chained at the peak were no more than a myth, and the dreadful moans were heard as only the voice of the wind. Surely no mortal man could find the Titan there, could free him. Yet the gifts of the Fire-bearer were known to all: not only smithcraft but pottery, medicine, and every craft that makes use of fire. Melas, if he were to succeed, would be redeeming a debt owed by them all.

The mountain was a sheer cliff newly thrust up from the sea, sharp-edged granite that wind and rain had not yet had time to weather. As he climbed, Melas soon found himself crawling up the bare rock face, groping for purchase, his knees and elbows scraped raw. The muscles of his arms ached with the effort of pulling his body upward, and the stone cut his fingers and left them bleeding.

Clinging to the sheer face, Melas could no longer see the peak above him. He had to turn his head to see the sky. And then he looked down. The sight made him reel with shock, for he had not realized how high he had already climbed. Seagulls wheeled through the air—below him—and the ocean's breakers were thin traces of white foam on an expanse of deepest green. At the foot of the cliff the huts of his village clustered, and he could barely make out his father's forge. The people below were no larger than insects. This, he realized, was how the gods must view humanity—as utterly insignificant.

He turned back quickly to the cliff, his heart pounding. Above him was black and white speckled granite, its crystals glinting in the sunlight. He had no way to judge how far he had come, how far he had yet to go before he reached the summit where the Titan was chained. He climbed on, finding purchase where he could, from crack to crack, from ledge to ledge. More than once he came to a place where he could not go any farther, and he had to climb back down the way he had come to seek out some other way up the mountain.

The harsh glare of the sun had dimmed. Soon Melas found himself enveloped in the white mist of a cloud, in a chill silence. When he looked down again his village was invisible, and the peak above him hidden in the thickening fog. *Cloud-gatherer!* he breathed, terror constricting his throat. Suddenly, alone on the cloud-shrouded mountain, the gods were overwhelmingly real, and present.

At that moment the sound of a thunderclap struck the mountainside, its echo making the stone tremble. The rage of Keraunos flashed through the sky. Melas clung to the rock, blinded, knowing that the god had seen his defiance. And though the wind raged around him on his exposed ledge, though the lightning made the living stone tingle beneath his feet and Melas expected at every moment that the charred, smoking cinder of his body would be hurled earthward by the god's wrath, yet the storm did not strike him.

For a while afterward fear held him motionless, incapable either of continuing his climb or descending back down through the cloud. The mountain faced him. He reached up for a handhold, grasped it. Slowly he resumed his ascent, and in a while the cloud was below him, a white billow cutting off his sight of the earth. Above, the peak glowed in the light of the lowering sun. Now, truly, he was in the realm of the gods.

There was a harsh cry, and he looked up. An eagle circled far over his head. "Yes, Keraunos," Melas whispered, "I'm here."

The sunset's glow upon the clouds was fading to purple when Melas was forced to admit to himself that he could not reach his goal before darkness. He halted on a ledge wide enough for him to lie down to sleep and rubbed his sore and bleeding hands, took out the cheese and olives he had carried in his pouch. By this time the day's heat was leaving the stone and he shivered in his woolen garment. The night on the mountain would be cold. Though he had the gift of fire, no fuel grew on the lifeless bare rock to feed it.

As darkness fell his thoughts returned to the forbearance of the Thunderer. The tales had it that his wrath had raised this very mountain up out of the sea. Surely he could have stricken a single mortal human clinging to its face. Was it that his power was less than men had believed? Melas had no answers. What did he really know of the gods? Only that they demanded worship and sacrifice from men, while granting little in return. If the tales were true, when the war against the Titans was finally won, Keraunos would have destroyed mankind along with the elder gods. Only Pyrophoros had intervened to save humanity, defying the Thunderer's will to bring down fire from heaven and earning the torment he now suffered.

Now Melas dared in his turn, a mortal interfering in the affairs of gods. He had not considered, when he set out to climb the mountain, what punishment he might incur for himself. Now, for the first time, he realized that there could be a worse fate than death awaiting him here on the mountain, whether or not he succeeded. What if he were to be chained in the Firebearer's place? Yet he was mortal, and death would come eventually to end his suffering. No such mercy would be granted the Titan, no such release. Only when the chains that held him were struck away would the torture be relieved.

Uneasy with such thoughts, Melas rested as well as he could. All through the hours of darkness the moon shone her pale light down on the narrow ledge where he lay, and before dawn the granite sparkled with a thin icy rime.

First light woke him, the dawn of a clear, cloudless day. As Melas huddled on the mountain's edge rubbing his hands to bring back life and warmth, a swift shadow fell over him. Looking up, he heard the chilling cry of the eagle. The bird circled above the crag, but Melas was now high enough that he could see its small black eyes and cruel, rending beak. It descended toward the peak where Pyrophoros was chained, and Melas sprang to his feet with a curse, stringing his bow, setting the arrow. It flew high, straight toward its target, but at the top of its flight it fell short, and the eagle disappeared behind the rock overhead.

A sound came then, a gasp of indescribable agony. The moans Melas had heard in his village below were only the faintest echoes of this cry, which brought the rocky heart of the mountain itself alive to tremble with the Titan's pain.

Flinging the bow across his back, Melas began to climb in desperate, reckless haste, cursing the eagle and the god its master. All the while the cries went on, building in intensity, wringing Melas's soul with pity, but he could do nothing but keep climbing, as helpless as the chained Titan to stop the torture.

In his impatience he lunged rashly for an outcrop, only to find his hands slipping. He slid, scraping across the rough raw face of the rock until his feet found purchase on a narrow shelf. He clung to the mountain, heart pounding as he realized how close he had come to death, but then he began the ascent once again, pulling his weight upward with bleeding fingers.

Then, directly over his head, came the rustle of feathers, a thunderclap of wings, and the eagle was flying directly at his head, talons extended, beak open in a scream.

Melas flung himself backward, almost off the mountain, and the eagle plunged past him, the wind of its passage striking his face. He wedged himself into a crack in the rock and braced himself with his legs as he reached behind him for his bow and set another arrow to the string, held it ready, waiting.

Again the bird stooped to strike, but Melas bent his bow with a swift, sure movement. The arrow flew straight, piercing the eagle through its breast, and the bird screamed out its pain and rage as it fell tumbling toward the surf so very far below.

Melas felt his hands tremble as he lowered the bow. He had come so far. He had killed the eagle, the instrument of the Fire-bearer's torment. Now he slung the bow again on his back and began the final ascent to the peak, all but overcome at what he had done, at what he was about to find there, risking the hope that in a little while he might actually succeed in releasing the Titan from his bondage.

He grasped a last edge of rock, wedging his toes into the stone for leverage, pulled his body upward, then swung a knee over the top. He raised his head.

The breath froze in his chest with horror and awe. He fell on the rock, unable to move. The Titan was a giant, twice the size of a mortal man, pinioned naked against the bare granite. His arms and legs were outstretched and shackled. A collar of bronze was around his throat. But worst of all, a brazen spike had been driven through his chest, directly into the living heart of the mountain, and from this wound ran glistening black blood where the eagle had torn away the flesh to savage the tortured god's heart.

Then he spoke. "Have you come then at last, Herakles, these many years before your birth?"

Melas rose to his knees. How should he address a god, even one chained? "Firebearer?" he asked uncertainly. "Pyrophoros? Has the Cloud-gatherer truly done all this to you, just for bringing men the gift of fire?"

The Titan's sigh was a soft wind. "My real crime was to defy his will. Ten thousand years bound to this rock, with only the sun and sky as companions. And the Thunderer's wind-riding eagle."

Melas's heart had contracted with pity and sympathy at the sight of the mutilated flesh. But the vulture of Keraunos was dead. It would never return to its cruel feast. Daring to feel pride, he held out his bow. "It will never be back again, Pyrophoros."

"Ah," said the Titan slowly. He laughed then, a faint, painful sound, but a laugh nonetheless. "I shall not miss its company."

Melas had not expected, of all things, that the Titan would jest. But the Firebearer's ravaged face went grave as he looked at the man standing before him. "I owe you thanks. I would know your name, Hero."

Melas shook his head. "Not a hero, not I. My name is Melas, and I'm only a bronzesmith from the village at the foot of the cliff. So often in the mornings I heard your pain, and . . ." He finished lamely, unfastening his tools from his belt, "I came to set you free."

"Ah," said the Titan again, shutting his eyes. "I fear . . ."

His eyes opened again. "But of course I am grateful. It has been so long."

Melas stepped closer, his gaze drawn against his will to the cruel spike that transfixed the Titan's chest, where the eagle had feasted on his beating heart.

"It will heal," Pyrophoros assured him. His voice held bitter pain. "Each morning it is whole again."

Melas shuddered. Again he hard the agonized cries, the newly healed wound being torn open once again, every morning for ten thousand years.

"How could you endure it?"

The Firebearer sighed again. "I endure it because I must. So many times I have envied your mortality. Such torment as this is possible only for the gods. Yet I cannot say I did not know my fate."

Melas was no longer held motionless by awe of the god, but now as he regarded the fetters on the Titan he grew more doubtful. Frowning, he set down his sack of tools and brought out his father's hammer.

"The tale is," he said, holding it up, "that this hammer was cast in the very fire stolen from heaven by Pyrophoros."

"Then," said the Titan, "perhaps after all . . ." He stirred, straining against his bonds. "Strike, smith!"

Melas already had seen that he could never loosen the massive spike that transfixed the Titan's chest. But if he could free his arms, perhaps the god's own strength might do what his could not.

The shackle around the Firebearer's wrist was thick and twice as broad as Melas's hand, held fast by a spike driven deep into the living granite. Straining to reach it, he set his chisel and swung his hammer with all his mortal strength. Once again the crags echoed with the ringing sound of bronze. The smith labored until his muscular arms were weak and the sweat of exertion ran down his sides. But the fetters chaining the Firekindler were of adamant, forged by Hephaistos himself. Mortal strength was too weak, mortal tools too soft to sunder them. The last of Melas's chisels was soon blunted and useless, but the shackle made by Hephaistos was still unmarred.

Melas fell to his knees, exhausted and weary with the shame of his failure. All his efforts had gone for nothing. The Firebearer was still held fast in his chains.

The god had closed his eyes. Resignation was in his voice as he told Melas, "Do not blame yourself. The day I am destined to be freed is yet to come. I have yet another name: Foresight, and I fear that the one who will release me is not yet born. It was only when I saw you here, that for a few moments I was able to hope that I might have been wrong."

Melas looked up at him, full of confusion. "Foresight? Prometheus? You can foresee your own fate?"

"Alas, too well!"

"But then you must have seen all of this, the chains, the eagle! How could you do it, then, when you knew what would happen? How could you still defy the Thunderer?"

The Titan's voice was distant, as if he were staring far back into the past. "Oh, yes. I knew. Yet I think I didn't know, really know, how bad it would be, how much pain . . ."

"Then why?" Melas exclaimed. Surely nothing could be worth this suffering!

The Titan's voice rose. "I was the last of us to be free. My brothers all lie chained in the darkness, crushed beneath the mountains, blasted by the Cloud-gatherer's lightning. I alone of all our race took his side in the wars. But he would have gone further and extinguished the whole race of humanity along with the Titans, for fear they might one day rebel against him. Yet the provenance of mankind was mine! Its future was my care. Yes! I defied him! I could not bow my head and yield to his will. Let him send what tortures he can devise, he can never make me submit!"

"This seems a heavy price to pay for your pride," Melas said slowly.

"So Hephaistos said, too, when he chained me here. He would have refused the task if he could. He wept with pity and grief at my fate, but nonetheless he did the will of Keraunos, against his own. *That* is the price of submission that I would not pay!

"I will tell you another thing, bronzesmith. The Thunderer is bound by these chains as surely as I am. For as long as I suffer here, the whole world must hear my cries and know the extent of his cruelty. And never will I beg for his forgiveness, not if I must stand here until the end of time! No, in the end, he will be the one to relent, he will be the one to know defeat!"

The Titan's voice reached a desperate intensity. He strained against his shackles. Melas gave his head a slight shake in awe of the Titan's intransigent pride. He could not believe that anyone, even a god, would willingly choose such suffering. Had not Pyrophoros, only hours before, urged him to try to strike off his fetters? Yet pride, in his chains, was all that remained to him.

The Titan had sagged in his bonds. Now he opened his eyes and asked calmly, "And what of you, Melas the bronzesmith, did you not also defy the Thunderer's will in coming here? Did you not fear his wrath?"

Melas tried to gather his thoughts into words. "Down there where men live, it's hard to feel the presence of the gods. Only your cries—those I knew, those I could hear." His voice dropped almost to a whisper. "Now, though, on the mountain . . ."

"Yes," said the Titan gravely. "I felt his anger."

"But I don't understand! He could shatter this mountain with his thunderbolt! Why does he stay his hand?"

"His own word binds him, when no other power could. The chains and the eagle are to be my punishment, not the lightning. By his own decree, he may not strike here."

Then the Cloud-gatherer's forbearance, Melas realized, had not been directed at him. He shook his head again, wearily, still burdened by his failure and knowing that punishment might yet strike him once he left the mountain. But not this day. And whatever the future might bring, he had done what he could.

He leaned back against the mountain and opened his pouch. He still had half a piece of cheese and a handful of olives. And there stood the Titan, fettered in this barren place for ten thousand years. Whether for the sake of humanity or his own pride, what did it matter? "I don't suppose—would you like some?" he offered, holding out the pouch. "It isn't much."

The Firebearer looked surprised, as if this was one thing he had not foreseen. "Yes, please," he said finally. "It is hard to remember the taste of food."

Melas reached up and held an olive to the Titan's sun-cracked lips. Pyrophoros swallowed, and a small shiver took him. "Ah," he said, closing his eyes.

So they shared the rest of the food while night fell over the mountain, knowing that in the morning Melas must begin his descent and the Titan must resume the loneliness of his punishment. As he took what shelter he could among the rocks, glad of his wool garment, Melas pitied the Firebearer, exposed to the ice-edged lash of the winds. Such agony, without end, that only an immortal could suffer, only a god could bear. He consoled himself that at least the eagle was no longer alive to rend the Titan's ever-healing flesh. His long punishment would be easier until the day the hero finally came who was destined to free him.

But Melas's sleep was uneasy, as throughout the night he could hear the ominous roll of distant thunderclaps.

He was awakened by a cry, an eagle's scream that chilled his spine with cold horror. Above his head, the long-winged bird circled in its descent.

Chained to the rock, the Titan sighed, his face drawn with despair. "Curse you, Cloud-gatherer," he said dully. And to Melas, "Ah, bronzesmith, I feared it would be so."

"No!" Melas cried, and then more grimly, "No." With deliberate haste he strung his bow. "Not as long as I'm here to stop it."

The arrow flew, the bird dropped heavily, broken-winged, to his feet. And above the peak the angry thunder crashed, the god denied his vengeance.

"He will send another tomorrow," said the Titan bleakly. "Yet I thank you, archer, for this day, the first in ten thousand years without that pain."

Melas bent down to the dead eagle and began with care to extract his arrow from its breast. "As I said," he declared slowly, "not as long as I'm here to stop it."

"You cannot stay here, bronzesmith! No mortal could survive on this rock. Go, man, while you can! You've done what you could. I brought this fate upon myself."

"As I will, now. Do you think I could go back down there and leave you, waiting for another vulture to come tomorrow? Should I turn my back and listen to your cries every morning of my life?"

"I have endured it already for ten thousand years! What real difference will another day make? Or however long you last?"

Melas shook his head, not replying. He had seen the Titan's face as the eagle began its descent. No pride could have masked that despair. He replaced the arrow carefully in his sheath.

"This is barren rock!" the Tital protested. "Nothing grows here, nothing lives. You're mortal, you have no more food. What would you eat?"

Melas took out his knife and began to skin the eagle's carcass. Then he laughed. "Look, here I am, reduced to eating raw flesh, as men must have lived before we had the gift of fire. Don't you see, Pyrophoros, how much we owe you? This is little enough that I can repay you, as long as I can."

"Men—you are creatures of a day."

"Yet we remember. After all these years, down there, we still remember your gift."

So he insisted, until darkness once more fell over the mountain peak, and god and man together looked down upon a thousand flickering hearthfires far below.

The Bully and the Beast

❖

Orson Scott Card

he page entered the Count's chamber at a dead run. He had long ago given up sauntering—when the Count called, he expected a page to appear immediately, and any delay at all made the Count irritable and likely to assign a page to stable duty.

"My lord," said the page.

"My lord indeed," said the Count. "What kept you?" The Count stood at the window, his back to the boy. In his arms he held a velvet gown, incredibly embroidered with gold and silver thread. "I think I need to call a council," said the Count. "On the other hand, I haven't the slightest desire to submit myself to a gaggle of jabbering knights. They'll be quite angry. What do you think?"

No one had ever asked the page for advice before, and he wasn't quite sure what was expected of him. "Why should they be angry, my lord?"

"Do you see this gown?" the Count asked, turning around and holding it up.

"Yes, my lord."

"What do you think of it?"

"Depends, doesn't it, my lord, on who wears it."

"It cost eleven pounds of silver."

The page smiled sickly. Eleven pounds of silver would keep the average knight in arms, food, women, clothing, and shelter for a year with six pounds left over for spending money.

"There are more," said the Count. "Many more."

"But who are they for? Are you going to marry?"

"None of your business!" roared the Count. "If there's anything I hate, it's a meddler!" The Count turned again to the window and looked out. He was shaded by a huge oak tree that grew forty feet from the castle walls. "What's today?" asked the Count.

"Thursday, my lord."

"The day, the day!"

"Eleventh past Easter Feast."

"The tribute's due today," said the Count. "Due on Easter, in fact, but today the Duke will be certain I'm not paying."

"Not paying the tribute, my lord?"

"How? Turn me upside down and shake me, but I haven't a farthing. The tribute money's gone. The money for new arms is gone. The travel money is gone. The money for new horses is gone. Haven't got any money at all. But gad, boy, what a wardrobe." The Count sat on the sill of the window. "The Duke will be here very quickly, I'm afraid. And he has the latest in debt collection equipment."

"What's that?"

"An army." The Count sighed. "Call a council, boy. My knights may jabber and scream, but they'll fight. I know they will."

The page wasn't sure. "They'll be very angry, my lord. Are you sure they'll fight?"

"Oh, yes," said the Count. "If they don't, the Duke will kill them."

"Why?"

"For not honoring their oath to me. Do go now, boy, and call a council."

The page nodded. Kind of felt sorry for the old boy. Not much of a Count, as things went, but he could have been worse, and it was pretty plain the castle would be sacked and the Count imprisoned and the women raped and the page sent off home to his parents. "A council!" he cried as he left the Count's chamber. "A council!"

In the cold cavern of the pantry under the kitchen, Bork pulled a huge keg of ale from its resting place and lifted it, not easily, but without much strain, and rested it on his shoulders. Head bowed, he walked slowly up the stairs. Before Bork worked in the kitchen, it used to take two men most of an afternoon to move the huge kegs. But Bork was a giant, or what passed for a giant in those days. The Count himself was of average height, barely past five feet. Bork was nearly seven feet tall, with muscles like an ox. People stepped aside for him.

"Put it there," said the cook, hardly looking up. "And don't drop it."

Bork didn't drop the keg. Nor did he resent the cook's expecting him to be clumsy. He had been told he was clumsy all his life, ever since it became plain at the age of three that he was going to be immense. Everyone knew that big people were clumsy. And i was true enough. Bork was so strong he kept doing things he never meant to do, accidentally. Like the time the swordmaster, admiring his strength, had invited him to learn to use the heavy battleswords. Bork hefted them easily, of course, though at the time he was only twelve and hadn't reached his full strength.

"Hit me," the swordmaster said.

"But the blade's sharp," Bork told him.

"Don't worry. you won't come near me." The swordmaster had taught a hundred knights to fight. None of them had come near him. And, in fact, when Bork swung the heavy sword the swordmaster had his shield up in plenty of time. He just hadn't counted on the terrible force of the blow. The shield was battered aside easily, and the blow threw the sword upward, so it cut off the swordmaster's left arm just below the shoulder, and only narrowly missed slicing deeply into his chest.

Clumsy, that was all Bork was. But it was the end of any hope of his becoming a knight. When the swordmaster finally recovered, he consigned Bork to the kitchen and the blacksmith's shop, where they needed someone with enough strength to skewer a cow end to end and carry it to the fire, where it was convenient to have a man who, with a double-sized ax, could chop down a large tree in half an hour, cut it into logs, and carry a month's supply of firewood into the castle in an afternoon.

A page came into the kitchen. "There's a council, cook. The Count wants ale, and plenty of it."

The cook swore profusely and threw a carrot at the page. "Always changing the schedule! Always making me do extra work." As soon as the page had escaped, the cook turned on Bork. "All right, carry the ale out there, and be quick about it. Try not to drop it."

"I won't," Bork said.

"He won't," the cook muttered. "Clever as an ox, he is."

Bork manhandled the cask into the great hall. It was cold, though outside the sun was shining. Little light and little warmth reached the inside of the castle. And since it was spring, the huge logpile in the pit in the middle of the room lay cold and damp.

The knights were beginning to wander into the great hall and sit on the benches that lined the long, pock-marked slab of a table. They knew enough to carry their mugs—councils were always well-oiled with ale. Bork had spent years as a child watching the knights practice the arts of war, but the knights seemed more natural carrying their cups than holding their swords at the ready. They were more dedicated to their drinking than to war.

"Ho, Bork the Bully," one of the knights greeted him. Bork managed a half-smile. He had learned long since not to take offense.

"How's Sam the stableman?" asked another, tauntingly.

Bork blushed and turned away, heading for the door to the kitchen.

The knights were laughing at their cleverness. "Twice the body, half the brain," one of them said to the others. "Probably hung like a horse," another speculated, then quipped, "Which probably accounts for those mysterious deaths among the sheep this winter." A roar of laughter, and cups beating on the table. Bork stood in the kitchen trembling. He could not escape the sound—the stones carried it echoing to him wherever he went.

The cook turned and looked at him. "Don't be angry, boy," he said. "It's all in fun."

Bork nodded and smiled at the cook. That's what it was. All in fun. And besides, Bork deserved it, he knew. It was only fair that he be treated cruelly. For he had earned the title Bork the Bully, hadn't he? When he was three, and already massive as a ram, his only friend, a beautiful young village boy named Winkle, had hit upon the idea of becoming a knight. Winkle had dressed himself in odds and ends of leather and tin, and made a makeshift lance from a hog prod.

"You're my destrier," Winkle cried as he mounted Bork and rode him for hours. Bork thought it was a fine thing to be a knight's horse. It became the height of his ambition, and he wondered how one got started in the trade. But one day Sam, the stableman's son, had taunted Winkle for his make-believe armor, and it had turned into a fist fight, and Sam had thoroughly bloodied Winkle's nose. Winkle screamed as if he were dying, and Bork sprang to his friend's defense, walloping Sam, who was three years older, along the side of his head.

Ever since then Sam spoke with a thickness in his voice, and often lost his balance; his jaw, broken in several places, never healed properly, and he had problems with his ear.

It horrified Bork to have caused so much pain, but Winkle assured him that Sam deserved it. "After all, Bork, he was twice my size, and he was picking on me. He's a bully. He had it coming."

For several years Winkle and Bork were the terror of the village. Winkle would constantly get into fights, and soon the village children learned not to resist him. If Winkle lost a fight, he would scream for Bork, and though Bork was never again so harsh as he was with Sam, his blows still hurt terribly. Winkle loved it. Then one day he tired of being a knight, dismissed his destrier, and be-

came fast friends with the other children. It was only then that
Bork began to hear himself called Bork the Bully; it was Winkle
who convinced the other children that the only villain in the
fighting had been Bork. "After all," Bork overheard Winkle say
one day, "he's twice as strong as anyone else. Isn't fair for him to
fight. It's a cowardly thing for him to do, and we mustn't have anything to do with him. Bullies must be punished."

Bork knew Winkle was right, and ever after that he bore the
burden of shame. He remembered the frightened looks in the other
children's eyes when he approached them, the way they pleaded
for mercy. But Winkle was always screaming and writhing in
agony, and Bork always hit the child despite his terror, and for that
bullying Bork was still paying. He paid in the ridicule he accepted
from the knights; he paid in the solitude of all his days and nights;
he paid by working as hard as he could, using his strength to serve
instead of hurt.

But just because he knew he deserved the punishment did not
mean he enjoyed it. There were tears in his eyes as he went about
his work in the kitchen. He tried to hide them from the cook, but
to no avail. "Oh, no, you're not going to cry, are you?" the cook
said. "You'll only make your nose run and then you'll get snot in
the soup. Get out of the kitchen for awhile!"

Which is why Bork was standing in the doorway of the great
hall watching the council that would completely change his life.

"Well, where's the tribute money gone to?" demanded one of
the knights. "The harvest was large enough last year!"

It was an ugly thing, to see the knights so angry. But the Count
knew they had a right to be upset—it was they who would have to
fight the Duke's men, and they had a right to know why.

"My friends," the Count said. "My friends, some things are
more important than money. I invested the money in something
more important than tribute, more important than peace, more
important than long life. I invested the money in beauty. Not to
create beauty, but to perfect it." The knights were listening now.
For all their violent preoccupations, they all had a soft spot in their

hearts for true beauty. It was one of the requirements for knight-hood. "I have been entrusted with a jewel, more perfect than any diamond. It was my duty to place that jewel in the best setting money could buy. I can't explain. I can only show you." He rang a small bell, and behind him one of the better-known secret doors in the castle opened, and a wizened old woman emerged. The Count whispered in her ear, and the woman scurried back into the secret passage.

"Who's she?" asked one of the knights.

"She is the woman who nursed my children after my wife died. My wife died in childbirth, you remember. But what you don't know is that the child lived. My two sons you know well. But I have a third child, my last child, whom you know not at all, and this one is not a son."

The Count was not surprised that several of the knights seemed to puzzle over this riddle. Too many jousts, too much prac-tice in full armor in the heat of the afternoon.

"My child is a daughter."

"Ah," said the knights.

"At first, I kept her hidden away because I could not bear to see her—after all, my most beloved wife had died in bearing her. But after a few years I overcame my grief, and went to see the child in the room where she was hidden, and lo! She was the most beau-tiful child I had ever seen. I named her Brunhilda, and from that moment on I loved her. I was the most devoted father you could imagine. But I did not let her leave the secret room. Why, you may ask?"

"Yes, why!" demanded several of the knights.

"Because she was so beautiful I was afraid she would be stolen from me. I was terrified that I would lose her. Yet I saw her every day, and talked to her, and the older she got, the more beautiful she became, and for the last several years I could no longer bear to see her in her mother's cast-off clothing. Her beauty is such that only the finest cloths and gowns and jewels of Flanders, of Venice, of Florence would do for her. You'll see! The money was not ill spent."

And the door opened again, and the old woman emerged, leading forth Brunhilda.

In the doorway, Bork gasped. But no one heard him, for all the knights gasped, too.

She was the most perfect woman in the world. Her hair was a dark red, flowing behind her like an auburn stream as she walked. Her face was white from being indoors all her life, and when she smiled it was like the sun breaking out on a stormy day. And none of the knights dared look at her body for very long, because the longer they looked the more they wanted to touch her, and the Count said, "I warn you. Any man who lays a hand on her will have to answer to me. She is a virgin, and when she marries she shall be a virgin, and a king will pay half his kingdom to have her, and still I'll feel cheated to have to give her up."

"Good morning, my lords," she said, smiling. Her voice was like the song of leaves dancing in the summer wind, and the knights fell to their knees before her.

None of them was more moved by her beauty than Bork, however. When she entered the room he forgot himself; there was no room in his mind for anything but the great beauty he had seen for the first time in his life. Bork knew nothing of courtesy. He only knew that, for the first time in his life, he had seen something so perfect that he could not rest until it was his. Not his to own, but his to be owned by. He longed to serve her in the most degrading ways he could think of, if only she would smile upon him; longed to die for her, if only the last moment of his life were filled with her voice saying, "You may love me."

If he had been a knight, he might have thought of a poetic way to say such things. But he was not a knight, and so his words came out of his heart before his mind could find a way to make them clever. He strode blindly from the kitchen door, his huge body casting a shadow that seemed to the knights like the shadow of death passing over them. They watched with uneasiness that soon turned to outrage as he came to the girl, reached out, and took her small white hands in his.

"I love you," Bork said to her, and tears came unbidden to his eyes. "Let me marry you."

At that moment several of the knights found their courage. They seized Bork roughly by the arms, meaning to pull him away and punish him for his effrontery. But Bork effortlessly tossed them away. They fell to the ground yards from him. He never saw them fall; his gaze never left the lady's face.

She looked wonderingly into his eyes. Not because she thought him attractive, because he was ugly and she knew it. Not because of the words he had said, because she had been taught that many men would say those words, and she was to pay no attention to them. What startled her, what amazed her, was the deep truth in Bork's face. That was something she had never seen, and though she did not recognize it for what it was, it fascinated her.

The Count was furious. Seeing the clumsy giant holding his daughter's small white hands in his was outrageous. He would not endure it. But the giant had such great strength that to tear him away would mean a full-scale battle, and in such a battle Brunhilda might be injured. No, the giant had to be handled delicately, for the moment.

"My dear fellow," said the Count, affecting a joviality he did not feel. "You've only just met."

Bork ignored him. "I will never let you come to harm," he said to the girl.

"What's his name?" the Count whispered to a knight. "I can't remember his name."

"Bork," the knight answered.

"My dear Bork," said the Count. "All due respect and every-thing, but my daughter has noble blood, and you're not even a knight."

"Then I'll become one," Bork said.

"It's not that easy, Bork, old fellow. You must do something ex-ceptionally brave, and then I can knight you and we can talk about this other matter. But in the meantime, it isn't proper for you to be holding my daughter's hands. Why don't you go back to the kitchen like a good fellow?"

Bork gave no sign that he heard. He only continued looking into the lady's eyes. And finally it was she who was able to end the dilemma.

"Bork," she said, "I will count on you. But in the meantime, my father will be angry with you if you don't return to the kitchen."

Of course, Bork thought. Of course, she is truly concerned for me, doesn't want me to come to harm on her account. "For your sake," he said, the madness of love still on him. Then he turned and left the room.

The Count sat down, sighing audibly. "Should have got rid of him years ago. Gentle as a lamb, and then all of a sudden goes crazy. Get rid of him—somebody take care of that tonight, would you? Best to do it in his sleep. Don't want any casualties when we're likely to have a battle at any moment."

The reminder of the battle was enough to sober even those who were on their fifth mug of ale. The wizened old woman led Brunhilda away again. "But not to the secret room, now. To the chamber next to mine. And post a double guard outside her door, and keep the key yourself," said the Count.

When she was gone, the Count looked around at the knights. "The treasury has been emptied in a vain attempt to find clothing to do her justice. I had no other choice."

And there was not a knight who would say the money had been badly spent.

The Duke came late that afternoon, much sooner than he was expected. He demanded the tribute. The Count refused, of course. There was the usual challenge to come out of the castle and fight, but the Count, outnumbered ten to one, merely replied, rather saucily, that the Duke should come in and get him. The messenger who delivered the sarcastic message came back with his tongue in a bag around his neck. The battle was thus begun grimly: and grimly it continued.

The guard watching on the south side of the castle was slacking. He paid for it. The Duke's archers managed to creep up to the huge oak tree and climb it without any alarm being given, and the first notice any of them had was when the guard fell from the battlements with an arrow in his throat.

The archers—there must have been a dozen of them—kept up a deadly rain of arrows. They wasted no shots. The squires dropped dead in alarming numbers until the Count gave orders for them to come inside. And when the human targets were all under cover, the archers set to work on the cattle and sheep milling in the open pens. There was no way to protect the animals. By sunset, all of them were dead.

"Dammit," said the cook. "How can I cook all this before it spoils?"

"Find a way," said the Count. "That's our food supply. I refuse to let them starve us out."

So all night Bork worked, carrying the cattle and sheep inside, one by one. At first the villagers who had taken refuge in the castle tried to help him, but he could carry three animals inside the kitchen in the time it took them to drag one, and they soon gave it up.

The Count saw who was saving the meat. "Don't get rid of him tonight," he told the knights. "We'll punish him for his effrontery in the morning."

Bork only rested twice in the night, taking naps for an hour before the cook woke him again. And when dawn came, and the arrows began coming again, all the cattle were inside, and all but twenty sheep.

"That's all we can save," the cook told the Count.

"Save them all."

"But if Bork tries to go out there, he'll be killed!"

The Count looked the cook in the eyes. "Bring in the sheep or have him die trying."

The cook was not aware of the fact that Bork was under sentence of death. So he did his best to save Bork. A kettle lined with cloth and strapped onto the giant's head; a huge kettle lid for a shield. "It's the best we can do," the cook said.

"But I can't carry sheep if I'm holding a shield," Bork said.

"What can I do? The Count commanded it. It's worth your life to refuse."

Bork stood and thought for a few moments, trying to find a way out of his dilemma. He saw only one possibility. "If I can't stop them from hitting me, I'll have to stop them from shooting at all."

"How!" the cook demanded, and then followed Bork to the blacksmith's shop, where Bork found his huge ax leaning against the wall.

"Now's not the time to cut firewood," said the blacksmith.

"Yes it is," Bork answered.

Carrying the ax and holding the kettle lid between his body and the archers, Bork made his way across the courtyard. The arrows pinged harmlessly off the metal. Bork got to the drawbridge. "Open up!" he shouted, and the drawbridge fell away and dropped across the moat. Bork walked across, then made his way along the moat toward the oak tree.

In the distance the Duke, standing in front of his dazzling white tent with his emblem of yellow in it, saw Bork emerge from the castle. "Is that a man or a bear?" he asked. No one was sure.

The archers shot at Bork steadily, but the closer he got to the tree, the worse their angle of fire and the larger the shadow of safety the kettle lid cast over his body. Finally, holding the lid high over his head, Bork began hacking one-handed at the trunk. Chips of wood flew with each blow; with his right hand alone he could cut deeper and faster than a normal man with both hands free.

But he was concentrating on cutting wood, and his left arm grew tired holding his makeshift shield, and an archer was able to get off a shot that slipped past the shield and plunged into his left arm, in the thick muscle at the back.

He nearly dropped the shield. Instead, he had the presence of mind to let go of the ax and drop to his knees, quickly balancing the kettle lid between the tree trunk, his head, and the top of the ax handle. Gently he pulled at the arrow shaft. It would not come backward. So he broke the arrow and pushed the stub the rest of the way through his arm until it was out the other side. It was excruciatingly painful, but he knew he could not quit now. He took hold of the shield with his left arm again, and despite the pain held it high as he began to cut again, girdling the tree with a deep white gouge. The blood dripped steadily down his arm, but he ignored it, and soon enough the bleeding stopped and slowed.

On the castle battlements, the Count's men began to realize that there was a hope of Bork's succeeding. To protect him, they began to shoot their arrows into the tree. The archers were well hidden, but the rain of arrows, however badly aimed, began to have its effect. A few of them dropped to the ground, where the castle archers could easily finish them off; the others were forced to concentrate on finding cover.

The tree trembled more and more with each blow, until finally Bork stepped back and the tree creaked and swayed. He had learned from his lumbering work in the forest how to make the tree fall where he wanted it; the oak fell parallel to the castle walls, so it neither bridged the moat nor let the Duke's archers scramble from the tree too far from the castle. So when the archers tried to flee to the safety of the Duke's lines, the castle bowmen were able to kill them all.

One of them, however, despaired of escape. Instead, though he already had an arrow in him, he drew a knife and charged at Bork, in a mad attempt to avenge his own death on the man who had caused it. Bork had no choice. He swung his ax through the air and discovered that men are nowhere near as sturdy as a tree.

In the distance, the Duke watched with horror as the giant cut a man in half with a single blow. "What have they got!" he said. "What is this monster?"

Covered with the blood that had spurted from the dying man, Bork walked back toward the drawbridge, which opened again as he approached. But he did not get to enter. Instead the Count and fifty mounted knights came from the gate on horseback, their armor shining in the sunlight.

"I've decided to fight them in the open," the Count said. "And you, Bork, must fight with us. If you live through this, I'll make you a knight!"

Bork knelt. "Thank you, my Lord Count," he said.

The Count glanced around in embarrassment. "Well, then. Let's get to it. Charge!" he bellowed.

Bork did not realize that the knights were not even formed in a line yet. He simply followed the command and charged, alone, toward the Duke's lines. The Count watched him go, and smiled.

"My Lord Count," said the nearest knight. "Aren't we going to attack with him?"

"Let the Duke take care of him," the Count said.

"But he cut down the oak and saved the castle, my lord."

"Yes," said the Count. "An exceptionally brave act. Do you want him to try to claim my daughter's hand?"

"But my lord," said the knight, "if he fights beside us, we might have a chance of winning. But if he's gone, the Duke will destroy us."

"Some things," said the Count, with finality, "are more important than victory. Would you want to go on living in a world where perfection like Brunhilda's was possessed by such a man as that?"

The knights were silent, then, as they watched Bork approach the Duke's army, alone.

Bork did not realize he was alone until he stood a few feet away from the Duke's lines. He had felt strange as he walked across the fields, believing he was marching into battle with the knights he had long admired in their bright armor and deft instruments of war. Now the exhilaration was gone. Where were the others? Bork was afraid.

He could not understand why the Duke's men had not shot any arrows at him. Actually, it was a misunderstanding. If the Duke had known Bork was a commoner and not a knight at all, Bork would have had a hundred arrows bristling from his corpse. As it was, however, one of the Duke's men called out, "You, sir! Do you challenge us to single combat?"

Of course. That was it—the Count did not intend Bork to face an army, he intended him to face a single warrior. The whole outcome of the battle would depend on him alone! It was a tremendous honor, and Bork wondered if he could carry if off.

"Yes! Single combat!" he answered. "Your strongest, bravest man!"

"But you're a giant!" cried the Duke's man.

"But I'm wearing no armor." And to prove his sincerity, Bork took off his helmet, which was uncomfortable anyway, and stepped forward. The Duke's knights backed away, making an opening for him, with men in armor watching him pass from both sides. Bork walked steadily on, until he came to a cleared circle where he faced the Duke himself.

"Are you the champion?" asked Bork.

"I'm the Duke," he answered. "But I don't see any of my knights stepping forward to fight you."

"Do you refuse the challenge, then?" Bork asked, trying to sound as brave and scornful as he imagined a true knight would sound.

The Duke looked around at his men, who, if the armor had allowed, would have been shuffling uncomfortably in the morning sunlight. As it was, none of them looked at him.

"No," said the Duke. "I accept your challenge myself." The thought of fighting the giant terrified him. But he was a knight, and known to be a brave man; he had become Duke in the prime of his youth, and if he backed down before a giant now, his duchy would be taken from him in only a few years; his honor would be lost long before. So he drew his sword and advanced upon the giant.

Bork saw the determination in the Duke's eyes, and marveled at a man who would go himself into a most dangerous battle instead of sending his men. Briefly Bork wondered why the Count had not shown such courage; he determined at that moment that if he could help it the Duke would not die. The blood of the archer was more than he had ever wanted to shed. Nobility was in every movement of the Duke, and Bork wondered at the ill chance that had made them enemies.

The Duke lunged at Bork with his sword flashing. Bork hit him with the flat of the ax, knocking him to the ground. The Duke cried out in pain. His armor was dented deeply; there had to be ribs broken under the dent.

"Why don't you surrender?" asked Bork.

"Kill me now!"

"If you surrender, I won't kill you at all."

The Duke was surprised. There was a murmur from his men.

"I have your word?"

"Of course. I swear it."

It was too startling an idea.

"What do you plan to do, hold me for ransom?"

Bork thought about it. "I don't think so."

"Well, what then? Why not kill me and have done with it?" The pain in his chest now dominated the Duke's voice, but he did not spit blood, and so he began to have some hope.

"All the Count wants you to do is go away and stop collecting tribute. If you promise to do that, I'll promise that not one of you will be harmed."

The Duke and his men considered in silence. It was too good to believe. So good it was almost dishonorable even to consider it. Still—there was Bork, who had broken the Duke's body with one blow, right through the armor. If he chose to let them walk away from the battle, why argue?

"I give my word that I'll cease collecting tribute from the Count, and my men and I will go in peace."

"Well, then, that's good news," Bork said. "I've got to tell the Count." And Bork turned away and walked into the fields, heading for where the Count's tiny army waited.

"I can't believe it," said the Duke. "A knight like that, and he turns out to be generous. The Count could have his way with the King, with a knight like that."

They stripped the armor off him, carefully, and began wrapping his chest with bandages.

"If he were mine," the Duke said, "I'd use him to conquer the whole land."

*   *   *

The Count watched, incredulous, as Bork crossed the field.

"He's still alive," he said, and he began to wonder what Bork would have to say about the fact that none of the knights had joined his gallant charge.

"My Lord Count!" cried Bork, when he was within range. He would have waved, but both his arms were exhausted now. "They surrender!"

"What?" the Count asked the knights near him. "Did he say they surrender?"

"Apparently," a knight answered. "Apparently he won."

"Damn!" cried the Count. "I won't have it!"

The knights were puzzled. "If anybody's going to defeat the Duke, I am! Not a damnable commoner! Not a giant with the brains of a cockroach! Charge!"

"What?" several of the knights asked.

"I said charge!" And the Count moved forward, his warhorse plodding carefully through the field, building up momentum.

Bork saw the knights start forward. He had watched enough mock battles to recognize a charge. He could only assume that the Count hadn't heard him. But the charge had to be stopped—he had given his word, hadn't he? So he planted himself in the path of the Count's horse.

"Out of the way, you damned fool!" cried the Count. But Bork stood his ground. The Count was determined not to be thwarted. He prepared to ride Bork down.

"You can't charge!" Bork yelled. "They surrendered!"

The Count gritted his teeth and urged the horse forward, his lance prepared to cast Bork out of the way.

A moment later the Count found himself in midair, hanging to the lance for his life. Bork held it over his head, and the knights laboriously halted their charge and wheeled to see what was going on with Bork and the Count.

"My Lord Count," Bork said respectfully. "I guess you didn't hear me. They surrendered. I promised them they could go in peace if they stopped collecting tribute."

From his precarious hold on the lance, fifteen feet off the ground, the Count said, "I didn't hear you."

"I didn't think so. But you *will* let them go, won't you?"

"Of course. Could you give a thought to letting me down, old boy?"

And so Bork let the Count down, and there was a peace treaty between the Duke and the Count, and the Duke's men rode away in peace, talking about the generosity of the giant knight.

"But he isn't a knight," said a servant to the Duke.

"What? Not a knight?"

"No. Just a villager. One of the peasants told me, when I was stealing his chickens."

"Not a knight," said the Duke, and for a moment his face began to turn the shade of red that made his knights want to ride a few feet further from him—they knew his rage too well already.

"We were tricked, then," said a knight, trying to fend off his lord's anger by anticipating it.

The Duke said nothing for a moment. Then he smiled. "Well, if he's not a knight, he should be. He has the strength. He has the courtesy. Hasn't he?"

The knights agreed that he had.

"He's the moral equivalent of a knight," said the Duke. Pride assuaged, for the moment, he led his men back to his castle. Underneath, however, even deeper than the pain in his ribs, was the image of the Count perched on the end of a lance held high in the air by the giant, Bork, and he pondered what it might have meant, and what, more to the point, it might mean in the future.

Things were getting out of hand, the Count decided. First of all, the victory celebration had not been his idea, and yet here they were, riotously drunken in the great hall, and even villagers were making free with the ale, laughing and cheering among the knights. That was bad enough, but worse was the fact that the knights were making no pretense about it—the party was in honor of Bork.

The Count drummed his fingers on the table. No one paid any

attention. They were too busy—Sir Alwishard trying to keep two village wenches occupied near the fire, Sir Silwiss pissing in the wine and laughing so loud that the Count could hardly hear Sir Braig and Sir Umlaut as they sang and danced along the table, kicking plates off with their toes in time with the music. It was the best party the Count had ever seen. And it wasn't for him, it was for that damnable giant who had made an ass of him in front of all his men and all the Duke's men and, worst of all, the Duke. He heard a strange growling sound, like a savage wolf getting ready to spring. In a lull in the bedlam he suddenly realized that the sound was coming from his own throat.

Get control of yourself, he thought. The real gains, the solid gains were not Bork's—they were mine. The Duke is gone, and instead of paying him tribute from now on, he'll be paying me. Word would get around, too, that the Count had won a battle with the Duke. After all, that was the basis of power—who could beat whom in battle. A duke was just a man who could beat a count, a count someone who could beat a baron, a baron someone who could beat a knight.

But what was a person who could beat a duke?

"You should be king," said a tall, slender young man standing near the throne.

The Count looked at him, making a vague motion with his hidden hand. How had the boy read his thoughts?

"I'll pretend I didn't hear that."

"You heard it," said the young man.

"It's treason."

"Only if the king beats you in battle. If *you* win, it's treason *not* to say so."

The Count looked the boy over. Dark hair that looked a bit too carefully combed for a villager. A straight nose, a pleasant smile, a winning grace when he walked. But something about his eyes gave the lie to the smile. The boy was vicious somehow. The boy was dangerous.

"I like you," said the Count.

"I'm glad." He did not sound glad. He sounded bored.

"If I'm smart, I'll have you strangled immediately."

The boy only smiled more.

"Who are you?"

"My name is Winkle. And I'm Bork's best friend."

Bork. There he was again, that giant sticking his immense shadow into everything tonight. "Didn't know Bork the Bully had any friends."

"He has one. Me. Ask him."

"I wonder if a friend of Bork's is really a friend of mine," the Count said.

"I said I was his best friend. I didn't say I was a good friend." And Winkle smiled.

A thoroughgoing bastard, the Count decided, but he waved to Bork and beckoned for him to come. In a moment the giant knelt before the Count, who was irritated to discover that when Bork knelt and the Count sat, Bork still looked down on him.

"This man," said the Count, "claims to be your friend."

Bork looked up and recognized Winkle, who was beaming down at him, his eyes filled with love, mostly. A hungry kind of love, but Bork wasn't discriminating. He had the admiration and grudging respect of the knights, but he hardly knew them. This was his childhood friend, and at the thought that Winkle claimed to be his friend Bork immediately forgave all the past slights and smiled back. "Winkle," he said. "Of course we're friends. He's my *best* friend."

The Count made the mistake of looking in Bork's eyes and seeing the complete sincerity of his love for Winkle. It embarrassed him, for he knew Winkle all too well already, from just the moments of conversation they had had. Winkle was nobody's friend. But Bork was obviously blind to that. For a moment the Count almost pitied the giant, had a glimpse of what his life must be like, if the predatory young villager was his best friend.

"Your Majesty," said Winkle.

"Don't call me that."

"I only anticipate what the world will know in a matter of months."

Winkle sounded so confident, so sure of it. A chill went up the Count's spine. He shook it off. "I won one battle, Winkle. I still have a huge budget deficit and a pretty small army of fairly lousy knights."

"Think of your daughter, even if *you* aren't ambitious. Despite her beauty she'll be lucky to marry a duke. But if she were the daughter of a king, she could marry anyone in all the world. And her own lovely self would be a dowry—no prince would think to ask for more."

The Count thought of his daughter, the beautiful Brunhilda, and smiled.

Bork also smiled, for he was also thinking of the same thing.

"Your Majesty," Winkle urged, "with Bork as your right-hand man and me as your counselor, there's nothing to stop you from being king within a year or two. Who would be willing to stand against an army with the three of us marching at the head?"

"Why three?" asked the Count.

"You mean, why me. I thought you would already understand that—but then, that's what you need me for. You see, your majesty, you're a good man, a godly man, a paragon of virtue. You would never think of seeking power and conniving against your enemies and spying and doing repulsive things to people you don't like. But kings *have* to do those things or they quickly cease to be kings."

Vaguely the Count remembered behaving in just that way many times, but Winkle's words were seductive—they *should* be true.

"Your majesty, where you are pure, I am polluted. Where you are fresh, I am rotten. I'd sell my mother into slavery if I had a mother and I'd cheat the devil at poker and win hell from him before he caught on. And I'd stab any of your enemies in the back if I got the chance."

"But what if my enemies aren't your enemies?" the Count asked.

"Your enemies are *always* my enemies. I'll be loyal to you through thick and thin."

"How can I trust you, if you're so rotten?"

"Because you're going to pay me a lot of money." Winkle bowed deeply.

"Done," said the Count.

"Excellent," said Winkle, and they shook hands. The Count noticed that Winkle's hands were smooth—he had neither the hard horny palms of a village workingman nor the slick calluses of a man trained to warfare.

"How have you made a living, up to now?" the Count asked.

"I steal," Winkle said, with a smile that said I'm joking and a glint in his eye that said I'm not.

"What about me?" asked Bork.

"Oh, you're in it, too," said Winkle. "You're the King's strong right arm."

"I've never met the King," said Bork.

"Yes you have," Winkle retorted. "That is the King."

"No he's not," said the giant. "He's only a count."

The words stabbed the Count deeply. *Only* a count. Well, that would end. "Today I'm only a count," he said patiently. "Who knows what tomorrow will bring? But Bork—I shall knight you. As a knight you must swear absolute loyalty to me and do whatever I say. Will you do that?"

"Of course I will," said Bork. "Thank you, my Lord Count." Bork arose and called to his new friends throughout the hall in a voice that could not be ignored. "My Lord Count has decided I will be made a knight!" There were cheers and applause and stamping of feet. "And the best thing is," Bork said, "that now I can marry the Lady Brunhilda."

There was no applause. Just a murmur of alarm. Of course. If he became a knight, he was eligible for Brunhilda's hand. It was unthinkable—but the Count himself had said so.

The Count was having second thoughts, of course, but he knew no way to back out of it, not without looking like a word-breaker. He made a false start at speaking, but couldn't finish. Bork waited expectantly. Clearly he believed the Count would confirm what Bork had said.

It was Winkle, however, who took the situation in hand. "Oh,

Bork," he said sadly—but loudly, so that everyone could hear. "Don't you understand? His Majesty is making you a knight out of gratitude. But unless you're a king or the son of a king, you have to do something exceptionally brave to earn Brunhilda's hand."

"But, wasn't I brave today?" Bork asked. After all, the arrow wound in his arm still hurt, and only the ale kept him from aching unmercifully all over from the exertion of the night and the day just past.

"You were brave. But since you're twice the size and ten times the strength of an ordinary man, it's hardly fair for you to win Brunhilda's hand with ordinary bravery. No, Bork—it's just the way things work. It's just the way things are done. Before you're worthy of Brunhilda, you have to do something ten times as brave as what you did today."

Bork could not think of something ten times as brave. Hadn't he gone almost unprotected to chop down the oak tree? Hadn't he attacked a whole army all by himself, and won the surrender of the enemy? What could be ten times as brave?

"Don't despair," the Count said. "Surely in all the battles ahead of us there'll be *something* ten times as brave. And in the meantime, you're a knight, my friend, a great knight, and you shall dine at my table every night! And when we march into battle, there you'll be, right beside me—"

"A few steps ahead," Winkle whispered discreetly.

"A few steps ahead of me, to defend the honor of my country—"

"Don't be shy," whispered Winkle.

"No, not my country. My kingdom. For from today, you men no longer serve a count! You serve a king!"

It was a shocking declaration, and might have caused sober reflection if there had been a sober man in the room. But through the haze of alcohol and torchlight and fatigue, the knights looked at the Count and he did indeed seem kingly. And they thought of the battles ahead and were not afraid, for they had won a glorious victory today and not one of them had shed a drop of blood. Except, of course, Bork. But in some corner of their collected opinions was a viewpoint they would not have admitted to holding, if anyone brought the subject out in the open. The opinion so well hidden from themselves and each other was simple: Bork is not like me. Bork is not one of us. Therefore, Bork is expendable.

The blood that still stained his sleeve was cheap. Plenty more where that came from.

And so they plied him with more ale until he fell asleep, snoring hugely on the table, forgetting that he had been cheated out of the woman he loved; it was easy to forget, for the moment, because he was a knight, and a hero, and at last he had friends.

It took two years for the Count to become King. He began close to home, with other counts, but soon progressed to the great dukes and earls of the kingdom. Wherever he went, the pattern was the same. The Count and his fifty knights would ride their horses, only lightly armored so they could travel with reasonable speed. Bork would walk, but his long legs easily kept up with the rest of them. They would arrive at their victim's castle, and three squires would hand Bork his new steel-handled ax. Bork, covered with impenetrable armor, would wade the moat, if there was one, or simply walk up to the gates, swing the ax, and begin chopping through the wood. When the gates collapsed, Bork would take a huge steel rod and use it as a crow, prying at the portcullis, bending the heavy iron like pretzels until there was a gap wide enough for a mounted knight to ride through.

Then he would go back to the Count and Winkle.

Throughout this operation, not a word would have been said; the only activity from the Count's other men would be enough archery that no one would be able to pour boiling oil or hot tar on Bork while he was working. It was a precaution, and nothing more—even if they set the oil on the fire the moment the Count's little army approached, it would scarcely be hot enough to make water steam by the time Bork was through.

"Do you surrender to His Majesty the King?" Winkle would cry.

And the defenders of the castle, their gate hopelessly breached and terrified of the giant who had so easily made a joke of their defenses, would usually surrender. Occasionally there was some token resistance—when that happened, at Winkle's insistence, the town was brutally sacked and the noble's family was held in prison until a huge ransom was paid.

At the end of two years, the Count and Bork and Winkle and their army marched on Winchester. The King—the real king—fled before them and took up his exile in Anjou, where it was warmer anyway. The Count had himself crowned king, accepted the fealty of every noble in the country, and introduced his daughter, Brunhilda, all around. Then, finding Winchester not to his liking, he returned to his castle and ruled from there. Suitors for his daughter's hand made a constant traffic on the roads leading into the country; would-be courtiers and nobles vying for positions filled the new hostelries that sprang up on the other side of the village. All left much poorer than they had arrived. And while much of that money found its way into the King's coffers, much more of it went to Winkle, who believed that skimming off the cream meant leaving at least a quarter of it for the King.

And now that the wars were done, Bork hung up his armor and went back to normal life. Not quite normal life, actually. He slept in a good room in the castle, better than most of the knights. Some of the knights had even come to enjoy his company, and sought him out for ale in the evenings or hunting in the daytime—Bork could always be counted on to carry home two deer himself, and was much more convenient than a packhorse. All in all, Bork was happier than he had ever thought he would be.

Which is how things were going when the dragon came and changed it all forever.

Winkle was in Brunhilda's room, a place he had learned many routes to get to, so that he went unobserved every time. Brunhilda, after many gifts and more flattery, was on the verge of giving in to the handsome young advisor to the King when strange screams and cries began coming from the fields below. Brunhilda pulled away from Winkle's exploring hands and, clutching her half-open gown around her, rushed to the window to see what was the matter.

She looked down, to where the screams were coming from, and it wasn't until the dragon's shadow fell across her that she looked up. Winkle, waiting on the bed, only saw the claws reach in and, gently but firmly, take hold of Brunhilda and pull her from the room. Brunhilda fainted immediately, and by the time Winkle got to where he could see her, the dragon had backed away from the window and on great flapping wings was carrying her limp body off toward the north whence he had come.

Winkle was horrified. It was so sudden, something he could not have foreseen or planned against. Yet still he cursed himself and bitterly realized that his plans might be ended forever. A dragon had taken Brunhilda who was to be his means of legitimately becoming king; now the plot of seduction, marriage, and inheritance was ruined.

Ever practical, Winkle did not let himself lament for long. He dressed himself quickly and used a secret passage out of Brunhilda's room, only to reappear in the corridor outside it a moment later. "Brunhilda!" he cried, beating on the door. "Are you all right?"

The first of the knights reached him, and then the King, weeping and wailing and smashing anything that got in his way. Brunhilda's door was down in a moment, and the King ran to the window and cried out after his daughter, now a pinpoint speck in the sky many miles away. "Brunhilda! Brunhilda! Come back!" She did not come back. "Now," cried the King, as he turned back into the room and sank to the floor, his face twisted and wet with grief. "Now I have nothing, and all is in vain!"

My thoughts precisely, Winkle thought, but I'm not weeping about it. To hide his contempt he walked to the window and looked out. He saw, not the dragon, but Bork, emerging from the forest carrying two huge logs.

"Sir Bork," said Winkle.

The King heard a tone of decision in Winkle's voice. He had learned to listen to whatever Winkle said in that tone of voice. "What about him?"

"Sir Bork could defeat a dragon," Winkle said, "if any man could."

"That's true," the King said, gathering back some of the hope he had lost. "Of course that's true."

"But will he?" asked Winkle.

"Of course he will. He loves Brunhilda, doesn't he?"

"He said he did. But Your Majesty, is he really loyal to you? After all, why wasn't he here when the dragon came? Why didn't he save Brunhilda in the first place?"

"He was cutting wood for the winter."

"Cutting wood? When Brunhilda's life was at stake?"

The King was outraged. The illogic of it escaped him—he was not in a logical mood. So he was furious when he met Bork at the gate of the castle.

"You've betrayed me!" the King cried.

"I have?" Bork was smitten with guilt. And he hadn't even meant to.

"You weren't here when we needed you. When *Brunhilda* needed you!"

"I'm sorry," Bork said.

"Sorry, sorry, sorry. A lot of good it does to say you're sorry. You swore to protect Brunhilda from any enemy, and when a really dangerous enemy comes along, how do you repay me for everything I've done for you? You hide out in the forest!"

"What enemy?"

"A dragon," said the King, "as if you didn't see it coming and run out into the woods."

"Cross my heart, Your Majesty, I didn't know there was a dragon coming." And then he made the connection in his mind. "The dragon—it took Brunhilda?"

"It took her. Took her half-naked from her bedroom when she leaped to the window to call to you for help."

Bork felt the weight of guilt, and it was a terrible burden. His face grew hard and angry, and he walked into the castle, his harsh footfalls setting the earth to trembling. "My armor!" he cried. "My sword!"

In minutes he was in the middle of the courtyard, holding out his arms as the heavy mail was draped over him and the breastplate and helmet were strapped and screwed into place. The sword was not enough—he also carried his huge ax and a shield so massive two ordinary men could have hidden behind it.

"Which way did he go?" Bork asked.

"North," the King answered.

"I'll bring back your daughter, Your Majesty, or die in the attempt."

"Damn well better. It's all your fault."

The words stung, but the sting only impelled Bork further. He took the huge sack of food the cook had prepared for him and fastened it to his belt, and without a backward glance strode from the castle and took the road north.

"I almost feel sorry for the dragon," said the King.

But Winkle wondered. He had seen how large the claws were as they grasped Brunhilda—she had been like a tiny doll in a large man's fingers. The claws were razor sharp. Even if she were still alive, could Bork really best the dragon? Bork the Bully, after all, had made his reputation picking on men smaller than he, as Winkle had ample reason to know. How would he do facing a dragon at least five times his size? Wouldn't he turn coward? Wouldn't he run as other men had run from *him?*

He might. But Sir Bork the Bully was Winkle's only hope of getting Brunhilda and the kingdom. If he could do anything to ensure that the giant at least *tried* to fight the dragon, he would do it. And so, taking only his rapier and a sack of food, Winkle left the castle by another way, and followed the giant along the road toward the north.

And then he had a terrible thought.

Fighting the dragon was surely ten times as brave as anything Bork had done before. If he won, wouldn't he have a claim on Brunhilda's hand himself?

It was not something Winkle wished to think about. Something would come to him, some way around the problem when the time came. Plenty of opportunity to plan something—*after* Bork wins and rescues her.

*　　*　　*

Bork had not rounded the second turn in the road when he came across the old woman, waiting by the side of the road. It was the same old woman who had cared for Brunhilda all those years that she was kept in a secret room in the castle. She looked wizened and weak, but there was a sharp look in her eyes that many had mistaken for great wisdom. It was not great wisdom. But she did know a few things about dragons.

"Going after the dragon, are you?" she asked in a squeaky voice. "Going to get Brunhilda back, are you?" She giggled darkly behind her hand.

"I am if anyone can," Bork said.

"Well, anyone can't," she answered.

"*I* can."

"Not a prayer, you big bag of wind!"

Bork ignored her and started to walk past.

"Wait!" she said, her voice harsh as a dull file taking rust from armor. "Which way will you go?"

"North," he said. "That's the way the dragon took her."

"A quarter of the world is north, Sir Bork the Bully, and a dragon is small compared to all the mountains of the earth. But I know a way you can find the dragon, if you're really a knight.

"Light a torch, man. Light a torch, and whenever you come to a fork in the way, the light of the torch will leap the way you ought to go. Wind or no wind, fire seeks fire, and there is a flame at the heart of every dragon."

"They *do* breathe fire, then?" he asked. He did not know how to fight fire.

"Fire is light, not wind, and so it doesn't come from the dragon's mouth or the dragon's nostrils. If he burns you, it won't be with his breath." The old woman cackled like a mad hen. "No one knows the truth about dragons anymore!"

"Except you."

"I'm an old wife," she said. "And I know. They don't eat human begins, either. They're strict vegetarians. But they kill. From time to time they kill."

"Why, if they aren't hungry for meat?"

"You'll see," she said. She started to walk away, back into the forest.

"Wait!" Bork called. "How far will the dragon be?"

"Not far," she said. "Not far, Sir Bork. He's waiting for you. He's waiting for you and all the fools who come to try to free the virgin." Then she melted away into the darkness.

Bork lit a torch and followed it all night, turning when the flame turned, unwilling to waste time in sleep when Brunhilda might be suffering unspeakable degradation at the monster's hands. And behind him, Winkle forced himself to stay awake, determined not to let Bork lose him in the darkness.

All night, and all day, and all night again Bork followed the light of the torch, through crooked paths long unused, until he came to the foot of a dry, tall hill, with rocks and crags along the top. He stopped, for here the flame leaped high, as if to say, "Upward from here." And in the silence he heard a sound that chilled him to the bone. It was Brunhilda, screaming as if she were being tortured in the cruelest imaginable way. And the screams were followed by a terrible roar. Bork cast aside the remnant of his food and made his way to the top of the hill. On the way he called out, to stop the dragon from whatever it was doing.

"Dragon! Are you there!"

The voice rumbled back to him with a power that made the dirt shift under Bork's feet. "Yes indeed."

"Do you have Brunhilda?"

"You mean the little virgin with the heart of an adder and the brain of a gnat?"

In the forest at the bottom of the hill, Winkle ground his teeth in fury, for despite his designs on the kingdom, he loved Brunhilda as much as he was capable of loving anyone.

"Dragon!" Bork bellowed at the top of his voice. "Dragon! Prepare to die!"

"Oh dear! Oh dear!" cried out the dragon. "Whatever shall I do?"

And then Bork reached the top of the hill, just as the sun topped the distant mountains and it became morning. In the light

Bork immediately saw Brunhilda tied to a tree, her auburn hair glistening. All around her was the immense pile of gold that the dragon, according to custom, kept. And all around the gold was the dragon's tail.

Bork looked at the tail and followed it until finally he came to the dragon, who was leaning on a rock chewing on a tree trunk and smirking. The dragon's wings were clad with feathers, but the rest of him was covered with tough gray hide the color of weathered granite. His teeth, when he smiled, were ragged, long, and pointed. His claws were three feet long and sharp as a rapier from tip to base. But in spite of all this armament, the most dangerous thing about him was his eyes. They were large and soft and brown, with long lashes and gently arching brows. But at the center each eye held a sharp point of light, and when Bork looked at the eyes that light stabbed deep into him, seeing his heart and laughing at what it found there.

For a moment, looking at the dragon's eyes, Bork stood transfixed. Then the dragon reached over one wing toward Brunhilda, and with a great growling noise he began to tickle her ear.

Brunhilda was unbearably ticklish, and she let off a bloodcurdling scream.

"Touch her not!" Bork cried.

"Touch her what?" asked the dragon, with a chuckle. "I will not."

"Beast!" bellowed Bork. "I am Sir Bork the Big! I have never been defeated in battle! No man dares stand before me, and the beasts of the forest step aside when I pass!"

"You must be awfully clumsy," said the dragon.

Bork resolutely went on. He had seen the challenges and jousts—it was obligatory to recite and embellish your achievements in order to strike terror into the heart of the enemy. "I can cut down trees with one blow of my ax! I can cleave an ox from head to tail, I can skewer a running deer, I can break down walls of stone and doors of wood!"

"Why can't I ever get a handy servant like that?" murmured the dragon. "Ah well, you probably expect too large a salary."

The dragon's sardonic tone might have infuriated other knights; Bork was only confused, wondering if this matter was less serious than he had thought. "I've come to free Brunhilda, dragon. Will you give her up to me, or must I slay you?"

At that the dragon laughed long and loud. Then it cocked its head and looked at Bork. In that moment Bork knew that he had lost the battle. For deep in the dragon's eyes he saw the truth.

Bork saw himself knocking down gates and cutting down trees, but the deeds no longer looked heroic. Instead he realized that the knights who always rode behind him in these battles were laughing at him, that the King was a weak and vicious man, that Winkle's ambition was the only emotion he had room for; he saw that all of them were using him for their own ends, and cared nothing for him at all.

Bork saw himself asking for Brunhilda's hand in marriage, and he was ridiculous, an ugly, unkempt, and awkward giant in contrast to the slight and graceful girl. He saw that the King's hints of the possibility of their marriage were merely a trick, to blind him. More, he saw what no one else had been able to see—that Brunhilda loved Winkle, and Winkle wanted her.

And at last Bork saw himself as a warrior, and realized that in all the years of his great reputation and in all his many victories, he had fought only one man—an archer who ran at him with a knife. He had terrorized the weak and the small, but never until now had he faced a creature larger than himself. Bork looked in the dragon's eyes and saw his own death.

"Your eyes are deep," said Bork softly.

"Deep as a well, and you are drowning."

"Your sight is clear." Bork's palms were cold with sweat.

"Clear as ice, and you will freeze."

"Your eyes," Bork began. Then his mouth was suddenly so dry that he could barely speak. He swallowed. "Your eyes are filled with light."

"Bright and tiny as a star," the dragon whispered. "And see; your heart is afire."

Slowly the dragon stepped away from the rock, even as the tip of his tail reached behind Bork to push him into the dragon's waiting jaws. But Bork was not in so deep a trance that he could not see.

"I see that you mean to kill me," Bork said. "But you won't have me as easily as that." Bork whirled around to hack at the tip of the dragon's tail with his ax. But he was too large and slow, and the tail flicked away before the ax was fairly swung.

The battle lasted all day. Bork fought exhaustion as much as he fought the dragon, and it seemed the dragon only toyed with him. Bork would lurch toward the tail or a wing or the dragon's belly, but when his ax or sword fell where the dragon had been, it only sang in the air and touched nothing.

Finally Bork fell to his knees and wept. He wanted to go on with the fight, but his body could not do it. And the dragon looked as fresh as it had in the morning.

"What?" asked the dragon. "Finished already?"

Then Bork felt the tip of the dragon's tail touch his back, and the sharp points of the claws pressed gently on either side. He could not bear to look up at what he knew he would see. Yet neither could he bear to wait, not knowing when the blow would come. So he opened his eyes, and lifted his head, and saw.

The dragon's teeth were nearly touching him, poised to tear his head from his shoulders.

Bork screamed. And screamed again when the teeth touched him, when they pushed into his armor, when the dragon lifted him with teeth and tail and talons until he was twenty feet above the ground. He screamed again when he looked into the dragon's eyes and saw, not hunger, not hatred, but merely amusement.

And then he found his silence again, and listened as the dragon spoke through clenched teeth, watching the tongue move massively in the mouth only inches from his head.

"Well, little man. Are you afraid?"

Bork tried to think of some heroic message of defiance to hurl at the dragon, some poetic words that might be remembered forever so that his death would be sung in a thousand songs. But Bork's mind was not quick at such things; he was not that accustomed to speech, and had no ear for gallantry. Instead he began to think it would be somehow cheap and silly to die with a lie on his lips.

"Dragon," Bork whispered, "I'm frightened."

To Bork's surprise, the teeth did not pierce him then. Instead, he felt himself being lowered to the ground, heard a grating sound as the teeth and claws let go of his armor. He raised his visor, and saw that the dragon was now lying on the ground, laughing, rolling back and forth, slapping its tail against the rocks, and clapping its claws together. "Oh, my dear tiny friend," said the dragon. "I thought the day would never dawn."

"What day?"

"Today," answered the dragon. It had stopped laughing, and it once again drew near to Bork and looked him in the eye. "I'm going to let you live."

"Thank you," Bork said, trying to be polite.

"Thank me? Oh no, my midget warrior. You won't thank me. Did you think my teeth were sharp? Not half so pointed as the barbs of your jealous, disappointed friends."

"I can go?"

"You can go, you can fly, you can dwell in your castle for all I care. Do you want to know why?"

"Yes."

"Because you were afraid. In all my life, I have only killed brave knights who knew no fear. You're the first, the very first, who was afraid in that final moment. Now go." And the dragon gave Bork a push and sent him down the hill.

Brunhilda, who had watched the whole battle in curious silence, now called after him. "Some kind of knight you are! Coward! I hate you! Don't leave me!" The shouts went on until Bork was out of earshot.

Bork was ashamed.

Bork went down the hill and, as soon as he entered the cool of the forest, he lay down and fell asleep.

Hidden in the rocks, Winkle watched him go, watched as the dragon again began to tickle Brunhilda, whose gown was still open as it had been when she was taken by the dragon. Winkle could not stop thinking of how close he had come to having her. But now, if even Bork could not save her, her cause was hopeless, and Winkle immediately began planning other ways to profit from the situation.

All the plans depended on his reaching the castle before Bork. Since Winkle had dozed off and on during the day's battle, he was able to go farther—to a village, where he stole an ass and rode clumsily, half-asleep, all night and half the next day and reached the castle before Bork awoke.

The King raged. The King swore. The King vowed that Bork would die.

"But Your Majesty," said Winkle, "you can't forget that it is Bork who inspires fear in the hearts of your loyal subjects. You can't kill him—if he were dead, how long would you be king?"

That calmed the old man down. "Then I'll let him live. But he won't have a place in this castle, that's certain. I won't have him around here, the coward. Afraid! Told the dragon he was afraid! Pathetic. The man has no gratitude." And the King stalked from the court.

When Bork got home, weary and sick at heart, he found the gate of the castle closed to him. There was no explanation—he needed none. He had failed the one time it mattered most. He was no longer worthy to be a knight.

And now it was as it had been before. Bork was ignored, despised, feared, he was completely alone. But still, when it was time for great strength, there he was, doing the work of ten men, and not thanked for it. Who would thank a man for doing what he must to earn his bread.

In the evenings he would sit in his hut, staring at the fire that pushed a column of smoke up through the hole in the roof. He remembered how it had been to have friends, but the memory was not happy, for it was always poisoned by the knowledge that the friendship did not outlast Bork's first failure. Now the knights spat when they passed him on the road or in the fields.

The flames did not let Bork blame his troubles on them, how-ever. The flames constantly reminded him of the dragon's eyes, and in their dance he saw himself, a buffoon who dared to dream of loving a princess, who believed that he was truly a knight. Not so, not so. I was never a knight, he thought. I was never worthy. Only now am I receiving what I deserve. And all his bitterness turned inward, and he hated himself far more than any of the knights could hate him.

He had made the wrong choice. When the dragon chose to let him go, he should have refused. He should have stayed and fought to the death. He should have died.

Stories kept filtering into the village, stories of the many heroic and famous knights who accepted the challenge of freeing Brunhilda from the dragon. All of them went as heroes. All of them died as heroes. Only Bork had returned alive from the dragon, and with every knight who died Bork's shame grew. Until he decided that he would go back. Better to join the knights in death than to live his life staring into the flames and seeing the vi-sions of the dragon's eyes.

Next time, however, he would have to be better prepared. So after the spring plowing and planting and lambing and calving, where Bork's help was indispensable to the villagers, the giant went to the castle again. This time no one barred his way, but he was wise enough to stay as much out of sight as possible. He went to the one-armed swordmaster's room. Bork hadn't seen him since he accidentally cut off his arm in sword practice years before.

"Come for the other arm, coward?" asked the swordmaster.

"I'm sorry," Bork said. "I was younger then."

"You weren't any smaller. Go away."

But Bork stayed, and begged the swordmaster to help him. They worked out an arrangement. Bork would be the swordmas-ter's personal servant all summer, and in exchange the swordmaster would try to teach Bork how to fight.

They went out into the fields every day, and under the sword-master's watchful eye he practiced sword-fighting with bushes, trees, rocks—anything but the swordmaster, who refused to let

Bork near him. Then they would return to the swordmaster's rooms, and Bork would clean the floor and sharpen swords and burnish shields and repair broken practice equipment. And always the swordmaster said, "Bork, you're too stupid to do anything right!" Bork agreed. In a summer of practice, he never got any better, and at the end of the summer, when it was time for Bork to go out in the fields and help with the harvest and the preparations for winter, the swordmaster said, "It's hopeless, Bork. You're too slow. Even the bushes are more agile than you. Don't come back. I still hate you, you know."

"I know," Bork said, and he went out into the fields, where the peasants waited impatiently for the giant to come carry sheaves of grain to the wagons.

Another winter looking at the fire, and Bork began to realize that no matter how good he got with the sword, it would make no difference. The dragon was not to be defeated that way. If excellent swordplay could kill the dragon, the dragon would be dead by now—the finest knights in the kingdom had already died trying.

He had to find another way. And the snow was still heavy on the ground when he again entered the castle and climbed the long and narrow stairway to the tower room where the wizard lived.

"Go away," said the wizard, when Bork knocked at his door. "I'm busy."

"I'll wait," Bork answered.

"Suit yourself."

And Bork waited. It was late at night when the wizard finally opened the door. Bork had fallen asleep leaning on it—he nearly knocked the magician over when he fell inside.

"What the devil are you—you waited!"

"Yes," said Bork, rubbing his head where it had hit the stone floor.

"Well, I'll be back in a moment." The wizard made his way along a narrow ledge until he reached the place where the wall bulged and a hole opened onto the outside of the castle wall. In wartime, such holes were used to pour boiling oil on attackers. In peacetime, they were even more heavily used. "Go on inside and wait," the wizard said.

Bork looked around the room. It was spotlessly clean, the walls were lined with books, and here and there a fascinating artifact hinted at hidden knowledge and arcane powers—a sphere with the world on it, a skull, an abacus, beakers and tubes, a clay pot from which smoke rose, though there was no fire under it. Bork marveled until the wizard returned.

"Nice little place, isn't it?" the wizard asked. "You're Bork, the Bully, aren't you?"

Bork nodded.

"What can I do for you?"

"I don't know," Bork asked. "I want to learn magic. I want to learn magic powerful enough that I can use it to fight the dragon."

The wizard coughed profusely.

"What's wrong?" Bork asked.

"It's the dust," the wizard said.

Bork looked around and saw no dust. But when he sniffed the air, it felt thick in his nose, and a tickling in his chest made him cough, too.

"Dust?" asked Bork. "Can I have a drink?"

"Drink," said the wizard. "Downstairs—"

"But there's a pail of water right here. It looks perfectly clean—"

"Please don't—"

But Bork put the dipper in the pail and drank. The water sloshed into his mouth, and he swallowed, but it felt dry going down, and his thirst was unslaked. "What's wrong with the water?" Bork asked.

The wizard sighed and sat down. "It's the problem with magic, Bork old boy. Why do you think the King doesn't call on me to help him in his wars? He knows it, and now you'll know it, and the whole world probably will know it by Thursday."

"You don't know any magic?"

"Don't be a fool! I know all the magic there is! I can conjure up monsters that would make your dragon look tame! I can snap my fingers and have a table set with food to make the cook die of envy. I can take an empty bucket and fill it with water, with wine, with gold—whatever you want. But try spending the gold, and they'll hunt you down and kill you. Try drinking the water and you'll die of thirst."

"It isn't real."

"All illusion. Handy, sometimes. But that's all. Can't create anything except in your head. That pail, for instance—" And the wizard snapped his fingers. Bork looked, and the pail was filled, not with water, but with dust and spider webs. That wasn't all. He looked around the room, and was startled to see that the book-shelves were gone, as were the other trappings of great wisdom. Just a few books on a table in a corner, some counters covered with dust and papers and half-decayed food, and the floor inches deep in garbage.

"The place is horrible," the wizard said. "I can't bear to look at it." He snapped his fingers, and the old illusion came back. "Much nicer, isn't it?"

"Yes."

"I have excellent taste, haven't I? Now, you wanted me to help you fight the dragon, didn't you? Well, I'm afraid it's out of the question. You see, my illusions only work on human beings, and occasionally on horses. A dragon wouldn't be fooled for a moment. You understand?"

Bork understood, and despaired. He returned to his hut and stared again at the flames. His resolution to return and fight the dragon again was undimmed. But now he knew that he would go as badly prepared as he had before, and his death and defeat would be certain. Well, he thought, better death than life as Bork the Coward, Bork the Bully who only has courage when he fights peo-ple smaller than himself.

The winter was unusually cold, and the snow was remarkably deep. The firewood ran out in February, and there was no sign of an easing in the weather.

The villagers went to the castle and asked for help, but the King was chilly himself, and the knights were all sleeping together in the great hall because there wasn't enough firewood for their barracks and the castle, too. "Can't help you," the King said.

So it was Bork who led the villagers—the ten strongest men, dressed as warmly as they could, yet still cold to the bone in the wind—and they followed in the path his body cut in the snow. With his huge ax he cut down tree after tree; the villagers set the wedges and Bork split the huge logs; the men carried what they could but it was Bork who made seven trips and carried most of the wood home. The village had enough to last until spring—more than enough, for, as Bork had expected, as soon as the stacks of firewood were deep in the village, the King's men came and took their tax of it.

And Bork, exhausted and frozen from the expedition, was carefully nursed back to health by the villagers. As he lay coughing and they feared he might die, it occurred to them how much they owed to the giant. Not just the firewood, but the hard labor in the farming work, and the fact that Bork had kept the armies far from their village, and they felt what no one in the castle had let himself feel for more than a few moments—gratitude. And so it was that when he had mostly recovered, Bork began to find gifts outside his door from time to time. A rabbit, freshly killed and dressed; a few eggs; a vast pair of hose that fit him very comfortably; a knife specially made to fit his large grip and to ride with comfortable weight on his hip. The villagers did not converse with him much. But then, they were not talkative people. The gifts said it all.

Throughout the spring, as Bork helped in the plowing and planting, with the villagers working alongside, he realized that this was where he belonged—with the villagers, not with the knights. They weren't rollicking good company, but there was something about sharing a task that must be done that made for stronger bonds between them than any of the rough camaraderie of the castle. The loneliness was gone.

Yet when Bork returned home and stared into the flames in the center of his hut, the call of the dragon's eyes became even stronger, if that were possible. It was not loneliness that drove him to seek death with the dragon. It was something else, and Bork could not think what. Pride? He had none—he accepted the verdict of the castle people that he was a coward. The only guess he could make was that he loved Brunhilda and felt a need to rescue her. The more he tried to convince himself, however, the less he believed it.

He had to return to the dragon because, in his own mind, he knew he should have died in the dragon's teeth, back when he fought the dragon before. The common folk might love him for what he did for them, but he hated himself for what he was.

He was nearly ready to head back for the dragon's mountain when the army came.

"How many are there?" the King asked Winkle.

"I can't get my spies to agree," Winkle said. "But the lowest estimate was two thousand men."

"And we have a hundred and fifty here in the castle. Well, I'll have to call on my dukes and counts for support."

"You don't understand, Your Majesty. These *are* your dukes and counts. This isn't an invasion. This is a rebellion."

The King paled. "How do they dare?"

"They dare because they heard a rumor, which at first they didn't believe was true. A rumor that your giant knight had quit, that he wasn't in your army anymore. And when they found out for sure that the rumor was true, they came to cast you out and return the old king to his place."

"Treason!" the King shouted. "Is there no loyalty?"

"I'm loyal," Winkle said, though of course he had already made contact with the other side in case things didn't go well. "But it seems to me that your only hope is to prove the rumors wrong. Show them that Bork is still fighting for you."

"But he isn't. I threw him out two years ago. The coward was even rejected by the dragon."

"Then I suggest you find a way to get him back into the army. If you don't, I doubt you'll have much luck against that crowd out there. My spies tell me they're placing wagers about how many pieces you can be cut into before you die."

The King turned slowly and stared at Winkle, glared at him, gazed intently in his eyes. "Winkle, after all we've done to Bork over the years, persuading him to help us now is a despicable thing to do."

"True."

"And so it's your sort of work, Winkle. Not mine. *You* get him back in the army."

"I can't do it. He hates me worse than anyone, I'm sure. After all, I've betrayed him more often."

"You get him back in the army within the next six hours, Winkle, or I'll send pieces of you to each of the men in that traitorous group that you've made friends with in order to betray me."

Winkle managed not to looked startled. But he *was* surprised. The King had somehow known about it. The King was not quite the fool he had seemed to be.

"I'm sending four knights with you to make sure you do it right."

"You misjudge me, Your Majesty," Winkle said.

"I hope so, Winkle. Persuade Bork for me, and you live to eat another breakfast."

The knights came, and Winkle walked with them to Bork's hut. They waited outside.

"Bork, old friend," Winkle said. Bork was sitting by the fire, staring in the flames. "Bork, you aren't the sort who holds grudges, are you?"

Bork spat into the flames.

"Can't say I blame you," Winkle said. "We've treated you ungratefully. We've been downright cruel. But you rather brought it on yourself, you know. It isn't *our* fault you turned coward in your fight with the dragon. Is it?"

Bork shook his head. "My fault, Winkle. But it isn't my fault the army has come, either. I've lost my battle. You lose yours."

"Bork, we've been friends since we were three—"

Bork looked up so suddenly, his face so sharp and lit with the glow of the fire, that Winkle could not go on.

"I've looked in the dragon's eyes," Bork said, "and I know who you are."

Winkle wondered if it was true, and was afraid. But he had courage of a kind, a selfish courage that allowed him to dare anything if he thought he would gain by it.

"Who I am? No one knows anything as it is, because as soon as it's known it changes. You looked in the dragon's eyes years ago, Bork. Today I am not who I was then. Today you are not who you were then. And today the King needs you."

"The King is a petty count who rode to greatness on my shoulders. He can rot in hell."

"The other knights need you, then. Do you want them to die?"

"I've fought enough battles for them. Let them fight their own."

And Winkle stood helplessly, wondering how he could possibly persuade this man, who would not be persuaded.

It was then that a village child came. The knights caught him lurking near Bork's hut; they roughly shoved him inside. "He might be a spy," a knight said.

For the first time since Winkle came, Bork laughed. "A spy? don't you know your own village, here? Come to me, Laggy." And the boy came to him, and stood near him as if seeking the giant's protection. "Laggy's a friend of mine," Bork said. "Why did you come, Laggy?"

The boy wordlessly held out a fish. It wasn't large, but it was still wet from the river.

"Did you catch this?" Bork said.

The boy nodded.

"How many did you catch today?"

The boy pointed at the fish.

"Just the one? Oh, then I can't take this, if it's all you caught."

But as Bork handed the fish back, the boy retreated, refused to take it. He finally opened his mouth and spoke. "For you," he said, and then he scurried out of the hut and into the bright morning sunlight.

And Winkle knew he had his way to get Bork into the battle.

"The villagers," Winkle said.

Bork looked at him quizzically.

And Winkle *almost* said, "If you don't join the army, we'll come out here and burn the village and kill all the children and sell the adults into slavery in Germany." But something stopped him; a memory, perhaps, of the fact that he was once a village child himself. No, not that. Winkle was honest enough with himself to know that what stopped him from making the threat was a mental picture of Sir Bork striding into battle, not in front of the King's army, but at the head of the rebels. A mental picture of Bork's ax biting deep into the gate of the castle, his huge crow prying the portcullis free. This was not the time to threaten Bork.

So Winkle took the other tack. "Bork, if they win this battle, which they surely will if you aren't with us, do you think they'll be kind to this village? They'll burn and rape and kill and capture these people for slaves. They hate us, and to them these villagers are part of us, part of their hatred. If you don't help us, you're killing them."

"I'll protect them," Bork said.

"No, my friend. No, if you don't fight with us, as a knight, they won't treat you chivalrously. They'll fill you full of arrows before you get within twenty feet of their lines. You fight with us, or you might as well not fight at all."

Winkle knew he had won. Bork thought for several minutes, but it was inevitable. He got up and returned to the castle, strapped on his old armor, took his huge ax and his shield, and, with his sword belted at his waist, walked into the courtyard of the castle. The other knights cheered, and called out to him as if he were their dearest friend. But the words were hollow and they knew it, and when Bork didn't answer they soon fell silent.

The gate opened and Bork walked out, the knights on horseback behind him.

And in the rebel camp, they knew that the rumors were a lie— the giant still fought with the King, and they were doomed. Most of the men slipped away into the woods. But the others, particularly the leaders who would die if they surrendered as surely as they would die if they fought, stayed. Better to die valiantly than as a coward, they each thought, and so as Bork approached he still faced an army—only a few hundred men, but still an army.

They came out to meet Bork one by one, as the knights came to the dragon on his hill. And one by one, as they made their first cut or thrust, Bork's ax struck, and their heads flew from their bodies, or their chests were cloven nearly in half, or the ax reamed them end to end, and Bork was bright red with blood and a dozen men were dead and not one had touched him.

So they came by threes and fours, and fought like demons, but still Bork took them, and when even more than four tried to fight him at once they got in each other's way and he killed them more easily.

And at last those who still lived despaired. There was no honor in dying so pointlessly. And with fifty men dead, the battle ended, and the rebels laid down their arms in submission.

Then the King emerged from the castle and rode to the battleground, and paraded triumphantly in front of the defeated men.

"You are all sentenced to death at once," the King declared.

But suddenly he found himself pulled from his horse, and Bork's great hands held him. The King gasped at the smell of gore; Bork rubbed his bloody hands on the King's tunic, and took the King's face between his sticky palms.

"No one dies now. No one dies tomorrow. These men will all live, and you'll send them home to their lands, and you'll lower their tribute and let them dwell in peace forever."

The King imagined his own blood mingling with that which already covered Bork, and he nodded. Bork let him go. The King mounted his horse again, and spoke loudly, so all could hear. "I forgive you all. I pardon you all. You may return to your homes. I confirm you in your lands. And your tribute is cut in half from this day forward. Go in peace. If any man harms you, I'll have his life."

The rebels stood in silence.

Winkle shouted at them "Go! You heard the King! You're free! Go home!"

And they cheered, and long-lived-the-King, and then bellowed their praise to Bork.

But Bork, if he heard them, gave no sign. He stripped off his armor and let it lie in the field. He carried his great ax to the stream, and let the water run over the metal until it was clean. Then he lay in the stream himself, and the water carried off the last of the blood, and when he came out he was clean.

Then he walked away, to the north road, ignoring the calls of the King and his knights, ignoring everything except the dragon who waited for him on the mountain. For this was the last of the acts Bork would perform in his life for which he would feel shame. He would not kill again. He would only die, bravely, in the dragon's claws and teeth.

The old woman waited for him on the road.

"Off to kill the dragon, are you?" she asked in a voice that the years had tortured into gravel. "Didn't learn enough the first time?" She giggled behind her hand.

"Old woman, I learned everything before. Now I'm going to die."

"Why? So the fools in the castle will think better of you?"

Bork shook his head.

"The villagers already love you. For your deeds today, you'll already be a legend. If it isn't for love or fame, why are you going?"

Bork shrugged. "I don't know. I think he calls to me. I'm through with my life, and all I can see ahead of me are his eyes."

The old woman nodded. "Well, well, Bork. I think you're the first knight that the dragon won't be happy to see. We old wives know, Bork. Just tell him the truth, Bork."

"I've never known the truth to stop a sword," he said.

"But the dragon doesn't carry a sword."

"He might as well."

"No, Bork, no," she said, clucking impatiently. "You know better than that. Of all the dragon's weapons, which cut you the deepest?"

Bork tried to remember. The truth was, he realized, that the dragon had never cut him at all. Not with his teeth nor his claws.

Only the armor had been pierced. Yet there had been a wound, a deep one that hadn't healed, and it had been cut in him, not by teeth or talons, but by the bright fires in the dragon's eyes.

"The truth," the old woman said. "Tell the dragon the truth. Tell him the truth, and you'll live!"

Bork shook his head. "I'm not going there to live," he said. He pushed past her, and walked on up the road.

But her words rang in his ears long after he stopped hearing her call after him. The truth, she had said. Well, then, why not? Let the dragon have the truth. Much good may it do him.

This time Bork was in no hurry. He slept every night, and paused to hunt for berries and fruit to eat in the woods. It was four days before he reached the dragon's hill, and he came in the morning, after a good night's sleep. He was afraid, of course; but still there was a pleasant feeling about the morning, a tingling of excitement about the meeting with the dragon. He felt the end coming near, and he relished it.

Nothing had changed. The dragon roared; Brunhilda screamed. And when he reached the top of the hill, he saw the dragon tickling her with his wing. He was not surprised to see that she hadn't changed at all—the two years had not aged her, and though her gown still was open and her breasts were open to the sun and the wind, she wasn't even freckled or tanned. It could have been yesterday that Bork fought with the dragon the first time. And Bork was smiling as he stepped into the flat space where the battle would take place.

Brunhilda saw him first. "Help me! You're the four hundred and thirtieth knight to try! Surely that's a lucky number!" Then she recognized him. "Oh, no. You again. Oh well, at least while he's fighting you I won't have to put up with his tickling."

Bork ignored her. He had come for the dragon, not for Brunhilda.

The dragon regarded him calmly. "You are disturbing my nap time."

"I'm glad," Bork said. "You've disturbed me, sleeping and waking, since I left you. Do you remember me?"

"Ah yes. You're the only knight who was ever afraid of me."

"Do you really believe that?" Bork asked.

"It hardly matters what I believe. Are you going to kill me today?"

"I don't think so," said Bork. "You're much stronger than I am, and I'm terrible at battle. I've never defeated anyone who was more than half my strength."

The lights in the dragon's eyes suddenly grew brighter, and the dragon squinted to look at Bork. "Is that so?" asked the dragon.

"And I'm not very clever. You'll be able to figure out my next move before I know what it is myself."

The dragon squinted more, and the eyes grew even brighter.

"Don't you want to rescue this beautiful woman?" the dragon asked.

"I don't much care," he said. "I loved her once. But I'm through with that. I came for you."

"You don't love her anymore?" asked the dragon.

Bork almost said, "Not a bit." But then he stopped. The truth, the old woman had said. And he looked into himself and saw that no matter how much he hated himself for it, the old feelings died hard. "I love her, dragon. But it doesn't do me any good. She doesn't love me. And so even though I desire her, I don't want her."

Brunhilda was a little miffed. "That's the stupidest thing I've ever heard," she said. But Bork was watching the dragon, whose eyes were dazzlingly bright. The monster was squinting so badly that Bork began to wonder if he could see at all.

"Are you having trouble with your eyes?" Bork asked.

"Do you think *you* ask the questions here? I ask the questions."

"Then ask."

"What in the world do I want to know from you?"

"I can't think of anything," Bork answered. "I know almost nothing. What little I do know, you taught me."

"Did I? What was it that you learned?"

"You taught me that I was not loved by those I thought had

loved me. I learned from you that deep within my large body is a very small soul."

The dragon blinked, and its eyes seemed to dim a little.

"Ah," said the dragon.

"What do you mean, 'Ah'?" asked Bork.

"Just 'Ah,' " the dragon answered. "Does every *ah* have to mean something?"

Brunhilda sighed impatiently. "How long does this go on? Everybody else who comes up here is wonderful and brave. You just stand around talking about how miserable you are. Why don't you fight?"

"Like the others?" asked Bork.

"They're so brave," she said.

"They're all dead."

"Only a coward would think of that," she said scornfully.

"It hardly comes as a surprise to you," Bork said. "Everyone knows I'm a coward. Why do you think I came? I'm of no use to anyone, except as a machine to kill people at the command of a king I despise."

"That's my father you're talking about!"

"I'm nothing, and the world will be better without me in it."

"I can't say I disagree," Brunhilda said.

But Bork did not hear her, for he felt the touch of the dragon's tail on his back, and when he looked at the dragon's eyes they had stopped glowing so brightly. They were almost back to normal, in fact, and the dragon was beginning to reach out its claws.

So Bork swung his ax, and the dragon dodged, and the battle was on, just as before.

And just as before, at sundown Bork stood pinned between tail and claws and teeth.

"Are you afraid to die?" asked the dragon, as it had before.

Bork almost answered *yes* again, because that would keep him alive. But then he remembered that he had come in order to die, and as he looked in his heart he still realized that however much he might fear death, he feared life more.

"I came here to die," he said. "I still want to."

And the dragon's eyes leaped bright with light. Bork imagined that the pressure of the claws lessened.

"Well, then, Sir Bork, I can hardly do you such a favor as to kill you." And the dragon let him go.

That was when Bork became angry.

"You can't do this to me!" he shouted.

"Why not?" asked the dragon, who was now trying to ignore Bork and occupied itself by crushing boulders with its claws.

"Because I insist on my right to die at your hands."

"It's not a right, it's a privilege," said the dragon.

"If you don't kill me, then I'll kill you!"

The dragon sighed in boredom, but Bork would not be put off. He began swinging the ax, and the dragon dodged, and in the pink light of sunset the battle was on again. This time, though, the dragon only fell back and twisted and turned to avoid Bork's blows. It made no effort to attack. Finally Bork was too tired and frustrated to go on.

"Why don't you fight!" he shouted. Then he wheezed from the exhaustion of the chase.

The dragon was panting, too. "Come on now, little man, why don't you give it up and go home. I'll give you a signed certificate testifying that I asked you to go, so that no one thinks you're a coward. Just leave me alone."

The dragon began crushing rocks and dribbling them over its head. It lay down and began to bury itself in gravel.

"Dragon," said Bork, "a moment ago you had me in your teeth. You were about to kill me. The old woman told me that truth was my only defense. So I must have lied before, I must have said something false. What was it? Tell me!"

The dragon looked annoyed. "She had no business telling you that. It's privileged information."

"All I ever said to you was the truth."

"Was it?"

"Did I lie to you? Answer—yes or no!"

The dragon only looked away, its eyes still bright. It lay on its back and poured gravel over its belly.

"I did then. I lied. Just the kind of fool I am to tell the truth and still get caught in a lie."

Had the dragon's eyes dimmed? Was there a lie in what he had just said?

"Dragon," Bork insisted, "if you don't kill me or I don't kill you, then I might as well throw myself from the cliff. There's no meaning to my life, if I can't die at your hands!"

Yes, the dragon's eyes were dimming, and the dragon rolled over onto its belly, and began to gaze thoughtfully at Bork.

"Where is the lie in that?"

"Lie? Who said anything about a lie?" But the dragon's long tail was beginning to creep around so it could get behind Bork.

And then it occurred to Bork that the dragon might not even know. That the dragon might be as much a prisoner of the fires of truth inside him as Bork was, and that the dragon wasn't deliberately toying with him at all. Didn't matter, of course. "Never mind what the lie is, then," Bork said. "Kill me now, and the world will be a better place!"

The dragon's eyes dimmed, and a claw made a pass at him, raking the air by his face.

It was maddening, to know there was a lie in what he was saying and not know what it was. "It's the perfect ending for my meaningless life," he said. "I'm so clumsy I even have to stumble into death."

He didn't understand why, but once again he stared into the dragon's mouth, and the claws pressed gently but sharply against his flesh.

The dragon asked the question of Bork for the third time. "Are you afraid, little man, to die?"

This was the moment, Bork knew. If he was to die, he had to lie to the dragon now, for if he told the truth the dragon would set him free again. But to lie, he had to know what the truth was, and now he didn't know at all. He tried to think of where he had gone astray from the truth, and could not. What had he said? It was true that he was clumsy; it was true that he was stumbling into death. What else then?

He had said his life was meaningless. Was that the lie? He had said his death would make the world a better place. Was that the lie?

And so he thought of what would happen when he died. What hole would his death make in the world? The only people who might miss him were the villagers. That was the meaning of his life, then—the villagers. So he lied.

"The villagers won't miss me if I die. They'll get along just fine without me."

But the dragon's eyes brightened, and the teeth withdrew, and Bork realized to his grief that his statement had been true after all. The villagers wouldn't miss him if he died. The thought of it broke his heart, the last betrayal in a long line of betrayals.

"Dragon, I can't outguess you! I don't know what's true and what isn't! All I learn from you is that everyone I thought loved me doesn't. Don't ask me questions! Just kill me and end my life. Every pleasure I've had turns to pain when you tell me the truth."

And now, when he had thought he was telling the truth, the claws broke his skin, and the teeth closed over his head, and he screamed. "Dragon! Don't let me die like this! What is the pleasure that your truth won't turn to pain? What do I have left?"

The dragon pulled away, and regarded him carefully. "I told you, little man, that I don't answer questions. I ask them."

"Why are you here?" Bork demanded. "This ground is littered with the bones of men who failed your tests. Why not mine? Why not mine? Why can't I die? Why did you keep sparing my life? I'm just a man, I'm just alive, I'm just trying to do the best I can in a miserable world and I'm sick of trying to figure out what's true and what isn't. End the game, dragon. My life has never been happy, and I want to die."

The dragon's eyes went black, and the jaws opened again, and the teeth approached, and Bork knew he had told his last lie, that this lie would be enough. But with the teeth inches from him Bork finally realized what the lie was, and the realization was enough to change his mind. "No," he said, and he reached out and seized the teeth, though they cut his fingers. "No," he said, and he wept. "I have been happy. I have." And, gripping the sharp teeth, the memories raced through his mind. The many nights of comradeship with the knights in the castle. The pleasures of weariness from working in the forest and the fields. The joy he felt when alone he won a victory from the Duke; the rush of warmth when the boy brought him the single fish he had caught; and the solitary pleasures, of waking and going to sleep, of walking and running, of feeling the wind on a hot day and standing near a fire in the deep of winter. They were all good, and they had all happened. What did it matter if later the knights despised him? What did it matter if the villagers' love was only a fleeting thing, to be forgotten after he died? The reality of the pain did not destroy the reality of the pleasure; grief did not obliterate joy. They each happened in their time, and because some of them were dark it did not mean that none of them was light.

"I have been happy," Bork said. "And if you let me live, I'll be happy again. That's what my life means, doesn't it? That's the truth, isn't it, dragon? My life matters because I'm alive, joy or pain, whatever comes, I'm alive and that's meaning enough. It's true, isn't it, dragon! I'm not here to fight you. I'm not here for you to kill me. I'm here to make myself alive!"

But the dragon did not answer. Bork was gently lowered to the ground. The dragon withdrew its talons and tail, pulled its head away, and curled up on the ground, covering its eyes with its claws.

"Dragon, did you hear me?"

The dragon said nothing.

"Dragon, look at me!"

The dragon sighed. "Man, I cannot look at you."

"Why not?"

"I am blind," the dragon answered. It pulled its claws away from its eyes. Bork covered his face with his hands. The dragon's eyes were brighter than the sun.

"I feared you, Bork," the dragon whispered. "From the day you told me you were afraid, I feared you. I knew you would be back. And I knew this moment would come."

"What moment?" Bork asked.

"The moment of my death."

"Are you dying?"

"No," said the dragon. "Not yet. You must kill me."

As Bork looked at the dragon lying before him, he felt no desire for blood. "I don't want you to die."

"Don't you know that a dragon cannot live when it has met a truly honest man? It's the only way we ever die, and most dragons live forever."

But Bork refused to kill him.

The dragon cried out in anguish. "I am filled with all the truth that was discarded by men when they chose their lies and died for them. I am in constant pain, and now that I have met a man who does not add to my treasury of falsehood, you are the cruelest of them all."

And the dragon wept, and its eyes flashed and sparkled in every hot tear that fell, and finally Bork could not bear it. He took his ax and hacked off the dragon's head, and the light in its eyes went out. The eyes shriveled in their sockets until they turned into small, bright diamonds with a thousand facets each. Bork took the diamonds and put them in his pocket.

"You killed him," Brunhilda said wonderingly.

Bork did not answer. He just untied her, and looked away while she finally fastened her gown. Then he shouldered the dragon's head and carried it back to the castle, Brunhilda running to keep up with him. He only stopped to rest at night because she begged him to. And when she tried to thank him for freeing her, he only turned away and refused to hear. He had killed the dragon because it wanted to die. Not for Brunhilda. Never for her.

At the castle they were received with rejoicing, but Bork would not go in. He only laid the dragon's head beside the moat and went to his hut, fingering the diamonds in his pocket, holding them in front of him in the pitch blackness of his hut to see that they shone with their own light, and did not need the sun or any other fire but themselves.

The King and Winkle and Brunhilda and a dozen knights

came to Bork's hut. "I have come to thank you," the King said, his cheeks wet with tears of joy.

"You're welcome," Bork said. He said it as if to dismiss them.

"Bork," the King said. "Slaying the dragon was ten times as brave as the bravest thing any man has done before. You can have my daughter's hand in marriage."

Bork looked up in surprise.

"I thought you never meant to keep your promise, Your Majesty."

The King looked down, then at Winkle, then back at Bork. "Occasionally," he said, "I keep my word. So here she is, and thank you."

But Bork only smiled, fingering the diamonds in his pocket. "It's enough that you offered, Your Majesty. I don't want her. Marry her to a man she loves."

The King was puzzled. Brunhilda's beauty had not waned in her years of captivity. She had the sort of beauty that started wars. "Don't you want *any* reward?" asked the King.

Bork thought for a moment. "Yes," he said. "I want to be given a plot of ground far away from here. I don't want there to be any count, or any duke, or any king over me. And any man or woman or child who comes to me will be free, and no one can pursue them. And I will never see you again, and you will never see me again."

"That's all you want?"

"That's all."

"Then you shall have it," the King said.

Bork lived all the rest of his life on his little plot of ground. People did come to him. Not many, but five or ten a year all his life, and a village grew up where no one came to take a king's tithe or a duke's fifth or a count's fourth. Children grew up who knew nothing of the art of war and never saw a knight or a battle or the terrible fear on the face of a man who knows his wounds are too deep to heal. It was everything Bork could have wanted, and he was happy all his years there.

Winkle, too, achieved everything he wanted. He married Brunhilda, and soon enough the King's sons had accidents and died, and the King died after dinner one night, and Winkle became King. He was at war all his life, and never went to sleep at night without fear of an assassin coming upon him in the darkness. He governed ruthlessly and thoroughly and was hated all his life; later generations, however, remembered him as a great king. But he was dead then, and didn't know it.

Later generations never heard of Bork.

He had only been out on his little plot of ground for a few months when the old wife came to him. "Your hut is much bigger than you need," she said. "Move over."

So Bork moved over, and she moved in.

She did not magically turn into a beautiful princess. She was foul-mouthed and nagged Bork unmercifully. But he was devoted to her, and when she died a few years later he realized that she had given him more happiness than pain, and he missed her. But the grief at her dying did not taint any of the joys of his memory of her; he just fingered the diamonds, and remembered that grief and joy were not weighed in the same scale, one making the other seem less substantial.

And at last he realized that Death was near; that Death was reaping him like wheat, eating him like bread. He imagined Death to be a dragon, devouring him bit by bit, and one night in a dream he asked Death, "Is my flavor sweet?"

Death, the old dragon, looked at him with bright and understanding eyes, and said, "Salty and sour, bitter and sweet. You sting and you soothe."

"Ah," Bork said, and was satisfied.

Death poised itself to take the last bite. "Thank you," it said.

"You're welcome," Bork answered, and he meant it.

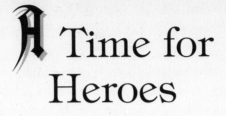

A Time for Heroes

❖

Richard Parks

imon the Black, demon of a thousand nightmares and master of none, came to a sudden understanding. "It's raining," he said. "And I'm cold."

He sounded surprised.

The dwarf Seb was not surprised. The chilling rain had started the moment they reached the foothills of the White Mountains and continued all afternoon. Seb's long fair hair hung limp about his face, and he peered out at the magician through a tangled mat like a runt wolf eyeing a lamb through a hedge. "At last he deigns to notice . . . I've been cold for hours! At the very least you could have been miserable with me."

"Sorry," Timon said. "You know I have trouble with some things."

Seb nodded. "'Here' and 'now' being two of them." Day-to-day practical matters were really Seb's responsibility, but there was comfort in complaining. In his years with Timon, Seb had learned to take comfort where he could.

Nothing else was said for a time, there being nothing to say. Seb, as usual, was the first to notice the failing light. "It's getting late. We'd better find somewhere dry to camp, if there be such in this wretched place."

It was beginning to look like a very wet night until Seb spotted a large overhang on a nearby ridge. It wasn't a true cave, more a remnant of some long-ago earthquake, but it reached more than forty yards into the hillside and had a high ceiling and dry, level floor. It wasn't the worst place they'd ever slept.

"I'll build a fire," the dwarf said, "if you will promise me not to look at it."

Timon didn't promise, but Seb built the fire anyway after seeing to their mounts and the pack train. He found some almost-dry wood near the entrance and managed to collect enough rainwater for the horses and for a pot of tea. He unpacked the last of their dried beef and biscuit, studied the pitiful leavings, and shook his head in disgust. Gold wasn't a problem, but they hadn't dared stop for supplies till well away from the scene of Timon's last escapade, and now what little food they'd had time to pack was almost gone.

Seb scrounged another pot and went to catch some more rain. When he had enough, he added the remnants of beef and started the pot simmering on the fire. The mixture might make a passable broth. If not, at least they could use it to soften the biscuit.

Timon inched closer to the fire, watching Seb out of the corner of his eye. The dwarf pretended not to notice. Timon was soaked, and neither of them had any dry clothing. Timon's catching cold or worse was the last thing Seb needed. As for the risk, well, when the inevitable happened it would happen and that, as it had been many times before, would be that.

"I never look for trouble, you know that," Timon said. It sounded like an apology.

"I know." Seb handed him a bowl of the broth and a piece of hard biscuit, and that small gesture was as close to an acceptance of the apology as the occasion demanded. They ate in comfortable silence for a while, but as the silence went on and on and the meal didn't, Seb began to feel definitely uncomfortable. He finally surrendered tact and leaned close.

"Bloody hell!"

It was the Long Look. Timon's eyes were glazed, almost like a blind man's. They focused at once on the flames and on nothing. Timon was seeing something far beyond the firelight, something hidden as much in time as distance. And there wasn't a damn thing Seb could do about it. He thought of taking his horse and leaving his friend behind, saving himself. He swore silently that one day he would do just that. He had sworn before, and he meant it no less now. But not this time. Always, not this time.

Seb dozed after a while, walking the edge of a dream of warmth and ease and just about to enter, when the sound of his name brought him back to the cold stone and firelight.

"Seb?"

Timon was back, too, from whatever far place he'd gone, and he was shivering again. Seb poured the last of the tea into Timon's mug. "Well?"

"I've seen something," Timon said. He found a crust of biscuit in his lap and dipped it in his tea. He chewed thoughtfully.

"Timon, is it your habit to inform me that the sun has risen? The obvious I can deal with; I need help with the Hidden Things."

"So do I," Timon said. "Or at least telling which is which. What do you think is hidden?"

"What you saw. What the Long Look has done to us this time."

Timon rubbed his eyes like the first hour of morning. "Oh, that . . . tragedy, Seb. That's what I saw in the fire. I didn't mean to. I tried not to look."

Seb threw the dregs of his own cup into the fire, and it hissed in protest. "I rather doubt it matters. If it wasn't the fire, it would be the pattern of sweat on your horse's back, or the shine of a dewdrop—" The dwarf's scowl suddenly cleared away, and he looked like a scholar who'd just solved a particularly vexing sum. "The Long Look is a curse, isn't it? I should have realized that long ago. What did you do? Cut firewood in a sacred grove? Make water on the wrong patch of flowers? What?" Seb waited but Timon didn't answer. He didn't seem to be listening. Seb shook his head sadly. "I'll wager it was a goddess. Those capable of greatest kindness must also have the power for greatest cruelty. That's balance."

"That's nonsense," said Timon, who was listening after all. "And a Hidden Thing, I see. So let me reveal it to you—there is one difference between the workings of a god and a goddess in our affairs. One only."

"And that is?"

"Us. Being men, we take the disfavor of a female deity more personally." Timon yawned and reached for his saddle and blanket.

Seb seized the reference. "Disfavor. You admit it."

Timon shrugged. "If it gives you pleasure. The Powers know you've had precious little of that lately." He moved his blanket away from a sharp rise in the stone and repositioned his saddle. "Where are we going?"

Seb tended the fire, looking sullen. "Morushe."

"Good. I'm not known there—by sight, anyway."

Seb nodded. "I was counting on that."

"It *will* make things easier . . ."

Seb knew that Timon was now speaking to himself, but he refused to be left out. "I know why we *were* heading toward Morushe—it was far away from Calyt. What business do we have there now?"

"We're going to murder a prince."

Seb closed his eyes. "Pity the fool who asked."

"I never look for trouble. You know that."

"I won't marry him and that's final!"

Princess Ashesa of Morushe spurred the big roan viciously, her long red hair streaming behind her like the wake of a Fury. She was dressed for the hunt and carried a short bow slung across her back, but the only notice she took of the forest was mirrored in a glare clearly meant to wither any tree impertinent enough to block her path.

Lady Margate—less sensibly attired—was having trouble keeping up, though she rode gamely enough. A large buck, frightened by the commotion, broke cover and leaped across their path.

"A buck!" shouted Margy, hopefully.

Ashesa didn't even pause. "I won't marry *him* either," she

snapped, "though I daresay if he ruled a big enough kingdom, Father would consider it." She grinned. "At least he's a *gentler* beast."

"That's no way to talk about your future husband!" reproved Margy. "Prince Daras is of ancient and noble lineage."

"So's my boar-hound," returned Ashesa sweetly. "We have the documents."

There had been almost no warning. Ashesa had barely time to hide her precious—and expressly forbidden—books away before her father had burst in to tell her the good news. The alliance between Morushe and the coastal realm of Borasur was agreed and signed. By breakfast King Macol had the date and was halfway done with the guest list. Ashesa couldn't decide between smashing dishes or going on her morning hunt. In the end she'd done both. But now half the crockery in her father's palace was wrecked, and her horse was not much better. Ashesa finally took pity on the poor beast and reined in at a small clearing. Margy straggled up looking reproachful and nearly as spent as Ashesa's mount.

"I just wish that someone had *asked* me. Father could have at least let me know what he was planning, *talked* to me. Was that asking for such a great deal?"

Lady Margate sighed deeply. "In Balanar town yesterday I saw a girl about your age. She would be even prettier than you are except she's already missing three teeth and part of an ear. She hawks ale and Heaven knows what else at a tavern near the barracks. If I were to tell her that the Princess Ashesa was going to be married to a prince without her permission, do you think that girl would weep for you?"

Ashesa looked sullen. "No need to go 'round the mulberry bush, Margy. I understand you."

"Then understand this—Morushe is a rich kingdom but not a strong one. Wylandia, among others, is all too aware of that. Without powerful friends, your people aren't safe. This marriage will help ensure that we have those friends."

"For someone who claims statecraft is no field for a woman, you certainly have a firm grasp of it," Ashesa said dryly.

"Common sense, Highness. Don't confuse the two." Margy

looked around them. "We should not be this far from the palace. Two high-born ladies, unescorted, in the middle of a wild forest . . ."

Ashesa laughed, and felt a little better for it. "Margy, Father's game park is about as 'wild' as your sewing room. Even the wolves get their worming dose every spring."

Lady Margate drew herself up in matronly dignity. "Never the—" She paused, her round mouth frozen in mid-syllable. She looked puzzled.

"Yes?" Ashesa encouraged, but Lady Margate just sat there, swaying ever so gently in her saddle. Ashesa slid from her mount and ran over to her nurse. "Margy, what is it?"

Ashesa saw the feathered dart sticking out of the woman's neck and whirled, drawing her hunting sword.

Too late.

Another dart hummed out of a nearby oak and stung her in the shoulder. Ashesa felt a pinprick of pain and then nothing. Her motion continued and she fell, stiff as a toppled statue, into the wildflowers, her eyes fixed upward at the guilty tree. Two short legs appeared below the leaves of a low branch, then the rest of a man not quite four feet high followed.

He wore fashionable hunting garb of brown and green immaculately tailored to his small frame, and in his hand was a blowpipe. He carried a small quiver with more darts at his belt.

Elf-shot . . . ? Ashesa's mind was all fuzzy; it was hard to think.

The small man reached the ground and nodded pleasantly in her direction, touched his cap, and whistled. Two normal-sized men in concealing robes appeared at the edge of the clearing and went to work with professional detachment. First they removed Lady Margate from her horse and propped her against the dwarf's oak, closing her eyes and tipping her hat forward to keep the sun off her face. Ashesa, half-mad with anger and worry, struggled against the drug until the veins stood out on her neck, but she could not move. The little man knelt beside her, looking strangely concerned.

"You'll only injure yourself, Highness. Don't worry about your friend—she'll recover, but not till we're well away." With that he gently plucked the dart from her shoulder and tossed it into the bushes.

"Who are you? Why are you doing this?"

The shout echoed in her head but nowhere else; she could not speak. The two silent henchmen brought Ashesa's horse as the dwarf pulled a small vial from his belt, popped the cork, and held it to her nose. An acrid odor stung her nostrils and she closed her eyes with no help at all.

Kings Macol and Riegar sat in morose silence in Macol's chambers. At first glance they weren't much alike: Macol was stout and ruddy, Riegar tall and gaunt with thinning gray hair. All this was only surface, for what they shared was obvious even without their crowns. Each man wore his responsibilities like a hair shirt.

Riegar finally spoke. "It was soon after you broke the news to your daughter, I gather?"

Macol nodded, looking disgusted. "I fooled myself into thinking she knew her duty. Blast, after her outburst this morning I'd almost think she cooked this up herself just to spite me!"

Riegar dismissed that. "We have the note, and the seal is unmistakable—"

The clatter on the stairs startled them both, and then they heard the sentry's challenge. They heard the answer even better—it was both colorful and loud.

"That will be Daras." Riegar sighed.

The crown prince of Borasur strode through the door, his handsome face flushed, his blue eyes shining with excitement. "The messenger said there was a note. Where is it?"

"Damn you, lad, you've barged into a room containing no fewer than two kings, one of whom is your father. Where are your manners?" Riegar asked.

Daras conceded a curt nod, mumbled an apology, and snatched the parchment from the table. For all his hurry the message didn't register very quickly. Daras read slowly, mouthing each word as if getting the taste of it. When he was done there was a grimness in his eyes that worried them. "Wylandia is behind this, Majesties. I'm certain!"

Macol and Riegar exchanged glances, then Macol spoke. "Prince, aren't you reading a great deal into a message that says only 'I have Ashesa—Timon the Black'?"

Daras looked surprised. "Who else has a reason to kidnap My Beloved Ashesa? The king of Wylandia would do anything to prevent our alliance." Daras said Ashesa's name with all the passion of a student reciting declensions, but he'd seen his intended only twice in his life and had as little say in the matter as she did.

Macol shook his head. "I know Aldair—he'll fight you with everything he has at the slightest provocation, but he won't stab you in the back. And Morushe and Borasur have so many trading ties that it amounts to alliance already. Aldair knows this; his negotiating position for Wylandia's use of our mountain passes is quite reasonable. We are close to agreement."

"If Aldair is not involved, then the kidnapping is not for reasons of state. And if not, then why was there no ransom demand? Why taunt us this way?"

Macol looked almost pleased. "A sensible question, Prince. Your father and I wonder about that ourselves. But no doubt this 'Timon' will make his demands clear in time, and I'll meet them if I can. In the meantime—"

"Of course!" Daras fairly glowed. "How long will it take to raise your army? May I lead the assault?"

"There will be no assault." Riegar's tone was pure finality.

"No assault!? Then what are we going to do?"

Macol sighed. "Prince, what can we do? Our best information—mere rumor—puts Timon in an old watchtower just inside the border of Wylandia. Do you honestly think His Majesty Aldair will negotiate tariffs during an invasion?"

"Has it ever been tried?" Daras asked mildly.

Riegar looked to heaven. "Sometimes I pray for a miracle to take a year from your age and add it to Galan's. I might keep what's left of my wits."

"My brother is a *clark*," snapped Daras, reddening. "Divine

Providence gave the inheritance to *me*, and when I'm king I'll show Wylandia and all else how a king deals with his enemies!" Daras nodded once and stalked out of the room.

Macol watched him go. "A bit headstrong, if I may say."

"You may." Riegar sighed. "Though it's too kind." He winced.

"Are you ill?"

"It's nothing . . . indigestion. Comes and goes." Riegar relaxed a bit as the pain eased, then said, "I've been thinking . . . Aldair won't tolerate an army on his border, but if the situation was explained to him, he might be willing to send a few men of his own."

"I daresay," Macol considered. "If this magician is operating in Aldair's territory without permission, Aldair's pride might even demand it. Yes, I'll have a delegation out tonight! After that, all a father can do is pray."

"As will I. But there is one other thing you can do," Riegar said "Would you be good enough to post a guard on Prince Daras's quarters tonight?"

"Certainly. But why?"

King Riegar of Borasur, remembering the look in his son's eyes, answered. "Oh, just a whim."

Prince Galan of Borasur strolled down a corridor in Macol's Castle, a thick volume under one arm. He didn't need much in the way of direction, though this was his first visit to Morushe. The fortress was of a common type for the period it was built; he'd made a study in his father's library before the trip. Finding his brother's quarters was easy enough, too. It was the one with the unhappy-looking soldier standing beside the door.

"Is Prince Daras allowed visitors?" he asked, smiling. The guard waved him on wearily, and Galan knocked.

"Enter if you must!"

The muffled bellow sounded close enough to an invitation. Galan went inside and found his brother pacing the stone floor. With both in the same room it was hard to imagine two men more different. Daras was the tall one, strong in the shoulders and arms from years on the tourney fields he loved so well. Galan by contrast had accepted the bare minimum of military training necessary for a Gentleman and no more. He was smaller, darker, with green eyes and a sense of calm. When the brothers were together, it was like a cool forest pool having conversation with a forest fire.

"It's intolerable!" Daras announced.

Galan didn't have to ask what was intolerable. He knew his brother's mind, even if he didn't really understand it. "Macol and Father don't want a war. Can you really fault them for that?"

Daras stopped pacing. He looked a little hurt. "You think I want a war?"

Galan shrugged. "Sometimes."

Daras shook his head. "Remember the heroic tales you used to read to me . . ." He apparently caught the reproach in Galan's eye and so amended, "The ones you still read from time to time? Even among all the nobility and sacrifice, the excitement of combat and rescue, I can see the destruction in my mind's eye. What sane man wants that? No. I blame Father and Macol for nothing except their shortsightedness. By the by, I called you a clark today in front of Father."

"It wouldn't be the first time. And not wholly wrong."

"Even so—I was angry and I'm sorry. Despite your faults I envy you in a lot of ways; you know so many things, whereas I know only one thing in this world for certain—wanted or no, a war with Wylandia is inevitable. I'd rather it be on our terms than Aldair's."

Galan changed the subject. He held up his prize. "Look what I found in Macol's library."

"A book. How odd."

Galan smiled. Sarcasm was another thing his brother knew for certain. "Not just a book. Borelane's *Tales of the Red King*. I've been trying to find a copy of this for years."

Daras showed a little more interest. "Perhaps . . ." he said, then finished, "perhaps you can read to me later."

"It'll have to be later. I'm for Wylandia tonight. Macol and Father are sending a delegation to Aldair. Father thought it might carry more weight if a Prince of the Blood went along."

"Not me, of course," Daras said bitterly.

"Be reasonable, Brother. You've no patience for diplomacy; action suits you better."

"It suits all men better."

Galan swallowed the casual insult by long habit. He'd long ago given up seeking approval from his older brother. He'd never quite given up wanting it. "We wouldn't want to do anything to endanger Ashesa." Her name brought back a little of the envy he'd always felt for Daras. The first time Galan had ever seen Ashesa was barely a year before, when Morushe's royal family paid a state visit to Borasur. He'd spent a month afterward writing bad poetry and staring at the moon.

"No," Daras agreed, though his thoughts were elsewhere.

Ashesa awoke in a room fit for a princess—a near perfect copy of her own. The big four-poster bed and the tapestry of the Quest of the Sunbeast were both in place; she was beginning to think she might have dreamed the whole abduction until she saw what was wrong. There were books, and they were not hidden.

She got up, still a little wobbly, and examined the first of them. They weren't hers, of course. She checked a few pages of each, just enough to know they were real books. She closed the last one and checked the door.

Barred.

Someone's gone to a great deal of trouble to make me feel comfortable was all she could think. Her head still ached and it was easier not to think at all. There was an arched window in the east wall, and she looked out.

The room was in a high tower somewhere in the mountains—somewhere, some mountains—and even in the dying light the view was breathtaking. The earth folded like a deflated bagpipe in all directions, and one peak snuggled up to the next with a bare knife-edge of a valley between them. The window was barred, too, but the glassed shutters worked. She opened them and took a breath of cool, head-clearing air.

Someone knocked on her door.

Odd manners for a kidnapper. And there was another thought. "I'm afraid you'll have to let yourself in," she said.

Nothing happened. Ashesa put her ear to the door and heard a faint creaking like an old oak in a breeze. The knock repeated.

"Come in, damn you!"

She heard a scrape as the bar lifted, then the clink of silverware. The door swung outward and there stood a figure in a black robe and hood, carrying a tray of food and wine. His face and hands were both covered—his face by the hood, his hands by leather gloves. He looked like one of the pair who had helped kidnap her. Ashesa stepped back, and the figure came in and set the tray on a little table by the bed. Ashesa considered trying to slip past him, but two more were in the corridor, steel spears glinting. She turned to the tray bearer, looking regal despite her rumpled condition.

"I demand to know who you are and why you've brought me here." Her jailor only shook his head slowly and turned toward the door. Ashesa stamped her foot and snatched at the hood. "Look at me when I speak to—"

There was no face under the hood. A stump of wood jutted through the neck of the robe, around which a lump of clay had been crudely shaped. A piece of it fell to the floor and shattered with a little puff of yellow dust. Ashesa screamed.

"Normally they don't wear anything, but I didn't want to upset you. I see I've failed."

A slightly chagrined man stood in the doorway. He was just past the full blood of youth, with features as fine and delicate as a girl's. His dark eyes were reddened and weak, as if he spent too many hours reading in poor light. None of these details registered as strongly in Ashesa's mind as her first impression—the man had an air of quiet certainty that she found infuriating.

"Very . . . considerate," Ashesa said, recovering her poise with great effort. "Would you please tell me *what* that is and who you are?"

He patted the simulacrum fondly. "That, Highness, is a stick golem. I learned the technique from a colleague in Nyas; you

should see what he can do with stone . . ." He stoped, clearly aware
that Ashesa had heard as much as she cared to on the subject. "My
apologies, Highness. I am called Timon the Black."

Ashesa almost screamed again. She scrambled to the other side
of the bed and snatched up a heavy gilt candlestick from the table.
She waved it with all the menace she could scrape together. "Don't
come near me, Fiend!"

"My reputation precedes me," the magician sighed. "What is
my most recent atrocity?"

Ashesa glared at him. "Do you deny that you sacrificed a virgin
girl to raise an army of demons against the Red Company?"

Timon smiled a little ruefully. "To start, they weren't demons
and she wasn't a virgin. Nor did I 'sacrifice' her . . . exactly. The
Red Company took a geld from half the kingdoms on the main-
land, so I don't recall hearing any objections at the time. No matter; it's water down the river. You must be hungry, Highness. Have
some supper."

In truth, the aroma from the tray was making Ashesa a little
giddy, but she eyed it with suspicion. Timon noticed the look.

"Be reasonable, Highness. Would I go to all this bother just to
poison you? And if I *were* in need of a virgin, there are certainly
others easier to hand than a Princess of the Blood, common
knowledge and barracks gossip not withstanding."

"You are a beast," she said.

"Red-eyed and howling every full moon. So I've heard."

Ashesa shrugged and sampled a beef pie. It was delicious. She
poured herself some wine as Timon dismissed his servant. He found
a chair and sat watching her, while she in turn glared at him between mouthfuls.

"Well?" she asked, finally. "Aren't you going to tell me why I'm
here?"

"You didn't ask, so I assumed you weren't interested. Pesky
things, assumptions," he said. "Let's see what others might be floating about, besides that silly misunderstanding about virginity . . .
Ransom? There's a common theme. Will I force your doting father
to surrender half his kingdom to save you?"

Ashesa took a sip of wine so he wouldn't see her smile. "No," she said from behind her goblet.

Timon looked genuinely surprised. "Why not?"

"Because we both know you wouldn't get it, break Father's heart though it would. And then there's all this . . ." She waved a capon leg at the room and furnishings. "That tapestry alone is of finer quality than my copy, and I *know* how much that one cost—poor Father nearly had a stroke. You obviously have great resources at your beck, Magician. That rules out any conventional ransom short of greed, and that's *one* sin I've never heard spoken of you. So. What do you want?"

There was open admiration in Timon's eyes. "You have an exceptional mind, Highness. It's really unfortunate that Daras will never allow you to use it. From what I've gathered of his philosophy, your duties will be to produce heirs and be ornamental at court."

"You seem to know a great deal about matters that don't concern you, Magician, but you still haven't answered my question. I wish you would because frankly I'm baffled. I hope for your sake it's more than a whim. They'll search for me, you know."

"And find you, too, since I was good enough to leave a note. I've also bought supplies openly; my location is common knowledge to half the hill crofters on the border. Diplomacy and protocol will delay your father, but Prince Daras will be along soon."

Ashesa was stunned. "Are you mad? As well to draw a map and have done!"

"No, Highness. I'm not mad, though it often seems so—even to me. But to avoid wearying you I'll speak plainly—I kidnapped you so that Prince Daras will try to rescue you. And he will try. His nature doesn't allow for any other option."

"But why—" Ashesa stopped. She knew. It was there for her to see in Timon's eyes.

"Quite right, Highness. I'm going to kill him."

The man Macol selected to watch Daras was a veteran: solid, trustworthy. A competent guard. Not a competent diplomat. The orders he had received in King Macol's throne room were quite beyond him.

"I want you to guard my son's quarters tonight," said King Riegar solemnly. "He is not to leave his room."

"But," added King Macol, "Prince Daras is an honored guest, not a prisoner. Treat him with respect."

Riegar nodded. "Certainly. But he may have it in his head to do something foolish. Use whatever force you must, within reason."

"But," again added Macol, "Prince Daras is heir to the throne of Borasur. He must on no account be harmed or you'll answer for it."

"Just keep him there," said Riegar.

"Without hurting or offending him," said Macol. "Now. Is all that clear?"

"Yes, Sire," the man lied. Later, as he stood at his post in the corridor, he placidly awaited the inevitable.

"Guard," Prince Daras called out, "lend some assistance in here, there's a good fellow."

The guard smiled and walked right in. The bump on his head was no less than he expected, and he was grateful for it. It seemed the simplest solution to a very complicated problem.

Princess Ashesa climbed the long spiral staircase to the top of Timon's fortress. Her hooded escort thumped along behind her like a child on stilts. Ashesa wasn't fooled. She'd stumbled once and the thing had snapped forward, supporting her, faster than she would have believed possible.

They passed several doors along the way. All unlocked, most empty, but Ashesa couldn't resist looking for something that might help her escape. One room was full of echoing voices in a language she didn't understand; another held a dark gray mist and she dared not enter. None of them contained anything useful.

Ashesa ran out of doors and stairs at about the same time. She and her golem escort stood on the parapet that wrapped around the outside off the highest level of the tower. The thin mountain wind whipped the golem's robes tight against its stick frame until it looked like a scarecrow flapping in a field. Ashesa looked over the railing and got a little dizzy.

"Too far to jump," said the wind.

Ashesa jumped anyway, but only a little. She didn't clear the railing.

The dwarf sat before a small canvas on the other side of the platform. He had changed his woodland green for an artist's smock stained with the remnants of an exploded rainbow. He concentrated on the canvas and painted with long smooth strokes, unperturbed by the gusts.

"That depends on your reason for jumping," returned Ashesa grimly.

The dwarf smiled, though he still wouldn't look at her. "A noble gesture, but it wouldn't keep Daras out of Timon's web even if he knew. Revenge has a longer pedigree than rescue."

"He's very certain of himself, your master."

"About some things," the dwarf agreed sadly. "He can't help it."

Ashesa considered a new tack. "How much is he paying you? Whatever your price, my father will meet it. Just help me escape and warn My Beloved Daras."

The dwarf cleaned one brush and selected another. "Would your father be willing to offer me the lucrative and entirely appropriate position of Court Fool?"

"Certainly!"

"Yes," the dwarf sighed. "I thought he might."

Ashesa frowned, and, even as she spoke the words, she wondered how many times they had passed her lips and her thoughts since the kidnapping. "I don't understand."

"My story is simple, Highness—my father sold me to a troupe of acrobats and thieves when I was seven. By twelve I was the best among them at both skills, but I still wore a cap and bells at every performance. Can you guess why?" He studied the canvas. "And when I couldn't abide that anymore I took to the streets on my own, and that's where Timon found me. We understood one another. Now he pays me with a little gold and a lot of hardship and aggravation, but part of the price is respect and an appreciation of my talents that totally ignores my height except when it's actually important. That's coin beyond your means, I'm afraid. Consider— we've been conversing for the better part of two minutes and you haven't even asked my name." He swirled the brush tip in a puddle of gold.

Ashesa stood in the presence of the man who'd kidnapped her, and yet for a moment she almost felt as if *he* were the injured party. It made her angry. "What is your name?"

He touched his cap and left a speck of gold there. "Seb, at your service," he said, making a quick dab at the canvas. "Up to a point."

"I'd like to know where that point is. Timon won't tell me why he plans to kill My Beloved Daras. Will you?"

"My Beloved . . . that's not what you were calling him during your little ride." Ashesa flushed but said nothing. Seb shrugged. "I know—it's the proper title for the betrothed and you do know your duty, even if you don't like it. So. Why not 'to prevent the marriage'? You suggested it yourself, Timon says."

The princess shook her head. "If he merely wanted that, killing me would have worked as well and been a lot less bother. I don't flatter myself by thinking he'd have hesitated."

"He wouldn't," confirmed Seb, "though it would grieve him bitterly. As it will when Daras is killed."

"But *why?* Why does Daras deserve to die?"

Seb smiled ruefully. "That's the saddest part. He doesn't. At least not in the sense of anything he's done. It's who he is, and what he is, and what that combination will make him do when the time comes. It's all here, Highness, if you care to look."

Seb moved to one side so she could see the canvas. Ashesa's mouth fell open in surprise when she recognized the portrait. It was Daras, mounted and armored in an archaic pattern. He held his helmet under one arm, his lance pointed to the sky.

"It's lovely," she said honestly, "but why the old armor?"

"That's the armor of the time of the Lyrsan wars. When the

folk of the Western Deserts pushed east against the Seven King-doms. That's when Daras should have lived. That was a time for heroes."

"Daras isn't a hero," Ashesa snapped. "That takes more than winning tournaments."

"More even than rescuing one princess," the dwarf agreed. "It's rather a full-time pursuit. It might even take, say, a long bloody war with Wylandia."

Ashesa put her hands on her hips. "Do you really expect me to believe that Daras would start a war just so he can be a hero?"

"He wouldn't be starting it, to his way of thinking. But the seeds are already there: real intrigues, imagined insults . . . mistrust. All waiting to take root in his mind until he firmly believes that Wylandia struck first. You see, Daras is already a hero in many ways. He's seen the soul of it in his brother's stories, and in that he sees himself. And why not? He's brave, strong, skilled in warlike pursuits and in no other. All he lacks to make his destiny complete is the one vital ingredient—need. If the need is not there, he will create it. He has no choice. And neither do we."

Most of the blood had deserted Ashesa's face, and she trem-bled. "You can't be sure! And even if you were, what right—"

"Timon is sure," interrupted Seb calmly. "It's his greatest power, and greatest curse. He knows, and he can't escape the responsibil-ity of knowing. That gives him the right."

"I . . . don't . . . believe . . . you!" Ashesa spat out each word like something foul.

Seb smiled. "Oh, yes, you do. More than you'd like, anyway. Far better to see this tale as history no doubt will—a foul crime done by foul folk. Forgive me, Highness, but I'm not as kind as Timon and see no reason why this should be any easier on you than the rest of us."

Ashesa's hands turned into fists, and she took a step toward the dwarf. In an instant the golem was between her and Seb, and the dwarf hadn't even blinked. Ashesa took several deep, calming breaths, and after a moment the golem moved aside. Ashesa groped for some shred of sweet reason to pull her thoughts out of the pit. "But . . . but Daras can't start a war on his own! Only the king can do that! Even if what you say is true, there's still time . . ."

While she spoke Seb made several deft strokes on the canvas, and when she saw what the dwarf had painted there her words sank into nothing.

"Time has run out, Highness. King Riegar—rest him—died in his sleep last night."

In the portrait, Daras wore the plain golden crown of Borasur.

Prince Daras had never been on a quest before and wasn't quite sure what to expect, but at least the scenery felt right—it was wild and strange. The forest that bordered the mountain foothills was very different from the tilting fields and well-groomed game parks he was accustomed to: the grass grew high and razor-edged, brambles clawed at his armored legs, and trees took root and reached for the sunlight wherever the notion took them. Daras stepped his charger through a tortured, twisty path, and when an arrow hummed out of the trees and twanged off his armor, that, too, seemed as it should be.

"Hah! Villains! At you!"

Daras spurred forward along the arrow's course as if his mount was as armored as he was. The second arrow showed that notion in error; Daras barely cleared the stirrups before the poor beast went down kicking. Another instant and he was among them.

They were men, of course. Forest bandits with no other skill and without enough sense to avoid a victim armed in proof. None of that mattered once the attack began. They were bodies attached to swords, meat in ragged clothes for the blooding, characters in a play of which Daras was the lead, existing only for their cue to dance a few steps and then die. It wasn't how he thought it would be; it wasn't horrible. Daras never saw their faces, never noticed their pain as he turned clumsy blows and struck sure ones, killing with the mad joy of a newfound sport. When it was over it was as if they had never lived at all.

Rather like a tournament, only they don't get up.

After the last bandit fell, Daras, catlike, lost interest. He cleaned his sword on a dead man's tunic, had a sip or two of weak wine, then resumed his quest on foot, whistling.

Ashesa didn't know what was different at first that morning. She only knew that *something* was not right. After a few moments she was awake enough to notice what was missing. Her clothes. The mantle and overdress she had laid out on the table the night before weren't there. In their place were two rather ethereal strips of cloth appliquéd with crescents and stars and glyphs of a rather suggestive nature.

Timon sat in her chair, looking unhappy.

"Magician, where are my clothes?"

He waved his hand at the table. "There, I'm afraid. It's the traditional sacrificial garb of an obscure fertility cult. You wouldn't have heard of it."

"And you're one of them?" she asked, as calmly as she could manage.

He shuddered delicately. "Certainly not. But as much as the prospect would delight *me*, I don't think Daras expects to burst in and find us discussing literature over a cup of tea. I had to come up with something suitably dreadful for you to be saved from. Think of it as a play, Highness. This is your costume for the final act."

Ashesa eyed the flimsy cloth with distaste. "Uninspired as this may sound—suppose I refuse?"

He shrugged. "I can't *force* you to wear it—it tears too easily—but bear in mind that you stretched out on the altar in all your natural glory would suit the play as well . . . no, better. I considered it, believe me. But clothed or no, you will play your part. You have no choice."

Ashesa, bedclothes wrapped tightly about her, gathered up the scanty garments. "I'm getting terribly weary of that catechism, Master Timon. Pray, is there any esoteric reason why I cannot at least get dressed in private?"

Timon looked even more unhappy. "Unfortunately, no."

* * *

Prince Daras hid behind a boulder and studied the gate. It was strongly built with oak posts set into the narrowest point of what was already a knife slash of a valley. Two robed guards stood outside, halberds crossed. Daras idly pulled at a chafing armor strap as he pondered a sigil carved into the gate. Just like the one on the kidnapper's note. Timon the Black, no question. Beyond the gate a tower rose on a rocky ridge above the valley.

Careless or arrogant?

The sigil was as good as an announcement; Daras couldn't decide what it meant, so he decided it didn't matter.

The prince sat with his back to the stone and considered. There was no way around the gate, nor could he climb the valley walls without being seen. The two guards at the gate had to be overpowered without raising an alarm, and he might have to scale the wall if neither had a key . . . There was cover—rocks and brush—until about ten yards from the guard post. *If* he could reach it unseen.

And unheard.

Slowly, reluctantly, Prince Daras began removing his armor.

"Ready, Highness?"

Ashesa studied her reflection, trying to arrange the material of her costume as efficiently as possible. The effect was dramatic despite her best efforts. She gave up. "Yes, damn you to hell."

Timon entered the room with two of his golem guards. The magician, damn him again, smiled at her. "Follow us, please."

He took her arm and led her down the corridor to the staircase, then around and down the spiral to ground level and out. They moved single file down a narrow path to the valley floor, golems in front and behind her, with Timon bringing up the rear. A single wall cut them off from the rest of the valley, and before that was a very suspicious-looking stone flanked by two upright stones of dark granite. A smaller building of stone blocks sat on the opposite side. Closer, Ashesa's fears were confirmed: the building was a small temple with a narrow oval doorway, the flat stone a massive altar with shackles bolted to the four corners.

Ashesa's mouth was suddenly dry. "You said you weren't a member of the cult."

"Props, Highness. Nothing more."

The golems led her to the altar. There was a stepping block to help her climb, and the top was smooth except for a groove cut for—she supposed—her heart's blood. Ashesa looked at the altar, then the guards. Their weapons gleamed brightly in the morning sun, but one held his a little farther away from his body. Ashesa judged the distance and her chances, but she made the mistake of glancing at Timon. His smile hadn't changed a whit, but there was a new and very clear message in his eyes.

Don't.

Ashesa lay down reluctantly and let the twig-fingered guards shackle her to the cold stone. As the last manacle clicked into place she heard a yelp like a hunting horn cut off in mid-note. Timon wasn't smiling now. There was something like worry on his face, perhaps even a touch of fear. Ashesa couldn't have imagined that a moment before.

"Daras is early . . . I'd better hurry and get into *my* costume, Highness. Won't be a moment."

The magician hurried off into the temple, leaving Ashesa alone with the golems. There was a commotion at the gate and Ashesa turned her head to look just as the gate burst open and something very much like brown rag sailed through, cartwheeling end over end to smash against the stones. Prince Daras of Borasur strode through.

His entrance made Ashesa skip a breath; she'd forgotten how handsome he was, but that wasn't all of it—a glory seemed to shine around him, like a saint etched in stained glass. He saw her then and rushed forward, all smooth motion and mad joy.

And this is what Timon wants to destroy.

She heard Timon but could not see him. "Stop him, my Pets!"

The golems set their halberds and charged. Ashesa finally recovered her wits. "Flee, My Beloved! It's a trap!"

Daras, of course, did nothing of the sort. He veered to the right and a golem's headlong rush carried it past. Daras struck a trailing blow without breaking stride and the golem's clay head exploded.

Ashesa watched, horrified but unable to look away. There was a battlelight on Daras's face, and his eyes were bright and wild. Ashesa's breath skipped a second time.

He's enjoying this!

The truth of it was like a cold slap in the face. It wasn't the rescue. It wasn't even herself as anything but an excuse. The prince was consumed with a mad ecstasy born of the clash of weapons and pleasure in his skill. He destroyed golems. He would destroy men with as little thought and the same wild joy. Ashesa tried not to think anymore, but it was a torrent held too long in check and the dams were breaking.

This is what Timon wants to destroy . . .

The second golem thrust past Daras's parry by brute force and the prince twisted his body like an acrobat. The halberd merely sliced a thin red line across the front of Daras's tunic, and the prince's return stroke left the golem broken and still.

A voice issued from the temple. It was Timon, and it wasn't Timon—it boomed like thunder across the valley. "Now you must die!"

Ashesa strained to turn her head and saw Timon step out of the shadows of the temple. He wore a robe decorated with glyphs like the ones on Ashesa's costume, and in his gloved hands he carried a long curved knife. It glowed with a blue balefire that still could not penetrate the blackness under Timon's hood.

Prince Daras studied the magician's knife, then looked at his own sword. Grinning, he dropped the sword and pulled his own long dagger. Ashesa wanted to scream but nothing came out—it was as if an invisible hand clapped itself over her mouth.

The fool, she thought wildly, *the bloody, senseless fool!*

What happened next was filled with terrible beauty. Daras charged the magician, and this time it was Timon who danced aside to let Daras hurtle past like a maddened bull. Timon's blade flicked out and then there was another line of red on the prince's chest. Daras snarled like a *berserk*, but kept some caution as he stopped himself and slowly circled, looking for an opening. Timon kept just out of reach, reacting with a speed Ashesa wouldn't have expected of him. The glow on Daras's face built to new heights of rapture, as if the magician's surprising skill fanned it like the bellows of a forge.

It was like the sword dance Ashesa had seen performed at her father's court—the flash of steel always averted, always eluded as if it *was* nothing more than a dance for her amusement instead of a fight to the death. Timon's knife traced its path through the air like a lightning flash, and Daras's dagger slashed and hummed in a silvered blur.

Then everything changed.

Timon broke from the fight and sprinted toward the altar. "The sacrifice must be made!"

What?

The wizard hurtled toward her, his knife burning away the distance to her heart. Ashesa closed her eyes.

Someone screamed and Ashesa opened her eyes again, surprised. She had meant to scream but never really managed. *Who?*

Timon. He lay sprawled at the foot of the altar, Daras's weapon buried almost to the hilt in his back. Bright, impossibly red blood oozed from around the steel. Ashesa felt a little sick, a lot relieved and a bit . . . well, guilty. Guilty for wondering why Timon's trap had failed, and for wondering—just for an instant—if it should have failed. And why the mad dash to the altar? Unless Timon had lied to her . . .

Prince Daras grinned down at her, his chest heaving like a bellows. "Did—did you see that throw?" he chortled. "Thirty paces, easily . . ." Daras seemed to forget about the throw all at once, as he got his first good look at Ashesa. The grin turned into something else.

Ashesa shivered. "For the love of heaven, stop staring and get me loose! There may be more of them."

"You're in no danger now, My Beloved Ashesa," Daras said, placing a hand on her bare shoulder. "And first thing's first."

"Get me loose." Ashesa repeated, all sweet reason. "We have to get away from here."

Daras nodded. "In time. His lackey today, Aldair himself tomorrow. That's the order of business. Right now there are other matters to attend to."

Ashesa spoke very clearly, very urgently. "You're wrong, Beloved. Wylandia had nothing to do with this. I must tell you—" She stopped. Daras's hand had departed her shoulder for a more southerly location. "What are you doing?!"

He looked a little surprised at her attitude. "That 'other matter' I mentioned. Surely you know that tradition demands a price for your rescue?"

"We're not married yet, Beloved," Ashesa pointed out.

Daras shrugged. "A rescue is a separate matter altogether, with its own traditions and duties. Binding, too. I'm afraid we don't have any choice."

That word.

It wasn't the act that Daras demanded, or even her feelings about Daras himself that mattered in what came next. It was the one word Daras had used. That made all the difference.

Sometimes, in those dark hours between waking and sleeping, when night closes in and the sound of their own heartbeats is much too clear, people have been known to wonder how close to the edge of the abyss they dwelled, and what it would take to push them over. In that moment, strapped to an altar under a warming sun, Ashesa became one of the lucky ones. That question would never trouble her again.

She looked at a soft patch of grass nearby, perfect for paying her debt. Very close to where Timon's dagger had fallen to lie mostly hidden. Yes, it was perfect.

"Free me," she said, "and you'll have your reward."

Ashesa leaned on the altar, trying to clear away a red haze from her mind. She tried not to look at Daras's body, tried not to remember the stunned surprise on his face before all expression ceased. Ashesa pulled herself around the stone until she came to

Timon's limp form, then her mouth set in a grim smile and she yanked the robes aside.

The blood came from a punctured animal bladder, and the stick skeleton was dappled with thick, blackening drops.

"Damn you!"

Timon stepped out of the temple again, but this time it was really him. Ashesa glared at him and all the world behind. "No one will believe you," she said, pale as snow and twice as cold.

Timon obviously considered the suggestion in questionable taste. "Did *I* suggest such a thing? No, Highness. But they will believe *you* as you relate—tearfully, I advise—how Daras fell in the rescue, slaying the fiend and freeing you with the strength of his dying breath. Will I spurt green ichor? I should think I would."

"I saw the fight—the real fight—while it lasted. Daras was good, but your golem could have killed him easily!" she accused. "But you knew I . . ." She couldn't finish it.

"What a mind," repeated Timon with deeper admiration. "And what you say is partly true, Highness. Once Daras took the bait he was finished, one way or another. For your sake take comfort—you can't kill a dead man. But I was curious about you, I admit it. Not everyone has the talent for knowing what must be done *when* it must be done. No, Highness. I didn't know. Add another sin to my head because I wanted to find out."

Ashesa saw the dwarf, Seb, coming down the mountain path. He led two horses packed for travel and two more saddled to ride, and he played out a grayish cord behind him from a large spool mounted on a stick.

"A few matters to attend, Highness," Timon said. "The first involves something new in the art of destruction. I think you'll be seeing it again." He nodded and Seb struck a flint to the cord. It sizzled with life and burned its way back to the tower. In a moment there was a dull roar and the earth trembled. The tower swayed on its foundation and then collapsed. Flames licked the exposed beams and flooring and soon the whole thing was burning merrily.

Ashesa stared. *Heavens.*

Timon pulled a vial from his robe and poured an acrid black

liquid on the golem. There was an instantaneous, nauseating stench and the cloth, wood, leather, and blood all hissed and bubbled and melted into a smoking mass.

Seb stared at the remnants of the tower wistfully. Timon laid a hand on his shoulder. "Sorry, but you knew it was only temporary. My magic would have to die with me. Expectations, you know." He turned back to Ashesa. "As cruel as assumptions in their way. They killed Daras as surely as we did."

"What about me?" Ashesa asked dully.

"Don't worry. If you'll wait here, I've no doubt that King Aldair and Prince Galan will follow the beacon of flames right to you, combining against the common foe under the push of a father's love. Have you met young Galan, by the way? A kind, intelligent lad by all report, though given to idle dreaming. Who can say? With a firm hand to guide him he might even make a king."

Seb handed Ashesa a cloak. "Master, we'd best be going."

They mounted and rode out the gate without a backward glance. Ashesa gathered the cloak about her and settled down to wait. As she waited, she thought about Timon, and Daras, and herself. Maybe she would talk to her father about Galan. Maybe. They would still want the alliance, but that didn't matter just then. She would meet Galan again, and she would decide. *She* would decide. Her father, whether he realized it or not, would just go along. She didn't really understand what was different now, but something was, and it wasn't because of her crime as such. It just came down to choice. Once you knew it existed there was no end to it. And no escape from it either.

Forgive me, Beloved, but Seb was right—this isn't a time for heroes.

Still, the Age that couldn't profit from a clever, determined princess had never dawned.

The Cup and the Cauldron

❖

Mercedes Lackey

ain leaked through the thatch of the hen-house; the same dank, cold rain that had been falling for weeks, ever since the snow melted. It dripped on the back of her neck and down under her smock. Though it was nearly dusk, Elfrida checked the nests one more time, hoping that one of the scrawny, ill-tempered hens might have been persuaded, by a miracle or sheer perversity, to drop an egg. But as she had expected, the nests were empty, and the hens resisted with natsy jabs of their beaks her attempts at investigation. They'd gotten quite adept at fighting, competing with and chasing away the crows who came to steal their scant feed over the winter. She came away from the hen-house with an empty apron and scratched and bleeding hands.

Nor was there remedy waiting for her in the cottage, even for that. The little salve they had must be hoarded against greater need than hers.

Old Mag, the village healer and Elfrida's teacher, looked up from the tiny fire burning in the pit in the center of the dirt-floored cottage's single room. At least the thatch here was sound, though rain dripped in through the smoke-hole, and the fire didn't seem to be warming the place any. Elfrida coughed on the smoke, which persisted in staying inside, rather than rising through the smoke-hole as it should.

Mag's eyes had gotten worse over the winter, and the cottage was very dark with the shutters closed. "No eggs?" she asked, peering across the room, as Elfrida let the cowhide down across the cottage door.

"None," Elfrida replied, sighing. "This spring—if it's this bad now, what will summer be like?"

She squatted down beside Mag, and took the share of barley-bread the old woman offered, with a crude wooden cup of bitter-tasting herb tea dipped out of the kettle beside the fire.

"I don't know," Mag replied, rubbing her eyes—Mag, who had been tall and straight with health last summer, who was now bent and aching, with swollen joints and rheumy eyes. Neither willow-bark nor eyebright helped her much. "Lady bless, darling, I don't know. First that killing frost, then nothing but rain—seems like what seedlings the frost didn't get, must've rotted in the fields by now. Hens aren't laying, lambs are born dead, pigs lay on their own young . . . what we're going to do for food come winter, I've no notion."

When Mag said "we," she meant the whole village. She was not only their healer, but their priestess of the Old Way. Garth might be hetman, but she was the village's heart and soul—as Elfrida expected to be one day. This was something she had chosen, knowing the work and self-sacrifice involved, knowing that the enmity of the priests of the White Christ might fall upon her. But not for a long time—Lady grant.

That was what she had always thought, but now the heart and soul of the village was sickening, as the village around her sickened. But why?

"We made the proper sacrifices," Elfrida said, finally. "Didn't we? What've we done or not done that the land turns against us?"

Mag didn't answer, but there was a quality in her silence that made Elfrida think that the old woman knew something—something important. Something that she hadn't yet told her pupil.

Finally, as darkness fell, and the fire burned down to coals, Mag spoke.

"We made the sacrifices," she said. "But there was one—who didn't."

"Who?" Elfrida asked, surprised. The entire village followed the Old Way—never mind the High King and his religion of the White Christ. That was for knights and nobles and suchlike. Her people stuck by what they knew best, the turning of the seasons, the dance of the Maiden, Mother and Crone, the rule of the Horned Lord. And if anyone in the village had neglected their sacrifices, surely she or Mag would have known!

"It isn't just our village that's sickening," Mag said, her voice a hoarse, harsh whisper out of the dark. "Nor the county alone. I've talked to the other Wise Ones, to the peddlers—I talked to the crows and the owls and ravens. It's the whole land that's sickening, failing—and there's only one sacrifice can save the land."

Elfrida felt her mouth go dry, and took a sip of her cold, bitter tea to wet it. "The blood of the High King," she whispered.

"Which he will not shed, come as he is to the feet of the White Christ." Mag shook her head. "My dear, my darling girl, I'd hoped the Lady wouldn't lay this on us . . . I'd prayed she wouldn't punish us for his neglect. But 'tisn't punishment, not really, and I should've known better than to hope it wouldn't come. Whether he believes it or not, the High King is tied to the land, and Arthur is old and failing. As he fails, the land fails."

"But—surely there's something we can do?" Elfrida said timidly into the darkness.

Mag stirred. "If there is, I haven't been granted the answer," she said, pausing as she spoke. "But perhaps—you've had Lady-dreams before, 'twas what led you to me . . ."

"You want me to try for a vision?" Elfrida's mouth dried again, but this time no amount of tea would soothe it, for it was dry from fear. For all that she had true visions, when she sought them, the experience frightened her. And no amount of soothing on Mag's part, or encouragement that the—things—she saw in the dark waiting for her soul's protection to waver could not touch her, could ever ease that fear.

But weighed against her fear was the very real possibility that the village might not survive the next winter. If she was worthy to be Mag's successor, she must dare her fear, and dare the dreams, and see if the Lady had an answer for them since High King Arthur did not. The land and the people needed her and she must answer that need.

"I'll try," she whispered, and Mag touched her lightly on the arm.

"That's my good and brave girl," she said. "I knew you wouldn't fail us." Something on Mag's side of the fire rustled, and she handed Elfrida a folded leaf full of dried herbs.

They weren't what the ignorant thought; herbs to bring visions. The visions came when Elfrida asked for them—these were to strengthen and guard her while her spirit rode the night winds, in search of answers. Foxglove to strengthen her heart, moly to shield her soul, a dozen others, a scant pinch of each.

Obediently, she placed them under her tongue, and while Mag chanted the names of the Goddess, Elfrida closed her eyes, and released her all-too-fragile hold on her body.

The convent garden was sodden, the ground turning to mush, and unless someone did something about it, there would be nothing to eat this summer but what the tithes brought and the King's Grace granted them. Outside the convent walls, the fields were just as sodden; so, as the Mother Superior said, "A tithe of nothing is still nothing, and we must prepare to feed ourselves." Leonie sighed, and leaned a little harder on the spade, being careful where she put each spadeful of earth. Behind the spade, the drainage trench she was digging between each row of drooping pea-seedlings filled with water. Hopefully, this would be enough to keep them from rotting. Hopefully, there would be enough to share. Already the eyes of the children stared at her from faces pinched and hungry when they came to the convent for Mass, and she hid the bread that was half her meal to give to them.

Her gown was as sodden as the ground; cold and heavy with water, and only the fact that it was made of good wool kept it from chilling her. Her bare feet, ankle-deep in mud, felt like blocks of stone, they were so cold. She had kirtled her gown high to keep the hem from getting muddied, but that only let the wind get at her legs. Her hair was so soaked that she had not even bothered with the linen veil of a novice; it would only have flapped around without protecting her head and neck any. Her hands hurt; she wasn't used to this.

The other novices, gently born and not, were desperately doing the same in other parts of the garden. Those that could, rather; some of the gently-born were too ill to come out into the soaking, cold rain. The sisters, as many as were able, were outside the walls, helping a few of the local peasants dig a larger ditch down to the swollen stream. The trenches in the convent garden would lead to it—and so would the trenches being dug in the peasants' gardens, on the other side of the high stone wall.

"We must work together," Mother Superior had said firmly, and so here they were, knight's daughter and villain's son, robes and tunics kirtled up above the knee, wielding shovels with a will. Leonie had never thought to see it.

But the threat of hunger made strange bedfellows. Already the convent had turned out to help the villagers trench their kitchen gardens. Leonie wondered what the village folk would do about the fields too large to trench, or fields of hay? It would be a cold summer, and a lean winter.

What had gone wrong with the land? It was said that the weather had been unseasonable and miserable all over the kingdom. Nor was the weather all that had gone wrong; it was said there was quarreling at High King Arthur's court; that the knights were moved to fighting for its own sake, and had brought their leman openly to many court gatherings, to the shame of the ladies. It was said that the Queen herself—

But Leonie did not want to hear such things, or even think of them. It was all of a piece, anyway; the knights fighting among themselves, the killing frosts and rain that wouldn't end, the threat of war at the borders, raiders and bandits within, and the starvation and plague hovering over all.

Something was deeply, terribly wrong.

She considered that, as she dug her little trenches, as she returned to the convent to wash her dirty hands and feet and change into a drier gown, as she nibbled her meager supper, trying to make it last, and as she went in to Vespers with the rest.

Something was terribly, deeply wrong.

When Mother Superior approached her after Vespers, she somehow knew that her feeling of *wrongness* and what the head of the convent was about to ask were linked.

"Leonie," Mother Superior said, once the other novices had filed away, back to their beds, "when your family sent you here, they told me it was because you had visions."

Leonie ducked her head and stared at her sandals. "Yes, Mother Magdalene."

"And I asked you not to talk about those visions in any way," the nun persisted. "Not to any of the other novices, not to any of the sisters, not to Father Peregrine."

"Yes, Mother Magdalene—I mean, no Mother Magdalene." Leonie looked up, flushing with anger. "I mean, I haven't."

She knew why the nun had ordered her to keep silence on the subject; she'd heard the lecture to her parents through the door. The Mother Superior didn't believe in Leonie's visions—or rather, she was not convinced that they were really visions. "This could simply be a young woman's hysteria," she'd said sternly, "or an attempt to get attention. If the former, the peace of the convent and the meditation and prayer will cure her quickly enough—if the latter, well, she'll lose such notions of self-importance when she has no one to prate to."

"I know you haven't, child," Mother Magdalene said wearily, and Leonie saw how the nun's hands were blistered from the spade she herself had wielded today, how her knuckles were swollen, and her cheekbones cast into a prominence that had nothing to do with the dim lighting in the chapel. "I wanted to know if you still have them."

"Sometimes," Leonie said hesitantly. "That was how—I mean, that was why I woke last winter, when Sister Maria was elf-shot—"

"Sister Maria was not elf-shot," Mother Magdalene said automatically. "Elves could do no harm to one who trusts in God. It was simply something that happens to the very old, now and again; it is a kind of sudden brain-fever. But that isn't the point. You're still having the visions—but can you still see things that you want to see?"

"Sometimes," Leonie said cautiously. "If God and the Blessed Virgin permit."

"Well, if God is ever going to permit it, I suspect He'd do so during Holy Week," Mother Magdalene sighed. "Leonie, I am going to ask you a favor. I'd like you to make a vigil tonight."

"And ask for a vision?" Leonie said, raising her head in sudden interest.

"Precisely." The nun shook her head, and picked up her beads, telling them through her fingers as she often did when nervous. "There is something wrong with us, with the land, with the kingdom—I want you to see if God will grant you a vision of what." As Leonie felt a sudden upsurge of pride, Mother Magdalene added hastily, "You aren't the only one being asked to do this—every order from one end of the kingdom to the other has been asked for visions from their members. I thought long and hard about asking this. But you are the only one in my convent who has ever had a tendency to visions."

The Mother Superior had been about to say something else, Leonie was sure, for the practical and pragmatic Mother Magdalene had made her feelings on the subject of mysticism quite clear over the years. But that didn't matter—what did matter was that she was finally going to be able to release that pent-up power again, to soar on the angels' wings. Never mind that there were as many devils "out there" as angels; her angels would protect her, for they always had, and always would.

Without another word, she knelt on the cold stone before the altar, fixed her eyes on the bright little gilded cross above it, and released her soul's hold on her body.

"What did you see?" Mag asked, as Elfrida came back, shivering and spent, to consciousness. Her body was lying on the ground beside the fire, and it felt too tight, like a garment that didn't fit anymore—but she was glad enough to be in it again, for there had been *thousands* of those evil creatures waiting for her, trying to prevent her from reaching . . .

"The Cauldron," she murmured, sitting up slowly, one hand on her aching head. "There was a Cauldron. . . ."

"Of course!" Mag breathed. "The Cauldron of the Goddess! But—" It was too dark for Elfrida to see Mag, other than as a shadow in the darkness, but she somehow felt Mag's searching eyes. "What about the Cauldron? When is it coming back? Who's to have it? Not the High King, surely—"

"I'm—supposed to go look for it," Elfrida said, vaguely. "That's what They said—I'm supposed to go look for it."

Mag's sharp intake of breath told her of Mag's shock. "But— no, I know you, when you come out of this," she muttered, almost as if to herself. "You can't lie. If you say They said for you to go, then go you must."

Elfrida wanted to say something else, to ask what it all meant, but she couldn't. The vision had taken too much out of her, and she was whirled away a second time, but this time it was not on the winds of vision, but into the arms of exhausted sleep.

"What did you see?" Mother Superior asked urgently.

Leonie found herself lying on the cold stone before the altar, wrapped in someone's cloak, with something pillowed under her head. She felt very peaceful, as she always did when the visions released her, and very, very tired. There had been many demons out there, but as always, her angels had protected her. Still, she was glad to be back. There had never been quite so many of the evil things there before, and they had frightened her.

She had to blink a few times, as she gathered her memories

and tried to make sense of them. "A cup," she said, hesitantly—then her eyes fell upon the Communion chalice on the altar, and they widened as she realized just what she truly had seen. "No—not *a* cup, *the* Cup! We're to seek the Grail! That's what They told me!"

"The Grail?" Mother Magdalene's eyes widened a little themselves, and she crossed herself hastily. "Just before you—you dropped over, you reached out. I thought I saw—I thought I saw something faint, like a ghost of a glowing cup in your hands."

Leonie nodded, her cheek against the rough homespun of the habit bundled under her head. "They said that to save the kingdom, we have to seek the Grail."

"We?" Mother Magdalene said, doubtfully. "Surely you don't mean—"

"The High King's knights and squires, some clergy and—me—" Leonie's voice trailed off, as she realized what she was saying. "They said the knights will know already and that when you hear about it from Camelot, you'll know I was speaking the truth. But I don't *want* to go!" she wailed. "I don't! I—"

"I'm convinced of the truth now," the nun said. "Just by the fact that you don't want to go. If this had been a sham, to get attention, you'd have demanded special treatment, to be cosseted and made much of, not to be sent off on your own."

"But—" Leonie protested frantically, trying to hold off unconsciousness long enough to save herself from this exile.

"Never mind," the Mother Superior said firmly. "We'll wait for word from Camelot. When we hear it, then you'll go."

Leonie would have protested further, but Mother Magdalene laid a cool hand across her hot eyes, and sleep came up and took her.

Elfrida had never been this far from her home village before. The great forest through which she had been walking for most of the day did not look in the least familiar. In fact, it did not look like anything anyone from the village had ever described.

And why hadn't Mag brought her here to gather healing herbs

and mushrooms? The answer seemed clear enough; she was no longer in lands Mag or any of the villagers had ever seen.

She had not known which way to go, so she had followed the raven she saw flying away from the village. The raven had led her to the edge of the woods, which at the time had seemed quite ordinary. But the oaks and beeches had turned to a thick growth of fir; the deeper she went, the older the trees became, until at last she was walking on a tiny path between huge trunks that rose far over her head before properly branching out. Beneath those spreading branches, thin, twiggy growth reached out skeletal fingers like blackened bones, while the upper branches cut off most of the light, leaving the trail beneath shrouded in a twilight gloom, though it was midday.

Though she was on a quest of sorts, that did not mean she had left her good sense behind. While she was within the beech and oak forest, she had gleaned what she could on either side of the track. Her pack now held two double-handfuls each of acorns and beechnuts, still sound, and a few mushrooms. Two here, three or four there, they added up.

It was just as well, for the meager supply of journey-bread she had with her had been all given away by the end of the first day of her quest. A piece at a time, to a child here, a nursing mother there . . . but she had the freedom of the road and the forest; the people she encountered were tied to their land and could not leave it. Not while there was any chance they might coax a crop from it.

They feared the forest, though they could not tell Elfrida why. They would only enter the fringes of it, to feed their pigs on acorns, to pick up deadfall. Further than that, they would not go.

Elfrida had known for a long time that she was not as magical as Mag. She had her visions, but that was all; she could not see the power rising in the circles, although she knew it was there, and could sometimes feel it. She could not see the halos of light around people that told Mag if they were sick or well. She had no knowledge of the future outside of her visions, and could not talk to the birds and animals as Mag could.

So she was not in the least surprised to find that she could sense nothing about the forest that indicated either good or ill. If there was something here, she could not sense it. Of course, the gloom of the fir-forest was more than enough to frighten anyone with any imagination. And while nobles often claimed peasants had no more imagination than a block of wood—well, Elfrida often thought that nobles had no more sense than one of their high-bred, high-strung horses, that would break legs, shying at shadows. Witless, useless—and irresponsible. How many of them were on their lands, helping their liegemen and peasants to save their crops? Few enough; most were idling their time away at the High King's Court, gambling, drinking, wenching, playing at tourneys and other useless pastimes. And she would wager that the High King's table was not empty; that the nobles' children were not going pinch-faced and hungry to bed. The religion of the White Christ had divorced master from man, noble from villager, making the former into a master in truth, and the latter into an income-producing slave. The villager was told by his priest to trust in God and receive his reward in heaven. The lord need feel no responsibility for any evils he did or caused, for once they had been confessed and paid for—usually by a generous gift to the priest—his God counted them as erased. The balance of duty and responsibility between the vassal and his lord was gone.

She shook off her bitter thoughts as nightfall approached. Without Mag's extra abilities Elfrida knew she would have to be twice as careful about spending the night in this place. If there were supernatural terrors about, she would never know until they were on her. So when she made her little camp, she cast circles around her with salt and iron, betony and rue, writing the runes as clear as she could, before she lit her fire to roast her nuts.

But in the end, when terror came upon her, it was of a perfectly natural sort.

Leonie cowered, and tried to hide in the folds of her robe. Her bruised face ached, and her bound wrists were cut and swollen around the thin twine the man who had caught her had used to bind her.

She had not gotten more than two days away from the convent—distributing most of her food to children and the sick as she walked—when she had reached the edge of the forest, and her vague visions had directed her to follow the path through it. She had seen no signs of people, nor had she sensed anything about the place that would have caused folk to avoid it. That had puzzled her, so she had dropped into a walking trance to try and sort out what kind of a place the forest was.

That was when someone had come up behind her and hit her on the head.

Now she knew why ordinary folk avoided the forest; it was the home of bandits. And she knew what her fate was going to be. Only the strength of the hold the chieftain had over his men had kept her from that fate until now. He had decreed that they would wait until all the men were back from their errands—and then they would draw lots for their turns at her. . . .

Leonie was so terrified that she was beyond thought; she huddled like a witless rabbit inside her robe and prayed for death.

"What's *this?*" the bandit chief said, loudly, startling her so that she raised her head out of the folds of her sleeves. She saw nothing at first; only the dark bulking shapes of men against the fire in their midst. He laughed, long and hard, as another of his men entered their little clearing, shoving someone in front of him. "By Satan's arse! The woods are sprouting wenches!"

Elfrida caught her breath at the curse; so, these men were not "just" bandits—they were the worst kind of bandit, nobles gone beyond the law. Only one who was once a follower of the White Christ would have used his adversary's name as an exclamation. No follower of the Old Way, either Moon or Blood-path, would have done so.

The brigand who had captured her shoved her over to land beside another girl—and once again she caught her breath, as her talisman-bag swung loose on its cord, and the other girl shrunk away, revealing the wooden beads and cross at the rope that served her as a belt. Worse and worse—the girl wore the robes of one who had vowed herself to the White Christ! There would be no help there . . . if she were not witless before she had been caught, she was probably frightened witless now. Even if she would accept help from the hands of a "pagan."

Leonie tried not to show her hope. Another girl! Perhaps between the two of them, they could manage to win freedom!

But as the girl was shoved forward, to drop to the needles beside Leonie, something swung free of her robe to dangle over her chest. It was a little bag, on a rawhide thong.

And the bandit chief roared again, this time with disapproval, seizing the bag and breaking the thong with a single, cruelly hard tug of his hand. He tossed it out into the darkness and backhanded the outlaw who had brought the girl in.

"You witless bastard!" he roared. "You brought in a witch!"

A *witch?*

Leonie shrunk away from her fellow captive. A witch? Blessed Jesu—this young woman would be just as pleased to see Leonie raped to death! She would probably call up one of her demons to help!

As the brigand who had been struck shouted and went for his chief's throat, and the others gathered around, yelling encouragement and placing bets, she closed her eyes, bowed her head, and prayed. *Blessed Mother of God, hear me. Angels of grace, defend us. Make them forget us for just a moment. . . .*

As the brainless child started in fear, then pulled away, bowed her head, and began praying, Elfrida kept a heavy hand on her temper. Bad enough that she was going to die—and in a particularly horrible way—but to have to do it in such company!

But—suddenly the outlaws were fighting. One of them appeared to be the chief; the other the one who had caught her. And they were ignoring the two girls as if they had somehow forgotten their existence. . . .

Blessed Mother, hear me. Make it so.

The man had only tied her with a bit of leather, no stronger than the thong that had held her herb-bag. If she wriggled just right, bracing her tied hands against her feet, she could probably snap it.

She prayed, and pulled. And was rewarded with the welcome release of pressure as the thong snapped.

She brought her hands in front of her, hiding them in her tunic, and looked up quickly; the fight had involved a couple more of the bandits. She and the other girl were in the shadows now, for the fire had been obscured by the men standing or scuffling around it. If she crept away quickly and quietly—

No sooner thought than done. She started to crawl away, got as far as the edge of the firelight, then looked back.

The other girl was still huddled where she had been left, eyes closed. Too stupid or too frightened to take advantage of the opportunity to escape.

If Elfrida left her there, they probably wouldn't try to recapture her. They'd have one girl still, and wouldn't go hunting in the dark for the one that had gotten away. . . .

Elfrida muttered an oath, and crawled back.

Leonie huddled with the witch-girl under the shelter of a fallen tree, and they listened for the sounds of pursuit. She had been praying as hard as she could, eyes closed, when a painful tug on the twine binding her wrists had made her open her eyes.

"Well, come on!" the girl had said, tugging again. Leonie had not bothered to think about what the girl might be pulling her into, she had simply followed, crawling as best she could with her hands tied, then getting up and running when the girl did.

They had splashed through a stream, running along a moonlit path, until Leonie's sides ached. Finally the girl had pulled her off the path and shoved her under the bulk of a fallen tree, into a little dug-out den she would never have guessed was there. From the musky smell, it had probably been made by a fox or badger. Leonie huddled in the dark, trying not to sob, concentrating on the pain in her side and not on the various fates the witch-girl could have planned for her.

Before too long, they heard shouts in the distance, but they never came very close. Leonie strained her ears, holding her breath, to try and judge how close their pursuers were, and jumped when the witch-girl put a hand on her.

"Don't," the girl whispered sharply. "You won't be going far with your hands tied like that. Hold still! I'm not going to hurt you."

Leonie stuttered something about demons, without thinking. The girl laughed.

"If I had a demon to come when I called, do you think I would have let a bastard like that lay hands on me?" Since there was no logical answer to that question, Leonie wisely kept quiet. The girl touched her hands, and then seized them; Leonie kept herself from pulling away, and a moment later, felt the girl sawing at her bonds with a bit of sharp rock. Every so often the rock cut into Leonie instead of the twine, but she bit her lip and kept quiet, gratitude increasing as each strand parted. "What were you doing out here, anyway?" the girl asked. "I thought they kept your kind mewed up like prize lambs."

"I had a vision," Leonie began, wondering if by her words and the retelling of her holy revelation, the witch-girl might actually be converted to Christianity. It happened that way all the time in the tales of the saints, after all. . . .

So while the girl sawed patiently at the bonds with the sharp end of the rock, Leonie told her everything, from the time she realized that something was wrong, to the moment the bandit took her captive. The girl stayed silent through all of it, and Leonie began to hope that she *might* bring the witch-girl to the Light and Life of Christ.

The girl waited until she had obviously come to the end, then laughed, unpleasantly. "Suppose, just suppose," she said, "I were to tell you that the *exact same* vision was given to me? Only it isn't some mystical cup that this land needs, it's the Cauldron of Cerridwen, the ever-renewing, for the High King refuses to sacrifice himself to save his kingdom as the Holy Bargain demands and only the Cauldron can give the land the blessing of the Goddess."

The last of the twine snapped as she finished, and Leonie

pulled her hands away. "Then I would say that your vision is wrong, evil," she retorted. "There is no goddess, only the Blessed Virgin—"

"Who is one face of the Goddess, who is Maiden, Mother and Wise One," the girl interrupted, her words dripping acid. "Only a fool would fail to see that. And your White Christ is no more than the Sacrificed One in one of *His* many guises—it is the Cauldron the land needs, not your apocryphal Cup—"

"Your cauldron is some demon-thing," Leonie replied, angrily. "Only the Grail—"

Whatever else she was going to say was lost, as the tree trunk above them was riven into splinters by a bolt of lightning that blinded and deafened them both for a moment.

When they looked up, tears streaming from their eyes, it was to see something they both recognized as The Enemy.

Standing over them was a shape, outlined in a glow of its own. It was three times the height of a man, black and hairy like a bear, with the tips of its outstretched claws etched in fire. But it was not a bear, for it wore a leather corselet, and its head had the horns of a bull, the snout and tusks of a boar, dripping foam and saliva, and its eyes, glowing an evil red, were slitted like a goat's.

Leonie screamed and froze. The witch-girl seized her bloody wrist, hauled her to her feet, and ran with her stumbling along behind.

The beast roared and followed after. They had not gotten more than forty paces down the road, when the witch-girl fell to the ground with a cry of pain, her hand slipping from Leonie's wrist.

Her ankle—Leonie thought, but no more, for the beast was shambling towards them. She grabbed the girl's arm and hauled her to her feet; draped her arm over her own shoulders, and dragged her erect. Up ahead there was moonlight shining down on something—perhaps a clearing, and perhaps the beast might fear the light—

She half-dragged, half-guided the witch-girl towards that promise of light, with the beast bellowing behind them. The thought crossed her mind that if she dropped the girl and left her, the beast would probably be content with the witch and would not chase after Leonie. . . .

No, she told herself, and stumbled onward.

They broke into the light, and Leonie looked up—

And sank to her knees in wonder.

Elfrida fell beside the other girl, half blinded by tears of pain, and tried to get to her feet. The beast—she had to help Leonie up, they had to run. . . .

Then she looked up.

And fell again to her knees, this time stricken not with pain, but with awe. And though she had never felt power before, she felt it now; humming through her, blood and bone, saw it in the vibration of the air, in the purity of the light streaming from the Cup.

The Cup held in the hand of a man, whose gentle, sad eyes told of the pain, not only of His own, but of the world's, that for the sake of the world, He carried on His own shoulders.

Leonie wept, tears of mingled joy and fear—joy to be in the Presence of One who was all of Light and Love, and fear, that this One was She and not He—and the thing that she held, spilling over the Light of Love and Healing was Cauldron and not Cup.

I was wrong—she thought, helplessly.

Wrong? said a loving, laughing Voice. *Or simply—limited in vision?*

And in that moment, the Cauldron became a Cup, and the Lady became the Lord, Jesu—then changed again, to a man of strange, draped robes and slanted eyes, who held neither Cup nor Cauldron, but a cup-shaped Flower with a jeweled heart—a hawk-headed creature with a glowing stone in His hand—a black-skinned Woman with a bright Bird—

And then to another shape, and another, until her eyes were dazzled and her spirit dizzied, and she looked away, into the eyes of Elfrida. The witch-girl—*Wise Girl* whispered the Voice in her mind, *And Quest-Companion*—looked similarly dazzled, but the joy in her face must surely mirror Leonie's. The girl offered her hand, and Leonie took it, and they turned again to face—

A Being of Light, neither male nor female, and a dazzling Cup as large as a Cauldron, the veil covering it barely dimming its brilliance.

Come, the Being said. *You have proved yourselves worthy.*

Hand in hand, the two newest Grail Maidens rose, and followed the shining beacon into the Light.

The Lands Beyond the World

Michael Moorcock

I

is bone-white, long-fingered hand upon a carved demon's head in black-brown hardwood (one of the few such decorations to be found anywhere about the vessel), the tall man stood alone in the ship's fo'csle and stared through large, slanting, crimson eyes at the mist into which they moved with a speed and sureness to make any mortal mariner marvel and become incredulous.

There were sounds in the distance, incongruent with the sounds of even this nameless, timeless sea: thin sounds, agonized and terrible, for all that they remained remote—yet the ship followed them, as if drawn by them; they grew louder—pain and despair were there, but terror was predominant.

Elric had heard such sounds echoing from his cousin Yyrkoon's sardonically named "Pleasure Chambers" in the days before he had fled the responsibilities of ruling all that remained of the old Melnibonéan Empire. These were the voices of men whose very souls were under siege; men to whom death meant not mere extinction, but a continuation of existence, forever in thrall to some cruel and supernatural master. He had heard men cry so when his salvation and his nemesis, his great black battle-blade Stormbringer, drank their souls.

He did not savor the sound: he hated it, turned his back away from the source and was about to descend the ladder to the main deck when he realized that Otto Blendker had come up behind him. Now that Corum had been borne off by friends with chariots which could ride upon the surface of the water, Blendker was the last of those comrades to have fought at Elric's side against the two alien sorcerers Gagak and Agak.

Blendker's black, scarred face was troubled. The ex-scholar, turned hireling sword, covered his ears with his huge palms.

"Ach! By the Twelve Symbols of Reason, Elric, who makes that din? It's as though we sail close to the shores of Hell itself!"

Prince Elric of Melniboné shrugged. "I'd be prepared to forego an answer and leave my curiosity unsatisfied, Master Blendker, if only our ship would change course. As it is, we sail closer and closer to the source."

Blendker grunted his agreement. "I've no wish to encounter whatever it is that causes those poor fellows to scream so! Perhaps we should inform the Captain."

"You think he does not know where his own ship sails?" Elric's smile had little humor.

The tall black man rubbed at the inverted V-shaped scar which ran from his forehead to his jawbones. "I wonder if he plans to put us into battle again?"

"I'll not fight another for him." Elric's hand moved from the carved rail to the pommel of his runesword. "I have business of my own to attend to, once I'm back on real land."

A wind came from nowhere. There was a sudden rent in the mist. Now Elric could see that the ship sailed through rust-colored water. Peculiar lights gleamed in that water, just below the surface. There was an impression of creatures moving ponderously in the depths of the ocean and, for a moment, Elric thought he glimpsed a white, bloated face not dissimilar to his own—a Melnibonéan face. Impulsively he whirled, back to the rail, looking past Blendker as he strove to control the nausea in his throat.

For the first time since he had come aboard the Dark Ship he was able clearly to see the length of the vessel. Here were the two great wheels, one beside him on the foredeck, one at the far end of the ship on the rear deck, tended now as always by the Steersman, the Captain's sighted twin. There was the great mast bearing the taut black sail, and fore and aft of this, the two deck cabins, one of which was entirely empty (its occupants having been killed during their last landfall) and one of which was occupied only by himself and Blendker. Elric's gaze was drawn back to the Steersman and not for the first time the albino wondered how much influence the Captain's twin had over the course of the Dark Ship. The man seemed tireless, rarely, to Elric's knowledge, going below to his quarters which occupied the stern deck as the Captain's occupied the foredeck. Once or twice Elric or Blendker had tried to involve the Steersman in conversation, but he appeared to be as dumb as his brother was blind.

The cryptographic, geometrical carvings covering all the ship's wood and most of its metal, from sternpost to figurehead, were picked out by the shreds of pale mist still clinging to them (and again Elric wondered if the ship actually generated the mist normally surrounding it) and, as he watched, the designs slowly turned to pale pink fire as the light from that red star, which forever followed them, permeated the overhead cloud.

A noise from below. The Captain, his long red-gold hair drifting in a breeze which Elric could not feel, emerged from his cabin. The Captain's circlet of blue jade, worn like a diadem, had turned to something of a violet shade in the pink light, and even his buff-colored hose and tunic reflected the hue—even the silver sandals with their silver lacing glittered with the rosy tint.

Again Elric looked upon that mysterious blind face, as unhuman, in the accepted sense, as his own, and puzzled upon the origin of the one who would allow himself to be called nothing but "Captain."

As if at the Captain's summons, the mist drew itself about the ship again, as a woman might draw a froth of furs about her body. The red star's light faded, but the distant screams continued.

Did the Captain notice the screams now for the first time, or was this a pantomime of surprise. His blind head tilted, a hand went to his ear. He murmured in a tone of satisfaction: "Aha!" The head lifted. "Elric?"

"Here," said the albino. "Above you."

"We are almost there, Elric."

The apparently fragile hand found the rail of the companion-way. The Captain began to climb.

Elric faced him at the top of the ladder. "If it's a battle . . ."

The Captain's smile was enigmatic, bitter. "It was a fight—or shall be one."

". . . we'll have no part of it," concluded the albino firmly.

"It is not one of the battles in which my ship is directly involved," the blind man reassured him. "Those whom you can hear are the vanquished—lost in some future which, I think, you will experience close to the end of your present incarnation."

Elric waved a dismissive hand. "I'll be glad, Captain, if you would cease such vapid mystification. I'm weary of it."

"I'm sorry it offends you. I answer literally, according to my instincts."

The Captain, going past Elric and Otto Blendker so that he could stand at the rail, seemed to be apologizing. He said nothing for a while but listened to the disturbing and confused babble from the mist. Then he nodded, apparently satisfied.

"We'll sight land shortly. If you would disembark and seek your own world, I should advise you to do so now. This is the closest we shall ever come again to your plane."

Elric let his anger show. He cursed, invoking Arioch's name, and put a hand upon the blind man's shoulder. "What? You cannot return me directly to my own plane?"

"It is too late." The Captain's dismay was apparently genuine. "The ship sails on. We near the end of our long voyage."

"But how shall I find my world? I have no sorcery great enough to move me between the spheres! And demonic assistance is denied me here."

"There is one gateway to your world," the Captain told him. "That is why I suggest you disembark. Elsewhere there are none at all. Your sphere and this one intersect directly."

"But you say this lies in my future?"

"Be sure—you will return to your own time. Here you are timeless. It is why your memory is so poor. It is why you remember so little of what befalls you. Seek for the gateway—it is crimson and it emerges from the sea off the coast of the island."

"Which island?"

"The one we approach."

Elric hesitated. "And where shall you go, when I have landed?"

"To Tanelorn," said the Captain. "There is something I must do there. My brother and I must complete our destiny. We carry cargo as well as men. Many will try to stop us now, for they fear our cargo. We might perish, but yet we must do all we can to reach Tanelorn."

"Was that not, then, Tanelorn, where we fought Agak and Gagak?"

"That was nothing more than a broken dream of Tanelorn, Elric."

The Melnibonéan knew that he would receive no more information from the Captain.

"You offer me a poor choice—to sail with you into danger and never see my own world again, or to risk landing on yonder island inhabited, by the sound of it, by the damned and those which prey upon the damned!"

The Captain's blind eyes moved in Elric's direction. "I know," he said softly. "But it is the best I can offer you, nonetheless."

The screams, the imploring, terrified shouts, were closer now, but there were fewer of them. Glancing over the side Elric thought he saw a pair of armored hands rising from the water; there was foam, red-flecked and noxious, and there was yellowish scum in which pieces of frightful flotsam drifted; there were broken timbers, scraps of canvas, tatters of flags and clothing, fragments of weapons and, increasingly, there were floating corpses.

"But where was the battle?" Blendker whispered, fascinated and horrified by the sight.

"Not on this plane," the Captain told him. "You see only the wreckage which has drifted over from one world to another."

"Then it was a supernatural battle?"

The Captain smiled again. "I am not omniscient. But, yes, I believe there were supernatural agencies involved. The warriors of half a world fought in the sea-battle—to decide the fate of the multiverse. It is—or will be—one of the decisive battles to determine the fate of Mankind, to fix Man's destiny for the coming Cycle."

"Who were the participants?" asked Elric, asking the question in spite of his resolve. "What were the issues as they understood them?"

"You will know in time, I think." The Captain's head faced the sea again.

Blendker sniffed the air. "Ach! It's foul!"

Elric, too, found the odor increasingly unpleasant. Here and there now the water was lit by guttering fires which revealed the faces of the drowning, some of whom still managed to cling to pieces of blackened driftwood. Not all the faces were human (though they had the appearance of having, once, been human): Things with the snouts of pigs and of bulls raised twisted hands to the Dark Ship and grunted plaintively for succor, but the Captain ignored them and the Steersman held his course.

Fires spluttered and water hissed; smoke mingled with the mist. Elric had his sleeve over his mouth and nose and was glad that the smoke and mist between them helped obscure the sights, for as the wreckage grew thicker not a few of the corpses he saw reminded him more of reptiles than of men, their pale, lizard bellies spilling something other than blood.

"If that is my future," Elric told the Captain, "I've a mind to remain on board, after all."

"You have a duty, as have I," said the Captain quietly. "The future must be served, as much as the past and the present."

Elric shook his head. "I fled the duties of an Empire because I sought freedom," the albino told him. "And freedom I must have."

"No," murmured the Captain. "There is no such thing. Not yet. Not for us. We must go through much more before we can even begin to guess what freedom is. The price for the knowledge alone is probably higher than any you would care to pay at this stage of your life. Indeed, life itself is often the price."

"I also sought release from metaphysics when I left Melniboné," said Elric. "I'll fetch the rest of my gear and take the land that's offered. With luck this Crimson Gate will be quickly found and I'll be back amongst dangers and torments which will, at least, be familiar."

"It is the only decision you could have made." The Captain's blind head turned towards Blendker. "And you, Otto Blendker? What shall you do?"

"Elric's world is not mine and I like not the sound of those screams. What can you promise me, sir, if I sail on with you?"

"Nothing but a good death." There was regret in the Captain's voice.

"Death is the promise we're all born with, sir. A good death is better than a poor one. I'll sail on with you."

"As you like. I think you're wise." The Captain sighed. "I'll say farewell to you, then, Elric of Melniboné. You fought well in my service and I thank you."

"Fought for what?" Elric asked.

"Oh, call it Mankind. Call it Fate. Call it a dream or an ideal, if you wish."

"Shall I never have a clearer answer?"

"Not from me. I do not think there is one."

"You allow a man little faith." Elric began to descend the companionway.

"There are two kinds of faith, Elric. Like freedom, there is a kind which is easily kept but proves not worth the keeping and there is a kind which is hard won. I agree, I offer little of the former."

Elric strode towards his cabin. He laughed, feeling genuine affection for the blind man at that moment. "I thought I had a penchant for such ambiguities, but I have met my match in you, Captain."

He noticed that the Steersman had left his place at the wheel and was swinging out a boat on its davits, preparatory to lowering it.

"Is that for me?"

The Steersman nodded.

Elric ducked into his cabin. He was leaving the ship with nothing but that which he had brought aboard, only his clothing and his armor were in a poorer state of repair than they had been, and his mind was in a considerably greater state of confusion.

Without hesitation he gathered up his things, drawing his heavy cloak about him, pulling on his gauntlets, fastening buckles and thongs, then he left the cabin and returned to the deck. The Captain was pointing through the mist at the dark outlines of a coast. "Can you see land, Elric?"

"I can."

"You must go quickly, then."

"Willingly."

Elric swung himself over the rail and into the boat. The boat struck the side of the ship several times, so that the hull boomed like the beating of some huge funeral drum. Otherwise there was silence now upon the misty waters and no sign of wreckage.

Blendker saluted him. "I wish you luck, comrade."

"You, too, Master Blendker."

The boat began to sink towards the flat surface of the sea, the pulleys of the davits creaking. Elric clung to the rope, letting go as the boat hit the water. He stumbled and sat down heavily upon the seat, releasing the ropes so that the boat drifted at once away from the Dark Ship. He got out the oars and fitted them into their rowlocks.

As he pulled toward the shore he heard the Captain's voice

calling to him, but the words were muffled by the mist and he would never know, now, if the blind man's last communication had been a warning or merely some formal pleasantry. He did not care. The boat moved smoothly through the water; the mist began to thin, but so, too, did the light fade.

Suddenly he was under a twilight sky, the sun already gone and stars appearing. Before he had reached the shore it was already completely dark, with the moon not yet risen, and it was with difficulty that he beached the boat on what seemed flat rocks, and stumbled inland until he judged himself safe enough from any inrushing tide.

Then, with a sigh, he lay down, thinking just to order his thoughts before moving on; but, almost instantly, he was asleep.

II

ELRIC DREAMED.

He dreamed not merely of the end of his world but of the end of an entire cycle in the history of the cosmos. He dreamed that he was not only Elric of Melniboné but that he was other men, too— men who were pledged to some numinous cause which even they could not describe. And he dreamed that he had dreamed of the Dark Ship and Tanelorn and Agak and Gagak while he lay exhausted upon a beach somewhere beyond the borders of Pikarayd and when he woke up he was smiling sardonically, congratulating himself for the possession of a grandiose imagination. But he could not clear his head entirely of the impression left by that dream.

This shore was not the same, so plainly something had befallen him—perhaps he had been drugged by slavers, then later abandoned when they found him not what they expected? But, no, the explanation would not do. If he could discover his whereabouts, he might also recall the true facts.

It was dawn, for certain. He sat up and looked about him.

He was sprawled upon a dark, sea-washed limestone pavement, cracked in a hundred places, the cracks so deep that the small streams of foaming saltwater rushing through these many narrow channels made raucous what would otherwise have been a very still evening.

Elric climbed to his feet, using his scabbarded runesword to steady himself. His bone-white lids closed for a moment over his crimson eyes as he sought, again, to recollect the events which had brought him here.

He recalled his flight from Pikarayd, his panic, his falling into a coma of hopelessness, his dreams. And, because he was evidently neither dead nor a prisoner, he could at least conclude that his pursuers had, after all, given up the chase, for if they had found him, they would have killed him.

Opening his eyes and casting about him, he remarked the peculiar blue quality of the light (doubtless a trick of the sun behind the gray clouds) which made the landscape ghastly and gave the sea a dull, metallic look.

The limestone terraces which rose from the sea and stretched above him shone intermittently like polished lead. On an impulse he held his hand to the light and inspected it. The normally lusterless white of his skin was now tinged with a faint, bluish luminosity. He found it pleasing and smiled as a child might smile, in innocent wonder.

He had expected to be tired, but he now realized that he felt unusually refreshed, as if he had slept long after a good meal, and, deciding not to question the fact of this fortunate (and unlikely) gift, he determined to climb the cliffs in the hope that he might get some idea of his bearings before he decided which direction he would take.

Limestone could be a little treacherous, but it made easy climbing, for there was almost always somewhere that one terrace met another.

He climbed carefully and steadily, finding many footholds, and seemed to gain considerable height quite quickly, yet it was noon before he had reached the top and found himself standing at the edge of a broad, rocky plateau which fell away sharply to form a close horizon. Beyond the plateau was only the sky. Save for sparse, brownish grass, little grew here and there were no signs at all of human habitation. It was now, for the first time, that Elric realized the absence of any form of wildlife. Not a single seabird flew in the air, not an insect crept through the grass. Instead, there was an enormous silence hanging over the brown plain.

Elric was still remarkably untired, so he decided to make the best use he could of his energy and reach the edge of the plateau in the hope that, from there, he would sight a town or a village. He pressed on, feeling no lack of food and water, and his stride was singularly energetic, still, but he had misjudged his distance and the sun had begun to set well before his journey to the edge was completed. The sky on all sides turned a deep, velvety blue and the few clouds that there were in it were also tinged blue, and now, for the first time, Elric realized that the sun itself was not its normal shade, that it burned blackish purple, and he wondered again if he still dreamed.

The ground began to rise sharply and it was with some effort that he walked, but before the light had completely faded he was on the steep flank of a hill, descending towards a wide valley which, though bereft of trees, contained a river which wound through rocks and russet turf and bracken. After a short rest, Elric decided to press on, although night had fallen, and see if he could reach the river where he might, at least, drink and, possibly, in the morning, find fish to eat.

Again, no moon appeared to aid his progress and he walked for two or three hours in a darkness which was almost total, stumbling occasionally into large rocks, until the ground leveled and he felt sure he had reached the floor of the valley.

He had developed a strong thirst by now and was feeling somewhat hungry, but decided that it might be best to wait until morning before seeking the river when, rounding a particularly tall rock, he saw, with some astonishment, the light of a camp fire.

Hopefully this would be the fire of a company of merchants, a trading caravan on its way to some civilized country which would allow him to travel with it, perhaps in return for his services as a mercenary swordsman (it would not be the first time, since he had left Melniboné, that he had earned his bread in such a way).

Yet Elric's old instincts did not desert him: he approached the fire cautiously and let no one see him. Beneath an overhang of rock, made shadowy by the flame's light, he stood and observed the group of fifteen or sixteen men who sat or lay close to the fire, playing some kind of game involving dice and slivers of numbered ivory.

Gold, bronze, and silver gleamed in the firelight as the men staked large sums on the fall of a die and the turn of a slip of ivory.

Elric guessed that, if they had not been so intent on their game, these men must certainly have detected his approach, for they were not, after all, merchants. By the evidence, they were warriors, wearing scarred leather and dented metal, their weapons ready to hand, yet they belonged to no army—unless it be an army of bandits—for they were of all races and (oddly) seemed to be from various periods in the history of the Young Kingdoms.

It was as if they had looted some scholar's collection of relics. An axman of the later Lormyrian Republic, which had come to an end some two hundred years ago, lay with his shoulder rubbing the elbow of a Chalalite bowman, from a period roughly contemporary with Elric's own. Close to the Chalalite sat a short Ilmioran infantryman of a century past. Next to him was a Filkharian in the barbaric dress of that nation's earliest times. Tarkeshites, Shazarians, Vilmirians, all mingled and the only thing they had in common, by the look of them, was a villainous, hungry cast to their features.

In other circumstances Elric might have skirted this encampment and moved on, but he was so glad to find human beings of any sort that he ignored the disturbing incongruities of the group, but yet he remained content to watch them.

One of the men, less unwholesome than the others, was a bulky, black-bearded, bald-headed sea warrior clad in the casual leathers and silks of the people of the Purple Towns. It was when this man produced a large, gold Melnibonéan wheel—a coin not minted, as most coins, but carved by craftsmen to a design both ancient and intricate—that Elric's caution was fully conquered by his curiosity.

Very few of those coins existed in Melniboné and none, that Elric had heard of, outside; for the coins were not used for trade with the Young Kingdoms. They were prized, even by the nobility of Melniboné.

It seemed to Elric that the bald-headed man could only have acquired the coin from another Melnibonéan traveler—and Elric knew of no other Melnibonéan who shared his penchant for exploration. His wariness dismissed, he stepped into the circle.

If he had not been completely obsessed by the thought of the Melnibonéan wheel he might have taken some satisfaction in the sudden scuffle to arms which resulted. Within seconds, the majority of the men were on their feet, their weapons drawn.

For a moment, the gold wheel was forgotten. His hand upon his runesword's pommel, he presented the other in a placatory gesture.

"Forgive the interruption, gentlemen. I am but one tired fellow soldier who seeks to join you. I would beg some information and purchase some food, if you have it to spare."

On foot, the warriors had an even more ruffianly appearance. They grinned among themselves, entertained by Elric's courtesy but not impressed by it.

One, in the feathered helmet of a Pan Tangian seachief, with features to match—swarthy, sinister—pushed his head forward on its long neck and said banteringly:

"We've company enough, white-face. And few here are over-fond of the man-demons of Melniboné. You must be rich."

Elric recalled the animosity with which Melnibonéans were regarded in the Young Kingdoms, particularly by those from Pan Tang who envied the Dragon Isle her power and her wisdom and, of late, had begun crudely to imitate Melniboné.

Increasingly on his guard, he said evenly: "I have a little money."

"Then we'll take it, demon." The Pan Tangian presented a dirty palm just below Elric's nose as he growled: "Give it over and be on your way."

Elric's smile was polite and fastidious, as if he had been told a poor joke.

The Pan Tangian evidently thought the joke better than did Elric, for he laughed heartily and looked to his nearest fellows for approval.

Coarse laughter infected the night and only the bald-headed, black-bearded man did not join in the jest, but took a step or two backward, while all the others pressed forward.

The Pan Tangian's face was close to Elric's own; his breath was foul and Elric saw that his beard and hair were alive with lice, yet he kept his head, replying in the same equable tone:

"Give me some decent food—a flask of water—some wine, if you have it—and I'll gladly give you the money I have."

The laughter rose and fell again as Elric continued:

"But if you would take my money and leave me with naught—then I must defend myself. I have a good sword."

The Pan Tangian strove to imitate Elric's irony. "But you will note, Sir Demon, that we outnumber you. Considerably."

Softly the albino spoke: "I've noticed that fact, but I'm not disturbed by it," and he had drawn the black blade even as he finished speaking, for they had come at him with a rush.

And the Pan Tangian was the first to die, sliced through the side, his vertebrae sheered, and Stormbringer, having taken its first soul, began to sing.

A Chalalite died next, leaping with stabbing javeline poised, on the point of the runesword, and Stormbringer murmured with pleasure.

But it was not until it had sliced the head clean off a Filkharian pikemaster that the sword began to croon and come fully to life, black fire flickering up and down its length, its strange runes glowing.

Now the warriors knew they battled sorcery and became more cautious, yet they scarcely paused in their attack, and Elric, thrusting and parrying, hacking and slicing, needed all of the fresh, dark energy the sword passed on to him.

Lance, sword, ax, and dirk were blocked, wounds were given

and received, but the dead had not yet outnumbered the living when Elric found himself with his back against the rock and nigh a dozen sharp weapons seeking his vitals.

It was at this point, when Elric had become somewhat less than confident that he could best so many, that the bald-headed warrior, ax in one gloved hand, sword in the other, came swiftly into the firelight and set upon those of his fellows closest to him.

"I thank you, sir!" Elric was able to shout, during the short respite this sudden turn produced. His morale improved, he resumed the attack.

The Lormyrian was cloven from hip to pelvis as he dodged a feint; a Filkharian, who should have been dead four hundred years before, fell with the blood bubbling from lips and nostrils, and the corpses began to pile one upon the other. Still Stormbringer sang its sinister battlesong and still the runesword passed its power to its master so that with every death Elric found strength to slay more of the soldiers.

Those who remained now began to express their regret for their hasty attack. Where oaths and threats had issued from their mouths, now came plaintive petitions for mercy and those who had laughed with such bold braggadocio now wept like young girls, but Elric, full of his old battle-joy, spared none.

Meanwhile the man from the Purple Towns, unaided by sorcery, put ax and sword to good work and dealt with three more of his one-time comrades, exulting in his work as if he had nursed a taste for it for some time.

"*Yoi!* But this is worthwhile slaughter!" cried the black-bearded one.

And then that busy butchery was suddenly done and Elric realized that none were left save himself and his new ally who stood leaning on his ax, panting and grinning like a hound at the kill, replacing a steel skullcap upon his pate from where it had fallen during the fight, and wiping a bloody sleeve over the sweat glistening on his brow, and saying, in a deep, good-humored tone:

"Well, now, it is we who are wealthy, of a sudden."

Elric sheathed Stormbringer still reluctant to return to its scabbard. "You desire their gold. Is that why you aided me?"

The black-bearded soldier laughed. "I owed them a debt and had been biding my time, waiting to pay. These rascals are all that were left of a pirate crew which slew everyone aboard my own ship when we wandered into strange waters—they would have slain me had I not told them I wished to join them. Now I am revenged. Not that I am above taking the gold, since much of it belongs to me and my dead brothers. It will go to their wives and their children when I return to the Purple Towns."

"How did you convince them not to kill you, too?" Elric sought amongst the ruins of the fire for something to eat. He found some cheese and began to chew upon it.

"They had no captain or navigator, it seemed. None are real sailors at all, but coast-huggers, based upon this island. They were stranded here, you see, and had taken to piracy as a last resort, but were too terrified to risk the open sea. Besides, after the fight, they had no ship. We had managed to sink that as we fought. We sailed mine to this shore, but provisions were already low and they had no stomach for setting sail without full holds, so I pretended that I knew this coast (may the Gods take my soul if I ever see it again after this business) and offered to lead them inland to a village they might loot. They had heard of no such village, but believed me when I said it lay in a hidden valley. That way I prolonged my life while I waited for the opportunity to be revenged upon them. It was a foolish hope, I know. Yet," grinning, "as it happened, it was well founded, after all! Eh?"

The black-bearded man glanced a little warily at Elric, uncertain of what the albino might say, hoping, however, for comradeship, though it was well known how haughty Melnibonéans were. Elric could tell that all these thoughts went through his new acquaintance's mind; he had seen many others make similar calculations. So he smiled openly and slapped the man on the shoulder.

"You saved my life, also, my friend. We are both fortunate."

The man sighed in relief and slung his ax upon his back. "Aye—lucky's the word. But shall our luck hold, I wonder?"

"You do not know the island at all?"

"Nor the waters, either. How we came to them I'll never guess. Enchanted waters, though, without question. You've seen the color of the sun?"

"I have."

"Well," the seaman bent to remove a pendant from around the Pan Tangian's throat, "you'd know more about enchantments and sorceries than I. How came you here, Sir Melnibonéan?"

"I know not. I fled from some who hunted me. I came to a shore and could flee no further. Then I dreamed a great deal. When next I awoke I was on the shore again, but of this island."

"Spirits of some sort—maybe friendly to you—took you to safety, away from your enemies."

"That's just possible," Elric agreed, "for we have many allies amongst the elementals. I am called Elric and I am self-exiled from Melniboné. I travel because I believe I have something to learn from the folk of the Young Kingdoms. I have no power, save what you see . . ."

The black-bearded man's eyes narrowed in appraisal as he pointed at himself with his thumb. "I'm Smiorgan Baldhead, once a sealord of the Purple Towns. I commanded a fleet of merchant-men. Perhaps I still do. I shall not know until I return—if I ever do return."

"Then let us pool our knowledge and our resources, Smiorgan Baldhead, and make plans to leave this island as soon as we can."

Elric walked back to where he saw traces of the abandoned game, trampled into the mud and the blood. From amongst the dice and the ivory slips, the silver and the bronze coins, he found the gold Melnibonéan wheel. He picked it up and held it in his outstretched palm. The wheel almost covered the whole palm. In the old days, it had been the currency of kings.

"This was yours, friend?" he asked Smiorgan.

Smiorgan Baldhead looked up from where he was still searching the Pan Tangian for his stolen possessions. He nodded.

"Aye. Would you keep it as part of your share?"

Elric shrugged. "I'd rather know from whence it came. Who gave it you?"

"It was not stolen. It's Melnibonéan, then?"

"Yes."

"I guessed it."

"From whom did you obtain it?"

Smiorgan straightened up, having completed his search. He scratched at a slight wound on his forearm. "It was used to buy passage on our ship—before we were lost—before the raiders attacked us."

"Passage? By a Melnibonéan?"

"Maybe," said Smiorgan. He seemed reluctant to speculate.

"Was he a warrior?"

Smiorgan smiled in his beard. "No. It was a woman gave that to me."

"How came she to take passage?"

Smiorgan began to pick up the rest of the money. "It's a long tale and, in part, a familiar one to most merchant sailors. We were seeking new markets for our goods and had equipped a good sized fleet, which I commanded, as the largest shareholder." He seated himself casually upon the big corpse of the Chalalite and began to count the money. "Would you hear the tale or do I bore you already?"

"I'd be glad to listen."

Reaching behind him, Smiorgan pulled a wine flask from the belt of the corpse and offered it to Elric who accepted it and drank sparingly of a wine which was unusually good.

Smiorgan took the flask when Elric had finished. "That's part of our cargo," he said. "We were proud of it. A good vintage, eh?"

"Excellent. So you set off from the Purple Towns?"

"Aye. Going east towards the Unknown Kingdoms. We sailed due east for a couple of weeks, sighting some of the bleakest coasts I have ever seen, and then we saw no land at all for another week. That was when we entered a stretch of water we came to call the Roaring Rocks—like the Serpent's Teeth off Shazar's coast, but much greater in expanse, and larger, too. Huge volcanic cliffs which rose from the sea on every side and around which the waters heaved and boiled and howled with a fierceness I've rarely experienced. Well, in short, the fleet was dispersed and at least four ships were lost on those rocks. At last we were able to escape those waters and found ourselves becalmed and alone. We searched for our sister ships for a while and then decided to give ourselves another week before turning for home, for we had no liking to go back into the Roaring Rocks again. Low on provisions, we sighted land at last—grassy cliffs and hospitable beaches and, inland, some signs of cultivation, so we knew we had found civilization again. We put into a small fishing port and satisfied the natives—who spoke no tongue used in the Young Kingdoms—that we were friendly. And that was when the woman approached us."

"The Melnibonéan woman?"

"If Melnibonéan she was. She was a fine-looking woman, I'll say that. We were short of provisions, as I told you, and short of any means of purchasing them, for the fishermen desired little of what we had to trade. Having given up our original quest, we were content to head westward again."

"The woman?"

"She wished to buy passage to the Young Kingdoms—and was content to go with us as far as Menii, our home port. For her passage she gave us two of those wheels. One was used to buy provisions in the town—Graghin, I think it was called—and after making repairs we set off again."

"You never reached the Purple Towns?"

"There were more storms—strange storms. Our instruments were useless, our lodestones were of no help to us at all. We became even more completely lost than before. Some of my men argued that we had gone beyond our own world altogether. Some blamed the woman, saying she was a sorceress who had no intention of going to Menii. But I believed her. Night fell and seemed to last forever until we sailed into a calm dawn beneath a blue sun. My men were close to panic—and it takes much to make my men panic—when we sighted the island. As we headed for it those pirates attacked us in a ship which belonged to history—it should have been on the bottom of the ocean, not on the surface. I've seen pictures of such craft in murals on a temple wall in Tarkesh. In ramming us, she stove in half her port side and was sinking even when they swarmed aboard. They were desperate, savage men, Elric—half-starved and blood-hungry. We were weary after our voyage but fought well. During the fighting the woman disappeared, killed herself, maybe, when she saw the stamp of our conquerors. After a long fight only myself and one other, who died soon after, were left. That was when I became cunning and decided to wait for revenge."

"The woman had a name?"

"None she would give. I have thought the matter over and suspect that, after all, we were used by her. Perhaps she did not seek Menii and the Young Kingdoms. Perhaps it was this world she sought, and, by sorcery, led us here."

"This world? You think it different to our own?"

"If only because of the sun's strange color. Do you not think so, too? You, with your Melnibonéan knowledge of such things, must believe it?"

"I have dreamed of such things," Elric admitted, but he would say no more.

"Most of the pirates thought as I—they were from all the ages of the Young Kingdoms. That much I discovered. Some were from the earliest years of the era, some from our own time—and some were from the future. Adventurers, most of them, who, at some stage in their lives, sought a legendary land of great riches which lay on the other side of an ancient gateway, rising from the middle of the ocean, but they found themselves trapped here, unable to sail back through this mysterious gate. Others had been involved in sea fights, thought themselves drowned and woken up on the shores of the island. Many, I suppose, had once had reasonable virtues, but there is little to support life on the island and they had become wolves, living off one another or any ship unfortunate enough to pass, inadvertently, through this gate of theirs."

Elric recalled part of his dream. "Did any call it the 'Crimson Gate'?"

"Several did, aye."

"And yet the theory is unlikely, if you'll forgive my skepticism," Elric said. "As one who has passed through the Shade Gate to Ameeron . . ."

"You know of other worlds, then?"

"I've never heard of this one. And I am versed in such matters. That is why I doubt the reasoning. And yet, there was the dream . . ."

"Dream?"

"Oh, it was nothing. I am used to such dreams and give them no significance."

"The theory cannot seem surprising to a Melnibonéan, Elric!" Smiorgan grinned again. "It's I who should be skeptical, not you."

And Elric replied, half to himself: "Perhaps I fear the implications more." He lifted his head and, with the shaft of a broken spear, began to poke at the fire. "Certain ancient sorcerers of Melniboné proposed that an infinite number of worlds coexist with our own. Indeed, my dreams, of late, have hinted as much!" He forced himself to smile. "But I cannot afford to believe such things. Thus, I reject them."

"Wait for the dawn," said Smiorgan Baldhead. "The color of the sun shall prove the theory."

"Perhaps it will prove only that we both dream," said Elric. The smell of death was strong in his nostrils. He pushed aside those corpses nearest to the fire and settled himself to sleep.

Smiorgan Baldhead had begun to sing a strong yet lilting song in his own dialect, which Elric could scarcely follow.

"Do you sing of your victory over your enemies?" the albino asked.

Smiorgan paused for a moment, half amused. "No, Sir Elric, I sing to keep the shades at bay. After all, these fellows' ghosts must still be lurking nearby, in the dark, so little time has passed since they died."

"Fear not," Elric told him. "Their souls are already eaten."

But Smiorgan sang on, and his voice was louder, his song more intense, than ever it had been before.

Just before he fell asleep, Elric thought he heard a horse whinny, and he meant to ask Smiorgan if any of the pirates had been mounted, but he fell asleep before he could do so.

III

RECALLING LITTLE OF HIS VOYAGE ON THE DARK SHIP, ELRIC WOULD never know how he came to reach the world in which he now found himself. In later years he would recall most of these experiences as dreams and, indeed, they seemed dreamlike even as they occurred.

He slept uneasily, and, in the morning, the clouds were heavier, shining with that strange, leaden light, though the sun itself was obscured. Smiorgan Baldhead of the Purple Towns was pointing upwards, already on his feet, speaking with quiet triumph:

"Will that evidence suffice to convince you, Elric of Melniboné?"

"I am convinced of a quality about the light—possibly about this terrain—which makes the sun appear blue," Elric replied. He glanced with distaste at the carnage around him. The corpses made a wretched sight and he was filled with a nebulous misery that was neither remorse nor pity.

Smiorgan's sigh was sardonic. "Well, Sir Skeptic, we had best retrace my steps and seek my ship. What say you?"

"I agree," the albino told him.

"How far had you marched from the coast when you found us?"

Elric told him.

Smiorgan smiled. "You arrived in the nick of time, then. I should have been most embarrassed by today if the sea had been reached and I could show my pirate friends no village! I shall not forget this favor you have done me, Elric. I am a Count of the Purple Towns and have much influence. If there is any service I can perform for you when we return, you must let me know."

"I thank you," Elric said gravely. "But first we must discover a means of escape."

Smiorgan had gathered up a satchel of food, some water and

some wine. Elric had no stomach to make his breakfast among the dead, so he slung the satchel over his shoulder. "I'm ready," he said.

Smiorgan was satisfied. "Come—we go this way."

Elric began to follow the sealord over the dry, crunching turf. The steep sides of the valley loomed over them, tinged with a peculiar and unpleasant greenish hue, the result of the brown foliage being stained by the blue light from above. When they reached the river, which was narrow and ran rapidly through boulders giving easy means of crossing, they rested and ate. Both men were stiff from the previous night's fighting; both were glad to wash the dried blood and mud from their bodies in the water.

Refreshed, the pair climbed over the boulders and left the river behind, ascending the slopes, speaking little so that their breath was saved for the exertion. It was noon by the time they reached the top of the valley and observed a plain not unlike the one which Elric had first crossed. Elric now had a fair idea of the island's geography: it resembled the top of a mountain, with an indentation near the center which was the valley. Again he became sharply aware of the absence of any wildlife and remarked on this to Count Smiorgan, who agreed that he had seen nothing—no bird, fish nor beast since he had arrived.

"It's a barren little world, friend Elric, and a misfortune for a mariner to be wrecked upon its shores."

They moved on, until the sea could be observed meeting the horizon in the far distance.

It was Elric who first heard the sound behind them, recognizing the steady thump of the hooves of a galloping horse, but when he looked back over his shoulder he could see no sign of a rider, nor anywhere that a rider could hide. He guessed that, in his tiredness, his ears were betraying him. It had been thunder that he had heard.

Smiorgan strode implacably onward, though he, too, must have heard the sound.

Again it came. Again, Elric turned. Again he saw nothing.

"Smiorgan? Did you hear a rider?"

Smiorgan continued to walk without looking back. "I heard," he grunted.

"You have heard it before?"

"Many times since I arrived. The pirates heard it, too, and some believed it their nemesis—an Angel of Death seeking them out for retribution."

"You don't know the source?"

Smiorgan paused, then stopped, and when he turned his face was grim. "Once or twice I have caught a glimpse of a horse, I think. A tall horse—white—richly dressed—but with no man upon his back. Ignore it, Elric, as I do. We have larger mysteries with which to occupy our minds!"

"You are afraid of it, Smiorgan?"

He accepted this. "Aye. I confess it. But neither fear nor speculation will rid us of it. Come!"

Elric was bound to see the sense of Smiorgan's statement and he accepted it, yet, when the sound came again, about an hour later, he could not resist turning. Then he thought he glimpsed the outline of a large stallion, caparisoned for riding, but that might have been nothing more than an idea Smiorgan had put in his mind.

The day grew colder and in the air was a peculiar, bitter odor. Elric remarked on the smell to Count Smiorgan and learned that this, too, was familiar.

"The smell comes and goes, but it is usually here in some strength."

"Like sulphur," said Elric.

Count Smiorgan's laugh had much irony in it, as if Elric made reference to some private joke of Smiorgan's own. "Oh, aye! Sulphur right enough!"

The drumming of hooves grew louder behind them as they neared the coast and at last Elric, and Smiorgan too, turned round again, to look.

And now a horse could be seen plainly—riderless, but saddled and bridled, its dark eyes intelligent, its beautiful white head held proudly.

"Are you still convinced of the absence of sorcery here, Sir Elric?" Count Smiorgan asked with some satisfaction. "The horse was invisible. Now it is visible." He shrugged the battle-ax on his shoulder into a better position. "Either that, or it moves from one world to another with ease, so that all we mainly hear are its hoof-beats."

"If so," said Elric sardonically, eyeing the stallion, "it might bear us back to our own world."

"You admit, then, that we are marooned in some Limbo?"

"Very well, yes. I admit the possibility."

"Have you no sorcery to trap the horse?"

"Sorcery does not come so easily to me, for I have no great liking for it," the albino told him.

As they spoke, they approached the horse, but it would let them get no closer. It snorted and moved backward, keeping the same distance between them and itself.

At last, Elric said: "We waste time, Count Smiorgan. Let's get to your ship with speed and forget blue suns and enchanted horses as quickly as we may. Once aboard the ship I can doubtless help you with a little incantation or two, for we'll need aid of some sort if we're to sail a large ship by ourselves."

They marched on, but the horse continued to follow them. They came to the edge of the cliffs, standing high above a narrow, rocky bay in which a battered ship lay at anchor. The ship had the high, fine lines of a Purple Towns merchantman, but its decks were piled with shreds of torn canvas, pieces of broken rope, shards of timber, torn-open bales of cloth, smashed wine-jars, and all manner of other refuse, while in several places her rails were smashed and two or three of her yards had splintered. It was evident that she had been through both storms and sea-fights and it was a wonder that she still floated.

"We'll have to tidy her up as best we can, using only the mains'l for motion," mused Smiorgan. "Hopefully we can salvage enough food to last us . . ."

"Look!" Elric pointed, sure that he had seen someone in the

shadows near the afterdeck. "Did the pirates leave any of their company behind?"

"None."

"Did you see anyone on the ship, just then?"

"My eyes play filthy tricks on my mind," Smiorgan told him. "It is this damned blue light. There is a rat or two aboard, that's all. And that's what you saw."

"Possibly." Elric looked back. The horse appeared to be unaware of them as it cropped the brown grass. "Well, let's finish the journey."

They scrambled down the steeply sloping cliff-face and were soon on the shore, wading through the shallows for the ship, clambering up the slippery ropes which still hung over the sides and, at last, setting their feet with some relief upon the deck.

"I feel more secure already," said Smiorgan. "This ship was my home for so long!" He searched through the scattered cargo until he found an unbroken winejar, carved off the seal and handed it to Elric. Elric lifted the heavy jar and let a little of the good wine flow into his mouth. As Count Smiorgan began to drink, Elric was sure he saw another movement near the afterdeck, and he moved closer.

Now he was certain that he heard strained, rapid breathing—like the breathing of one who sought to stifle their need for air rather than be detected. They were slight sounds, but the albino's ears, unlike his eyes, were sharp. His hand ready to draw his sword, he stalked towards the source of the sound, Smiorgan now behind him.

She emerged from her hiding place before he reached her. Her hair hung in heavy, dirty coils about her pale face; her shoulders were slumped and her soft arms hung limply at her sides, while her dress was stained and ripped.

As Elric approached, she fell on her knees before him. "Take my life," she said humbly, "but I beg you—do not take me back to Saxif D'Aan, though I know you must be his servant or his kinsman."

"It's she!" cried Smiorgan in astonishment. "It's our passenger. She must have been in hiding all this time."

Elric stepped forward, lifting up the girl's chin so that he could study her face. There was a Melnibonéan cast about her features, but she was, to his mind, of the Young Kingdoms; she lacked the pride of a Melnibonéan woman, too. "What name was that you used, girl?" he asked kindly. "Did you speak of Saxif D'Aan? Earl Saxif D'Aan of Melniboné?"

"I did, my lord."

"Do not fear me as his servant," Elric told her. "And as for being a kinsman, I suppose you could call me that—on my mother's side—or rather my great-grandmother's side. He was an ancestor. He must have been dead for two centuries, at least!"

"No," she said. "He lives, my lord."

"On this island?"

"This island is not his home, but it is in this plane that he exists. I sought to escape him through the Crimson Gate. I fled through the gate in a skiff, reached the town where you found me, Count Smiorgan, but he drew me back once I was aboard your ship. He drew me back and the ship with me. For that, I have remorse—and for what befell your crew. Now I know he seeks me. I can feel his presence growing nearer."

"Is he invisible?" Smiorgan asked suddenly. "Does he ride a white horse?"

She gasped. "You see! He *is* near! Why else should the horse appear on this island?"

"He rides it?" Elric asked.

"No, no! He fears the horse almost as much as I fear him. The horse pursues him!"

Elric produced the Melnibonéan gold wheel from his purse. "Did you take this from Earl Saxif D'Aan?"

"I did."

The albino frowned.

"Who is this man, Elric?" Count Smiorgan asked. "You describe him as an ancestor—yet he lives in this world. What do you know of him?"

Elric weighed the large gold wheel in his hand before replacing it in his pouch. "He was something of a legend in Melniboné. His story is part of our literature. He was a great sorcerer—one of the greatest—and he fell in love. It's rare enough for Melnibonéans to fall in love, as others understand the emotion, but rarer for one to have such feelings for a girl who was not even of our own race. She was half-Melnibonéan, so I heard, but from a land which was, in those days, a Melnibonéan possession, a western province close to Dharijor. She was bought by him in a batch of slaves he planned to use for some sorcerous experiment, but he singled her out, saving her from whatever fate it was the others suffered. He lavished his attention upon her, giving her everything. For her, he abandoned his practices, retired to live quietly away from Imrryr, and I think she showed him a certain affection, though she did not seem to love him. There was another, you see, called Carolak, as I recall, and also half-Melnibonéan, who had become a mercenary in Shazar and risen in the favor of the Shazarian court. She had been pledged to this Carolak before her abduction . . ."

"She loved him?" Count Smiorgan asked.

"She was pledged to marry him, but let me finish my story . . ." Elric continued: "Well, at length Carolak, now a man of some substance, second only to the king in Shazar, heard of her fate and swore to rescue her. He came with raiders to Melniboné's shores and, aided by sorcery, sought out Saxif D'Aan's palace. That done, he sought the girl, finding her at last in the apartments Saxif D'Aan had set aside for her use. He told her that he had come to claim her as his bride, to rescue her from persecution. Oddly, the girl resisted, suggesting that she had been too long a slave in the Melnibonéan harem to readapt to the life of a princess in the Shazarian court. Carolak scoffed at this and seized her. He managed to escape the castle and had the girl over the saddle of his horse and was about to rejoin his men on the coast when Saxif D'Aan detected them. Carolak, I think, was slain, or else a spell was put on him, but Saxif D'Aan, in his terrible jealousy and certain that the girl had planned the escape with a lover, ordered her to die upon the Wheel of Chaos—a machine rather like that coin in design.

Her limbs were broken slowly and Saxif D'Aan sat and watched, through long days, while she died. Her skin was peeled from her flesh, and Earl Saxif D'Aan observed every detail of her punishment. Soon it was evident that the drugs and sorcery used to sustain her life were failing and Saxif D'Aan ordered her taken from the Wheel of Chaos and laid upon a couch. 'Well,' he said, 'you have been punished for betraying me and I am glad. Now you may die.' And he saw that her lips, blood-caked and frightful, were moving, and he bent to hear her words."

"Those words? Revenge? An oath?" asked Smiorgan.

"Her last gesture was an attempt to embrace him. And the words were those she had never uttered to him before, much as he had hoped that she would. She said simply, over and over again, until the last breath left her: 'I love you. I love you. I love you.' And then she died."

Smiorgan rubbed at his beard. "Gods! What then? What did your ancestor do?"

"He knew remorse."

"Of course!"

"Not so, for a Melnibonéan. Remorse is a rare emotion with us. Few have ever experienced it. Torn by guilt, Earl Saxif D'Aan left Melniboné, never to return. It was assumed that he had died in some remote land, trying to make amends for what he had done to the only creature he had ever loved. But now, it seems, he sought the Crimson Gate, perhaps thinking it an opening into Hell."

"But why should he plague me!" the girl cried. "I am not she! My name is Vassliss. I am a merchant's daughter, from Jharkor. I was voyaging to visit my uncle in Vilmir when our ship was wrecked. A few of us escaped in an open boat. More storms seized us. I was flung from the boat and was drowning when . . ." she shuddered—"when *his* galley found me. I was grateful, then . . ."

"What happened?" Elric pushed the matted hair away from her face and offered her some of their wine. She drank gratefully.

"He took me to his palace and told me that he would marry me, that I should be his Empress forever and rule beside him. But I was frightened. There was such pain in him—and such cruelty, too. I thought he must devour me, destroy me. Soon after my capture, I took the money and the boat and fled for the gateway, which he had told me about . . ."

"You could find this gateway for us?" Elric asked.

"I think so. I have some knowledge of seamanship, learned from my father. But what would be the use, sir? He would find us again and drag us back. And he must be very near, even now."

"I have a little sorcery myself," Elric assured her, "and will pit it against Saxif D'Aan's, if I must." He turned to Count Smiorgan. "Can we get a sail aloft quickly?"

"Fairly quickly."

"Then let's hurry, Count Smiorgan Baldhead. I might have the means of getting us through this Crimson Gate and free from any further involvement in the dealings of the dead!"

IV

WHILE COUNT SMIORGAN AND VASSLISS OF JHARKOR WATCHED, Elric lowered himself to the deck, panting and pale. His first attempt to work sorcery in this world had failed and had exhausted him.

"I am further convinced," he told Smiorgan, "that we are in another plane of existence, for I should have worked my incantations with less effort."

"You have failed."

Elric rose with some difficulty. "I shall try again."

He turned his white face skyward; he closed his eyes; he stretched out his arms and his body tensed as he began the incantation again, his voice growing louder and louder, higher and higher, so that it resembled the shrieking of a gale.

He forgot where he was; he forgot his own identity; he forgot those who were with him as his whole mind concentrated upon the summoning. He sent his call out beyond the confines of the world, into that strange plane where the elementals dwelled— where the powerful creatures of the air could still be found—the *sylphs* of the breeze, and the *sharnahs*, who lived in the storms, and the most powerful of all, the *h'Haarshanns*, creatures of the whirl-wind.

And now at last some of them began to come at his summons, ready to serve him as, by virtue of an ancient pact, the elementals had served his forefathers. And slowly the sail of the ship began to fill, and the timbers creaked, and Smiorgan raised the anchor, and the ship was sailing away form the island, through the rocky gap of the harbor, and out into the open sea, still beneath a strange, blue sun.

Soon a huge wave was forming around them, lifting up the ship and carrying it across the ocean, so that Count Smiorgan and the girl marveled at the speed of their progress, while Elric, his crimson eyes open now, but blank and unseeing, continued to croon to his unseen allies.

Thus the ship progressed across the waters of the sea, and at last the island was out of sight and the girl, checking their position against the position of the sun, was able to give Count Smiorgan sufficient information for him to steer a course.

As soon as he could, Count Smiorgan went up to Elric, who still straddled the deck, still as stiff-limbed as before, and shook him.

"Elric! You will kill yourself with this effort. We need your friends no longer!"

At once the wind dropped and the wave dispersed and Elric, gasping, fell to the deck.

"It is harder here," he said. "It is so much harder here. It is as if I have to call across far greater gulfs than any I have known be-fore."

And then Elric slept.

He lay in a warm bunk in a cool cabin. Through the porthole filtered diffused blue light. He sniffed. He caught the odor of hot food and, turning his head, saw that Vassliss stood there, a bowl of broth in her hands. "I was able to cook this," she said. "It will im-prove your health. As far as I can tell, we are nearing the Crimson

Gate. The seas are always rough around the gate, so you will need your strength."

Elric thanked her pleasantly and began to eat the broth as she watched him.

"You are very like Saxif D'Aan," she said. "Yet harder in a way—and gentler, too. He is so remote. I know why that girl could never tell him that she loved him."

Elric smiled. "Oh, it's nothing more than a folktale, probably, the story I told you. This Saxif D'Aan could be another person altogether—or an imposter, even, who has taken his name—or a sorcerer. Some sorcerers take the names of other sorcerers, for they think it gives them more power."

There came a cry form above, but Elric could not make out the words.

The girl's expression became alarmed. Without a word to Elric, she hurried from the cabin.

Elric, rising unsteadily, followed her up the companionway.

Count Smiorgan Baldhead was at the wheel of his ship and he was pointing towards the horizon behind them. "What do you make of that, Elric?"

Elric peered at the horizon, but could see nothing. Often his eyes were weak, as now. But the girl said in a voice of quiet despair:

"It is a golden sail."

"You recognize it?" Elric asked her.

"Oh, indeed I do. It is the galleon of Earl Saxif D'Aan. He has found us. Perhaps he was lying in wait along our route, knowing we must come this way."

"How far are we from the Gate?"

"I am not sure."

At that moment, there came a terrible noise from below, as if something sought to stave in the timbers of the ship.

"It's in the forward hatches!" cried Smiorgan. "See what it is, friend Elric! But take care, man!"

Cautiously Elric prized back one of the hatch covers and peered into the murky fastness of the hold. The noise of stamping and thumping continued and, as his eyes adjusted to the light, he saw the source.

The white horse was there. It whinnied as it saw him, almost in greeting.

"How did it come aboard?" Elric asked. "I saw nothing. I heard nothing."

The girl was almost as white as Elric. She sank to her knees beside the hatch, burying her face in her arms.

"He has us! He has us!"

"There is still a chance we can reach the Crimson Gate in time," Elric reassured her. "And once in my own world, why I can work much stronger sorcery to protect us."

"No," she sobbed, "it is too late. Why else would the white horse be here? He knows that Saxif D'Aan must soon board us."

"He'll have to fight us before he shall have you," Elric promised her.

"You have not seen his men. Cutthroats all. Desperate and wolfish! They'll show you no mercy. You would be best advised to hand me over to Saxif D'Aan at once and save yourselves. You'll gain nothing from trying to protect me. But I'd ask you a favor."

"What's that?"

"Find me a small knife to carry, that I may kill myself as soon as I know you two are safe."

Elric laughed, dragging her to her feet. "I'll have no such melodramatics from you, lass! We stand together. Perhaps we can bargain with Saxif D'Aan."

"What have you to barter?"

"Very little. But he is not aware of that."

"He can read your thoughts, seemingly. He has great powers!"

"I am Elric of Melniboné. I am said to possess a certain facility in the sorcerous arts, myself."

"But you are not as single-minded as Saxif D'Aan," she said simply. "Only one thing obsesses him—the need to make me his consort."

"Many girls would be flattered by the attention—glad to be an

Empress with a Melnibonéan Emperor for a husband." Elric was sardonic.

She ignored his tone. "That is why I fear him so," she said in a murmur. "If I lost my determination for a moment, I could love him. I should be destroyed! It is what *she* must have known!"

V

THE GLEAMING GALLEON, SAILS AND SIDES ALL GILDED SO THAT IT seemed the sun itself pursued them, moved rapidly upon them while the girl and Count Smiorgan watched aghast and Elric desperately attempted to recall his elemental allies, without success.

Through the pale blue light the golden ship sailed relentlessly in their wake. Its proportions were monstrous, its sense of power vast, its gigantic prow sending up huge, foamy waves on both sides as it sped silently towards them.

With the look of a man preparing himself to meet death, Count Smiorgan Baldhead of the Purple Towns unslung his battle-ax and loosened his sword in its scabbard, setting his little metal cap upon his bald pate. The girl made no sound, no movement at all, but she wept.

Elric shook his head and his long, milk-white hair formed a halo around his face for a moment. His moody, crimson eyes began to focus on the world around him. He recognized the ship; it was of a pattern with the golden battle-barges of Melniboné—doubtless the ship in which Earl Saxif D'Aan had fled his homeland, searching for the Crimson Gate. Now Elric was convinced that this must be that same Saxif D'Aan and he knew less fear than did his companions, but considerably greater curiosity. Indeed, it was almost with nostalgia that he noted the ball of fire, like a natural comet, glowing with green light, come hissing and spluttering towards them, flung by the ship's forward catapult. He half expected to see a great dragon wheeling in the sky overhead, for it was with dragons and gilded battlecraft like these that Melniboné had once conquered the world.

The fireball fell into the sea a few inches from their bow and was evidently placed there deliberately, as a warning.

"Don't stop!" cried Vassliss. "Let the flames slay us! It will be better!"

Smiorgan was looking upwards. "We have no choice. Look! He has banished the wind, it seems."

They were becalmed. Elric smiled a grim smile. He knew now what the folk of the Young Kingdoms must have felt when his ancestors had used these identical tactics against them.

"Elric?" Smiorgan turned to the albino. "Are these your people? That ship's Melnibonéan without question!"

"So are the methods," Elric told him. "I am of the blood royal of Melniboné. I could be Emperor, even now, if I chose to claim my throne. There is some small chance that Earl Saxif D'Aan, though an ancestor, will recognize me and, therefore, recognize my authority. We are a conservative people, the folk of the Dragon Isle."

The girl spoke through dry lips, hopelessly: "He recognizes only the authority of the Lords of Chaos, who give him aid."

"All Melnibonéans recognize that authority," Elric told her with a certain humor.

From the forward hatch, the sound of the stallion's stamping and snorting increased.

"We're besieged by enchantments!" Count Smiorgan's normally ruddy features had paled. "Have you none of your own, Prince Elric, you can use to counter them?"

"None, it seems."

The golden ship loomed over them. Elric saw that the rails, high overhead, were crowded not with Imrryrian warriors but with cutthroats equally as desperate as those he had fought upon the island, and, apparently, drawn from the same variety of historical periods and nations. The galleon's long sweeps scraped the sides of the smaller vessel as they folded, like the legs of some water insect, to enable the grappling irons to be flung out. Iron claws bit into the timbers of the little ship and the brigandly crowd overhead cheered, grinning at them, menacing them with their weapons.

The girl began to run to the seaward side of the ship, but Elric caught her by the arm.

"Do not stop me, I beg you!" she cried. "Rather, jump with me and drown!"

"You think that death will save you from Saxif D'Aan?" Elric said. "If he has the power you say, death will only bring you more firmly into his grasp!"

"Oh!" The girl shuddered and then, as a voice called down to them from one of the tall decks of the gilded ship, she gave a moan and fainted into Elric's arms, so that, weakened as he was by his spell-working, it was all that he could do to stop himself falling with her to the deck.

The voice rose over the coarse shouts and guffaws of the crew. It was pure, lilting and sardonic. It was the voice of a Melnibonéan, though it spoke the common tongue of the Young Kingdoms, a corruption, in itself, of the speech of the Bright Empire.

"May I have the captain's permission to come aboard?"

Count Smiorgan growled back: "You have us firm, sir! Don't try to disguise an act of piracy with a polite speech!"

"I take it I have your permission then." The unseen speaker's tone remained exactly the same.

Elric watched as part of the rail was drawn back to allow a gangplank, studded with golden nails to give firmer footing, to be lowered from the galleon's deck to theirs.

A tall figure appeared at the top of the gangplank. He had the fine features of a Melnibonéan nobleman, was thin, proud in his bearing, clad in voluminous robes of cloth-of-gold, an elaborate helmet in gold and ebony upon his long, auburn locks. He had gray-blue eyes, pale, slightly flushed skin, and he carried, so far as Elric could see, no weapons of any kind.

With considerable dignity, Earl Saxif D'Aan began to descend, his rascals at his back. The contrast between this beautiful intellectual and those he commanded was remarkable. Where he walked with straight back, elegant and noble, they slouched, filthy, degenerate, unintelligent, grinning with pleasure at their easy victory. Not a man amongst them showed any sign of human dignity; each was overdressed in tattered and unclean finery, each had at least three weapons upon his person, and there was much evidence of looted jewelry, of noserings, earrings, bangles, necklaces, toe- and finger-rings, pendants, cloak-pins and the like.

"Gods!" murmured Smiorgan. "I've rarely seen such a collection of scum, and I thought I'd encountered most kinds in my voyages. How can such a man bear to be in their company?"

"Perhaps it suits his sense of irony," Elric suggested.

Earl Saxif D'Aan reached their deck and stood looking up at them to where they still positioned themselves, in the poop. He gave a slight bow. His features were controlled and only his eyes suggested something of the intensity of emotion dwelling within him, particularly as they fell upon the girl in Elric's arms.

"I am Earl Saxif D'Aan of Melniboné, now of the Islands Beyond the Crimson Gate. You have something with you which is mine. I would claim it from you."

"You mean the Lady Vassliss of Jharkor?" Elric said, his voice as steady as Saxif D'Aan's.

Saxif D'Aan seemed to note Elric for the first time. A slight frown crossed his brow and was quickly dismissed. "She is mine," he said. "You may be assured that she will come to no harm at my hands."

Elric, seeking some advantage, knew that he risked much when he next spoke, in the High Tongue of Melniboné, used between those of the blood royal. "Knowledge of your history does not reassure me, Saxif D'Aan."

Almost imperceptibly, the golden man stiffened and fire flared in his gray-blue eyes. "Who are you, to speak the Tongue of Kings? Who are you, who claims knowledge of my past?"

"I am Elric, son of Sadric, and I am the four-hundred-and-twenty-eighth Emperor of the folk of R'lin K'ren A'a, who landed upon the Dragon Isle ten thousand years ago. I am Elric, your Emperor, Earl Saxif D'Aan, and I demand your fealty." And Elric held up his right hand, upon which still gleamed a ring set with a single Actorios stone, the Ring of Kings.

Earl Saxif D'Aan now had firm control of himself again. He

gave no sign that he was impressed. "Your sovereignty does not extend beyond your own world, noble emperor, though I greet you as a fellow monarch." He spread his arms so that his long sleeves rustled. "This world is mine. All that exists beneath the blue sun do I rule. You trespass, therefore, in my domain. I have every right to do as I please."

"Pirate pomp," muttered Count Smiorgan, who had understood nothing of the conversation but had gathered something of what passed by the tone. "Pirate braggadocio. What does he say, Elric?"

"He convinces me that he is not, in your sense, a pirate, Count Smiorgan. He claims that he is ruler of this plane. Since there is apparently no other, we must accept his claim."

"Gods! Then let him behave like a monarch and let us sail safely out of his waters!"

"We may—if we give him the girl."

Count Smiorgan shook his head. "I'll not do that. She's my passenger, in my charge. I must die rather than do that. It is the Code of the Sealords of the Purple Towns."

"You are famous for your adherence to that Code," Elric said. "As for myself, I have taken this girl into my protection and, as hereditary emperor of Melniboné, I cannot allow myself to be browbeaten."

They had conversed in a murmur, but, somehow, Earl Saxif D'Aan had heard them.

"I must let you know," he said evenly, in the common tongue, "that the girl is mine. You steal her from me. Is that the action of an Emperor?"

"She is not a slave," Elric said, "but the daughter of a free merchant in Jharkor. You have no rights upon her."

Earl Saxif D'Aan said: "Then I cannot open the Crimson Gate for you. You must remain in my world forever."

"You have closed the gate? Is it possible?"

"To me."

"Do you know that the girl would rather die than be captured by you, Earl Saxif D'Aan? Does it give you pleasure to instill such fear?"

The golden man looked directly into Elric's eyes as if he made some cryptic challenge. "The gift of pain has ever been a favorite gift amongst our folk, has it not? Yet it is another gift I offer her. She calls herself Vassliss of Jharkor, but she does not know herself. I know her. She is Gratyesha, Princess of Fwem-Omeyo, and I would make her my bride."

"How can it be that she does not know her own name?"

"She is reincarnated—soul and flesh are identical—that is how I know. And I have waited, Emperor of Melniboné, for many scores of years for her. Now I shall not be cheated of her."

"As you cheated yourself, two centuries past, in Melniboné?"

"You risk much with your directness of language, brother monarch!" There was a hint of a warning in Saxif D'Aan's tone, a warning much fiercer than any implied by the words.

"Well," Elric shrugged, "you have more power than we. My sorcery works poorly in your world. Your ruffians outnumber us. It should not be difficult for you to take her from us."

"You must give her to me. Then you may go free, back to your own world and your own time."

Elric smiled. "There is sorcery here. She is no reincarnation. You'd bring your lost love's spirit from the netherworld to inhabit this girl's body. Am I not right? That is why she must be given freely, or your sorcery will rebound upon you—or might—and you would not take the risk."

Earl Saxif D'Aan turned his head away so that Elric might not see his eyes. "She is the girl," he said, in the High Tongue. "I know that she is. I mean her soul no harm. I would merely give it back its memory."

"Then it is stalemate," said Elric.

"Have you no loyalty to a brother of the royal blood?" Saxif D'Aan murmured, still refusing to look at Elric.

"You claimed no such loyalty, as I recall, Earl Saxif D'Aan. If you accept me as your emperor, then you must accept my decisions. I keep the girl in my custody. Or you must take her by force."

"I am too proud."

"Such pride shall ever destroy love," said Elric, almost in sympathy. "What now, King of Limbo? What shall you do with us?"

Earl Saxif D'Aan lifted his noble head, about to reply, when from the hold the stamping and the snorting began again. His eyes widened. He looked questioningly at Elric, and there was something close to terror in his face.

"What's that? What have you in the hold?"

"A mount, my lord, that is all," said Elric equably.

"A horse? An ordinary horse?"

"A white one. A stallion, with bridle and saddle. It has no rider."

At once Saxif D'Aan's voice rose as he shouted orders for his men. "Take those three aboard our ship. This one shall be sunk directly. Hurry! Hurry!"

Elric and Smiorgan shook off the hands which sought to seize them and they moved towards the gangplank, carrying the girl between them, while Smiorgan muttered: "At least we are not slain, Elric. But what becomes of us now?"

Elric shook his head. "We must hope that we can continue to use Earl Saxif D'Aan's pride against him, to our advantage, though the gods alone know how we shall resolve the dilemma."

Earl Saxif D'Aan was already hurrying up the gangplank ahead of them.

"Quickly," he shouted. "Raise the plank!"

They stood upon the decks of the golden battle-barge and watched as the gangplank was drawn up, the length of rail replaced.

"Bring up the catapults," Saxif D'Aan commanded. "Use lead. Sink that vessel at once!"

The noise from the forward hold increased. The horse's voice echoed over ships and water. Hooves smashed at timber and then, suddenly, it came crashing through the hatch-covers, scrambling for purchase on the deck with its front hooves, and then standing there, pawing at the planks, its neck arching, its nostrils dilating and its eyes glaring, as if ready to do battle.

Now Saxif D'Aan made no attempt to hide the terror on his

face. His voice rose to a scream as he threatened his rascals with every sort of horror if they did not obey him with utmost speed. The catapults were dragged up and huge globes of lead were lobbed onto the decks of Smiorgan's ship, smashing through the planks like arrows through parchment so that almost immediately the ship began to sink.

"Cut the grappling hooks!" cried Saxif D'Aan, wrenching a blade from the hand of one of his men and sawing at the nearest rope. "Cast loose—quickly!"

Even as Smiorgan's ship groaned and roared like a drowning beast, the ropes were cut. The ship keeled over at once, and the horse disappeared.

"Turn about!" shouted Saxif D'Aan. "Back to Fhaligarn and swiftly, or your souls shall feed my fiercest demons!"

There came a peculiar, high-pitched neighing from the foaming water, as Smiorgan's ship, stern uppermost, gasped and was swallowed. Elric caught a glimpse of the white stallion, swimming strongly.

"Go below!" Saxif D'Aan ordered, indicating a hatchway. "The horse can smell the girl and thus is doubly difficult to lose."

"Why do you fear it?" Elric asked. "It is only a horse. It cannot harm you."

Saxif D'Aan uttered a laugh of profound bitterness. "Can it not, brother monarch? Can it not?"

As they carried the girl below, Elric was frowning, remembering a little more of the legend of Saxif D'Aan, of the girl he had punished so cruelly, and of her lover, Prince Carolak. The last he heard of Saxif D'Aan was the sorcerer crying:

"More sail! More sail!"

And then the hatch had closed behind them and they found themselves in an opulent Melnibonéan day-cabin, full of rich hangings, precious metal, decorations of exquisite beauty and, to Count Smiorgan, disturbing decadence. But it was Elric, as he lowered the girl to a couch, who noticed the smell.

"Augh! It's the smell of a tomb—of damp and mold. Yet nothing rots. It is passing peculiar, friend Smiorgan, is it not?"

"I scarcely noticed, Elric." Smiorgan's voice was hollow. "But I would agree with you on one thing. We are entombed. I doubt we'll live to escape this world now."

VI

AN HOUR HAD PASSED SINCE THEY HAD BEEN FORCED ABOARD. THE door had been locked behind them and, it seemed, Saxif D'Aan was too preoccupied with escaping the white stallion to bother with them. Peering through the lattice of a porthole, Elric could look back to where their ship had been sunk. They were many leagues distant, already, yet he still thought, from time to time, that he saw the head and shoulders of the stallion above the waves.

Vassliss had recovered and sat pale and shivering upon the couch.

"What more do you know of that horse?" Elric asked her. "It would be helpful to me if you could recall anything you have heard."

She shook her head. "Saxif D'Aan spoke little of it, but I gather he fears the rider more than he does the horse."

"Ah!" Elric frowned. "I suspected it! Have you ever seen the rider?"

"Never. I think that Saxif D'Aan has never seen him, either. I think he believes himself doomed if that rider should ever sit upon the white stallion."

Elric smiled to himself.

"Why do you ask so much about the horse?" Smiorgan wished to know.

Elric shook his head. "I have an instinct, that is all. Half a memory. But I'll say nothing and think as little as I may, for there is no doubt Saxif D'Aan, as Vassliss suggests, has some power of reading the mind."

They heard a footfall above, descending to their door. A bolt was drawn and Saxif D'Aan, his composure fully restored, stood in the opening, his hands in his golden sleeves.

"You will forgive, I hope, the peremptory way in which I sent you here. There was danger which had to be averted at all costs. As a result, my manners were not all that they should have been."

"Danger to us?" Elric asked. "Or to you, Earl Saxif D'Aan."

"In the circumstances, to all of us, I assure you."

"Who rides the horse?" Smiorgan asked bluntly. "And why do you fear him?"

Earl Saxif D'Aan was master of himself again, so there was no sign of a reaction. "That is very much my private concern," he said softly. "Will you dine with me now?"

The girl made a noise in her throat and Earl Saxif D'Aan turned piercing eyes upon her. "Gratyesha, you will want to cleanse yourself and make yourself beautiful again. I will see that facilities are placed at your disposal."

"I am not Gratyesha," she said. "I am Vassliss, the merchant's daughter."

"You will remember," he said. "In time, you will remember." There was such certainty, such obsessive power in his voice that even Elric experienced a frisson of awe. "The things will be brought to you, and you may use this cabin as your own until we return to my palace on Fhaligarn. My lords . . ." He indicated that they should leave.

Elric said: "I'll not leave her, Saxif D'Aan. She is too afraid."

"She fears only the truth, brother."

"She fears you and your madness."

Saxif D'Aan shrugged insouciantly. "I shall leave first then. If you would accompany me, my lords . . ." He strode from the cabin and they followed.

Elric said, over his shoulder: "Vassliss, you may depend upon my protection." And he closed the cabin doors behind him.

Earl Saxif D'Aan was standing upon the deck, exposing his noble face to the spray which was flung up by the ship as it moved with supernatural speed through the sea.

"You called me mad, Prince Elric? Yet you must be versed in sorcery, yourself?"

"Of course. I am of the blood royal. I am reckoned knowledgeable in my own world."

"But here? How well does your sorcery work?"

"Poorly, I'll admit. The spaces between the planes seem greater."

"Exactly. But I have bridged them. I have had time to learn how to bridge them."

"You are saying that you are more powerful than am I?"

"It is a fact, is it not?"

"It is. But I did not think we were about to indulge in sorcerous battles, Earl Saxif D'Aan."

"Of course. Yet, if you were to think of besting me by sorcery, you would think twice, eh?"

"I should be foolish to contemplate such a thing at all. It could cost me my soul. My life, at least."

"True. You are a realist, I see."

"I suppose so."

"Then we can progress on simpler lines, to settle the dispute between us."

"You propose a duel?" Elric was surprised.

Earl Saxif D'Aan's laughter was light. "Of course not—against your sword? That has power in all worlds, though the magnitude varies."

"I am glad that you are aware of that," Elric said significantly.

"Besides," added Earl Saxif D'Aan, his golden robes rustling as he moved a little nearer to the rail, "you would not kill me—for only I have the means of your escaping this world."

"Perhaps we'd elect to remain," said Elric.

"Then you would be my subjects. But, no—you would not like it here. I am self-exiled. I could not return to my own world now, even if I wished to do so. It has cost me much, my knowledge. But I would found a dynasty here, beneath the blue sun. I must have my wife, Prince Elric. I must have Gratyesha."

"Her name is Vassliss," said Elric obstinately.

"She thinks it it."

"Then it is. I have sworn to protect her, as has Count Smiorgan. Protect her we shall. You will have to kill us all."

"Exactly," said Earl Saxif D'Aan with the air of a man who has been coaching a poor student towards the correct answer to a problem. "Exactly. I shall have to kill you all. You leave me with little alternative, Prince Elric."

"Would that benefit you?"

"It would. It would put a certain powerful demon at my service for a few hours."

"We should resist."

"I have many men. I do not value them. Eventually, they would overwhelm you. Would they not?"

Elric remained silent.

"My men would be aided by sorcery," added Saxif D'Aan. "Some would die, but not too many, I think."

Elric was looking beyond Saxif D'Aan, staring out to sea. He was sure that the horse still followed. He was sure that Saxif D'Aan knew, also.

"And if we gave up the girl?"

"I should open the Crimson Gate for you. You would be honored guests. I should see that you were borne safely through, even taken safely to some hospitable land in your own world, for even if you passed through the gate there would be danger. The storms."

Elric appeared to deliberate.

"You have only a little time to make your decision, Prince Elric. I had hoped to reach my palace, Fhaligarn, by now. I shall not allow you very much longer. Come, make your decision. You know I speak the truth."

"You know that I can work some sorcery in your world, do you not?"

"You summoned a few friendly elementals to your aid, I know. But at what cost? Would you challenge me directly?"

"It would be unwise of me," said Elric.

Smiorgan was tugging at his sleeve. "Stop this useless talk. He knows that we have given our word to the girl and that we *must* fight him!"

Earl Saxif D'Aan sighed. There seemed to be genuine sorrow in his voice. "If you are determined to lose your lives . . ." he began.

"I should like to know why you set such importance upon the speed with which we make up our minds," Elric said. "Why cannot we wait until we reach Fhaligarn?"

Earl Saxif D'Aan's expression was calculating, and again he looked full into Elric's crimson eyes. "I think you know," he said, almost inaudibly.

But Elric shook his head. "I think you give me too much credit for intelligence."

"Perhaps."

Elric knew that Saxif D'Aan was attempting to read his thoughts; he deliberately blanked his mind, and suspected that he sensed frustration in the sorcerer's demeanor.

And then the albino had sprung at his kinsman, his hand chopping at Saxif D'Aan's throat. The earl was taken completely off guard. He tried to call out, but his vocal chords were numbed. Another blow, and he fell to the deck, senseless.

"Quickly, Smiorgan," Elric shouted, and he had leapt into the rigging, climbing swiftly upwards to the top yards. Smiorgan, bewildered, followed, and Elric had drawn his sword, even as he reached the crow's nest, driving upwards through the rail so that the lookout was taken in the groin scarcely before he realized it.

Next, Elric was hacking at the ropes holding the mainsail to the yard. Already a number of Saxif D'Aan's ruffians were climbing after them.

The heavy golden sail came loose, falling to envelop the pirates and take several of them down with it.

Elric climbed into the crow's nest and pitched the dead man over the rail in the wake of his comrades. Then he had raised his sword over his head, holding it in his two hands, his eyes blank again, his head raised to the blue sun, and Smiorgan, clinging to the mast below, shuddered as he heard a peculiar crooning come form the albino's throat.

More of the cutthroats were ascending, and Smiorgan hacked at the rigging, having the satisfaction of seeing half a score go flying down to break their bones on the deck below, or be swallowed by the waves.

Earl Saxif D'Aan was beginning to recover, but he was still stunned.

"Fool!" he was crying. "Fool!" But it was not possible to tell if he referred to Elric or to himself.

Elric's voice became a wail, rhythmical and chilling, as he chanted his incantation, and the strength from the man he had killed flowed into him and sustained. His crimson eyes seemed to flicker with fires of another, nameless color, and his whole body shook as the strange runes shaped themselves in a throat which had never been made to speak such sounds.

His voice became a vibrant groan as the incantation continued, and Smiorgan, watching as more of the crew made efforts to climb the mainmast, felt an unearthly cold creep through him.

Earl Saxif D'Aan screamed from below:

"You would not dare!"

The sorcerer began to make passes in the air, his own incantation tumbling from his lips, and Smiorgan gasped as a creature made of smoke took shape only a few feet below him. The creature smacked its lips and grinned and stretched a paw, which became flesh even as it moved, towards Smiorgan. He hacked at the paw with his sword, whimpering.

"Elric!" cried Count Smiorgan, clambering higher so that he grasped the rail of the crow's nest. "Elric! He sends demons against us now!"

But Elric ignored him. His whole mind was in another world, a darker, bleaker world even than this one. Through gray mists, he saw a figure, and he cried a name. "Come!" he called in the ancient tongue of his ancestors. "Come!"

Count Smiorgan cursed as the demon became increasingly substantial. Red fangs clashed and green eyes glared at him. A claw stroked his boot and no matter how much he struck with his sword, the demon did not appear to notice the blows.

There was no room for Smiorgan in the crow's nest, but he stood on the outer rim, shouting with terror, desperate for aid. Still Elric continued to chant.

"Elric! I am doomed!"

The demon's paw grasped Smiorgan by his ankle.

"Elric!"

Thunder rolled out at sea; a ball of lightning appeared for a second and then was gone. From nowhere there came the sound of a horse's hooves pounding, and a human voice shouting in triumph.

Elric sank back against the rail, opening his eyes in time to see Smiorgan being dragged slowly downward. With the last of his strength he flung himself forward, leaning far out to stab downwards with Stormbringer. The runesword sank cleanly into the demon's right eye and it roared, letting go of Smiorgan, striking at the blade which drew its energy from it and, as that energy passed into the blade and thence to Elric, the albino grinned a frightful grin so that, for a second, Smiorgan became more frightened of his friend than he had been of the demon. The demon began to dematerialize, its only means of escape from the sword which drank its life force, but more of Saxif D'Aan's rogues were behind it, and their blades rattled as they sought the pair.

Elric swung himself back over the rail, balanced precariously on the yard as he slashed at their attackers, yelling the old battle-cries of his people. Smiorgan could do little but watch. He noted that Saxif D'Aan was no longer on deck and he shouted urgently to Elric:

"Elric! Saxif D'Aan. He seeks out the girl."

Elric now took the attack to the pirates, and they were more than anxious to avoid the moaning runesword, some even leaping into the sea rather than encounter it. Swiftly the two leapt from yard to yard until they were again upon the deck.

"What does he fear? Why does he not use more sorcery?" panted Count Smiorgan, as they ran towards the cabin.

"I have summoned the one who rides the horse," Elric told him. "I had so little time—and I could tell you nothing of it, knowing that Saxif D'Aan would read my intention in your mind, if he could not in mine!"

The cabin doors were firmly secured from the inside. Elric began to hack at them with the black sword.

But the door resisted as it should not have resisted. "Sealed by sorcery and I've no means of unsealing it," said the albino.

"Will he kill her?"

"I don't know. He might try to take her into some other plane. We must—"

Hooves clattered on the deck and the white stallion reared behind them, only now it had a rider, clad in bright purple and yellow armor. He was bareheaded and youthful, though there were several old scars upon his face. His hair was thick and curly and blond and his eyes were a deep blue.

He drew tightly upon his reins, steadying the horse. He looked piercingly at Elric. "Was it you, Melnibonéan, who opened the pathway for me?"

"It was."

"Then I thank you, though I cannot repay you."

"You have repaid me," Elric told him, then drew Smiorgan aside as the rider leaned forward and spurred his horse directly at the closed doors, smashing through as though they were rotted cotton.

There came a terrible cry from within and then Earl Saxif D'Aan, hampered by his complicated robes of gold, rushed from the cabin, seizing a sword from the hand of the nearest corpse, darting Elric a look not so much of hatred but of bewildered agony, as he turned to face the blond rider.

The rider had dismounted now and came from the cabin, one arm around the shivering girl, Vassliss, one hand upon the reins of his horse, and he said, sorrowfully:

"You did me a great wrong, Earl Saxif D'Aan, but you did Gratyesha an infinitely more terrible one. Now you must pay."

Saxif D'Aan paused, drawing a deep breath, and when he looked up again, his eyes were steady, his dignity had returned.

"Must I pay in full?" he said.

"In full."

"It is all I deserve," said Saxif D'Aan. "I escaped my doom for many years, but I could not escape the knowledge of my crime. She loved me, you know. Not you."

"She loved us both, I think. But the love she gave you was her entire soul and I should not want that from any woman."

"You would be the loser, then."

"You never knew how much she loved you."

"Only—only afterwards . . ."

"I pity you, Earl Saxif D'Aan." The young man gave the reins of his horse to the girl, and he drew his sword. "We are strange rivals, are we not?"

"You have been all these years in Limbo, where I banished you—in that garden on Melniboné?"

"All these years. Only my horse could follow you. The horse of Tendric, my father, also of Melniboné, and also a sorcerer."

"If I had known that, then, I'd have slain you cleanly and sent the horse to Limbo."

"Jealousy weakened you, Earl Saxif D'Aan. But now we fight as we should have fought then—man to man, with steel, for the hand of the one who loves us both. It is more than you deserve."

"Much more," agreed the sorcerer. And he brought up his sword to lunge at the young man who, Smiorgan guessed, could only be Prince Carolak himself.

The fight was predetermined. Saxif D'Aan knew that, if Carolak did not. Saxif D'Aan's skill in arms was up to the standard of any Melnibonéan nobleman, but it could not match the skill of a professional soldier, who had fought for his life time after time.

Back and forth across the deck, while Saxif D'Aan's rascals looked on in open-mouthed astonishment, the rivals fought a duel which should have been fought and resolved two centuries before, while the girl they both plainly thought was the reincarnation of Gratyesha watched them with as much concern as might her original have watched when Saxif D'Aan first encountered Prince Carolak in the gardens of his palace, so long ago.

Saxif D'Aan fought well, and Carolak fought nobly, for on many occasions he avoided an obvious advantage, but at length Saxif D'Aan threw away his sword, crying: "Enough. I'll give you your vengeance, Prince Carolak. I'll let you take the girl. But you'll not give me your damned mercy—you'll not take my pride."

And Carolak nodded, stepped forward, and struck straight for Saxif D'Aan's heart.

The blade entered clean and Earl Saxif D'Aan should have died, but he did not. He crawled along the deck until he reached the base of the mast, and he rested his back against it, while the blood pumped from the wounded heart. And he smiled.

"It appears," he said faintly, "that I cannot die, so long have I sustained my life by sorcery. I am no longer a man."

He did not seem pleased by this thought, but Prince Carolak, stepping forward and leaning over him, reassured him. "You will die," he promised, "soon."

"What will you do with her—with Gratyesha?"

"Her name is Vassliss," said Count Smiorgan insistently. "She is a merchant's daughter, from Jharkor."

"She must make up her own mind," Carolak said, ignoring Smiorgan.

Earl Saxif D'Aan turned glazed eyes on Elric. "I must thank you," he said. "You brought me the one who could bring me peace, though I feared him."

"Is that why, I wonder, your sorcery was so weak against me," Elric said. "Because you wished Carolak to come and release you from your guilt."

"Possibly, Elric. You are wiser in some matters, it seems, than am I."

"What of the Crimson Gate?" Smiorgan growled. "Can that be opened? Have you still the power, Earl Saxif D'Aan?"

"I think so." From the folds of his bloodstained garments of gold, the sorcerer produced a large crystal which shone with the deep colors of a ruby. "This will not only lead you to the gate, it will enable you to pass through, only I must warn you . . ." Saxif D'Aan began to cough. "The ship—" he gasped, "the ship—like my body—has been sustained by means of sorcery—therefore . . ." His head slumped forward. He raised it with a huge effort and stared beyond them at the girl who still held the reins of the white stallion. "Farewell, Gratyesha, Princess of Fwem-Omeyo. I loved you." The eyes remained fixed upon her, but they were dead eyes now.

Carolak turned back to look at the girl. "How do you call yourself, Gratyesha?"

"They call me Vassliss," she told him. She smiled up into his youthful, battle-scarred face. "That is what they call me, Prince Carolak."

"You know who I am?"

"I know you now."

"Will you come with me, Gratyesha? Will you be my bride, at last, in the strange new lands I have found, beyond the world?"

"I will come," she said.

He helped her up into the saddle of his white stallion and climbed so that he sat behind her. He bowed to Elric of Melniboné. "I thank you again, Sir Sorcerer, though I never thought to be helped by one of the royal blood of Melniboné."

Elric's expression was not without humor. "In Melniboné," he said, "I'm told it's tainted blood."

"Tainted with mercy, perhaps."

"Perhaps."

Prince Carolak saluted them. "I hope you find peace, Prince Elric, as I have found it."

"I fear my peace will more resemble that which Saxif D'Aan found," Elric said grimly. "Nonetheless, I thank you for your good words, Prince Carolak."

Then Carolak, laughing, had ridden his horse for the rail, leapt it, and vanished.

There was a silence upon the ship. The remaining ruffians looked uncertainly, one to the other. Elric addressed them:

"Know you this—I have the key to the Crimson Gate—and only I have the knowledge to use it. Help me sail the ship, and you'll have freedom from this world! What say you?"

"Give us our orders, captain," said a toothless individual, and he cackled with mirth. "It's the best offer we've had in a hundred years or more!"

VII

IT WAS SMIORGAN WHO FIRST SAW THE CRIMSON GATE. HE HELD the great red gem in his hand and pointed ahead.

"There! There, Elric! Saxif D'Aan has not betrayed us!"

The sea had begun to heave with huge, turbulent waves and, with the mainsail still tangled upon the deck, it was all that the crew could do to control the ship, but the chance of escape from the world of the blue sun made them work with every ounce of energy and, slowly, the golden battle-barge neared the towering crimson pillars.

The pillars rose from the gray, roaring water, casting a peculiar light upon the crests of the waves. They appeared to have little substance, and yet stood firm against the battering of the tons of water lashing around them.

"Let us hope they are wider apart than they look," said Elric. "It would be a hard enough task steering through them in calm waters, let alone this kind of sea."

"I'd best take the wheel, I think," said Count Smiorgan, handing Elric the gem, and he strode back up the tilting deck, climbing to the covered wheelhouse and relieving the frightened man who stood there.

There was nothing Elric could do but watch as Smiorgan turned the huge vessel into the waves, riding the tops as best he could, but sometimes descending with a rush which made Elric's heart rise to his mouth. All around them, then, the cliffs of water threatened, but the ship was taking another wave before the main force of water could crash onto her decks. For all this, Elric was quickly soaked through and, though sense told him he would be best below, he clung to the rail, watching as Smiorgan steered the ship with uncanny sureness towards the Crimson Gate.

And then the deck was flooded with red light and Elric was half blinded. Gray water flew everywhere; there came a dreadful scraping sound, then a snapping as oars broke against the pillars. The ship shuddered and began to turn, sideways to the wind, but Smiorgan forced her round and suddenly the quality of the light changed subtly, though the sea remained as turbulent as ever and Elric knew, deep within him, that overhead, beyond the heavy clouds, a yellow sun was burning again.

But now there came a creaking and a crashing from within the bowels of the battle-barge. The smell of mold, which Elric had noted earlier, became stronger, almost overpowering.

Smiorgan came hurrying back, having handed over the wheel. His face was pale again. "She's breaking up, Elric," he called out, over the noise of the wind and the waves. He staggered as a huge wall of water struck the ship and snatched away several planks from the deck. "She's falling apart, man!"

"Saxif D'Aan tried to warn us of this!" Elric shouted back. "As he was kept alive by sorcery, so was his ship. She was old before he sailed her to that world. While there, the sorcery which sustained her remained strong—but on this plane it has no power at all. Look!" And he pulled at a piece of the rail, crumbling the rotten wood with his fingers. "We must find a length of timber which is still good."

At that moment a yard came crashing from the mast and struck the deck, bounding, then rolling towards them.

Elric crawled up the sloping deck until he could grasp the spar and test it. "This one's still good. Use your belt or whatever else you can and tie yourself to it!"

The wind wailed through the disintegrating rigging of the ship; the sea smashed at the sides, driving great holes below the waterline.

The ruffians who had crewed her were in a state of complete panic, some trying to unship small boats which crumbled even as they swung them out, others lying flat against the rotted decks and praying to whatever gods they still worshiped.

Elric strapped himself to the broken yard as firmly as he could and Smiorgan followed his example. The next wave to hit the ship full-on lifted them with it, cleanly over what remained of the rail and into the chilling, shouting waters of that terrible sea.

Elric kept his mouth tight shut against swallowing too much water and reflected on the irony of his situation. It seemed that, having escaped so much, he was to die a very ordinary death, by drowning.

It was not long before his senses left him and he gave himself up to the swirling and somehow friendly waters of the ocean.

He awoke, struggling.

There were hands upon him. He strove to fight them off, but he was too weak. Someone laughed, a rough, good-humored sound.

The water no longer roared and crashed around him. The wind no longer howled. Instead there was a gentler movement. He heard waves lapping against timber. He was aboard another ship.

He opened his eyes, blinking in warm, yellow sunlight. Red-cheeked Vilmirian sailors grinned down at him. "You're a lucky man—if man you be!" said one.

"My friend?" Elric sought for Smiorgan.

"He was in better shape than were you. He's down in Duke Avan's cabin now."

"Duke Avan?" Elric knew the name but, in his dazed condition, could remember nothing to help him place the man. "You saved us?"

"Aye. We found you both drifting, tied to a broken yard carved with the strangest designs I've ever seen. A Melnibonéan craft, was she?"

"Yes, but rather old."

And with a smile, more tranquil than most, he fell back into his slumbers.

About the Authors

C.J. CHERRYH

C.J. Cherryh is the creator of the encompassing Union-Alliance future-history series, which chronicles the interplay of intergalactic commerce and politics several millennia hence. Praised for its inventive extrapolations of clinical and social science and deft blends of technology and human interest, the series enfolds a number of celebrated subseries, including her Faded Sun trilogy (*Kesrith, Shon'jir, Kutath*). Her Chanur cycle (*The Pride of Chanur, Chanur's Venture, The Kif Strikes Back, Chanur's Homecoming, Chanur's Legacy*), also part of the series, tells of a race of sentient lionlike creatures and is notable for its alien viewpoint and illuminating perspectives on the human race rendered from outside it. Much of her fiction is concerned with the impact of environment—family, politics, culture—on the values and ideologies of the individual. Cherryh has also authored the four-volume Morgaine heroic fantasy series and the epic Galisien sword-and-sorcery trilogy, which includes *Fortress in the Eye of Time, Fortress of Eagles*, and *Fortress of Owls*. She is the creator of the *Merovingian Nights* shared-world series and co-creator of the multivolume *Heroes in Hell* shared-world compilations.

KARL EDWARD WAGNER

Karl Edward Wagner (1945–1994) wrote the first of what was later to be termed "dark fantasy" fiction with his series character Kane, who is based on the biblical Cain, a wandering immortal who takes up arms for his own side in the eternal battle of good versus evil. He also collaborated with other authors, notably David Drake in the space alien meets Roman Empire adventure novel *Killer*. He continued the exploits of one of the pulp era's mightiest heroes, Conan the Barbarian. A prolific editor, his annual *Best Horror Stories* anthology showcased the most powerful tales of terror for more than two decades, and continued until his untimely death. A four-time recipient of the British Fantasy Award, he also won the World Fantasy Award twice.

POUL ANDERSON

Mention the name Poul Anderson and instantly dozens of excellent science fiction novels and short stories spring to mind. However, like many authors, he has also tried his hand at fantasy fiction, with equally impressive results. Two of his novels that deserve mention are *Three Hearts and Three Lions* and *The Broken Sword*, the latter based on the Norse eleven myths. He has also written in universes as diverse as Shakespeare's comedies and Robert E. Howard's Conan mythos. A seven-time winner of the Hugo Award, he has been awarded three Nebulas and the Tolkien Memorial Award.

CHARLES L. FONTENAY

Charles L. Fontenay is best known for his Kipton series, a young-adult collection of books featuring a girl solving mysteries and out-witting villains in a science fiction universe. He has also contributed to several anthologies, including *CatFantastic III* and *IV*, *Barbarians II*, and such noted magazines as *If*, *Analog*, and *The Magazine of Fantasy and Science Fiction*. He lives and writes in St. Petersburg, Florida.

TANYA HUFF

Tanya Huff lives and writes in rural Ontario with her partner, four cats, and an unintentional Chihuahua. After sixteen fantasies, she's written her first space opera, *Valor's Choice,* and is currently working on a sequel to *Summon the Keeper* called *The Second Summoning.* In her spare time she gardens and complains about the weather.

NEIL GAIMAN

Neil Gaiman is, quite simply, a world-class fantasist. Whether in his graphic novel series *The Sandman* or in his prose novels or story collections, he shows us—and the world around us—in the slightly skewed perspective that writers from Lord Dunsany to Ray Bradbury to Clive Barker to Terry Prachett favor. In truth, his unique voices manage to incorporate just about every major strain of traditional and modern fantasy and yet remain just that: unique, and unlike anyone else's. Recent books include *The Day I Swapped My Dad for Two Goldfish, Stardust,* and the *New York Times*–bestselling *American Gods.*

LOIS TILTON

Lois Tilton is an author who has made a name for herself in the fantasy and horror fields. Other work by her appears in *Grails: Quests, Visions and Occurrences, Witch Fantastic, Enchanted Forests,* and *Alternate Generals.* She lives in Illinois.

ORSON SCOTT CARD

Although best known for his Nebula and Hugo Award-winning science fiction novels *Ender's Game* and *Speaker for the Dead,* Orson Scott Card is also an accomplished fantasy and horror writer. Among his other achievements are two Locus Awards, a Hugo Award for nonfiction, and a World Fantasy Award. Currently he is working on the Tales of Alvin Maker series, which chronicles the history of an alternate nineteenth-century America where magic works. The Alvin Maker series, like the majority of his work, deals with messianic characters and their influence on the world around them. His short fiction has been collected in the anthology *Maps in a Mirror.*

RICHARD PARKS

Richard Parks lives in Mississippi, works with computers, and writes. He has a wife named Carol, whose first date with him was a campus screening of *Psycho*. As for other details of his personal existence, well, the less said the better. He firmly believes that his stories, which can be found in *Robert Bloch's Psychos*, *Elf Magic*, *Realms of Fantasy*, *Isaac Asimov's Science Fiction Magazine*, and *Amazing Stories*, are much more interesting than he is.

MERCEDES LACKEY

Mercedes Lackey was born in Chicago and has worked as a lab assistant, security guard, and computer programmer before turning to fiction writing. Her first book, *Arrows of the Queen*, the first in the Valdemar series, was published in 1985. She has since written more than thirty-five novels, and won the Lambda Award for *Magic's Price* and Science Fiction Book Club Book of the Year for the *The Elvenbane*, co-authored with Andre Norton. Along with her husband, Larry Dixon, she is a federally licensed bird rehabilitator, specializing in the care of wild birds. She shares her home with a menagerie of parrots, cats, and a Schutzhund-trained German shepherd. Recent novels include *The Serpent's Shadow* and *Take a Thief*.

MICHAEL MOORCOCK

Michael Moorcock's elegantly dark fantasies and science fiction have been garnering him awards and legions of fans ever since his first novel, *The Golden Barge*, which, strangely, wasn't published until more than a decade after it was written. Be that as it may, from the beginning he has explored a multidimensional universe (what he calls the "multiverse") that is unlike anything else in fantasy. His tragic, doomed heroes include the albino lord Elric of Melniboné, forever cursed with the knowledge that he was responsible for destroying his own race; the medieval adventurer, soldier, and killer Graf Ulrich von Bek; and Corum, who fights his own epic battle against the gods of Chaos. Along the way he has won the British Science Fiction Association Award, the Nebula Award, the *Guardian* fiction prize, the Campbell Memorial Award, the World Fantasy Lifetime Achievement Award, and been a four-time recipient of the Derleth Award. He has also edited many excellent anthologies, including the critically lauded *New Worlds* series.